KILTl

Dermid Strain

www.publishnation.co.uk

Kiltman is for Georgie, Max and Bruce

Anne, Angie, Margaret, John

And for Mum and George, who keep a watchful eye on all of us

Prologue

Field of Dreams

He could not ignore the sharp, painful parchment which once was a throat. It begged for lubrication. Vertical was the only option. Mustering all the strength his legs had to offer, he moved to place his feet under his body, ready to raise himself into a fighter's position, a pugilist of one too many blows to the head. It took less than a second to perform a somersault perfect in every way except grace, crunching his right shoulder down onto the hardened roots of the hedge he had fallen into six hours earlier.

Blood, no less than forty percent proof, rushed from his head to legs no longer pointing skyward, released from the pivotal role they had played in keeping their owner balanced across the foliage he had collapsed into during the third verse of a tuneless but heartfelt "Wild Rover". His legs lurched into life, cushions of pain, pins and needles. Grimacing at the discomfort, he made a note to self not to sleep upside down in a cold, damp field again.

Rising to his feet, the tightness around his lower stomach reminded him of the numerous beers consumed in the isolation of his misery just one day earlier. It ended when…

When? That was a good question. The last thing he could remember was lifting a whisky to his lips just as he turned to smile at the barmaid. Or were there two barmaids? His threadbare Pogues T-shirt was still stained with the dribbles of drinks he had gorged on to achieve mindless oblivion.

Now his groin was coming back to life, his bladder stretched to bursting point. Raising his pounding head oblivious to anyone who may have witnessed his resurrection, he attacked the grass that had never done him any harm. Good for the grass, he thought, as he watered generously.

Until the waft of his overworked liver reminded Kenny Morgan that drink had become the urination of him, his life and everything he had once loved.

I

The World at his Feet

The Graduate

He stopped and looked at her as if for the first time. Leaning towards an ear drooping with last year's birthday present, he whispered, "Fiona, I love you so much. I can't imagine life without you."

"Kenny Morgan, you're such a romantic," she answered, tilting her head at an angle as if trying to comprehend him. An unruly curl of red hair cascaded over her brow, framing the honesty in her eyes. On a dazzlingly bright day like this her auburn hair reflected in her eyes, turning them into a deep reddish-brown, above a nose sprinkled generously with freckles threatening to join up on the next sunny day.

"Who would've thought you were Scottish with all that soppiness! Come on, let's go. They'll be calling your name in a minute."

Arms linked, they walked through the Glasgow University colonnades oblivious to their surroundings. The current version of the university had been christened a Gothic Revival in the nineteenth century, capturing an age when pride was an acceptable sin. The buildings were of a granite magnificence shunned by architects for years. Strong, lasting, positioned with care, the bricks supported the pillars of learning, and the students who walked among them. Adam Smith, James Watt, John Logie Baird, and James Herriot were a testament to the wealth of social energy clearly portrayed in all creatures, great and small. Kenny had once used that line on Fiona, expecting her to laugh. She had looked at him quizzically wondering why he was smiling and what he was waiting for.

He guided her into the austerity of an atrium filled with shuffling feet and nervous coughs. The reality of the moment was exaggerated by the unsettling odour of scores of graduates sitting in neat rows of red velvet, cushioned chairs. Many chatted in loud whispers, while the remainder looked straight ahead in anticipation at the shallow platform. From the doorway, Kenny could see Donald, his fellow chemistry student, muttering to himself. Donald's eyes shifted erratically from ceiling to floor as if searching for a hole to disappear into. While he appeared oblivious to the sea of humanity crushed

2

into the cramped hall, the truth was he was drowning in it. Kenny knew Donald was only there to please his parents. On the one occasion Kenny had met them they quizzed him for hours on what subjects their son should study, but not a single question as to how he was enjoying the student life or, God forbid, whether he had a girlfriend. After his discussion with them, Kenny knew they wanted their son to be happy. As long as his happiness provided them with the indispensable, after-dinner sound bites to impress their guests. They accepted his increasing levels of manic paranoia as long as it did not interfere with his return on their investment. This morning could not pass quickly enough for Donald. He had opened up to Kenny about his stress early in second year, when Kenny had found him hiding in the corner of the library afraid to walk home. Kenny knew where he was going to sit on graduation day, whether Donald wanted him to or not.

"I'll be with Tommy and your mum. Make us proud!" Fiona whispered as she uncoupled her arm and kissed him on the cheek to go in search of the stairs leading to the balcony. He turned and crossed the room towards Donald. He was not surprised to find the seats on Donald's left and right were both free.

"How you doing, big man? You coming to the beer bar after this to celebrate?" he asked Donald, extending his hand forcefully.

Donald considered handshakes a societal oxymoron, germs and niceties incongruously intertwined. Despite his anxieties, he grabbed Kenny's hand as if sinking into a pit of quicksand, his own hand soaked in nervous dampness. Whenever Kenny saw Donald he seemed to age in front of him. He was now showing the signs of premature balding. Smooth temples arched unnaturally into the sides of his forehead, long strands of hair barely covering the middle ground. The draft in the hall played with Donald's receding tresses just as they had done when he had encountered a Van de Graaff generator in their science class. His downtrodden features made him look like a distraught Einstein, manically masterful while anxiously awkward. He could barely control the nerves in his face, the odd twitch escaping to indicate the underlying stress.

3

"You joking, Kenny? After this, I'm going into hibernation." He paused before looking deep into Kenny's eyes. "Do me a favour, will you?"

"Maybe. Depends what you're after, pal."

"I can't go up there. You know what I'm like. Can you do it for me? Please, I'm begging you."

He studied Donald's agitated face, eyebrows begging his friend to help him out. Kenny knew he was the only one who could help him. He touched Donald on the shoulder, compassionate and empathetic to the discomfort he was suffering.

"No way, you silly scientist!"

Donald's pained look swiftly became panic-stricken, not believing that the one person he trusted most in university would let him down so callously.

"You get yourself up there. You're the smartest guy in this hall. Wee bit off your head, mind you, but you worked harder than anyone to be here. Remember, the first step on a long journey can be the hardest." Kenny grimaced at the cliché but knew he had to be cruel to be kind. "Make your family proud."

A brief flicker of sadness coloured Donald's dark brown eyes before he said, "Kenny, my parents don't care what I do. They haven't for a long time. Ever since I didn't become a priest, they've treated me with contempt."

"You were going to be a priest?" Kenny's wide-eyed gape would have been considered exaggerated in other circumstances, but with Donald, Kenny always invested in overstated expression to keep the dialogue flowing.

"Aye, I studied at a seminary for a couple of years. I was only young. Although that didn't matter to them. They thought their son was going to be the Pope."

"Well, forget about them. Today's all about you. You've worked your socks off to be here. I want to see you do some breakdancing when you pick up your scroll!" Kenny punched him on the shoulder. "You're da man! It'll all be over in a few seconds then you can get on with the rest of your life."

"You're so full of it, Kenny," Donald said with a hint of a smile. "I'm going to tell you something I haven't told anyone." Donald looked at his hands before he spoke again. He had

4

stopped trying to conceal the tremble dancing along to the tips of his fingers.

"I'm being followed. I know you'll find this crazy, but listen."

A wave of sadness hit the pit of Kenny's stomach. Donald was in a bad place.

"I think they're Russian. I overheard them talking one day when they were sitting outside my apartment. I used the parabolic reflector I created in the lab to pick up on what they were saying. I couldn't understand anything, but it was definitely a Slavic language. It all started about six months ago. At first I didn't want to believe it because I know I can get paranoid at the least wee thing."

Serious understatement, Kenny mused. He decided to play along.

"So, what you going to do?"

"I'm checking into Gartnavel Royal Infirmary next week. I'm going to convince my parents to section me under the Mental Health Act. It's the only way I can be sure of protection. Otherwise I might be away the crow road."

His immediate reaction was to talk Donald out of the impending section, but his crow road reference made him reconsider. There was no denying his twitching and nervous tics seemed more acute than ever. But did he really think he was in mortal danger? At the very least, he needed protection from himself. Gartnavel Royal was created in the early nineteenth century by the Glasgow Lunatic Asylum to deal with serious psychiatric cases. Donald seemed to be as serious a case as he could imagine.

"Donald. I'm really sorry. If there's anything I can do..." Inadequacy simmered underneath Kenny's mortar board.

"What's done is done, Kenny. Let's get this over with." Donald turned back to face the stage, as if the conversation had never happened.

Kenny forced himself to look away from Donald. In direct contrast to Donald's woes, he studied rows of youthful faces underneath angled mortar boards, happy students in the realisation of their dreams. The rector had begun the droll roll

5

call of every name imaginable, the Crawfords and Ramsays of the world taking more than their fair share.

"It's with great pleasure," the rector announced, "that I ask Donald Mackenzie to come to the stage for a well-deserved First Prize in Chemistry."

Donald would still be sitting in the chair if Kenny had not had the presence of mind to jab him with a straightened paperclip he had found in his trouser pocket. Donald jumped to attention, before practically running to the stage, sporting a flowing, black, Dracula-esque robe with a mortar board threatening mutiny. The congratulatory applause swiftly changed to cheers as Donald ran past the rector, grabbing the medal and scroll en route to the door. The cloak would not touch ground until he was locked in his darkened Byres Road flat, cowering in a musky corner. It was over in an instant, the slam of the atrium's heavy door a signal for the rector to move on to the next graduate. Next time Kenny would devote time to Donald would be when he attended his funeral on a bleak winter's day a year later. Gartnavel provided a perfect mix of drugs and medicines, readily available for someone determined to bring life to a premature end. Few words were spoken after the funeral, family and "friends" wondering what they could, or should, have done differently.

"Kenny Morgan, First Class Honours in Chemistry," announced the rector rhythmically. Standing to attention, Kenny felt his heart swell as he stepped onto the well-trodden aisle en route to the next step he would take in life's great adventure. This was his baptism into the real world.

He walked slowly along the bruised red carpet, feasting on the polite applause of the audience, mostly strangers. He let it soak in like gravy on mash. For four years he had forfeited the social temptations his classmates flagrantly indulged in. The toga parties, cheese and wine nights and midweek sessions in the beer bar had been tempting. He had conceded to the odd beer to acknowledge he was living the student lifestyle at least to the point of acceptability. He could not afford to immerse himself in wasted socialising, there had been too much to lose.

Stepping onto the podium, he was awakened from his self-indulgent reverie by a shout from the gods, "Well done, wee man!"

Even before he turned, he knew Tommy would be standing on his chair in the balcony, waving his hands in the air. It was the telltale can of Tennent's lager dripping over the side onto hired robes in the stalls he did not expect to see. Tommy's excitement had reached the beer spilling stage. He had not gone to bed after leaving the club the night before, deciding to continue the celebration on his own. Kenny had left him sitting in the kitchen singing a ballad at three in the morning, as he was prone to do when he had talked everyone else into submission. This one was the usual score of wrist-slitting verses, yet Tommy could make it sound like a chirpy folk song:

"I cry myself to sleep each night,
Wishing you would hold me tight.
I feel so lonesome,
Since you went awa-a-ay..."

Tommy MacGregor had an underlying sense of positivity developed over the years. At the age of sixteen he had been running for Scotland in cross country championships, beating the best in the world. His fuel was comprised of twenty percent stamina, thirty percent determination and fifty percent madness, confirming what Kenny had known from the outset: Tommy was half mad. At nineteen, it all started to go horribly wrong when the seventy mile per week training regime took its toll on young, underdeveloped shins and knees. At twenty, the dream was over. While the madness remained, the stamina and determination were devoted to partying.

Although his legs may have succumbed to the proliferation of mileage, he was otherwise a young man at his physical peak: lean, good-looking, restless with the energy previously spent on country roads. Tommy was on a trail somewhere in the middle of his own forest, impatient to find his way out. At that moment in a hall full of love and pride, Kenny was proud of Tommy being proud of him.

Sitting alongside Tommy, hardly registering his friend's characteristically outrageous behaviour, Kenny's mother, Molly, sparkled with loving tears, because she knew. She knew

7

how much Kenny had laboured to reach graduation. That first experiment in the kitchen when he had boiled milk in a pressurised cooker, crammed with marshmallows and strawberry gateau, could easily have seen off his dreams of success. His mother would have been a lesser person not to have seen the potential in those creamy red splatterings around the walls and ceiling. Her good sense in encouraging experiments outside the kitchen had proved significant in Kenny's success as a chemist – and in assuring Safeway ready meals were always high on his shopping list.

Turning to accept his certificate, he caught the rector's raised eyebrow, his humourless acknowledgement of the vocal lager lout. Kenny did not care. As he wrapped his fingers around the document, he felt he had just received the baton on his lifelong relay. Inspired, optimistic, proud, strong, in love, he intended to take the baton to the university union beer bar.

Celebrate

"Excuse me!" slurred Tommy.

"Aye, what is it?" sneered the barman, bitter at having to serve beers to snobby students who spent all his taxes.

"Look, Zed," said Tommy, noticing a well-worn badge on a scruffy waistcoat. "Do you think you can put a whisky in each of these pints?"

"I suppose I could," he answered quizzically. "Bit bizarre behaviour even for a student. If you pay me though, I'll not argue."

"So why the hell," Tommy smiled, "did you not fill them with beer? Get them filled up or you'll be wearing them. Please."

Zed knew better than to argue with such a steely glare, realising his customer was most definitely not a student; he understood the value of money. This alcohol displacement theory on the other hand would probably have made a good experiment in the physics department, where they could have applied his practical view of weights and measures.

"Eh, sorry, pal, I didn't realise. Been a long day," Zed muttered. He topped up the two pints to the brim of the glass allowing a slight overflow to ensure his customer was satisfied.

By the time Tommy made it back to the table with the tray the extra beer had spilled and was splashing against a finely balanced array of drinks. But that was not the point.

Fiona and Kenny waited patiently with Molly. She was the quietest person at the table, but no-one had any doubt she was the architect of her son's success. Recently retired, she had worked till the last day possible cleaning the local high school, while keeping the house afloat. The years of hard graft had resulted in her size belying an underlying emotional and physical strength. Her small, round face was creased with laughter lines around the eyes, above dimples that had once appeared only when she smiled but were now a permanent part of her expression.

She sat humble yet steadfast at the table sipping on her wee goldie, enjoying the sense of achievement her hard work had inspired. She had spent her whole life praying for Kenny. While he had interpreted the prayers to be related to professional success, for her they maxed out at health and happiness. She was proud that he had met a lovely girl, strong of back, firm of hip. Other than that, she was happy about the things he had not done rather than the paper achievements. He had avoided jail, drug addiction, alcoholism, and crime. That was what she was celebrating.

Tommy had left a conversation vacuum at the table when he went to the bar. He invested so enthusiastically in any discussion that once he stopped, the silence became a welcome shelter until he returned. Truth was the pub was quieter than at any other time during the year. The majority of graduates had opted for one of the West End's overpriced hotels for a "memorable" lunch washed down with a glass of "oh-go-on-then" bubbly. The beer bar was sparsely populated with a handful of groups not requiring to overinvest, or overborrow, to celebrate their child's achievement. The quiet, comfortable air of the bar reflected their happiness more than Dom Perignon could ever do.

Handing drinks around the table, Tommy shouted, "Clink! Clink! I want to make a toast!"

"Hey, I don't drink whisky," Kenny managed to say through a mouth beginning to take its own path on the day's journey. "I'll stick to the pints."

"Go on, get it down you. It's your big day, but wait till I say a few words," Tommy soldiered on, as Fiona and Molly rolled their eyes to a flaky, whitewashed ceiling.

"I've known you since you were knee-high to a grasshopper. Right enough you haven't grown very much since then." He pretended to look at Kenny as if for the first time, as if only now noticing how vertically challenged his friend really was.

Turning to Molly, he continued. "Molly, I hate to tell you, but you should never have brought him up on a diet of shortbread and condensed milk. Instead of blankets, you should have put him to bed in a Fisons grow bag."

Molly and Fiona giggled along with Tommy's guffaw. Kenny tried to remember if he had heard this comment more or less than one hundred times.

10

"All the way through school, you never changed, wee man. You worked your nu…eh, really hard, to get through the exams to make it to university. You were rarely tempted by the… entertainment your fellow students enjoyed. You never drank cans of Kestrel round the back of the huts, or smoked the Woodbine butts we collected from our dad's pockets. You did have the odd snog with the girls, right enough…"

Tommy glanced at Fiona awaiting a reaction, disappointed that she did not even flinch.

"Hah, got you there! Just checking you were listening, Fiona. I'm only joking. We all thought Kenny was going to become a priest, because he never looked at the girls. I don't know how he could've resisted all those braces, freckles and acne. He must've had some willpower."

"Anyway," he announced, before taking a large mouthful of lager, his audience by now resigned to the rest of the monologue. "I just wanted to say that I'm proud of you, Kenny me boy! I knew you could do it. This is a big day, not just for you, but for me too. I think Molly and Fiona are a wee bit happy as well. You've got the world at your feet, wee man. Go on out there! Make it happen!"

He stopped for a half second. He lifted his whisky glass in the air and waited. Kenny knew it was a self-control measure Tommy employed when his emotions threatened to get the better of him. The glistening in his eye confirmed Kenny's hunch.

"Congratulations, Kenny! Our own university superhero."

"Well done, son!" Molly reached across to grasp Kenny's hand, her eyes awash with tears of Famous Grouse pride. Fiona beamed her heartwarming, pearly smile across to him, blowing him a kiss with a subtle purse of lips only Kenny recognised. Still holding his certificate, Kenny looked at Fiona. He saw their dreams coming together. Molly watched her dreams being realised in front of her eyes. Kenny had a good woman and had avoided temptation. Tommy's dreams would be realised when he met a young lass at the over twenty-fives disco later that night.

Touching glasses loudly, Tommy shouted, "Sláinte!" All four knew this moment was special. While they were there to

11

congratulate Kenny, they were also celebrating their love for each other. A love that would be tested to the limit in the years ahead.

Separate Ways

The shriek rebounded from the ceiling to the floor of the bar. It was either a strangulated peacock or... Lulu had just arrived. *Lulu* was short for Louise Loughrey, to whom Kenny had a debt he would never be able to repay. She had introduced him to Fiona back in their early student days, when he was a serial fumbler and spotty teenager.

Lulu dived on Fiona squashing her with her trademark bear hug. She believed everyone she met needed a good bone-crushing to let them know they were loved. Fiona's vain attempts not to spill her drink were dashed when she hoisted it into orbit, overpowered by a lunging Lulu. Most of the Bacardi landed on Tommy's arm, which he instinctively licked without missing a word or breaking eye contact with Molly, as they compared the unsubtlety of the Highland clearances with the clandestine population control of the Irish famine.

"Hi, Lulu! You look terrific," Fiona croaked.

The words had the desired effect. Lulu stepped back from the table to make an off-Broadway twirl. While Fiona felt the blood flow back into her arms.

"Do you like it?" Lulu stretched the bottom corners of her sweater to show there were even more colours in the folds above her skirt. "A penny short of four pounds out of What Every Woman Wants. A right bargain." The ultimate female bonding experience had just been accomplished. New item of clothing. Very low price. Not embarrassed to admit, or rather boast, about it. Fiona linked arms with the technicolour sweater and escorted Lulu to the bar.

Kenny felt for Lulu. Despite her seemingly extrovert personality, she oozed vulnerability. In the early days, their discussions would range around a host of subjects usually focused on saving the planet, a subject very dear to Lulu's heart. Over time Kenny learned not to disagree with her. He would search for a diplomatic reason to disengage from the debate. Recently she had become more sensitive, so much so that any dissent was viewed as a personal attack on her and her values. He had bitten his tongue on a number of occasions electing not to rise to the challenge. He knew the real reason for

13

her exaggerated public persona was less to do with the ozone layer than her exasperation at Hugh Quinn, known to his campus colleagues as Shuggy.

As if on cue, Shuggy walked into the bar. He stepped elegantly between the tables, lifting a hand to acknowledge Kenny. It was always evident when he entered a public place. Heads turned, girls smiled, some blushed, and an imaginary voiceover spoke, "Shuggy Quinn is sporting a summer look all young men will want to wear this year. Open-necked polo shirt, light woollen, beige sweater draped across his shoulders and faded Brutus jeans."

Good-looking did not begin to describe him. He had a Clark Gable intensity interwoven with a Paul Newman twinkle. He carried himself with an air of grace and self-confidence he could not have accomplished if he realised how desired he was. The name "Shuggy" spoke volumes for his view of himself as down to earth, one of the boys, yet appreciated for the good looks and charm he carried effortlessly. He was a god.

Which was ironic, since God was his life.

After the summer, Shuggy would go to Rome, to exercise his vocation for the Roman Catholic Church. He had studied theology at Glasgow for three years. With each passing year, he had become more convinced that his vocation was in the priesthood. This would have been an obvious match, since Shuggy's personality, sense of justice, and love of others made him the perfect candidate. The only barrier had been the fact that after fifteen hundred years the church still expected the vow of celibacy. He had come to terms with it. He loved God in a special way and that meant making special sacrifices, which made all the sense in the world to Shuggy. But made no sense to Lulu. She knew that on the day Shuggy sent off his application to the Glasgow archdiocese, their love would know no physical expression other than a hug or a timid holding of hands.

It broke her heart when he said that he had to follow his own, where he would always keep a unique place for his love for her. When she said that his being in Rome, shackled with a dog collar, would not keep her warm on a winter's night, he wept. Shuggy reminded himself that Jesus had also wept for the sacrifices he had to make.

Lulu's decision to herd elephants across Africa for the next two years, she insisted, had nothing to do with Shuggy. She was going to do her bit for the environment. It just so happened to be half a planet away in a far-flung country without a telephone or church for hundreds of miles.

"Hi, Father, can you turn this into a glass of your best Cana 30? AD of course!" Tommy handed a glass of tap water to Shuggy as he reached the table.

"Good one, Tommy," he answered. "Don't you know my time has not yet come? By the way, before you start, you're not my mother, so you've got no chance!" He smiled a row of perfect white teeth and winked at Tommy. Kenny was sure he could detect a ripple across the room as female breasts heaved.

"Congratulations, Kenny!" Shuggy extended his hand, which Kenny shook slowly, enjoying the envy of the room.

"Thanks, Shuggy. Glad you could make it."

"Wouldn't have missed it for the world. You look well. I see the party's been... eh... going on for a wee while. Eh, Kenny?"

"What?"

"You can stop shaking my hand now, people might start talking. Celibacy applies to me no matter what my sexual leaning. By the way, you look dashing in that gown, you might make me reconsider."

"Oh, right, got a bit carried away there. Do you want a drink?"

"No thanks, I see Lulu at the bar. I'll go up to say hello." Shuggy's barely raised eyebrow spoke volumes about the ever-increasing awkwardness of conversations with Lulu.

Kenny turned to tell Tommy that his water to wine comment would test the patience of a saint, let alone a student priest. The two hands on his shoulders stopped him in his tracks. Fingers began to work their way through gnarled muscles, victims of a posture punished by endless nights bent double over formulae and test tubes. He did not twist his neck to confirm it was Grant. The spontaneous massage energetically imposed on lumpy tissue was enough. After the first ten seconds of

15

kneading clumps of flesh, Grant ran out of ideas. He patted Kenny on the back. "I bet that relieved the tension, Kenny!"

"Aye, Grant, just what I needed." Kenny felt a twinge of pain above his left shoulder where Grant had most probably pinched a nerve. Grant was not much taller than Kenny but had been gifted with forearms larger than his biceps. Handshakes and back rubs were to be avoided at all costs. Grant was not a classically good-looking guy, but the straw-coloured floppy hair dangling across an intense pair of green eyes guaranteed him a second look. His unremitting enthusiasm shone through in his features, giving him a worldly-wise appearance, which he used to his full advantage. His energy combined with an unremitting passion for whatever he tried guaranteed him a place in the university football team, albeit second string. His inconsistent, flamboyant performances earned him the nickname of "Nearly"... nearly a good football player.

"Learned how to do that last year when I was hiking in Tibet. You'll get the full benefit tomorrow morning when you wake up. So how you been?" Grant surveyed the room, his arm resting on Kenny's shoulder the only indication the question was directed at him.

"Fine," Kenny answered, realising that his audience was not listening. Silently they studied the room to see that most tables were busy. When they had arrived earlier that afternoon, they were among a population of ten. The atmosphere was building; the smell of celebration was sharp, tinged with the sadness of graduation goodbyes and farewells.

"Last time I saw the bar this busy was when Sean Connery popped in for a pint one day. He had been shopping in Glasgow." Grant waited for Kenny to ask a question. Kenny did not ask, but looked quizzically at Grant. Nobody asked Grant questions any more.

"I managed to have a couple of pints with him before the hordes converged on the place once they'd heard he was here. It's ridiculous that he can't have a quiet drink without people bothering him."

Grant's pained expression meant he was either reliving or most probably imagining the scene. If Kenny had a genuine question, it would have been "why on earth would Sean

16

Connery pop into this beer bar?" Kenny struggled to keep his face straight, fighting a rebellious twitch at the corner of his mouth. He opted for a situation saving question. "I thought he only drank martinis, shaken but not stirred?"

"No, you daft pillock. That's only in the films, only the Bond films. I did ask him about that. He said he'd never had one in real life because Martini Bianco's a woman's drink."

"But it's not Martini Bianco he drinks. It's a martini cocktail, which has got gin in it," Kenny said.

"Aye, whatever. Point is, he never drinks them. Anyway, how's the graduation going?" A Grant sidestep was in process. "I'm off to the bar. Do you want a drink?"

"No thanks. Not even if they do real martinis here."

Grant, oblivious to the lesson in martinis, walked off towards Shuggy and Lulu, where he would provide an unconsciously funny, appreciated distraction. No doubt at some point in the evening he would get to use his well-worn chat-up line: "Hi, my name's Grant. You can have any wish you want."

There was probably a name for the condition Grant suffered from, although Kenny had never heard of it. He did not embellish stories in the hope of impressing a member of the opposite sex, which conceivably was the only valid reason to exaggerate. Grant did not exaggerate. The safe houses he had guarded in Belfast during the troubles were not an exaggeration. The second-hand car dealership he set up to launder IRA funds was not an overstatement of facts. He could never be accused of overtly magnifying the truth. He just told lies: massive, fantastically unbelievable, and ludicrously lacking in detail, with hugely unrealistic webs of wondrous fabrication.

Grant had already graduated earlier that week. In journalism.

"Hey, Hassan!" Kenny heard Tommy shout towards the door. Tommy stood and walked towards a figure silhouetted against the evening twilight. The white robes billowed gently in the evening breeze as he considered the bar while listening to the lively crowd, which had been forced to a murmur by the austerity of his glare. The figure held the tasbih, a set of Muslim prayer beads, rolling them leisurely between thumb and

17

forefinger. Kenny was surprised his friend had turned up considering it was Ramadan.

"Hi, Tommy, good to see you," Hassan said quietly. He extended a hand, which was ignored and replaced with a crushing hug. Tommy chose those whom he respected very carefully. When it came to Hassan, Tommy oozed admiration.

Kenny waited patiently for him to unlock himself from Tommy's embrace, then leant in to give Hassan a gentle man hug. He was having none of it, and squeezed Kenny tightly, lifting him in the air.

"Congratulations, Kenny. I am so proud of you, pal," he said with genuine emotion in his voice, his eyes glistening.

"Great to see you, buddy. It's been a while," Kenny whispered as he extricated himself from the hug. Hassan was a dedicated individual who did nothing by halves. When he had joined the university football team, he had been an austere, God-fearing Muslim who prayed regularly. Such was his charisma, games were arranged deliberately not to conflict with his prayer sessions. Otherwise, he would take himself off mid-game to face east and fall into a semi-trance. Kenny had learned to read his mood by watching him shuffle a set of beads between his fingers; he could not remember a meeting when Hassan was beadless.

One year into university after attending scores of post-football nights out, more as an observer than participant, he had decided that austerity would no longer guide his life's choices. During the wild days, the prayer beads remained although they had to compete with beer, cigarettes, and countless girls who could not avoid the hypnotic force of his darkly passionate, searching eyes. When it came to partying he had applied the same degree of focus as his faith had required from him, far outstripping his fellow revellers in both capacity and that Holy Grail of revellers – recovery. He did not know the meaning of the word "hangover", or the embarrassment of missing a class through the excesses of the night before.

The last year of university had found Hassan regretting the rejection of his faith. He decided to return to the Muslim religion with even more fervour to make up for the time and grace he had lost. While no-one would have described him as an extremist, Kenny knew he was an extreme version of the Muslim who had arrived from Turkey three years earlier. It was rumoured that he had his robes coated on the inside with horse hair to irritate him during the day, as a constant reminder that he should never have turned his back on his beliefs.

"Kenny, I've just popped in to say congratulations and goodbye. You've been a good friend. I will remember you fondly." Kenny saw his eyes moisten.

"Goodbye? What do you mean? You off somewhere?"

"I fly to Afghanistan next week. There is a group of Muslims with the same interpretation of the faith as me. I am going to become a member of that community." Hassan's chest rose slightly with the pride he felt at his decision.

"Afghanistan? You're joking! That place is in ruins. You'll get murdered." Kenny knew that tact was not going to help convince him to change his mind.

"Yes, but from great ruins come great beginnings. There are many good Muslims changing the face of our religion. I want to be part of it. Take care, my friend. May your god go with you!" They smiled at each other knowing their oft-quoted Dave Allen quip was more relevant than ever.

Out of the corner of his eye Kenny spotted a figure climb up onto a stool. Tommy was up to his antics again. "Everyone! Attention! Please!" Tommy's hands were cupped around his mouth as he shouted above the din of the beer bar. He was competing with a conversational momentum inspired by alcohol, not in the mood to be interrupted.

"Fire! Fire!" seemed to do the trick as it created a hiatus in noise large enough for him to continue. "Only joking, there's no fire! But equally as important is why we are all here today." He seemed to speak to the whole bar when there was a grand total of eight people there to celebrate Kenny's graduation. "It's only right that Kenny makes a speech to tell us how much he loves us." All eight, and some friendly strangers in the bar, clapped as he lowered himself from the stool.

Kenny had not realised just how drunk he was until he stepped onto a chair to teeter above a table full of drinks. The room began to see-saw in front of him as he worked his feet into a position wide enough to avoid a spectacular crash.

"You all know I'm not a man of words, so I will be short," Kenny began.

"You certainly are!" Tommy shouted over his shoulder on his way to the bar. Sniggers and hoots were barely drowned out by the banter starting again around the room.

"Today's not just a celebration for me, but for every one of us. We all move onto new, greener pastures this summer. I won't go into the detail of what each of us will do next, but we will have fun and face into a few adventures. Even Tommy might find a job."

The unspoken ouch from the crowd was tangible. It would have ruined the rest of Kenny's words if Tommy had not shouted, "I'm going to join Hassan's local prayer group, I am sure he doesn't want to be considered sectarian."

Hassan shook his head slowly, pinching the top of his nose, stifling a grin.

Kenny continued. "Thank you all for the last four years of friendship. I'm looking forward to the future, growing through life with the best bunch of friends a graduate could ask for. We'll have lots of reunions. Cheers!"

Kenny raised his glass and the eight cheered in unison. The reunions would not happen. At least, not en masse like the university union bar event. Ad hoc, rare moments of connection would happen, some fun, and some much more sinister.

The Dark Side

Why do I hate him so much? Is it jealousy? There is something about his achievement that twists a knife deep inside. Not so much the quantity of success, but the quality. Kenny came from a challenging background, quietly enjoying a passage into the land of dreams his peers had shunned.

On the face of it, he has remained true to his ideals and values.

But has he?

At the end of the day, what matters to Kenny is Kenny. He allows other people to step within his force field but does he truly acknowledge or care for them? He has been fortunate enough to identify his skills at an early age, finding a career path to pursue life at his own pace. But does he care for those around him trying to do the same?

He has become an end in himself, self-serving, arrogant. Others are ingredients in his recipe for success. He sucks them in, spins them around then spews out an unrecognisable gunge of human form. He pretends not to know he does it.

He has that hypnotic influence. I wish I could tell him what I think of him. Instead I do the opposite and treat him like something special. I treat him like a friend. He confuses me.

The more time spent in his company, the more difficult it becomes to ignore him. You become for his self-esteem what space is for a black hole. His magnetism polarises others. It is as if everything revolves around him, a source of energy, exploding with all the mass of an imploded sun too big for its own good. His light creates dark, brooding, self-absorbed, uninteresting shadows.

And that is what I will be. I will be that twisted shape created by Kenny: the dark side. I will be his shadow.

A Life-Changing Gift

The television blaring in the bedroom meant either Tommy or Fiona had let themselves in with the key from under the mat. It had crossed his mind that this was not the wisest place to leave it, but on further reflection he saw no reason to be concerned. An enterprising burglar would need to be thicker than the scaffolding surrounding the façade of the building to enter a smelly stairwell through a broken "security" door, oblivious to walls decorated by graffiti courtesy of Finnieston's Bundy. Boys United Never Die Young were more fearsome in name than action, and overly focused on informing all who entered that they could write their names in twenty-five different ways. Anyone unfortunate enough to burgle a flat in this block would most probably decide to leave something out of pity rather than add more misery to this Finnieston favela.

Finnieston is sandwiched between Glasgow's bustling city centre and the colourful, vibrant West End. While there were plenty of pubs and grocers in a couple of square miles of interwoven streets, in these halcyon days of student living Finnieston seemed to have a permanent tumbleweed atmosphere. Most of its inhabitants, living in three and four-storey tenements, enjoyed the night life on either side of Finnieston rather than the cheapest drink prices and highest number of characters per square mile in Glasgow on their own doorstep. It had been Kenny's home for three years providing him with access to as many life stories and regrets as people he would meet leaning against bars in the Ben Nevis or Grove at the end of his street.

He was greeted by Tommy lying on his bed, propped up against the pillows, stretched under the same duvet Fiona had shared with Kenny that morning. Kenny felt there was something sacrilegious about how his friend had turned his bed into an opportunity to munch furiously on pork scratchings while sipping a Tennent's, hand cradling the naked form of an embossed blonde model flattened onto the side of the can. Kenny wondered when someone would call the brewery to account on overstepping the political correctness line.

"Oh, aye, been letting the moths out, then?" Tommy sprayed crumbs over the bedspread Kenny had washed just last month, as he witnessed the cluster of bags Kenny dropped onto the floor.

"Bought myself a few things. Getting ready for the first day in my new job tomorrow!"

"Don't tell me, you were down in Partick, giving it Marvin Hagler with the poor shopkeepers." Tommy shook his head in disgust. "Those guys hardly get a customer all day. Then you turn up to squeeze their rent money out of them. No wonder the Scots have a reputation for being tight. Did you know that two Aberdonians fighting over a penny resulted in copper wire being invented?"

"Aye, Tommy. You have mentioned it, just about every time I go out shopping. By the way, how did you get on last night?" Kenny stopped him in mid-flow.

"What a night! I ended up meeting a wee lassie in the Savoy. A right wee cracker. She wants to see me again, but I'm playing hard to get."

"Hard to get?" Kenny laughed. "Tommy Cooper's jokes are harder to get than you! What you mean is that you can't afford it."

"Exactly!" Tommy responded. "Although I'll need to wait. I've just been signing on today at the Broo. My cheque's in the post. Why do you think I'm hanging out with you? Free beer, even though it's boring old Tennent's. After you start your new job, I'll be looking forward to a fridge full of Grolsch or Stella."

Kenny turned to his formica covered wardrobe shaking his head at this warped sense of reality. He prised opened the door of a shaky MFI wardrobe, stuggling to stay upright due to a frame distorted by the dampness of the room. Pushing an array of shirts and jeans to the side he created space for the Slater's suit that fell on the right side of one hundred pounds. He still had to figure out how to turn the legs up without resorting to needle and thread, unsure whether to use a roll of masking tape from under the sink or the stapler buried beneath his papers on the desk.

He kept most of his clothes in the wardrobe rather than in drawers. The dampness of the room encouraged him to hang his jeans, shirts, and T-shirts avoiding the process of ironing, one small benefit he had found in three years of cold nights and damp mornings. He began to close the door when he noticed something at the end of the row of worn attire. A light-blue material peeked out from between his worn jeans and Springsteen Wembley 1988 T-shirt. He knew each item of clothing intimately and could not recollect a bright, blue garment. He reached in to remove the object from the hanger. His hand felt a textile of contrasting materials. Rugged, yet smooth. Heavy, but nicely weighted. He was not sure what to think, studying what was arguably the most beautiful piece of attire he had ever laid eyes on. Colourful, but subtly so. The light-blue was criss-crossed with grey creating a black and blue tartan with thin red lines economically woven into the fabric. It was avant-garde versus traditional, historic but yet a contemporary icon.

Male with more than a hint of female.

A kilt.

Turning to show it to Tommy, he saw his friend standing in the middle of the room, duvet on the floor. Can of Tennent's in hand, Tommy stood proud in his own red and black kilt. While individually the colours were muted, the combination resulted in a garment of attitude and character. Perfect for his bizarre friend. Kenny knew it was MacGregor Rob Roy tartan as Tommy had pointed it out to him one evening in a Hope Street shop window a year earlier. In the middle of the MacGregor colours, hanging from a thin chain wrapped around his waist, sat a sporran in all its glory, with as much hair as a Highland cow in winter. The kilt reached down to just above his knees. His athletic legs stood sturdy above a pair of thick white socks pushed all the way down to his ankles.

"I got us one each, from that shop in Hope Street. They're both ex-hire, but you would never know they had ever been used. There's a sporran on the floor in the plastic bag."

Kenny was speechless.

After a minute, he looked up from the kilt. "But, Tommy, you can't afford this. Don't get me wrong, it's beautiful. It's even Morgan tartan. I'm lost for words."

"No bother, wee man. I've been saving for a while. I thought it would make a fine graduation present. Guess what, I managed to convince them to give me two for the price of one. I might not have your negotiating skills, but you did teach me a few tricks up the Yoker market." Kenny grinned at the memory of explaining to Tommy the secret of haggling for socks and Y-fronts: concentrate on reducing the price of a single item before seeking an additional discount on volume when you up the quantity from one to ten.

"Come here, you mad Highlander," Kenny said, stretching his arms wide.

The two friends hugged awkwardly, before stepping apart hurriedly.

"So, what do we do now, then?" Kenny asked between self-conscious coughs. He would have thrown himself into the bonding moment more energetically, if he had realised what the future held in store for their friendship.

Tommy raised his hands in the air and said, as if the answer was obvious, "We have a kilt night, Kenny-boy!"

The Power of the Kilt

Kenny could not remember ever having felt so free. Striding down Byres Road, arguably Glasgow's most popular street, he enjoyed the brush of fabric against his outer thigh, while the edge of the kilt tickled the top of his knees. The best sensation of all, the cause of his sense of freedom, was the breeze created by his fast-paced walk circulating around parts of the body otherwise imprisoned from the world outside. He tingled with the newness of the experience, particularly the sporran. With each step, the sporran lifted then fell like a gentle pulse. With each stride he realised no other garment could make a man feel quite so sexy and liberated.

In reality, it was a well-known fact that while the kilt was the birthright of every Scotsman, arguably the most famous national dress in the world, it was rarely worn in public in Scotland other than for a wedding or official celebration. Hence, without exception, bystanders watched the two kilts until they turned right onto Ashton Lane to avail themselves of a couple of real ales in the Chip. The Ubiquitous Chip catered for all types, ages and sizes, where nothing ever seemed out of place, where difference was encouraged. Chatting as they walked through the door, the welcoming hum of unfettered discussion stopped long enough for the clientele to survey the kilted lads. Eyes measured them until an older gent at the bar stuck his thumb in the air and shouted, "Now, that's a sight for sore eyes! Good on you, lads!"

They smiled self-consciously at the hint of acknowledgement as the drinkers turned back to their company, the briefest of smiles registering their acceptance. Kenny's new job would start the next day, it felt good to be out with Tommy having a quiet refreshment to calm his nerves. They squeezed through to the bar, where they sank the first two pints in minutes. A nice layer of alcohol-induced confidence coasting through their veins, it was not long before they mingled with other groups, encouraged to comment on everything from Scotland's best football manager to devolution. Until Tommy decided to merge the two discussions and enjoy an opportunity to enlighten a handful of people they had only just met.

"Look, to me it's quite simple. Take the analogy of Scotland's football team then apply it to a devolved government. The situation becomes crystal. The Scotland football team represents us on the world stage. Every so often, well once actually, we'll score a goal that is remembered. The wearing of the jersey inspires our team to do great things by taking on the biggest and strongest in the world. Ten out of ten for guts and bravery. The truth is though, that we never win a World Cup or a European championship, we rarely ever get to the knock out stages. We end up making up the numbers. In a strange way, despite what other nations might regard as embarrassing failure, we can still be proud, even somehow optimistic. But it's not really optimism, it's hope, it's love. Above all, it's pride. We're proud of still being able to hope. Our history won't let us do anything else." Tommy paused and took a long, slow drink from his glass. His audience waited.

"So then there's devolution. People argue that by being part of the union we have a greater say in world affairs. We can participate on the world stage. Our economy is stronger because we are allowed to spend our own oil revenues, at least partially. Why on earth, we're told, would we want to disconnect our umbilical cord with Westminster and Buckingham Palace? We would fall into discord, a state of dismay, disrepair, and disappointment. In fact, the number of dis-es in our lives would be so disproportionate to other countries that our only point of distinction would be a disregard for how many dis-es we were distinguished for."

Kenny smiled as Tommy's audience listened more out of a sense of bewilderment than interest in Scotland's future government.

"In other words, why can't we apply our hopes, dreams and faith in our football team to a home-grown government? Of course, there will be failures, but the odd moment of success will provide enough momentum to make it work. We would become a force to be reckoned with and, who knows, maybe one day respected."

Tommy's silenced listeners studied him, realising that his speech had been one big non-sequitur. Until the old man at the bar shouted, "Archie Gemmill for first President of Scotland!"

The audience laughed, shook their heads, and erupted into an analysis of Scotland's football exploits. The governmental status and independence of the nation fell off the agenda at that moment, eclipsed by Gemmill's 1978 goal against Holland.

Kenny was very different in a kilt. He felt not only liberated but empowered, with a heightened self-awareness and poise. A shy, kilted Scotsman was a contradiction. The kilt, as they found out that evening milling around the pub talking to whoever would listen, was a magnet. It attracted people who would normally not have the energy or desire to make the effort. Barriers did not exist between Scotland's national dress and the outside world. It represented the ultimate in transparency. It encouraged friendship, trust, and reminded others that the reputation of the Scots was of an outgoing, honest, humorous, personable yet slightly vulnerable race of people. When you put on the kilt, Kenny realised as he leant against the bar, you had better be prepared to live up to the high expectations that came with it. Snapping out of his reverie, he tapped Tommy on the shoulder as he explained to his new found friends why Scotland's drinking culture should be cherished, even encouraged, since it kept drugs at bay.

"Look, Tommy, I'm going to head home. It's been a great night, but I need to be a wee bit sensible."

"Aye alright, wee man. This has been a rare night! Good luck tomorrow."

"Cheers, pal!"

Kenny walked down the Chip's steep steps and sauntered out onto the damp cobblestones of Ashton Lane, feeling slightly unsteady underfoot. He placed his back against the wall sucking greedily on the freshness of the air. Two hours of stale pub smoke had taken its toll. He enjoyed the cool night on his cheeks as he listened to the hum of car engines reverberating off the surrounding tenements. Around the corner a busker strummed murderously on a guitar. It may have been "Bridge over Troubled Water" but Kenny was unsure. Whether it would be convincing enough to encourage the generosity of the drinkers spilling out of the pubs dotted around the lane, time would tell. As he closed his eyes to enjoy the cocktail of sounds, the mellow evening was shattered by a high-pitched, blood-curdling wail. That is one cat, Kenny thought, he would rather not tread on. Especially when he was in his kilt. Stepping away from the wall, Kenny measured the road ahead for his walk back home ready to step into the stride he had developed that evening to make the most of his amorous sporran.

Then he heard it again. This time it seemed less animalistic, more a shriek than a howl. Before he could formulate the thought lurking in the recesses of his subconscious, he was suddenly left in no doubt.

"Noooooooo!" rang out weakly until it drifted into the night, a desperate, helpless cry.

It resounded in his ears for seconds after it had stopped. The word created ice-cold fingers wrapping themselves around his spine. It may have come from the end of the lane. He could not be sure. Realising whatever was happening to the owner of the scream would not wait until he called the police, he ran towards it. Adrenalin flowed freely, taking over from where alcohol had recently been in charge, his heart beating hard and fast. The kilt rose behind him as he sprinted along the cobbles. He covered the fifty yards silently, thankful to have worn his trainers rather than his hobnailed boots, which would have eliminated the element of surprise he sensed he would need.

Reaching the end of the lane, he looked to his left at the stairs leading to the university campus. At the top, he could see a commotion, a frenzy of limbs grappling for control. His eyes adjusting to the darkness, he saw a youth kneeling on a young girl's arms, pinning her to the ground, while another, wearing an army camouflage jacket, emptied the contents of her handbag onto the ground. Both thugs faced the wall unaware of Kenny watching them from the bottom of the stairs.

The camouflage-jacketed youth towered over the girl, the air misting with the strain of his short, sharp breaths. Kenny focused on staying motionless, not moving a muscle. He studied the scene. It was frightening. Worst of all, it was happening now with Kenny as a hidden, trembling spectator.

He stared as if viewing a widescreen cinema, atmospheric sounds and cold air wafting into the auditorium. This was his moment to turn, walk away, to focus on getting home to bed, well-rested before his first day at work.

29

This was also Kenny's chance to be the man the kilt demanded him to be. There was only one thing he could do. Taking the stairs two at a time, he reached the camouflage jacket in seconds. Before the attacker had a chance to turn, Kenny grabbed the rough flannel, yanking hard at its collar. It was enough to put the attacker off balance and send him toppling backwards down the steps.

Kenny wasted no time to watch how he had landed as the other thug was turning to see what had happened. Kenny saw the side of his head, a profile of twisted, scarred features. He had never punched another person before that moment but, in classic southpaw stance, he balled his fist to crunch a nose that had seen plenty of action in the past. The splinter of bone sounded satisfyingly pleasing in the cool night air. Although not nearly as comforting as the crack of his skull when it connected with the wall behind. Goodnight, Kenny thought.

He could hear the girl whimper, pulling her legs up to her body, into a protective, foetal position. He wished he could have helped her but his priorities lay elsewhere. He spun round to see the youth at the bottom of the stairs try to stand up, rage boiling on a face arguably uglier than the one belonging to his unconscious friend. Kenny launched himself into the air, kilt flailing behind him, to land nimbly on the fourth step from the bottom. As he landed on his left leg, he unleashed the full force of his right, connecting with a bewildered face. The thug fell to the ground in a crumpled daze, blood seeping from a gash on the side of his head.

Kenny watched his still form for a second then turned to the girl, who was now sitting upright, knees held tight to her chest. Her confusion emanated from soft, terrified features, as she sobbed soundlessly. He was not sure what to do. He wanted to reach out to hold and comfort her but hesitated, conscious she may not be ready for male tenderness.

He walked up the steps slowly extending his hand. "It's okay. It's all over now. Let's get you away from here." She gripped his fingers tightly, allowing herself to be pulled to her feet. He placed his arm gently around her shoulders and led her down the steps onto the lane, stepping over a motionless body. Her shivering frame brought a lump to his throat. He held her, letting her cry into his chest, hands raised to her face.

Her tearful gulps were quickly interrupted by the commotion of what sounded like a stampede of horses on the cobbled stones. He looked over her head to see three policemen and a policewoman run down the street batons in hand. Behind them, strangely decorative in the night scene, ran a youth with rope-like dreadlocks holding a guitar. Kenny guessed that this was the murderer of Simon and Garfunkel's greatest hits.

"Right, you!" the tallest policeman shouted. "Stop right there!"

Kenny raised his hand in the air, open palmed. He spoke softly. "On the stairs. There are two guys. They tried to…" He stopped speaking, pointing at the dark hair of the girl in his arms.

The policeman locked eyes with Kenny for the briefest of seconds before turning to study the stairs, littered with two unconscious thugs. "You did this?"

"I got lucky, I suppose. They were focused on other things."

"Okay," the policeman answered, a hint of admiration in his eyes. "Don't go anywhere, we need a statement from you."

The policewoman gently placed her arm around the girl's shoulders saying, "Come on, love, let's go for a cup of tea. Everything's all right now. Kiltman came to your rescue." Kenny smiled self-consciously at the superhero reference. He would remember this comment in the future when he would have cause to consider the irony of her words.

Looking up into his eyes, the girl smiled uncertainly, then whispered, "Thank you. You're a very brave man." He looked at her properly for the first time. He saw a deeply attractive young girl with large, brown soulful eyes. She had a small mole to the right of her mouth, which briefly disappeared into a dimple on her cheek as she spoke.

"Not brave," Kenny answered, "but in the right place at the right time." Thanks to Tommy's kilt night. "I'm only glad I could do something."

The policewoman holding the girl allowed her and Kenny to lock eyes, both dealing with what had just happened until there were no more words to be spoken. Turning away, she squeezed her hero's hand. Kenny watched as she disappeared into the night.

Someone Else's Plan

How could something so simple go so horribly wrong? This has been planned for weeks, just waiting for the right moment. Tonight was perfect. But no, they could not listen to my simple instructions. The only thing they were able to do was alert Kenny as planned. But they then had to get carried away with the girl letting Kenny take advantage of their distraction. I had to call the police in the end like a lame citizen who does not have the guts to take action himself.

The Glasgow police were pathetically slow. They allowed Kenny to become the hero. They gave him the opportunity to save the damsel in distress. "Kiltman" the policewoman said with melodramatic respect in her eyes. My stomach churned watching him hold the girl, comfortably nestled in his arms. She seemed to regret leaving him to go to the policewoman. Leaving her saviour, whose claim to fame was to be in the right place at the right time. All of which was orchestrated by me.

The hatred bubbles up inside, desperate to escape. I want to scream at him. Tell him how he can no longer suck my energy; make himself stronger at my expense. But that would foil my plans, ruin everything. I must retreat once again into the darkness, blend into the walls and sanctuary of the lane. I need little to be invisible to the human eye. I have found the means to do this when it has mattered; those closest to me have taught me well. My time to put Kenny in his place has not yet come. I need a bigger moment, something more catastrophic, more memorable. I will bide my time and enjoy manipulating my prey, preparing for his day of destiny.

First Day on the Job

Morning came faster than he had ever remembered. He pulled himself out of bed with what felt like superhuman strength. Sitting on its edge, he rested elbows on knees, head in hands. What a night! By the time he had left Partick police station, it was on the wrong side of three in the morning. He had slept less than four hours but was already beginning to feel the pulse of energy in his head.

As a youth he had avoided brawls and confrontations preferring the diplomatic, and at times, reverse gear options. He could not explain from where his cool detachment and pseudo-martial arts moves had come from. Adrenalin really is a funny thing. Bottom line though, the girl was safe. He did not see her after she was led away by the policewoman. He probably would not see her again since he had asked the policeman to keep his identity private, avoid disclosing his details if not required. He would have liked to have had a coffee with her and get to know her a little, but the circumstances of their meeting somehow precluded that scenario.

His request for anonymity was mainly to avoid his new employer hearing how his new chemist had spent the night before his first day. The heroism of the evening would quickly be smothered by the kilt and pints, with many witnesses as to the quantity consumed. If he was required as a witness then he would of course step up, but otherwise he preferred to remain incognito.

One hour later, after a quick shower, shave, and a neater than expected application of masking tape to his trousers, he took a bus from Glasgow to the hinterlands of the western suburbs. The bus hurtled and bumped between traffic lights and stops, the driver apparently oblivious to the extra thirty feet of bus behind his seat and the floor above his head. The catnap he had hoped to enjoy was replaced by a tour of Partick, Scotstoun, Yoker and Clydebank. He studied the buildings on either side of the street realising that the vast majority of Glaswegians lived in tenement accommodation, testament to the Glaswegian's famed ability to get on with others; it was in-bred. Literally.

The bus drove into Duntocher terminus just as he stood to approach the door. The driver made one last effort to throw his passengers onto the aisle before braking abruptly. Kenny gripped the steel pole above his seat as he swung round full circle to land on the seat in front. The alternative of scraping his new suit across a wet, filthy floor would have made his first day more awkward than it was going to be already.

He stepped gingerly from the bus to walk through Duntocher towards his first real job. Duntocher, a small village nestled in the slopes of the Old Kilpatrick hills, famous for its close-knit community, lay eight miles to the west of Glasgow city centre, far enough away to retain its independence.

After a short walk along a quiet, house-lined Stark Avenue, he stopped in his tracks to absorb the clutch of buildings and sheds dotted across the welcoming hillside. Wallace Distillers sat snug under an overhang of the Old Kilpatrick hills, with a view along the Firth of Clyde towards Greenock. On a clear day such as this the river was spectacular, sun glistening off glassy water, mirroring the beautiful foliage and islands. The distillery used the contours of the land to protect it from the biting north wind in the winter. The façade was of exaggerated proportions, dotted with turrets, porous with windows in a range of shapes and sizes. He had already been to the building several months earlier for the interview. There was something about whisky that inspired him. It was Scotland. Up there with the kilt. He knew he could work in Wallace Distillers.

The sweat on his palm felt uncomfortable. No matter how many times he wiped it along the sleeve of his new jacket, it still remained clammy. He took a deep breath, stepped through the door and walked towards a shiny, beige reception desk, encouraged by a beaming, freckled girl sporting frail headphones and a slim microphone.

"Good morning, sir. How can I help you?"

Sir!

"Yes, good morning. My name is Kenny Morgan. I'm starting here today. Mr. Wallace is expecting me."

"Welcome to Wallace Distillers, Mr. Morgan."

Smiling pleasantly, she pushed a book towards him. "Just sign here. I'll give you a visitor's pass, which you can use for today until you have your ID completed. I'll call Mr. Wallace."

"Okay, thanks."

As Kenny signed his name, the receptionist whispered, "You may want to take the toilet paper off your face. You only get one chance to make a first impression."

"Oh, thanks," Kenny muttered awkwardly, gently peeling four pink corners of toilet paper from his chin and cheeks. "I was in a hurry this morning. There were no fresh blades at home. Em... okay... I'll just wait over here."

Settling gently into a soft, leather armchair, he felt his cheeks redden. He hoped the rush of blood would not start the nicks bleeding again. He did not have long to wait. A round man of excessive proportions bounded down the stairs. His tie flapped in the air before landing on a shirt bulging with determined buttons, flecks of breakfast speckled across his midriff. Before Kenny had a chance to stand up, he boomed, "Kenny Morgan! Welcome to Wallace Distillers. I've been looking forward to your first day just as much as you have, I bet."

Kenny scrambled to his feet extending his hand. "Thanks, Mr. Wallace. It's great to be here."

"Come now, Kenny, if you're going to do the great things for us I expect, then you better start by calling me Wullie. Let me show you the distillery."

Half an hour later, after a tour of the building enthusiastically delivered by his new boss, Kenny placed his briefcase on a semi-circular desk dominating a corner office. Outside the door lay a complex array of machines, tubes and glass cylinders. To the layman's eye, it might have looked as though a group of pre-school children had been let loose for two hours, but to Kenny the lab was exactly as it should be, especially because of the row upon row of clear bottles containing whisky of varying ages and blends dominating all four walls. He felt at home. He was impatient to play with this room full of toys of the trade. There was so much he wanted to achieve, but above all he wanted to create. He was feeling upbeat after his conversation with Wullie during their tour. He had only understood half of what he had said, but enough to know he had been hired for a reason.

"Right, Kenny, it's important you understand what motivates us here in Wallace. We work to a mission statement that quite simply states, 'Wallace Whiskies inspire long-term success for our customers and satisfaction for our consumers'. This means we can't remain stagnant in an ever-changing whisky industry. Our volume and value shares have been declining in both the home and export markets due to competitors finding ways to excite consumers and make the whisky experience relevant. They are also beating us hands down with new products. Their growth is driven by an in-depth understanding of what the consumer wants, creating a sales story through cutting-edge marketing programmes which we struggle to match. The reality is we don't have enough in the pipeline to keep up with an industry driven by multinational players, funded beyond our wildest dreams. While we're proud of the fact we run our business as a family, at the end of the day this may also be our Achilles heel. It's becoming a tough battlefield. Wallace Distillers needs some more weaponry to take on the big guns. We have a motto, which we live, breathe and by God, we work by: 'Unique blends grow great Wallaces'."

Seeing Kenny's worried face, Wullie said, "No pressure, eh?" He laughed aloud then slapped him on the back.

"Eh, just a wee bit, Wullie, but I am optimistic. I've already got a few ideas that I'm ready to work on."

"Good lad. Having said all that, let's take one day at a time. If there's one thing I've learned is that where there's a will… there's a dead body! Ha! Ha! Ha! Ha!"

Wullie walked off around the corner guffawing, shaking his head while Kenny turned to study the view from his window. Watching the gentle water of the River Clyde, he could not decide if the Wallace motto was better or worse than the mission statement. It seemed that Wullie had been on one management training course too many.

Kenny felt a sense of fear mingle with optimism. The pressure was all too evident. Wullie's jovial demeanour was a classic Scottish trait of bottling up the pain by putting a brave

36

face on it. The reality was that the company was in serious trouble. The year on year stagnation and lack of growth reported in the company's financial statements were evident in the worry lines and dark circles around Wullie's eyes. He was confident enough in his own abilities to know that he could not make the situation worse, but could add another dimension to the business. He actually surprised himself at how upbeat he felt considering his understanding of the whisky industry had been more focused on theory than practicalities. Now he was in an environment where the scent seeped through his clothes and filled his nostrils. The ever-present aroma of grain made him realise he would live and breathe his job more than most.

The Mother of Invention

The dampness of the bus seeped through the fabric of Kenny's new suit as the driver skilfully manoeuvred the bus over every pothole worth hitting on Kenny's journey back to Glasgow's West End. Kenny studied the fellow passengers he would become accustomed to on his return commute. The youth sitting at the back of the bus, also wearing his "first suit", loosened his tie, listening to a very audible Guns N' Roses, in subtle rebellion against the inevitability of his first job. A girl, head resting against a damp window, breathed seductively, misting the window with each exhalation, until yet another pothole would shake her awake. Ten seconds later sleep would take over. Her head would end up back on the window. Behind her sat a man in a pinstripe suit with an umbrella that would most probably accompany him in hail, rain or shine, clearly aspiring to work in "the city".

The bus dropped Kenny at the corner of Dumbarton Road where he took the opportunity to buy the most expensive bottle of wine on a local grocer's shelf. Ten minutes later he sat at a table laden with plates, cutlery, and candles, listening to Fiona sing along in the kitchen to a worn tape playing Phil Collins' "You Can't Hurry Love". She had picked it especially for the occasion. The smell of lamb and onions wafted into the dining room, as Kenny sipped on a glass of the nation's first true foray into the world of wine, Mateus Rosé. Bubbles tingled the front of his tongue, leaving him slightly dry at the back of the throat. He rarely drank wine, especially when it made his eyes water. He felt comfortable in his lack of awareness of it. Considering he had spent £6 on the bottle, the only flavour he tasted was that of annoyance he had not haggled to a lower price.

"Okay, my man! Let's eat!" Fiona announced as she walked through the door carrying plates steaming with flavours he had been inhaling during his wine-sipping moments. One of the plates, which Kenny knew immediately was his, was loaded with mashed potatoes, leg of lamb, and more than a splash of mint sauce. Wisps of steam spiralled up into the cold air of her apartment. Double-glazing was an unaffordable, and as far as

West End landlords were concerned, unnecessary luxury in student accommodation.

Halfway through dinner, Kenny offered, "Do you want to hear about my latest idea to turn Wallace Distillers around?"

"Sure! Don't tell me, you're going to invent a formula that produces whisky to cater for all tastes. You know, like chocolate flavour for women. Or maybe an Irn Bru version for the young drinkers. Or what about a beans on toast flavour for the student population?"

"Actually, your idea is not far off the mark." Kenny was enthusiastic, globules of mash dropping from his lips as he spoke. "Whisky is popular in Scotland with two types of consumer. The first is with the half and halfers, those guys who down a few whiskies with a beer. They don't really care what it tastes like as long as it goes okay with their half pint of heavy. The second consumer likes whisky because of the taste and the smell. In many cases because it brings them a moment of Scottishness. You know, they'll close their eyes, imagining the glen or river or even the deer standing noble on the hillside, antlers held high."

Hesitating a moment watching the laws of gravity compete with those of determination, he loaded a fork with a mound of mash and lamb, easily twice the size of the space his mouth offered. Once he had wiped his chin and nose clean of gravy, he continued.

"The half and halfers are unchangeable, they are quite happy in their ways. They want a taste that works well alongside a beer. They are less inclined to explore whisky.

"So far, so good." Fiona listened attentively as she refilled their glasses with something very similar to Mateus. Flat Mateus, the bottle had been open for over an hour already.

"So, I'm going after the second group. Let's take it one stage further. Imagine that your mind's eye is looking at the deer, except you are not in Scotland, but in a remote prairie land of midwest USA at the end of a hard day's corn cutting, or even in a bar at four in the morning in New York City on your own without a friend you can trust for miles. I could go on, but you get the picture. These people call whisky Scotch. They want to believe they are living vicariously in Scotland. They smell the smells, they hear the sounds, they sense the history."

Kenny paused for effect.

"Eh, okay, keep going," Fiona encouraged, holding Kenny's upturned hand, playing with his fingers distractedly.

"History," Kenny repeated.

"What about history?" Fiona asked.

"Exactly!" he said, animatedly. "The Scots are famous the world over, for being fearless warriors, inventors of world-changing technology, even peacekeepers and explorers. In many cases, your average whisky drinker, especially the American Scotch drinker, doesn't have a clue what Scotland brought to the world. Imagine a whisky that inspired the picture in your head of William Wallace lunging at the English, driving a beaten, weary yet hopeful race of wounded Scots forward into enemy territory. Pride, sheer strength of will make the difference as the battle goes on endlessly with casualties strewn across the field, until... until the Scots rise triumphant, the Saltire in tatters billowing in a breeze of hazy smoke."

"Wow!" Fiona enthused. "You've got me sold. I have one question, which may sound silly, but..."

"Go ahead, lass!"

"How do you get all that into a bottle, or even a glass?"

"Marketing!"

"Oh... it's as simple as that?"

"Not exactly. Look!" Kenny shifted in his seat, preparing to enter phase two of his plan. "Targeted marketing makes people dream of those things they may not otherwise have imagined they want. How can so many people drink brown sugary water while dreaming of sports events and sharing pleasant moments with friends? Coke spends enormous amounts on advertising. Successfully, I may add. Why not do something similar with whisky but play on the history and sense of Scottishness?

"Let's follow the example of William Wallace and Wallace Distillers. Which is not a bad analogy since whisky was invented around the time Wallace was fighting the English. We call this brand of whisky 'Freedom'. The label depicts a hand holding a sword, above Wallace's famous quote *'Dico Tibi Verum Libertas – Freedom in Truth, I say to you'*. The main commercial will be a ferocious battle where you hear the screams, practically feel the blows. At the end Wallace picks up a crystal glass, and yes, the contrasting luxury is deliberate. He raises it to the sky then screams 'Freedom!' before downing a whisky and smashing the glass off the helmet of a dead English soldier."

"You've really thought this through, Kenny. I like it, except you may want to drop the smashing glass bit, especially off a dead soldier's head. Bit too close to the bone, no pun intended. And it might alienate your English consumers... just a tad."

Kenny nodded his acknowledgement. He had not fully considered the anti-English element.

"The other thing I don't get is that this is all about marketing. You're a chemist, you aim to be an inventor. What would you do to make this happen?"

"Ah-hah! This is the beauty of it all. I create the whisky by going first to the battlefield, Stirling Bridge in this example, where I will collect pieces of foliage and earth and add them to the whisky. Imagine a whisky that smells and tastes of the battle. The remains of the warriors blended into the water of life for today's consumers."

Kenny waited expectantly for Fiona's reaction.

Her smile told him all he needed to know.

"The best part of what you've explained," she said with a glint in her eye, "is that you're passionate about your vision. Passion makes the world go round."

She dropped her voice. "Let's leave the dishes till morning. You should sleep on this idea so that you can sell it to Mr. Wallace with a clear mind tomorrow."

Turning to rise from the table, Fiona stepped softly in her pink, cotton socks into the bedroom to await her special brand of malt. Looking over her shoulder, she called, "Well, are you coming or not, inventor-boy? All this talk of whisky makes a shy girl frisky."

Whisky Religion

"Goodness me, young lad! I think you've got something there."

If Wullie was struggling to conceal his enthusiasm, he was no Laurence Olivier. "Of course, we need to keep this secret. I mean, no-one else inside, or out, of Wallace Distillers should know about this idea. If this were to leak, the competition would be all over it like a rash. With their state of the art technology, they would beat us to the market without a thought. No, this is ours. Ours alone."

Wullie reached down into the bottom drawer of his desk and produced two strong, dimpled, crystal glasses and an opaque bottle three quarters full of Glentocher twelve year old, the company's first product in the world of double-figured malts. He filled both glasses, pushing one across the table to Kenny.

"I'm not really a drinker, Wullie." Kenny knew it would be a faux pas to actually admit to disliking whisky. Especially at ten o'clock on a Tuesday morning. "But thanks any…"

"Nonsense!" Wullie bellowed as he lifted a glass to his lips. "Two things I expect of my employees here at Wallace. To be able to share a dram at any time of the day or night. The second is the capacity to hold their drink. If you're going to convince anyone to drink the water of life, then you need to be baptised in it every day! Sláinte!"

Angling the glass to allow a robust mouthful to slip through his lips, Wullie's glass caught a ray of sun shining through the window behind his head. The amber fluid burned bright in the light, inviting Kenny to raise his own. Pouring it gently onto his tongue, he nurtured the malt in the corners of his mouth, before letting it slide down to awaken the back of his throat. He was surprised at how smooth and warm the combination of taste and texture felt. He held the glass high in front of his line of vision, nodding his endorsement of this special malt. When describing it later that day to Tommy, he would refer to it as his Columbus moment: a new experience, a new world and a new vision.

"Ha! Ha! We could even have a whisky called Glen John the Baptist!" Wullie continued.

Seeing the twinkle in his eye, enjoying the whisky melt into the lining of his stomach, blasphemously mixed with rice krispies and burned toast, Kenny answered, "Aye, we could even go to the Sea of Galilee to collect some water for each bottle!"

"There you go. We could put a picture on the label of a head on a platter, two beady eyes staring back at you. Hah!" Wullie guffawed.

"Aye. How about putting red food dye into it as well, to make it look like two thousand-year old blood?" Kenny felt very relaxed.

"Just hold on a minute, laddie!" Wullie held his hand up, not a hint of a smile on his granite features. "You've just taken this a bit too far!"

Kenny was surprised at the serious look on his boss's face, sensing he had stepped unwittingly across an imaginary line where you could not play with the amber colour of whisky. Meekly, he placed the glass back on the desk, saying, "Eh, sorry, Wullie. I didn't mean to…"

"Ha! Ha! Ya daft pillock, ye! Ah'm only pulling your leg!" Wullie slapped his hand off the desktop, lifted his head and laughed uproariously.

At ease in his chair, Kenny sipped the whisky, studying his mentor. He knew at that moment this relationship would either make or break him. In truth, it did not look like it was going to be an easy ride. Nevertheless, he was up for it. He loved a challenge.

"Cheers, Wullie!" Kenny raised his glass, smiling back at his jolly boss. "Here's to Wallace Distillers – born again!"

"Aye, born again, laddie!"

They clinked their glasses for the first, and far from last time that day. Or that decade.

Born Again

Warrior Whiskies would become Wallace's flagship brand portfolio, capitalising on the Scottish reputation as fearless warriors winning battles against massive odds, fighting for honour to the death. After a swashbuckling day with the enemy, Kenny had no doubts the Scots would have sat at a peat fire reliving their heroics, nursing a whisky in an earthenware cup, anaesthetising war-torn limbs and settling stomachs, churned to sickness by hunger and nerves.

Until they fell asleep, wearied but satisfied.

The concept was to cater for the premium consumers, where whisky merged with mind and body. He already knew the battles and heroes he would bring to life in the drinker's palate. It would be a spiritual trinity, a sacred moment. He would put the dram in their drama of whisky-laden dreams and inspirational history.

Wullie was fully aware of the risks they were taking. He had realised that if they did not take this chance, they would be dead in the water. When he explained this to Kenny, he made the analogy of a drowned whisky. No matter how good the whisky, if you added more than the correct amount of water you ruined the taste rather than improved it. He also advised Kenny that while he might be a chemist, he knew very little about the art of whisky making. He had teamed Kenny up with Frank Strachan, a stalwart of Wallace Distillers who should have retired ten years earlier, but whose nose for blending was so powerful that Wullie pleaded with him to stay. When Kenny met Frank, he knew the nose was perfect for something. Every vein and blood vessel told a tale of a man devoted to his job. The unnaturally large and colourful appendage above his upper lip would one day make a splendid donation to whisky science.

The one frustration niggling him was the time required to produce a good whisky, specifically a good malt. No less than eight years. Even if he could find a way to do it in less time, he would kill a significant barrier to entry of the whisky making process. It would abort his creation long before it saw the light of day. The discerning whisky drinker would not allow corner-cutting, especially in an ancient process dating back half a millennium. He had to accept that this was a small price to pay for a legacy of designer whiskies to enrich palates for centuries to come.

Then there were the plans he had for blended whisky, to take existing Wallace Malts and Grains and revisit the mixing process. He would add special ingredients to bring out the best of them while making a connection in the drinker's mind's eye to an area dominated by Scots: invention. Television, Telephone, Gramophone, Tarmac, Penicillin, Antiseptic, Golf. The list was full of life-changing, life-saving inventions. Kenny would be busy, there were so many to celebrate and create, each would have a unique taste.

They had been in discussions for several months already about the new brands. Only a month earlier, Wullie had placed a letter on Kenny's desk. The offer was no less than spectacular. He had doubled his salary, layering in a series of staggered bonuses targeted to the various stages and tasks to be completed over the coming years. In addition, at the bottom of the page just above the signature line, Wullie had inserted an exceptionally generous clause to show his confidence in his new chemist.

Kenny had been satisfied with the contract and signed immediately. A month down the line as a more permanent employee, he looked away from the river, along the Old Kilpatrick hills to where the overhang connected perpendicularly with a larger mound of rock. They had already made good progress on the "generous clause". The ground had been cleared and they were now in process of laying the foundation of his new home. Kenny was going to call the house "Uisge Beatha", the Gaelic words mutating into English language as "whisky", the water of life. It was the least he could do after such a magnanimous gesture by Wullie. In his own discreet manner, Wullie had stated that the contractual rewards would be delivered as long as the "undersigned" agreed to stay with Wallace Distillers for a minimum of ten years, while respecting the confidentiality of any proprietary information shared. The conditions were exactly that, conditional on Kenny delivering. If the well dried up, then Kenny would be subject to various payback clauses and compromises. The contract was only as good as the success achieved.

Kenny's ideas would be Wallace's ideas.

On the day he signed the contract, he could not get to Fiona's flat fast enough to tell her the news about Wullie's gift of a house. Her first reaction was to shriek (à la Lulu) before hugging and kissing him. After a couple of minutes she asked, "Does that mean I will only see you once in a blue moon, when you decide to come to Glasgow? Wullie's not so daft, building you a house right beside the distillery so he can get as much out of you as he needs."

He smiled and touched her hand gently, then said, "They're building a large bedroom on the top floor, overlooking the Clyde valley. For the first time in my life, I'll have room for a double bed. Young lady, I want you in it."

"Of course, a double bed would be very comfy at the weekends," she answered, with a twinkle of curiosity in her eye.

"No, not just the weekends." He paused.

"Because, Fiona..." Kenny pushed his chair back from the table and descended slowly onto his right knee, his eyes not leaving Fiona's bewildered face. "...would you please marry me? Make me an honest and very lucky man."

He was surprised at how nervous he had felt, asking this question to someone he had spent years with, who knew him better than he did himself. His tongue was stuck to the roof of his mouth, saliva replaced by superglue.

A tear broke free from the corner of her right eye. As she spoke the words, "I would love to become Mrs. Morgan," Kenny made a mental note that he would create a whisky called Fiona Tears.

Reflecting on that life-changing moment that had happened only a month earlier, he chastised himself at thinking of work during what was supposed to be a romantic proposal. He also considered how Fiona had changed practically overnight. She had become a fiancée of unashamed energy and focus. Who should be invited, what church and hotel should be booked? Her constant and successful haggling with photographers and wedding car companies was impressive. She had studied Kenny all too well. The worst part of the planning process was the time spent endlessly reading magazines. Wedding magazines. Kenny had known they existed, but had never considered their volume or how they could say the same thing a thousand times while still making it seem unique every week. He was even struggling to remember what they had done before the wedding bliss/blitz had kicked in. He wished for the impromptu nights in the pub or cinema or down at the local restaurant. Bottom line, while he was happy, he needed some moral support to see things in perspective.

He snapped out of his reflection and called Tommy for some wedding wisdom.

"Hi, Tommy."

"Wee man, how are the wedding jitters? Don't tell me, Fiona's gone crazy wedding planning."

"Yes, that was what I was going to talk to you about. She's..."

"...marrying the man of her dreams. Not everybody's dreams, mind you, but there's no accounting for taste," Tommy offered.

"Aye, but, it's like she's become very emotional, getting weepy for the least wee thing. She even manages me like I'm an admin assistant." Kenny felt hopelessly overwhelmed.

"You have to get smarter, Kenny my boy. The more you feed the monster, the hungrier it gets. You've got to ration your wedding energy in a way that Fiona understands, respects even."

"Easier said than done! You've got no idea what I'm dealing with here. I get goose bumps when I'm sitting with Fiona and we hear the ice cream van, because the tune sounds like the wedding march. It's only a matter of time before we start sending letters to people asking them what songs they want at the wedding, in the church, at the reception. I mean, she's so out of control that I'm becoming out of control, so I think that she's more out of control than she actually is, which makes me even more out of control, when probably she's never been as bad as I thought, so then it's only me that's lost the plot, but I'm so far out of it that I forget where it all started and..."

47

"Enough!" Tommy said. "Okay, two things I'll say to you, wee man. First thing is that you're like an apprentice electrician in John Brown's shipyard. Your gaffer's telling you to get this, get that, check the plugs, make the tea, get the sarnies, turn off the mains, clock him in when he's at the pub, sort out his toolbox. You can't win. You have to take the initiative. Find ways of managing upwards."

Kenny heard Tommy take a drink of what was most likely his early morning Irn Bru hit, then continue. "Next time you both sit down to talk, you've got to go in with a pre-emptive strike. Instead of waiting for her to bombard you with wedding waffle, you should reach across, touch her hand, and look her in the eyes, then say, 'Fiona, my love, I was thinking about your wedding dress today at work. You really should try to get something that shows the curves of your fantastic wee body. I know it's not my place to speak because this is totally bridal territory, but something traditional yet slightly risqué would suit you perfectly.'

"Then sit back. Watch what happens. Her mind'll be racing ten to the dozen as she makes that her priority. You'll get her off your back for at least two weeks. By then you can move on to a tiara, headdress, the bridesmaids' dresses, presents for the helpers and so on. She'll be happy to look into that stuff, since you're driving the ideas. All she'll want from you is your agreement when she finds something."

"I think you're onto a winner, pal! I'll try that and let you know. By the way, you said you had two things to say. What was the second?"

"Oh, aye," Tommy nodded. "Can you make sure that one of the slow songs at the end of the night is 'Don't You Make My Brown Eyes Blue'? I usually get a lumber with that one, brings out my best moves!"

Kenny put the phone down and contemplated this counsel as he surveyed the Clyde valley all the way down to the last definable object in the landscape, Dumbarton Rock, an extinct volcano. Sitting there as a promontory in the ancient capital of Strathclyde, the rock belied the potency that once rose from its belly. The last time it had erupted was estimated at a couple of millennia pre-Christ. Atop the rock sat a small yet sturdy castle built in the lasting confidence that its foundation was going to be around forever, just like his love for Fiona. Considering Fiona was further up the Clyde in the other direction, he smiled when he realised he truly was caught between a rock and a hard place. Thanks to Tommy's advice, he felt he could manage the hard place much better now.

He turned from the window, and the rock. A rock that would one day in the future bear witness to an incident that would require all of Kenny's strength and guile in the face of inexplicable evil and danger.

He looked at the three white boards dominating his office. They were a massacre of words, brand names, connecting lines, doodles and colourful smudges where he could not be bothered using a cloth, rubbing with the edge of his hand instead. He had been brainstorming every minute of his waking hours taking him further into the unknown. The journey was exciting, a safari of discovery into spectacular landscapes of invention.

He raised a crystal tumbler to his lips letting the malt flow freely across his tongue seeping gently into expectant taste buds. There was nothing more invigorating than a twelve year old malt tickling a dry throat, the subtle warmth delivering a sense of well-being. While the experience was not unique to whisky, Kenny had found that his best ideas would come once he had allowed the second whisky of the day to flow freely through his veins to awaken that small corner of the brain, the Ideas Department.

The boards made him feel comfortable that he had enough ideas to put the production plans together. They helped him see where he joined the dots on his inventions. Wullie had been a great support over the last month. He was not a naturally impatient man, but considering the pressure he was under to turn the company around, and bearing in mind the concept they were sitting on, most general managers would have been knocking Kenny's door down to get the latest.

The only problem was the next morning when Kenny attempted to decipher a spider-scrawl of writing on the board, victim of the third, fourth, fifth etc. malts which had turned a stream of ideas into a hieroglyphic maelstrom.

49

A Stag Wasn't Built in a Day

Kenny lifted the glass ceremoniously, peering into the deep red of Chianti. It was going down well, considering they had arrived only two hours earlier. A quick check-in to a scruffy pensione near Rome's central station told them that they would be spending most of their time outdoors, the price of paying bottom dollar for the experience of a weekend in the eternal city. There was something incongruous about wandering around some of the oldest buildings in history, allowing power, imperialism and religion to seep into your bones. For it all to be snuffed out when you walked into a stale-smoke-perfumed room with a single bed squeezed between the wall and a rickety table. Made alright by the Virgin Mary staring down placidly from the wall, hands clasped, and eyes gently comforting in a tilted, humble head.

"What d'you think, eh? Not bad for the stag weekend. When you think how cheaply I got the package, you'll have much more dosh for a few beers into the bargain!" Tommy had said when they entered the pensione, before leaving three minutes later after having dropped bags and opened windows in each of their rooms.

Kenny took a deep breath and filled his lungs with the acrid smell left by whining Vespas. Life could be significantly worse than dining on the Piazza Navona in the centre of historical Rome. History, art and culture screamed from every building, fountain, church and cobbled street. The piazza had originally been constructed as a circus maximus to host the best chariot racers in the Roman Empire as they pitted wits against skill and strength. He wished he could have been in the same square two thousand years earlier when they had fought their way around the tight curves, armed with whips. Today the atmosphere was different, reflecting a more post-medieval architecture, brought to life by a myriad of characters milling around as artists, caricaturists, and street performers. Even the policemen were a form of entertainment, providing uniformed eye candy for the drooling female tourists dripping ice cream seductively onto their shoes. Kenny was already beginning to feel less self-conscious after allowing himself to be talked into wearing his kilt by his eager friend. In fact, he was beginning to enjoy the looks from some of the carabinieri's groupies as they spotted Kenny's hairy legs and Tommy's chiselled athletic calves.

"Complimenti dal tuo amico!" A smiling waiter extracted a bottle of Moet from an ice bucket. He ceremoniously began to wipe it down with a cloth.

"Sorry." Kenny, disturbed from his reverie, waved his hand. "We didn't order champagne."

"I know," said the waiter. "A friend bought this for you. He no wanna me give you name!"

"We'll take it!" Tommy blurbed. "Ya beauty!"

Strange, thought Kenny. The only person he knew of in Rome was the Pope, which was very much a one-way relationship. How bizarre. They discussed this philanthropic gesture through the rest of lunch. Their final conclusion was that an exiled Scot, probably wanted on all continents by Interpol for being an international assassin, had become homesick at seeing the kilts, finding solace in recognising his ancestry from a distance.

The warm, carefree high of the bubbly lasted well into the afternoon. It added a heightened swagger to their walk around town on a whirlwind tour of each of Rome's historical periods, from latest to earliest. They had already covered the Spanish Steps and Trevi Fountain. The most interesting had been their jaunts down side streets and off-piste piazzas, which had proven particularly rewarding due to the sense of a quiet oasis in a city bustling with people. On one of these side street walks they were surprised to find an obscure square near the Trevi Fountain with a plaque explaining that the house was connected to the House of Stuart. Kenny's two years of Latin had been sufficient to translate every fifth word, but still left them in the dark as to why the Stuarts would be honoured in Rome. Kenny decided he would study the Stuart connection when he returned to Scotland, this would make a nice one-liner in the wedding speech. Kenny the gallant, Bonnie Prince and Fiona his precious Flora, an island jewel. He was enjoying the sensation of how "Rome-antic" he was feeling.

Their walking tour carried them to the immensity of the Colosseum, dominating the far end of the Forum. They leaned against the side of an ice cream van licking frenziedly on cornettos before they dripped onto their kilts. Every so often a cool breeze tingled their sunburnt cheeks. In true Scottish fashion they had not let the side down, by avoiding suntan lotion to achieve a "good" sunburn before going home to impress Fiona and whoever Tommy was "seeing" at that moment in time.

Kenny was spellbound by the magnificence of this dilapidated building. His first reaction was bemusement that one third of the Colosseum's outer wall was missing. Until he realised that his old Finnieston flat was two thousand years younger and in significantly worse condition.

"Kenny, look at this." Tommy pointed to a wall leading from the Forum to the Colosseum.

"Unbelievable!" Kenny answered.

On the edge of the piazza three marble maps of Europe sat side by side, each providing a different stage in the chronological journey of how the Roman Empire had grown in its desire to Romanise the world, the defeated countries coloured in white. It showed clearly that while they had been given a hard time by the Saxons and the Gauls, they still managed to overpower them. By the time they had reached the height of their power most of Europe's map was white and under Roman rule, except for...

Scotland.

In fact, as Kenny looked more closely, it was not so much Scotland as Duntocher and the hinterlands to its north. The Romans could not find a way to get past Duntocher to take on the Highlanders. In the back of his mind, he recalled seeing some signs on the way to work pointing towards a wall built through the village centuries earlier by someone called Antoninus. He had always wanted to explore the wall, but since it was three stops before the distillery he had not taken the opportunity to do so, more content on getting to work instead.

"Tommy, let's sit on that grassy knoll," Kenny said, pointing at a mound of earth across from the Colosseum.

"Grassy knoll! That's the first time I've heard that expression used outside of a report on JFK's assassination." Tommy laughed. "Do you not want to go into the Colosseum?"

"No," Kenny answered, "I'm fine just sitting here people watching."

Twisting his head to the side, he looked at Tommy, placing a hand on his friend's shoulder. "Hey, mate, I couldn't have asked for a better stag weekend. Thanks a million!"

"No problem, wee man. You deserve it! If I couldn't do this for you, then I couldn't do it for anybody." Tommy patted Kenny's hand. "I thought we should push the boat out a wee bit."

Kenny wondered what world Tommy lived in – what boat "we" had pushed out. As he studied the square in front of the entrance, something caught his attention. A group of five gypsy youths dressed in gaudy robes and adorned with ostentatious jewellery wandered apparently aimlessly around the square. Carrying a sheet of flattened cardboard, the leader, a weather-beaten lass of around sixteen, steered the group towards a handful of tourists, whose tartan/plaid clothing identified them as most probably American.

It happened in an instant. The gypsies approached the tallest man in the group, the cardboard extended in front of the sixteen year-old. She twitched it aggressively as if it might fly away. The eccentricity of the movement captivated the tourist for one second longer than was wise. In that second, a classic split second, each member of the gyspy pack had descended on him, then withdrew.

Tommy and Kenny looked at each other, knowing immediately what had happened. Their eyes met with the realisation of what they had to do. They jumped down from the grassy knoll (they would later laugh at how a "grassy knoll" improved the quality of their adventure). They ran towards the youths who were picking up pace, aiming to round the corner of the Colosseum before losing themselves among hordes of tourists.

"Stop there!" Kenny shouted, knowing they could not speak English, but sure they would get the message.

To his surprise, they stopped in their tracks. Kenny liked to think it was the forcefulness of his voice, but knew it was probably more to do with kilt-shock. Stepping forward he held his hand out to the eldest girl. "Wallet, now!"

Her blank expression spoke nonchalance bordering on defiance.

"Now, I said!" His voice belied the lack of a contingency plan for non-cooperation.

"Look! I've had enough of this!" Tommy barged through pushing Kenny to the side. He grabbed a handful of shirt of one of the gypsies, a younger, smaller boy, obviously learning his apprenticeship. He practically lifted the youth into the air before pushing him back against the wall of the Colosseum. If this kind of behaviour had been permitted a couple of millennia earlier, then he was sure it would be alright that afternoon.

As Tommy held the boy firmly against, Kenny saw the victim approach. He was ruffled and confused, ambling uncertainly towards them. A small group of his fellow tourists advanced slowly.

"Did you lose something?" Kenny asked. "Check your pockets. All your pockets. I think they took something from you."

He put his hand inside his jacket pocket, which he had thought was a safe haven for his valuables.

"My wallet's gone, and my passport too. I've lost everything. What's going on here?" he answered in a broad, deep-south American accent. His confused expression was understandable in the face of two kilts, a handful of gypsies and a sheet of cardboard. In the shadow of the Colosseum. Kiltman and the American turned at the same time to Tommy, who had been holding the boy fixed against the wall.

"Right!" Tommy screamed, a rivulet of white saliva escaping the corner of his mouth. Kenny had last seen this trick in primary six. With his free hand Tommy held what looked like a stick, but was a tightly rolled *Herald Tribune* which he had not read but carried to impress any foreign girls he might meet that day. Somehow he believed the newspaper would win over the heart of a woman walking around Rome looking for a future husband who read newspapers. He cracked the paper several times against the wall beside the boy's head. Each blow made the boy jump till tears streamed down his cheeks. He screamed with genuine fear, "No! No!"

54

"Ou est le wallet?" Tommy shouted, thinking that a mixture of French and English would cross the language barrier into Italian.

"No! No!" cried the boy again.

"Hey, wait a goddamn minute!" interrupted the perplexed American, trying to insert an element of fair play into the escalating scenario.

"Shut it!" Tommy shouted over his shoulder. "I'm gonnae kill this toerag!" He then lifted the *Tribune* into the air before screaming, "Aaaaaaaaaaggggghhhhhh!"

It was clearly a war cry prior to delivering a lethal blow that would leave *"enubirT dlareH"* embedded on the boy's sweaty forehead.

"Please to stop!" came a shriek from somewhere in the middle of the gypsy group. All eyes turned to see a very pregnant teenager push her way through to the front. Without another word she placed her hand carefully down the front of her gown. She extracted a black wallet bulging with cards, lira and dollars. Handing it to the American she looked annoyed rather than contrite.

"Check it, mister," said Kenny, "before my hie'land warrior takes the boy's head off."

He took it from her warily then inspected the contents.

"Yup, it's all here. Now can someone tell me what kind of show we're involved in here?"

Kenny and Tommy, who had now lowered the *Tribune,* looked at each other. They rolled their eyes, wondering how to explain real life was not another button on the remote.

Tommy turned to the youths, who had never intended to take on the tartan army. "Beat it. Next time it's the carbonara!" The group ran in unison escaping in various directions. Kenny wished he could have been a fly on the wall of their caravan as they told the tale of the men in skirts who threatened them with a newspaper.

"Go back to your hotel, folks, it's all over for today," Kenny said to the tourists, making his best NYPD face.

Without a word, the Americans walked away. Kenny turned to Tommy. "What a performance! Good cop, bad cop! We had them from the beginning."

55

"Aye, I know. I was really scared that I'd need to hit that wee boy. Bloody hell, that was close."

"By the way, amico," Kenny asked. "What was that about 'carbonara'?"

"I wanted to frighten them with the police, that was all," Tommy answered. "I think it worked."

Slapping him across the head, Kenny laughed, "You daft eejit! You meant carabinieri! Carbonara is a plate of pasta with egg sauce and bacon bits! You offered to get them dinner the next time they stole a wallet when you were around!"

"Oh, aye, right!" Tommy mused. "Beers are on you for that! You're a right Italian-speaking dobber!"

"Absolutely," Kenny replied. "No wonder the police never arrest anyone in Italy, they've all got egg on their faces."

"Okay! I get it, let's move on."

"Maybe all they want to do is save someone's bacon…"

"Right, enough!" Tommy screamed, pretending to be angry as Kenny launched into a series of puns aimed at making sure his friend remembered one word in the Italian language at least.

After a few more minutes of Kenny's pun repertoire, Tommy held his hands up. "I'll let you off this time since it's your stag. God help poor wee Fiona, what she's got to put up with! Now, are we going to get bevvied or what?"

Kenny extended his hand. "Okay, mate, I've got it out my system. Let's go for a wee dram!"

"Aye, alright."

"You know, one day they might call us the Scottish Fusiliers."

"Maybe," Tommy answered, blissfully unaware.

Stalking

What a dump!

Look at that godawful wallpaper, yeuch! And those fifties tasselled lampshades thick with years of passive smoke only a Roman pensione could allow. I don't care if I never hear another scooter or horn. No matter how tightly I close the window the obnoxious noise seeps through its cracks. Sleep will not come easily tonight. But I don't care for sleep any more, not when I am working out my plan.

The champagne worked a treat. Kenny did not have a clue as to how masterfully it had been done. The waiter did well not to say anything. It was a small price to pay for the chance to play with Kenny's mind.

What does Fiona see in him? She seems oblivious to his self-centred, egotistical ways. This is not surprising. I myself fell into the same trap. If I am to be truthful, I should admit that while the champagne was a way to toy with my prey, I also felt a need to congratulate Kenny in a manner befitting of someone who had wanted to be a friend. I hate me! Why are my emotions so confused? Why can I not despise him outright? Why must my loathing be tinged by this ounce of respect? If only I could enjoy one hundred percent hatred; pure, unadulterated. Then I could be free to create a distance from him.

How I felt the burning anger in the pit of my stomach when Kenny came out of the gypsy clash the hero, the orchestrator of the wallet retrieval. By the time he returns to Fiona's bosom his narcissistic smugness will have been cemented by the events at the Colosseum, another story for the grandchildren. That is, if he will be around long enough to enjoy them.

I lie in this cheap, disgusting pensione counting rhythmically his deep snores drifting through the thin wall. My prey drops deeper into sleep, oblivious to his days being numbered.

The Big Day

"D'you want to give me the rings to hold onto?" Tommy whispered.

Kenny had been studying the cross on the wall, depicting one of the most horrific deaths known to man. He would gladly have offered up the meatball standing on his right to a similar torture.

Kenny turned stiffly, the starched collar digging into the side of his neck. "What did you say?"

"The rings," Tommy said. "Give them to me. I'll look after them till that bit in the wedding."

"I gave them to you yesterday in the pub!" Kenny's whisper was loud enough for the first few rows to stop complimenting each other's hats. Panic rose in his chest, perspiration adding to the irritation caused by the collar. "You are a total…"

Kenny caught the twinkle in his best man's eye, just before Tommy said, "I'm only winding you up, you plonker! Ha! Got you, eh?"

Kenny shook his head, not sure whether to be angry or relieved. "Let me see them!"

Tommy put his hand into his inside pocket and extracted two gold bands. The larger more robust ring would easily accommodate Kenny's premature middle age, his personal contribution to the food and drink industry. His waistline was already moving in the right direction. The kilt was digging irritatingly into his side. Post-honeymoon, he would get back on track by joining the Antonine Sports Centre, a mile from the distillery, built alongside the Roman wall. He would become the Spartacus of the gym!

Snapping out of his mind-wandering, he looked at the other ring glinting in Tommy's hand. Much more slender, it was sprinkled with twenty-four tiny diamonds glistening in the light. Each diamond represented a year in Fiona's life, developing and perfecting her beauty.

Turning back to the cross he considered the last two years since graduation. He could not have asked for more. Today was the most important day of his life. The fact it was happening when his job was going so well made it even sweeter. They knew they were on the road to success and the opportunity to expose their brands to a whole new swathe of consumers. The fun was in identifying who those consumers were; why they drank whisky and how to link that interest to a Scottish warrior, inventor or event. Most evenings ended with Kenny falling asleep on the couch in Wullie's office. He and Frank would sit with Wullie into the wee small hours working the finer detail of their designer whiskies, defining the whisky industry's future. Frank was a genius. Any early inhibitions he had at sharing his hard-earned knowledge with Kenny were quickly dispelled when he saw Kenny's talents in the lab. They were a powerful team. They celebrated their expected success most nights, witnessed by the bottles of twelve or eighteen year old lying in the middle of the table. They called their meetings "whisky wanderings". It was only right that their inspiration came from the water of life, ideas conceived by the product itself in a natural selection, self-protection kind of way.

Fiona had been a stalwart throughout, encouraging Kenny to work hard and make the most of the opportunity his intelligence had provided. He deliberately avoided telling her about the bottles of whisky they used as fuel for their creativity, knowing she would not understand. Besides, there were some things that should be secret in any relationship. With him, it was whisky.

With Fiona it was the baby. She had already been two months pregnant before she mentioned it to him. That was only last week. She said it was because she did not want to tempt fate, but he knew that she had been afraid of Kenny's reaction. What she could not have expected was for Kenny to shout, "Ya beauty!" He pulled her to him, hugging her until she had to say, "Kenny! The baby's going to pop out right now if you don't let go!"

The organ's hollow sound blasted across the church. Kenny wheeled round, not able to think about his nervousness, it was so overwhelming.

Fiona walked slowly on her father's arm. She was going to enjoy every minute of this amazing day she had dreamed about since she had been a little girl. As she walked towards the front of the church, the dress seemed motionless, the silk splayed around her in all directions. When she eventually reached the altar, Kenny lifted her veil. A soft, tanned face full of hope and joy looked back at him. This really was the first day of the rest of their lives. Lives enriched with joy and laughter, before being consumed by anger and sorrow. And ultimately danger.

II

Self-destruct Button

Missing

The curtain was torn and tattered, admitting a meagre sprinkling of brightness through shredded gaps in its worn canvas. He felt he had been projected light years into the next galaxy, the Milky Way just a cluster of cloud behind him, surrounded by stars burning themselves into oblivion. He loved the universe, his precocious curiosity never satisfied by reruns of *Star Trek* and *Battlestar Galactica*, barely capturing the wonder of such a vast expanse of space. He had an urge to study the heavens and all its cosmic miracles.

He felt someone's breath on his neck, a friend exhaling softly lest he generate a hint of noise. He looked to his right along a row of nervous faces speckled with light from the holes in the curtain. Then to his left, to more hopeful faces struggling to keep silent amidst a sea of humanity. It would not be long now, he thought. He heard the shuffling and coughing stutter to a slow halt, the silence of the universe not knowing where to land in a vacuum so dense and all-encompassing.

Suddenly the Aurora Borealis exploded in front of them with the raised curtain, dazzling and mesmerising, accompanied by the Big Bang. The cymbals clashed as the piano erupted into the melodic harmonies of "HMS Pinafore". The audience burst into screams and shouts. Parents' chests swelled with pride, eyes twinkled with tears of joy at how their primary school children could look so adult in their little white naval uniforms. Young Roddy Morgan felt a hint of awkwardness wishing the galaxy would come back rather than have to sing along to Mr. Sweeters on the piano, bobbing his head so fervently he was sure it would fall off.

Roddy belted out the chorus to chirpy songs, many of which he was sure he could have written in his sleep. His eyes became accustomed to the lights. Nervously, he began at the left of the school hall scanning the faces of parents, brothers and sisters, searching for the one face that would make this night even more special. In the centre of the third row from the front, he saw his mother beaming up at him, encouraging him with her wide smile and hand clapping. Beside his mother was an empty seat. As he sang along to a tune imprinted on his brain after countless hours of rehearsals, Roddy saw someone in a long trench coat stumble along the row, standing on feet, no doubt kicking handbags while knocking over drinks. At least that was what Roddy did when late for the cinema. He was sure this figure, with its back towards the stage, was doing the same, bending awkwardly to avoid eclipsing parents' precious moments of pride. It seemed like an eternity before the person plopped into the chair, face half-covered by a scarf, hat drooped over a lowered head.

Roddy concentrated on allowing his lungs to fill to bursting point as he prepared to sing the next ensemble, wanting to impress his father, give him a reason to sport a proud smile just like the other parents. As Mr. Sweeters raised his hand to strike the keys, Roddy smiled, watching the latecomer swiftly discard the scarf and hat before squeezing his mum's shoulder. The smile lasted no longer than it took for Roddy to realise that it was not his father. It was not even a man. It was a woman dressed in a man's clothes. The oxygen waiting expectantly in his chest escaped from nose and mouth, the droop of young shoulders heavy with the weight of disappointment. In a futile gesture of hope, he looked to the seat on his mother's right, filled by another parent. He realised that if his mother had expected Dad, then she would have made sure to keep that one free. Mum had already decided he was not coming to the performance. Roddy was sure he could see a streak of resigned mascara running down her left cheek as Mum's friend, Lulu, wrapped an arm around her and gave her a knowing, sisterly hug.

At the End of Her Tether

"What could be more important than your son's big night? Don't you know how hard he worked to make it so special? Did you see the hurt on his face when he went to bed tonight? No, of course you didn't! Because you didn't come home till midnight. You're pathetic! You don't even understand how sensitive a wee boy's emotions are, do you?"

Fiona banged the kettle on the worktop. She breathed deeply before turning around to face him. Kenny sat at the table sipping on a strong coffee, his head spinning with the onslaught of accusations and guilt-incurring weaponry his wife wielded so articulately. Why could he not find something to say, there must be some excuse to explain his behaviour that night? But it was not just that night. Her anger and Roddy's disappointment were the product of many let-downs. In the beginning, the absent-minded inventor role, while not acceptable, had been a more palatable excuse. It had eventually become less effective when it became clear that the family were not his priority. How else could he explain not being there, Fiona asked on more than one occasion.

If only she could look into my heart, Kenny would plead, to see the love he held for his wife and son. She had responded that she should not have to perform an endoscopy to find her husband's love. She always had an answer – until Kenny had stopped trying to conjure up another inventive story for the fact he was not there.

Now, the normal pattern was for Kenny to accept the onslaught without responding, until Fiona went to bed. He would fall asleep on the sanctuary of the couch. After finishing whatever brand of whisky had been tucked neatly into the lining of his overcoat.

"Kenny!"

"Yes?"

"Look," she continued, purposefully drying tears on her cheek with the ball of her left hand. "I made a decision tonight."

Kenny raised the lids of his bloodshot eyes, desperately trying to focus on one of her two pretty faces merging and separating while he blinked slowly. He could feel his left eyelid rebelling, struggling to open wide enough to allow him to see her clearly.

"I'm taking Roddy. We're going to stay with Lulu. There are no more words that can help us. I'm all talked out. You've heard it before. I never wanted to become a nag..."

"Lulu! Where the heck did she pop up from?"

"If you had been paying attention to what goes on in my life, you would've known that I've been spending a lot of time with her. She's helped me deal with this. With you. With us."

"Oh, great, so you're now taking marital counsel from an elephant herder gone radical." Last time Kenny spoke to Lulu was a year earlier when she was going to New York to protest at the United Nation's apparent reticence to stopping poverty in Africa. In the process of doing her Hannibal impersonation years earlier, she had realised there was an even bigger issue than elephants in Africa. Since then, her life had been devoted to tying herself to lampposts and carrying a banner that read "Stop Poverty in Africa".

"Lulu has been a good friend to me. She has been a strong support over the years, filling the gap that you left. If you had been the least bit interested you would have spent some time with her as well, rather than condemn her as some sort of revolutionary. She cares, Kenny. It's more than can be said about you."

"Okay, okay. I'm sorry. Look, I'm a stupid man and I've messed up. What..."

"That's an understatement, Kenny. Whatever you say will never be enough. Your drinking is out of control. You're a torment to yourself and those around you. The worst thing you could've done is work with Wallace Distillers. You never had the strength to be bigger than the demons you created."

"Come on, Fiona, look around you. This house, the cars, the holidays, my whisky wanderings made this happen. It's a dream come true."

"Holidays? We haven't had a family holiday in three years. What planet are you on? You send us off to Disney World for Roddy to ride on umpteen machines, while I cry every time he turns around to search for a father to take pride in him? Can you not see how you're breaking both our hearts?"

Taking a deep breath, she said, "I promised myself not to start shouting or keep going over old ground. I'm not going to let you drag me into that zone ever again. I don't need this any more. Roddy and I are going to move to Lulu's house. Roddy is already there with her, waiting for me. You can stay here. Enjoy all the trappings and furnishings you worked... and sacrificed for."

"Please, Fiona, don't do this. I can change! There's so much more inside me waiting to get out. I'll stop working so much, stop drink..."

"Kenny! You're a workaholic turned alcoholic. You no longer have a role in this family other than to create pain and sadness. Let it go. Get some help, I'm pleading with you. Do it for yourself, not for me and Roddy. We'll survive. But the way you're going, you won't."

Fiona's exit from the kitchen left Kenny staring at the wall, trying hard to comprehend the seriousness of the moment. Murmuring to himself, he pushed his hands against the table and lifted himself up to move through to the living room to find his overcoat, his blanket. Also his source of liquid anaesthesia. He slipped his hand through a silken pocket of the coat, wrapped his fingers round the neck of one of his own creations and pulled it gently from the material. Twisting off the red top, he raised the ribbed bottle to his mouth. The sound of his greedy gulps filled the silence of the room as he poured a hefty helping down his throat. The sensation of energy and grainy tang no longer accompanied the flow of amber. He rarely tasted the whisky, let alone enjoyed the subtlety of flavours he had woven into the blend.

Settling back onto the couch, head angled awkwardly, he drifted into sleep, listening to Fiona's opening and shutting of bedroom drawers. Closing his eyes, his hand lost control of the bottle, spilling whisky onto his overcoat and the couch, the irony of the label created to celebrate Roddy's birth staring up at him: "Sun Dew Eight Year Old, when a new day brings dreams and hopes together, forever".

66

The Final Blow

The door slammed with all the force of despair and frustration. The internal pressure on his temples meant the car's disappearing hum of tyres on gravel barely registered. Opening his eyes, he scanned the living room. He became aware of things he had barely noticed before: Roddy's bookcase filled with books and periodicals depicting every heavenly body known to man, ordered from largest to smallest. In the corner, Fiona's magazines on home furnishings and gardening bore witness to her uncomplicated view of life.

He pushed himself up from the couch more a man in possession of a bus pass than a thirty-something. Physically he had never been in such bad shape, his girth drooping unnaturally over a worn leather belt. He recalled remarking to Tommy that if anyone wanted to know his age they could just call in a tree surgeon. By dissecting his stomach, they would find a ring of over-indulgence for every year he had lived. To which Tommy had retorted, "But at least a tree has something planted firmly on the ground. You've become rootless!"

A comment Kenny tried to laugh off with, "Steady, Tommy... I think you're barking up the wrong tree."

This did not elicit the faintest of smiles from Tommy, who shook his head as he walked to the door. Tommy had been busy putting the finishing touches to his trip to Estonia, when he decided to visit Kenny a couple of days earlier. He explained to Kenny that he was going to the former eastern bloc to find his fortune. The curtain had been pulled back on a land of opportunity for entrepreneurs from the west. He had been saving and planning for several years. He was not going to miss this chance. It was the Soviet bloc's equivalent of the Oregon Trail and he had finally decided to take up the challenge. He would become a pioneer.

Turning to his friend, he had said, "Kenny, you were born to do amazing things, not to mess your life up in amazingly stupid ways. Get it together, man!"

How right Tommy had been. Their friendship had drifted into a catalogue of distant memories that became too painful to reminisce over. Kenny blamed himself for the onslaught of selfishness that seeped into every fibre of his being. How could he explain the absence of sadness at his best friend leaving without asking for an address or number? He had resigned their friendship to the status of passing acquaintances. Yet, despite this, Tommy still made that last-ditch attempt to talk to Kenny before he left, in his own way leaving a door open for friendship. While he may not have slammed it shut, Kenny may as well have disconnected the bell.

Standing on two shaky legs, he felt ready to pass out. Staggering to the bathroom, he bumped into obstacles that seemed to have appeared from nowhere: doors, walls and stairs. Reaching the sink, he took what seemed an age to place the plug in its hole, twisting the cold tap for a torrent of water to crash noisily against the porcelain. Once filled, Kenny placed his head in the water, listening to the blood pump inside his ears, in what he used to tell Roddy was a Jules Verne journey.

Lifting his head, eyes tight shut he barely registered the overspill on the floor, as he searched for a towel. His skull began to shake. Two large hands had taken a grip of his head rubbing it with a towel as if shining a bowling ball, although not too dissimilar, considering the premature baldness settling into the crown and forehead. The touch was not the soft, loving caress of Fiona, but had the strength and punishing energy of…

"Wullie!" Kenny shouted, as he pulled his head from under the towel.

"Aye, Kenny. Your door was open. I'm going to the kitchen to put the kettle on, see you there in a minute." Wullie's elephantesque footsteps reverberated off the walls, just before Kenny heard the clatter of kettle and crockery on the marble worktop.

Moments later, they sat at the corner of the wooden table staring into their cups.

"Kenny, there's no easy way to say this."

Kenny had been waiting for this moment for over a year, surprised it had taken so long.

"This can't go on. This is not about Wallace Distillers, before you think this is some sort of manager-employee tête-à-tête. I'm coming at this from the angle of Kenny Morgan."

68

"Wullie, if you're going to fire me, then get it over with. Stop pretending to do me a favour." Kenny tried to pull a determined chin but gave up when he realised it probably made him look even more pathetic than he felt already.

"Kenny, you've been the engine behind Wallace Distillers' turnaround. Over these last years you and Frank have given us whiskies to be proud of. We've become the world's first true designer whisky producer. Frank's retirement last year was long overdue. Fortunately he has still got the energy to enjoy his grandchildren. You on the other hand have given up everything in the process."

Wullie reached across to place a fatherly hand on Kenny's.

"Fiona called me this morning. She told me. I'm really sorry…"

God, so it really was true, Kenny thought. Why was this horrible nightmare turning out to be so real?

"It's okay, Wullie. I know I've messed up, but I'll get them back. I just need to…"

"Kenny! Wake up, laddie! They're not coming back. Fiona has moved on, don't you see that?"

Kenny struggled to comprehend. He had faced a similar vacuum of understanding when he had studied metaphysics at university, until one day it all fell into place. He could sense this was very different and infinitely more complex.

"But, Wullie…"

"Look, Kenny. I love you like a son, you've treated me with nothing but respect over the years. I would surrender all the success Wallace has enjoyed just to see you back on your feet and in control. It's clear that for the last couple of years you've been struggling. You've been drunk at your desk on a regular basis. There have been days no-one can find you because you've been unable to get out of bed. So I've had to make a decision." Wullie paused to take a deep breath. "It's all over, Kenny. I'm eliminating your position at Wallace, which means you'll be entitled to a substantial redundancy package. The whisky world is not for you, you can't handle it."

Kenny shook his head. He looked down into the depths of his dark coffee.

"So this is it?"

"Look, it's for your own good. I'll always be there for you, wee man." He paused to take a deep breath. "If you're not going to make this decision on your own, then someone has to do it for you. Don't you see that? I want you back on your feet; you're dying in front of me. I can't bear to see it."

"Aye, I get it, Wullie. You have what you need from me so you're now moving on with Wallace. See that 'substantial' redundancy package? You can keep it! Don't dare insult me."

Kenny pushed himself back from the table. He stood pointing towards the door.

"Now, please leave me to deal with my own life."

"Look, lad…"

"Don't laddie me, Wullie. Just close the door behind you."

Wullie slid his chair back and stepped away from the table. Kenny refused to register the tear that streaked Wullie's cheek. When the door closed gently, Kenny barely acknowledged another loved one leaving the building.

Farewell to the Prey

He had what I could never have and threw it down the drain. I respected him more than any other. His own self-love took over in the end. I knew it would happen at some point. The self-destruct button was so large, wherever he moved he would hit it. I heard every word through the kitchen window as Fiona read him the riot act. He deserved all that she said, even more besides. I saw the look on Roddy's face. The disappointment at the school play was there for all to see.

He is on a downward spiral, all the way into the pit of despair and angst awaiting him. My focus on the miserable Kenny is over. There is no way I would save him from the torture of realising how much he has lost. I, on the other hand, will one day have it all. My power will be all-encompassing on a much larger landscape. The stalking is history: I have lived vicariously enough to allow the self-determination and energy Kenny once had to become part of my armoury.

I have already completed most of the groundwork in my plan. Now it is time to leave this country. I will meet with my accomplices, poor fools, one last time. Kenny is a goner, a no-hoper. Hah! Who would have thought I would out-perform this wonder boy. In truth, who would have thought I could have invested so much time in something so worthless? But it had been necessary. It had allowed me the chance to hone my skills, ideas, and armoury to the point where I am now a viable force to be reckoned with. My days as the underdog are over.

Goodbye, Kenny, you useless piece of humanity. You served me well, but now are not even a thought in my head. My time has come. By the powers vested in me I will change the world. It will not be long now until I become a household name that strikes respect and fear into those who dare cross me. The world will soon take notice.

The End of the Beginning

What did Wullie know? Kenny mused. His heart was in the right place, but his head full of nonsense. Okay, so he took a wee drink, but he relished the empowerment it provided, enabling him to become a stronger man. At least he would never go mad on it, or hurt anyone, particularly someone he loved. At least not physically.

Lifting a glass to his mouth, he sipped from what had become a poisoned chalice. It was his conscience's self-preservation reaction. Feeling a twinge of remorse, another mouthful of the golden liquid would push the thought a fuzzy step further into the recesses of his mind, only to bounce back in the morning under an avalanche of guilt. Then the same process would start all over again.

It had been over a year since his world had imploded. Every waking day since then he had endured the guilt-drink-bed routine. He wished he could interrupt the cycle, find a glimmer of hope, but the light at the end of that tunnel had been snuffed out when his front door closed behind Fiona. He had tried to call them at Lulu's every day for the first month, until Lulu, in her polite but firm manner, advised, "Kenny, you're not helping by calling. Leave them alone." Click.

He wanted to tell them about his private project in the basement. He had been working on it before Fiona left, but had kept it secret. The basement was his lair, she never went near it, considering it his laboratory. She was afraid of what she would find there. If she knew now what it was, she would see this as another sign Kenny was on a downward spiral, just adding another link to the chain of events she saw as his self-destruction. Kenny was not strong enough to argue, nor even believe she was wrong. All he knew is he had to complete it. Somehow it would signal the start of his recovery, the source of his rebirth.

So why had he been drinking so much more lately? The last year had been punctuated by bouts of depression while his experiment bubbled along on its own. This project had been something he started years earlier as a hobby more than anything else. Now, bereft of the things that truly mattered, it had become his life's focus. He should have felt excited about it, energetic to share its results.

Previously he would not have considered going to Sweeneys for a drink since he knew it was the local for many Wallace employees. He preferred not to mix business with pleasure. Hah! he thought. Pleasure. Now what was that again? It had little to do with him raising glass after glass to a stubbled mouth.

It was nearing eleven o'clock. Last orders had just been called. His timing had once again been perfect since oblivion was creeping in. As per every other night, he sat alone in the corner of the pub. Customers were already leaving, glasses piling up on the bar at his elbow.

"Right, boys. Drink up! Do your talking while you're walking." Maureen was an affable barmaid, Kenny thought.

"Aye, Maureen. You run a good pub," Kenny shouted, to the smiles and whispers of the other customers donning their coats.

"Come on, Kenny, you've got three sitting in front of you. Knock them back or give them to me. I'll save them for you for tomorrow. There's a good man."

"Don't you touch them, Maureen. I'll have these hoovered up in a jiffy." His efforts to pour them into the same glass resulted in the majority seeping onto the bar's surface.

Punching his fist on the bar, Kenny raised the other to the air, cradling a neat Scotch. "A toast!" he announced.

If he was expecting a captive audience, he would have been disappointed. The door slamming against its hinges was the last customer but one leaving. Kenny was always the last to stagger out the door.

"Okay, Kenny, what's the toast? Is it to your favourite barmaid in Duntocher?" Maureen smiled, immediately relaxed to see her shift nearly over.

"Of course!" he said. "Maureen, the gorgeous lass o' Duntocher!" He sipped then raised the glass high once more, the sudden change in limb positioning forcing him to grab hold of the bar to save himself from falling onto cigarette butts and broken glass littering the floor.

"I've got one more toast as well, though!"

"Oh, aye. What could that be?" Maureen enjoyed Kenny's nonsensical banter.

"Maureen. Tonight's my last night in Sweeneys. You won't see me here again."

A fleeting panic made Maureen look carefully at Kenny. "What do you mean?"

"Don't worry, I'm not that brave. It's much simpler than that. Ha-ha-ha!" He chuckled loudly. He was so proud of himself.

"I've got a wee project I'm working on in the house. It'll be ready tomorrow. Sssshhhh! Don't tell anybody. Big secret! It'll mean no more Sweeneys nights, or days for that matter, sitting in the corner as the pub imbecile. I'll be able to sit at home as a wholly different kind of imbecile, with nobody to bother except myself."

"If you're saying you're going on the wagon, then I'm proud of you, Kenny." Maureen reached across and touched his arm. "You're a very special man with a lot to offer. You have to put your troubles behind you and move on, this pub scene is not for you."

"Maureen, if only you knew. You with your cute wee face and cheeky eyes. One day, I'll pop in and tell you what I'm up to. It's all a secret for the moment, so no amount of whisky you might offer would encourage me to tell you." Kenny winked, tapping his recently emptied glass with a bent forefinger.

"Ya sneaky rascal!" Maureen pulled the glass away from him. "If you think you're going to make me pour you another after the bell then you're off your head. Now, get away up the road. I have to get home to let the babysitter go. My wee Sarah will be snoozing away. I've not given her a cuddle since this afternoon. Now, off you go!"

"Alright, young lady! It was worth a try." Struggling to lift himself from the stool, Kenny stood on two unsteady feet. Tugging on the sides of his coat, he grimaced before weaving his way to the exit. He raised his hand and waved back at Maureen, without daring to take his eyes off the carpet between himself and the door. "Goodnight! Give Sarah a wee kiss from me!"

"Goodnight," Maureen called. Poor Kenny, she thought, running the glass under a tepid tap, would give anything to be tucking up his own wee boy in bed.

Fresh air hit the spot as Kenny stepped out onto the car park. By the end of Dalgliesh Avenue he knew his legs would not make the climb to his home on the hill. It seemed to get further away every night. On his left, beckoning him, was a field that allowed a short cut to his house. It was full of deep holes and boggy turf, which would have stopped a right-minded walker from even considering its crossing. Kenny was far from right of mind. He decided to take the chance. Stumbling towards the field, he realised his greatest challenge was in finding a way across a bushy, untamed hedge of twisted branches sprinkled with prickly leaves. He lifted his leg high in an attempt to drape it across the foliage. In the process he forgot to keep his other leg on the ground. It was all over in a second. The somersault that landed him head first in the hedge was the worst example of awkward acrobatics.

Embedded in the branches, exhaustion and alcohol allowed him to ignore the predicament. Sleep, that great saviour of troubled consciences, took over. His last thoughts as he drifted off into the escape he had worked hard for since morning were of the lovely barmaid and her wee Sarah. Maureen somehow respected him even though he had lost respect for himself.

III

Hair o' the Dog

Still Waters

Walking through the door of Uisge Beathe he felt strange. This was the first time in a long time he had a sense of purpose. He was about to bring his project to completion. The excitement bubbled somewhere deep inside his chest. Passing the hall mirror, he nearly jumped at the horror story it told him about the night before. Studying his reflection, he realised he should not be shocked at the muck and leaves embedded in his face, not even by the damp streak stretching down the side of his jacket and jeans. Lying unconscious for six hours in a weather-beaten hedge was bound to leave some sort of mark. He looked as if he had spent a week making a British Army recruitment commercial.

Entering the living room was the worst part, the most difficult moment of each day. Roddy's toys and books were dotted around the shelves. Some even still lay open on the table akin to the children's quarters on the *Marie Celeste*. The pain of losing his son was indescribable. Each day was like a prison sentence. He knew he had to work to get him back, but lacked the strength to change his habits. It was a no-brainer. Young, adorable, loving son. Or the booze and a life of solitude. Oh, let me think... Yes, I'll have another drink, please.

It had been like that since they left. This self-destructive downward spiral. It was as if he had to go all the way to the bottom before he could find solid ground to place his feet before pushing back to begin again. Would today be that day? Every day he asked himself that question.

He also missed Fiona. Her sense of order had been the constant in their family equation, letting the variables come and go, but maintaining the formula. Until Kenny turned into a parabolic nightmare. He knew they had fallen out of love several years ago, but had refused to accept it. Roddy had become the unwitting decision maker, all things for his happiness, while he played with spacecrafts and solar systems. He had become HAL in the Morgan family's space odyssey.

One day he would emerge from the guilt to ask Fiona for her forgiveness for his selfishness. They would never be a couple again and, he realised, he was okay with that. One thing he knew was that he could not live the lie he had shared with her over the last few years. They had grown out of love in the most natural way possible. Combined with Kenny's overzealous commitment to whisky production, this had been enough to seal their fate.

Clutching a towel he had already used more than enough that month, he stepped purposefully to the shower room. With each step he discarded another article of clothing to various piles around the floor. The coldness of the bathroom tiles barely registered on the soles of his feet. Turning the dial to full power he awaited the sharpness of the cold water against his scalp and shoulders. True to form, it unleashed its torrent with a vengeance, making Kenny gasp for breath. The pain felt good. Self-flagellation could never be this satisfying.

By the end of the shower Kenny's flesh was numb to the bone. Hypothermia would have been next, if the decision to eat had not convinced him to abandon the torture and seek out the kitchen. After rummaging around in cupboards Kenny wandered down to the basement carrying a tray laden with stale misshapen bread, half a margherita pizza, black coffee, and a family-sized packet of Quavers. If he was going to complete his project today he would need sustenance to see him through till evening. He had long ago sacrificed the quality of calories for the more practical quantity aspect. Today was to be no exception.

His right foot deftly pressed against the basement door, he applied enough pressure to open it slowly. He closed his eyes and took a deep inhalation of the refreshingly pungent aroma of the grain. The sheer strength of the smell told him his project would be successful. He had never sensed anything quite so wonderful in all the years he had spent at Wallace. He was not sure why the aroma was so special. He had originally thought the house added its own ingredient to the bouquet. However, recently his antics had proven to be less than fragrant, hence he had discounted this idea. Whatever it was, something was making his home brew whisky particularly unique.

He had created the still as a hobby several years ago, not considering it would realistically become a source of personal consumption until recently. The first bottle would be produced today: it was a very special moment for Kenny. This would be the first thing he had achieved in a long time. He intended to enjoy it to the full. Or at least until he was full.

The wafting odour was hypnotically powerful. Maybe he had invented the first whisky you inhaled rather than drank. It calmed him, putting him at ease, ready to proceed. It was time to get to work. A good whisky waits for no man, he thought, as he rolled his sleeves up, chewing determinedly on fossilised pizza, while studying the drip of golden nectar into the bottle placed strategically under a thin plastic tube. The steady flow of the liquid reminded him of a blood transfusion in a hospital surgery, giving life and hope to the recipient. Kenny was most definitely blood type H, he thought. As in H for Hair o' the Dog. He smirked at the name he decided would best define his new creation. Scribbled on the back of one of Roddy's school jotters was the label for the first bottle, which he intended to cut out and glue on later that day:

Hair o' the Dog's First Cut

He settled into the armchair placed deliberately in the front lounge for this moment. He studied the other side of the river as if he had set eyes on it for the first time. Planes landed periodically at the airport, bringing businessmen and tourists to Strathclyde to enjoy an opaque sunny day, balmy with the afternoon's lingering warmth. Dusk was approaching, clearly on the promise that a T-shirt evening was in store for the people who yearned for such things. Nature's little treats.

Along the river across from Dumbarton Rock he could make out the jut of land appropriately named Langbank, little country houses and villas sprinkled across its outline, like seeds popping up for sustenance. The river moved slowly underneath the canopy of hills adding an ease to the summer's evening. It was time, he thought.

He had already poured a glass of Hair o' the Dog, pleasantly enjoying its scent as it drifted into every corner of the room. His taste buds were juicing up nicely as he toyed with the bliss of ignorance. In moments he would know if he had created something truly special or had wasted years of research and work. It had been more difficult than he had imagined. The water had been the hardest part. It would have been easy to take it from the tap, but he wanted to use the water running down the hills behind his house.

He looked at the faint scars on his hands smiling ruefully at how difficult it had been to lay a pipe from the top of the hill down through the heather to Uisge Beathe. He had found the stream when he was walking on a Sunday morning fighting the demons in his head for the umpteenth time. Never had anything seemed so inviting than that crystal water cascading haphazardly across multi-coloured pebbles. He had placed two cupped hands in the water and raised them to his lips religiously. The experience was Lourdesesque. Miraculous. It was at that moment he had decided to turn this very special stream into his grandest whisky.

He placed the glass to his lips, tilting it to match the angle of his head. The whisky meandered slowly into his mouth, before slipping down into his parched and tortured throat. Kenny closed his eyes ready to settle into his chair for the evening. Pouring himself a top up, he let his mind drift into a drowsy dream world, allowing the drink to take control.

His muscles and joints seemed to relax and exhale years of tension through every pore in his body. His mind wandered into a peacefulness he had never known before, as he experienced a calming sense of tranquillity. He enjoyed a feeling of hope, a sensation he could not remember feeling in years. His body and mind fused into one as if floating above the armchair.

He began to see a tunnel, a long, dark but inviting tunnel. At its end a light shone, beckoning him to explore. A shape began to formulate almost immediately. It was a woman, with a look of anguish written across her face. In her arms she held a child, a screaming infant, a pathetic bundle of helplessness. He tried to make out the woman's face, he seemed to recognise her. The more he tried, the longer the tunnel stretched, the further away they drifted. He made one last effort to pull the image towards him. Just as he did so, and before he accepted the welcome arms of sleep, he saw her more clearly. For the second night in a row he dreamed of Maureen. But this time he saw her fear.

The Morning After

His eyelids opened without the least struggle. This was not normal. For the last year, he had battled every morning with congealed lashes and eyes fearful of the light. Now they opened of their own volition, hungry for the new day. How odd, he thought, waiting for the slow, incessant thump on his temples that would grow into a roar when he reached vertical. Not this morning. Only one day earlier he had greeted morning from a hedge, but today he felt he had woken up in a different body.

The sun greeted him through half-closed curtains as it had done many times in the past, except he felt he was noticing it for the first time in a long time. This was all a bit too much. Then he realised what was wrong, he was probably still drunk from the night before. The Hair o' the Dog must have been stronger than he expected. Boy, did it taste good. It truly was amber nectar, honey of the dogs.

Ten minutes later he sat on the edge of the table studying his bottle of home brew. His theory of still being under the influence was quashed when he saw that he had barely touched the whisky. Also the glass was half full, which, in a strange way, captured his view of the world this morning. Furrowed eyebrows belied the excitement and bewilderment he felt as he recalled his last thoughts from the day before. He remembered raising the glass to his lips, enjoying the scent and essence of the whisky. Then he felt the soft, welcoming blanket of sleep massage his nerve endings and softly caress his skin. He barely remembered falling asleep in a carefree mood, but yet…

How had he ended up in bed, undressed and the beneficiary of a full night's sleep? On numerous occasions in the past he had not remembered going to bed, but that would be accompanied by a massive hangover and scratches from a fight with foliage on his way home. He would need to revisit the mix of ingredients in the whisky; something had become enmeshed in there that added a massive feel-good factor. Or maybe not, he considered. It could also be that after the first sip, his body was so worn from constant abuse that it had closed down in an effort to rebuild parts broken and weary from processing poisons of the alcoholic variety.

Then it hit him, like a cannonball driven at a hundred miles per hour into the middle of his stomach. Hunger. At first he did not recognise it. Since he had only ever eaten of late because he knew he should do so. A desire for food had always been second to self-destruction. Now, he acknowledged, it felt good to be hungry. Lifting his jacket from the chair, he hurried to the front door. There was no need to search the kitchen for something to eat, since he had feasted on the best of the Uisge Beathe fayre the evening before. He smirked to himself on recalling how he had munched on week old pizza, only stopping himself when he realised he had seamlessly migrated from solidified pizza to eating cardboard for the best part of ten minutes, which had been significantly more flavourful and less rubbery.

After a brisk walk, he entered the corner shop in the heartland of Duntocher, the mainstay for locals. He felt energised as he collected the eggs, bacon, sausage, and potato scones his stomach screamed for. Thank goodness for the local shop, rather than have to negotiate aisle upon aisle of supermarkets that turned a shopping trip into an expedition to find the milk. Placing the groceries on the counter, a young sprightly girl earning her pocket money greeted him. "Hello, Mr. Morgan. Haven't seen you here in a while."

"Hi, Shona. I've been busy working on a project up at the house. I've not been out too much."

"We're all expecting some sort of Frankenstein monster to escape from your house one of these days and come to terrorise the village," she laughed self-consciously.

Kenny smiled back at her coy face, understanding that she had only recently started to crack jokes with adults. "Ha! Ha! Good one! No, I'll be keeping him locked up for a while longer. He still needs to be house trained."

Kenny knew that some of the local parents threatened, or rather enticed, their kids into behaving by saying they would ask Mr. Morgan if they could borrow Morganstein.

"What do you think of Kiltman, Mr. Morgan?"

"What? Sorry?" he asked.

"Kiltman, it's in the paper, here. I'll put it in your bag. You'll need something to read when you eat your breakfast."

"Okay, Shona, I'll take it. You'll make a good salesman, or is it saleswoman. What is it? I never know these days." Scratching his head, he was aware of how absent-minded he must have sounded.

"Salesperson, Mr. Morgan! It's a new world now, you know. Enjoy your breakfast."

Back in his kitchen, he had unravelled the bacon in seconds, flipping the switch on the gas cooker at the same time. So much for men not being able to do two things at once, he mused. Everything seemed easier this morning. Not only that. There was something else. Walking to and from the shop, he had heard the chirping of the birds blend in a waltz Strauss would have been proud of. He would go for a walk later in a quest to understand why the birds were so alive this morning.

For the moment, breakfast was the priority. Hunger was taking over his thought processes, demanding he eat otherwise he would not be able move a muscle. Within minutes he had covered the largest plate in the house with the breakfast food. He felt in such a good mood that he arranged the fry up in the shape of a face. Strips of bacon for eyebrows sat quizzically above saucer-shaped fried egg eyes, one half shut due to the yolk splitting as he placed it on the plate. The mouth was full and smiling, made up of four sausages parted seductively in the middle, underneath a pointed mushroom nose. The triangular potato scone made a perfect chin. He thought carefully about the square sausage left on the pan. Realising he could not fit it onto the plate, he dropped it gently onto a slice of bread watching the butter melt appetisingly. Stepping back from his creation, he was sure his breakfast winked at him before he went to work with the knife and fork. Once he had finished, he felt the warm sense of a stomach satisfied. A short belch and a wipe of grease from his chin later, he picked up the paper. He felt his curiosity pique as he read the headline out loud: "Kiltman Rescues Woman and Child from Blaze!"

Shona had not been joking after all, he thought. As he read through the story, he became increasingly gripped by the near tragedy that had unfolded the previous night on Bouverie Street, Yoker, only a few miles from Duntocher. A woman and child had been saved from a fire accidentally caused by a chip pan overheating. The woman explained in her own words what had happened:

"The windows were locked tight. I couldn't open them for love nor money. The whole kitchen was in flames. The kitchen was between our bedroom and the door. We were trapped. We couldn't get out. I wrapped the wean up in a blanket. Then we lay on the floor hoping for a miracle. The smoke was terrible, it was choking us. The heat was unbearable. Then he appeared. I heard the front door crash against the wall as it nearly came off its hinges. Next thing I know, we're being lifted by something, somebody. He covered our heads with a blanket then picked us up and carried us as if we were toy dolls. He jumped through the open door and ran down the stairs onto the street. God, the air was so good, and the wean was crying. I've never been so happy to hear her scream. I'll never complain again.

"Then I looked at our saviour. I thought I was imagining things. He stood there in a kilt, smiling at us, tickling the wean's chin. 'You'll be alright now,' he said. It was then I could hear the fire engine and ambulance coming. The strangest thing though was not the kilt. It was his face. It was covered in blue paint with a white cross in the middle. I couldn't see what he looked like. I didn't care. He was our hero.

"Before I could thank him, he ran away. Literally, ran down the street, without a word, before everyone else arrived."

Kenny's enjoyment of the story was sharply brought to a halt when he read the last line of the article.

Who was Kiltman? Will we ever know? Will we ever see him again? One thing's for sure, Maureen and Sarah will never forget their kilted hero.

Maureen and Sarah, Bouverie Street. It was his favourite barmaid and daughter. They had come so close to…

His mind raced. It was a depressing image, the world without such innocent, beautiful people. He closed his eyes for a second to say a small prayer in thanks for the person who had saved their lives. While Kenny and God were never going to be bosom buddies, they did have the odd moment together when they wanted the same thing. This was one of those moments.

He walked into the bedroom, dropping his clothing on the floor in his now habitual fashion, heading towards the shower. Out of the corner of his eye, he noticed a colourful blue garment draped across the back of the bedroom chair. Where did that come from, he thought? He could not remember the last time he had worn his kilt. It must have been a couple of months earlier, at a party in Sweeneys. It was odd that it was still out on the chair, although in retrospect Kenny had not been particularly house proud of late. There were, no doubt, lots of surprises lying in the wrong place in the house. He shivered slightly as he thought about how much work would be needed to get the house back in shipshape. Then he felt good that he was having the thought in the first place.

Stepping onto the tiled bathroom floor, he did not make it as far as the shower. His eyes drifted to the sink which he knew was encrusted with months of blackened grime. Splashed around the sink and mirror were blue stains. The last time Kenny had seen these stains was when Roddy dressed as a Scottish warrior at Halloween. He had been determined to take on the might of the English, while earning some sweeties into the bargain. He had painted his face – with blue paint.

Kenny's mind was racing, picking up pace. He remembered the whisky, the comforting taste as it hit the back of his tongue. His last thoughts came back to him slowly, timidly. Maureen and Sarah. Danger.

Turning on his heel, he ran to the bedroom. He lifted the kilt to his face. The smell was unmistakeable, chilling. He touched the soft material gently noticing an area rougher and more uneven than the rest. Studying it for what seemed like an age, Kenny tried to ignore the smell of smoke and singed fabric. He found it hard to accept what he could not understand. What had happened last night?

Then he realised.

Hair o' the Dog had wagged its tail.

A Tartan Jigsaw

The brazen bottle seemed to look at him, with nought but the words "Hair o' the Dog's First Cut" scawled on a bruised jotter cover, covering its nakedness. Kenny could not stop staring back. This had been going on for half an hour, Kenny racking his brain to make sense of this potion that drove him to scale burning buildings in a kilt. How had he known Maureen was in danger? He had faded into a peaceful sleep, as far from a hero as he could imagine. Yet, it had happened; he now knew it was true. The kilt and blue paint were only part of it. The breakfast news had reported the Kiltman story with more specifics than the newspaper, adding the detail of a cape bearing the blue and white of the Saint Andrew's cross. There were no surprises when he entered Roddy's room to check the Saltire on the wall. The Saltire, Scotland's national flag, had been carried to all World Cup tournaments from the seventies to the early nineties, autographed by players stretching from Law to Nicholas until Scotland's luck disappeared with its goal scoring abilities. Kenny had given it to Roddy in the hope that his son would live long enough to cheer Scotland on at a World Cup. Kenny was not convinced it would happen in his own lifetime. When he had nailed it to the wall of the bedroom, he had hoped it would not become a permanent fixture.

Those nails were no longer in the wall but spread across the bedside table. The flag had been draped across the bed. It pained him to see that the fire had erased patches of the flag. Archie Gemmill's autograph no longer existed. The fact that Alan Rough's autograph had also gone barely compensated for this loss.

His mind was racing. There were two potential explanations to the madcap Kiltman escapade: one was that Kenny had finally gone over the edge, although this still left many unexplained questions. He was a chemist, a scientist, everything was explainable. The second was the whisky. Hair o' the Dog had a lot to answer for, he was convinced. He had already placed a sample in his homemade mass spectrometer, christened Sonny since he had built it primarily from various parts of Sony equipment around the house. Sonny's gentle whirr told him that it was quickly analysing the whisky in the hope of identifying whether there had been an unusual mix of ingredients. Even if it did find something strange, it would not make sense since he had checked and rechecked the formula, continuing to test it over the years of distilling. There had never been a hint of a problem, until he drank the blighter!

Ding! Sonny sounded that it had concluded its analysis, the bell a direct transfer from the microwave he had found in the attic when looking for parts. He heard the comforting hum of printing. Two pages spilled out onto the tray. He pored over the information that would have made sense to no-one other than him. Another quirk he had built into Sonny was that the data printed in a code only Kenny could understand. With his capability to create the finest of whisky, he wanted no-one to steal the idea and turn it into a commercial venture.

Scanning the data, he should have been satisfied since the ingredients he expected to see checked out correctly as they should have done. However, at the bottom of the page in bold print he was baffled when he read:

Unidentified Ingredient

His mind raced, his fingers skirting over the keyboard directing Sonny to run a series of tests on the makeup of the unidentified ingredient. His eyebrows furrowed when the answer came back on the display in red neon letters: "Unknown rock-based mineral substance".

He asked several other questions, each one leading him back to the same conclusion. The whisky contained something "unknown". Whatever it was had not been identified in any of the geology dictionaries he had programmed into Sonny's memory. The only way the mineral could have gatecrashed the distillation party was by hijacking the water, slipping through the early tests unnoticed. This was the only possibility. Kenny had decided not to eliminate any of the natural minerals in the water as he wanted the whisky to be one hundred percent Duntocher.

Where did he go from here? The stream he had used for Hair o' the Dog meandered all the way down from the highest points of the Old Kilpatrick Hills. There was no way he could check the mineral content of every rock strewn across the stream. He considered adopting a sample approach, choosing stones at random. However, the thought of an exercise of this scale made him weary.

He paced the room staring the bottle down. Okay, he was a scientist, that meant he should think practically. The facts were as follows: the mineral was in the water; there was enough of it to impact the distilling process; the stream was very fast-flowing, not hanging around anywhere to be overly influenced by a rogue rock. Yet something had got in there. What?

Then it hit him. Running towards the door, he grabbed his overcoat from the floor where it had fallen off its hook. He sprinted up the hill towards the stream, oblivious to the mud and wet heather creeping up his trouser legs. Within ten minutes he reached a clearing where he had first noticed the stream, when he had drunk thirstily of its sweetness. The crevice was about ten feet by twenty, more a small pond than a fracture in the earth. The stream cascaded into the pond like a miniature waterfall, yet barely registered a ripple on its surface, indicating the pond was deeper than it appeared. On its other side the water drifted casually out over the edge to tumble down the hillside gathering momentum until it reached the first of the pipes leading to the still.

He studied the water, trying to identify how long it stayed in the pond before it flowed out over its edge. Realising he was attempting the impossible he plucked a leaf from a nearby weed. He placed it carefully a yard up the incoming stream before watching it topple into the pond. He kept his eyes on it until it disappeared with the plunging force of the water. He waited impatiently, biting at a loose fingernail, searching for where the leaf popped back up to the surface. It seemed like an age, but after ten minutes the leaf eventually appeared. It drifted slowly to the edge before being carried by the stream down the hill. Assuming the lifetime of the leaf in the pond was indicative of how long the water spent there, he felt comfortable he had found a potential source of change in the mineral content.

Searching the pond for rocks of an unusual colouring or structure, he noticed the same combination of boulders, stones, and moss that littered the hills. Of course, he thought, withdrawing a penknife from his coat pocket. The ones on the outskirts of the pond would be the same as the surrounding area.

Whatever had created this pond would be inside, at the bottom. He knew the water would be cold, but he also acknowledged he was the proverbial nutty professor. Taking off his coat he wrapped it around a hefty boulder tying the sleeves and belt together in a tight knot.

Foolhardy or not, he thought, nothing as exciting as this had happened to him since Roddy had been born. Just like Roddy's birth, he would not have missed it for the world. As he jumped into the pond, arms wrapped around the weighted jacket, he hoped not to have a repeat of when he passed out at Roddy's birth. The sharpness of the icy-cold water made him grimace. But it did not dampen the curiosity pushing him onwards. It seemed like an eternity before his feet touched solid ground, the cold darkness tightening around him. Without wasting time, he crawled along the bottom of the pond, holding the weighted jacket in one hand, running his free hand across the underwater foliage. Until his hand touched a large rock, smooth and ever so slightly spongy. He had never touched a texture like this, eerily silken, not a blemish or lump to impede his hand's caress.

He deftly levered the knife out of his trouser pocket holding it tight. He pushed the blade into its surface, scraping hard to free up a particle large enough for a lab test. Sensing a nodule break free, he gripped it between his thumb and forefinger. He felt the tension rise in his chest with the combination of cold and lack of oxygen. Placing his feet against the rock, he dropped the overcoat and pushed with all his might. In seconds he burst through the surface gasping for fresh air which seemed to want to puncture his lungs. He pulled himself out of the pond before he checked the sample was intact. He held the rogue mineral in his hand. It flickered from bright green to deep black, depending on how it caught the light. He had never seen anything like it before. It was hypnotically beautiful.

Crawling from the pond, he placed what he could only consider a jewel safely in his jeans pocket. As he did so, he noticed, worryingly, that the lower half of his body was numb with cold. Forcing himself to put one leg in front of the other, he stumbled back to the house determined to bring to life the fragment he had dislodged. After he had done the same to his own lifeless body parts.

89

His Time Had Come

Over the next three days he barely slept or left the lab. After painstaking testing and foraging into the molecular construction of hundreds of rock types he knew his gut reaction had been correct. Leaning back in his chair he held it to the light watching it shimmer and darken with each twist of his thumb. The rigour of geological analysis he had been able to execute, courtesy of university geology modules and encyclopedias accumulated over the years, provided the indisputable result. The rock at the bottom of the pool was a meteorite.

Kenny did not dare to age it since that was a whole other field of research he was not qualified for. Only through a lengthy process of elimination was he able to determine that it was not of earthly origin. Considering it was exactly the same mineral he had discovered in the whisky convinced him he had found the source of his kilted madness.

Why had the same heroic inclination not happened when he drank from the water years earlier? Surely he was not the first to wander across the hills stopping for a thirst-quenching break at the pond. Why had no-one reported it? Or maybe there were hundreds of kilted men saving people throughout West Scotland, while he had been in such a state of oblivion and self-loathing that it had bypassed him.

None of this made sense. It had to have something to do with the distilling process: somehow this had catalysed the power of the rock, which at that moment he christened "MacMeteor" due to it being the son of a heavenly body. He had scaled the outside of a building to save a mother and daughter doomed to die. While he was proud of what he had done, there were many more people who had performed significantly greater achievements. Without the power of MacMeteor.

The next step in the analysis was clear. If he had been working in the university chemistry department he would post a notice asking for volunteers to take part in an experiment. They would be asked to sign a waiver, while rewarding them with enough money for an Indian curry and half a dozen cans of Grolsch. Their reactions to the test would be analysed and turned upside down to extract as much information as possible. Such was the desire for Indian curry and the coolant effects of Grolsch, there was never a shortage of student guinea pigs.

Kenny sighed as he poured a thimbleful of Hair o' the Dog into a shot glass. In all his years of drinking, he had never seen a smaller dram. He knew his ancestors would be spinning in their hie'land graves, aghast at his miserliness. His objective, however, was not to enjoy the amber fluid, but rather to gauge its effects. The other evening's inexplicable rashness, he was convinced, was due in no small measure to the quantity he had poured down his throat.

Raising the glass to his lips he let the liquid drip onto his tongue. God, it was exquisite. The aroma and taste were beyond words. The fusion of two worlds into one substance had breathed life into something more wondrous than any distillery could have created. As the whisky drifted into his bloodstream, Kenny waited for the Mr. Hyde moment. He had cleared away any of the breakable items in the lab just in case his reaction was to drag his arms across the table, smash test tubes and scatter notes akimbo, before he tore his clothing and punched the mirror.

He waited twenty minutes, sitting upright in the chair. The temptation to pour another dram to provoke a reaction was strong. He resisted, encouraging the scientist to take over. He needed to remain focused on the objective of the experiment. Taking his log in hand, he scribbled the date, time and quantity consumed, before adding a footnote: "No short-term noticeable, physiological reaction". More than slightly disappointed, he rose from the chair to leave the house for the first time in days.

The fresh air tasted good, sweeter than he remembered. He inhaled greedily of the breezes buffeting him on a fresh, Scottish morn. Stepping along a roughly hewn path, the Firth of Clyde rising up on his right in all its glory, he felt a warm glow emanate from his lower abdomen. Hair o' the Dog had settled in. He wandered down towards Duntocher's main street, only slightly wider than the other village streets, abstractedly enjoying a profound sense of well-being.

"Morning, Kenny!"

"Good morning, Mrs. Campbell!" He held a rusty gate open for one of the village's oldest residents as she hobbled from her house, gently placing a walking stick onto the first step. "Can I give you a hand there?"

"Oh, no. If I start letting people help me then I'll just get lazy. The doctor told me that I needed to walk on my own to make sure my new hip healed quickly. Thanks anyway. I haven't seen you for a while. How have you been since you've been on your own?"

Kenny saw the hook, line and bait in Mrs. Campbell's question. He had no doubt his reputation for self-destruction was widespread in the village. Even in the senior citizens' community. His search to find a suitable avoidant answer was thankfully interrupted by a sound filtering up from further down the hill. The hairs on the back of his neck rose when he realised the sound was the screech of tyres followed by the grinding crash of metal on metal.

"Did you hear that, Mrs Campbell?" Kenny asked as he spun round to face the direction of the sound.

"What? No, I heard nothing, but then that's to be expected since my hearing aid has been playing..." She began to twiddle with her earpiece while muttering under her breath about getting new batteries.

Kenny focused on the source of the noise. It had come from the dual carriageway at the bottom of the village. Listening intently, he could hear the neigh and splutter of a horse. He sensed the panic and fear in the animal's hooves crashing frantically against a steel surface. If he had thought about it, he would have questioned why he could hear the sounds so clearly and know instinctively what they were. But he had no time for that.

"Mrs. Campbell, sorry, but I need to run!"

"Oh, well, it was nice to..."

Kenny had not run in years and was surprised that his legs remembered what to do as they carried him towards what was becoming a cacophony of noise pounding in his ears. He sprinted past Sweeneys and arrived at the main street in time to see a horse thrashing and kicking to escape from an upturned trailer. To the side of the trailer, the nose of a jeep was embedded in a low, rocky wall, the driver stepping from the seat shakily, clearly concussed. Kenny knew immediately what had happened. The driver had been travelling too fast when he negotiated the curve in the carriageway. He had lost control and drove straight onto the pavement, dislodging the trailer on impact.

By the time Kenny had processed what had happened, the animal had freed itself from the wreckage. He saw the blood drip from above its shin as it raised itself onto its hind legs and howled at a pitch more akin to a wolf than a proud steed. Fear and pain burned in its eyes as it dropped its front legs onto the tarmac and began its run towards him.

Kenny knew he had time to escape its path by diving behind a blue Audi parked just off the street, but then he heard the faint rhythm of footsteps behind him. He looked over his shoulder to see that young Martin was walking towards him captivated by the unfolding scene, licking an ice cream. Martin was about forty years old and had been christened "young" due to his permanent state of childhood. He had Down's syndrome and was without doubt the most loved person in the neighbourhood. He was seconds away from being trampled.

As the horse approached at a ferocious pace, Kenny was already leaning back conscious of the importance of his balance being perfect for what he needed to do. It threw its head up and down frantically, grunting and spluttering, its hooves pounding noisily on the road. Kenny focused on mustering every ounce of power in his body and directing it into his legs. As the wild animal galloped past him, saliva and steam pouring from its damp nostrils, Kenny jumped onto its back. He could not remember ever having moved so quickly. Wrapping his legs around the broad midriff he grabbed a handful of soft mane. Hunching down over its head he could feel his pulse race as he looked between its ears to see Martin's figure loom larger by the second. He was directly in the horse's path and had not grasped the peril of the situation. In fact as Kenny focused more closely he could see Martin smiling and waving.

Kenny had not been on a horse since he had gone to the fairground as a child and even then that Clydesdale had been so old any chance of sudden movements was non-existent.

Working on instinct, he ran his hands along the sides of its head before stopping just underneath its ears. He pressed his thumbs into the tough flesh, closing his eyes and squeezing his legs around its stomach, all the time making a combination of sounds he did not recognise himself. He felt the tension escape from the horse's muscles as it slowed from a gallop to a trot. It stopped as it drew level with a relaxed, enthusiastic Martin.

"Nice boy! Nice boy!" Martin patted its head and placed his ice cream cone underneath a drooling mouth, oblivious to the near-death experience he had avoided. Kenny watched the horse eat hungrily of the ice cream before he dropped down from its back.

"Mr. Morgan, you were like John Wayne!" Martin spoke earnestly, watching a huge tongue finish the last of his cornetto. "I love cowboy films. He's a great actor. His best film was *True Grit*."

"I liked that one too, Martin." Kenny spoke while catching his breath. He heard steps behind him as the driver arrived coughing and wheezing, holding a handkerchief to a cut above his head.

"Thank God! Are you both alright?" The driver was in his mid-fifties wearing a crumpled, Barbour jacket. A weather-beaten complexion and broad shoulders were the telltale signs of someone more comfortable in the countryside than the city.

"Yes, we're fine, but we need to get your trusted steed some help. And yourself by the look of things." Kenny inspected the gash above the man's head.

"How did you do that?" The man looked directly into Kenny's eyes as he patted the horse's flank. He was not able to conceal his astonishment. "Have you worked in stables before?"

Kenny had been wondering himself. "No, but my uncle taught me years ago where the pressure points were behind the ears." Kenny felt a white lie was the best ploy.

"Look, mister. This is a racehorse. I'm Jimmy Burns, the owner and trainer. He's called Wild Donegal because his temperament is completely unpredictable. My jockeys have struggled to calm him down before a race. He's the finest stallion I've ever seen that can't race. I've decided to put him out to stud rather than compete. What exactly did you do to stop him? More to the point, how would you fancy a job?"

As the owner wiped the blood away from Wild Donegal's leg, to find a superficial cut rather than a deep gash, Martin patted and stroked its head watching it nuzzle into the soft flesh of his hand.

"Jimmy, I think you may have found a willing stable boy for Wild Donegal in this man here, not in me."

Kenny nodded towards Martin staring deep into the animal's eyes, whispering, "Lovely boy! John Wayne would love you. I'll be John Wayne and you're my horse. We're a team. We'll beat the baddies, won't we?"

Wild Donegal neighed his acknowledgement, enjoying the tender strokes and soft voice of his new found friend.

"Sometimes it's not about pressure points, Jimmy, but just having the right person on the right wavelength. Just like Martin here." Kenny nodded at Martin again.

"Young man," Jimmy touched Martin's arm. "Would you like to spend some time out at the stables?"

"Oh, yeah! Wicked!" Martin's wide, childlike grin made the owner smile for the first time that afternoon. As Wild Donegal spluttered its own reaction to Martin, Jimmy turned to Kenny. "Strange how things happen, but I think we may have just found a solution to Wild Donegal's fits. He's taken to Martin like old friends." He paused before rubbing his chin with a strong, tanned hand. "By the looks of things we may also have a chance to share Wild Donegal with someone who deserves him."

"I think you're right, Jimmy. See you later, son." Kenny squeezed Martin's shoulder as he turned to walk back to his house. He began to notice the birds again. Their sounds were melodious, somehow knitted together as if they sang this way every day. He was listening to nature's harmony, the orchestra of the bird section in full flight.

He realised that Hair o' the Dog had come to his senses.

IV

Kiltman vs Cullen Skink

Tunnel Vision

"Good evening. I am Grant MacTavish reporting to you live from the Clyde Tunnel, Glasgow, witnessing what can only be described as devastation on a horrendous scale."

Grant could barely disguise his concern at the scene unfolding behind him. His furrowed brow and wide eyes also indicated he relished being the man on the scene. Behind him, ambulances and fire engines competed for space, while white and red uniforms hastily set up tables and workstations, working to emergency routines they had prepared for but prayed not to apply in practice.

"Only one hour ago the Whiteinch section of the tunnel collapsed. This is the first major incident to hit this tunnel since it was built in the sixties. We are receiving reports of an explosion just before the collapse. As you can see, the entrance behind me has completely caved in. We understand that another section has collapsed fifty yards further into the tunnel. It is believed as many as one hundred people may be trapped in their vehicles between the two sections. Fortunately, on the Govan side of this incredible structure the vehicles have been evacuated and people, while in a state of shock, have been evacuated and confirmed as safe and well with only minor injuries.

"There are two key questions here right now. Are there any remaining survivors? And if so, what medical treatment will be required as soon as the emergency services can find a way of getting them out?"

Grant touched his ear, and with it his worried expression conveyed a deeper angst.

"I am just now getting reports that the remaining infrastructure is so damaged it may completely collapse and allow the waters of the River Clyde to rage through the Govan end and flood the town. I don't need to tell you how disastrous that would be as there would be nothing to stem the flow of the Clyde waterway before it swamps the streets and surrounding houses."

As he finished his sentence the camera panned left from the reporter and zoomed in on a motorcycle arriving at the scene in the midst of the emergency services.

"This is incredible!" he continued. The camera focused on the bike rider beginning at his head and slowly moving to his feet. The colourful costume seemed out of place against the backdrop of disaster. A full mask adorned with a Saint Andrew's cross hid his identity. His blue cape flowed freely to his feet, shimmering in a damp autumn breeze. Across his chest an interwoven K and M in bright green and a dark black indicated his identity, the insignia perched neatly above a belly protruding sufficiently to stress that even a superhero is allowed some excesses in life.

The true measure of identity was not in the insignia but in the kilt that reached down to the middle of two sturdy, hairy legs. A lighter shade of blue than the cape, MacTavish wanted to describe the combination of colours as a sun rising over a windswept Highland morning. His producer that day was a particularly unimaginative type so he opted to leave it for another occasion.

"It is the first time we have captured Kiltman on TV. You are watching live on BBC Scotland." MacTavish could not believe his journalistic good fortune: his first ever scoop, far from the vanilla variety. This was the real deal. At any other time he could have turned this into a humorous scene.

In his ear MacTavish could hear his producer screaming, "Capitalise! Capitalise! Improvise! Make it meaningful!"

The camera panned backwards to bring the reporter back into the frame with Kiltman in the background.

"Eh, yes, well this is certainly an unexpected turn of events." MacTavish's mind was racing, collating any and every Kiltman anecdote from the recesses of his memory.

"Kiltman first became a household name a couple of years ago when he saved the lives of a mother and daughter fighting ferocious flames in their flat in the West End of Glasgow." Nice use of alliteration, MacTavish thought to himself.

"At the time, he was seen as a quirky hero who happened to be in the right place at the right time. Since then, however, we have come to realise that we have our very own superhero

98

living in our midst. He saved four climbers trapped on the Cairngorms during pre-Christmas storms, which at the time were regarded as apocalyptic in their ferocity."

"Steady, son, just stick to the facts, less of the Jackanory angle." His producer was in no mood for Grant's freestyle reporting.

"Yes, Kiltman was able to detect the exact location of the climbers even while flying high above them in the Mountain Rescue Team helicopter. While no-one is quite sure how he managed to identify the overhang where they were trapped, it is widely believed his extraordinary vision identified their location by searching out the rapidly diminishing heat of their bodies.

"This was quickly followed by the school bus incident near the Duke's Pass outside Aberfoyle. Thirty children were trapped on a coach that had gone out of control after the driver suffered a heart attack at the wheel. The bus sat precipitously balanced on the hillside facing a sharp fall down into Loch Achray."

"MacTavish! This isn't a politics report! No words with more than three syllables. Keep it simple, stupid!"

"This was when we truly realised Kiltman's hidden powers. Somehow, he managed to pull the bus back from the edge, where one wrong move by the children could have tilted its balance and created a horrific tragedy. Since then, he has regularly been involved in helping Strathclyde Police foil bank raids, burglaries and the kidnapping earlier this year of the Lord Provost's son. No-one knows his story, where he comes from or why he has dedicated his life to making ours safer. Above all, no-one quite knows the full extent of his powers, since he seems to have something different in his bag of tricks every time he is called upon to help.

"Today, we are faced with a disaster altogether more challenging than Kiltman has seen before. Just what he can do to avert doom is anybody's guess."

"Get that camera back on Kiltman!" screamed the producer, unable to control his impatience at MacTavish's attempts to hog precious airtime. MacTavish was getting too fond of his own lilting Highland accent.

The cameraman zoomed from the wounded reporter towards Kiltman, leaning against a police car. He was listening intently to the on-site Detective Inspector.

"Our current estimates are that around one hundred people are trapped between the two collapses. Whether they are alive or dead is impossible to tell at this stage. Until the engineers have performed their assessment of the damage, we can't even begin to remove the debris lest we collapse the middle section on top of any potential survivors. This could get a lot worse before it gets any better." The DI was struggling to contain his emotion. Until this moment, the worst accident he had seen was a ten-vehicle pileup on the M8 during rush hour. This was infinitely more distressing.

"It's okay, laddie." Kiltman squeezed his shoulder. "Let's see what we can do here before we think the worst. Can you get me up on top of the tunnel? And when I'm there, make sure no-one makes a sound. I need total silence."

"Right, Kiltman. You've got it."

Fifteen minutes later, Kiltman was gliding above the entrance to the tunnel on a chair at the end of a long, hopeful tentacle attached to a fire engine, his blue and white cape shimmering in the air behind him. The intensity of the moment was magnified by the stillness of the emergency services and onlookers. The whirr of the mechanised chair was the only noise to breach the silence imposed by the police.

He stepped gingerly onto a rock-strewn clearing above the tunnel. Kneeling on the flattest surface he could find, he placed the palm of his hands in front of him. Closing his eyes, he remained motionless for five minutes. Rising slowly, he began an even-paced walk along the top of the tunnel stopping every few minutes to repeat the kneeling and concentration. Twenty minutes later, his was back above the entrance stepping into the chair again to be lowered back to a crowd barely daring to breathe.

"Officer," he said when he stepped from the chair, "show me the tunnel plans."

He showed no emotion or acknowledgement of what he had learned.

The DI led him to a table where plans were spread evenly, rocks strategically placed against an unpredictable breeze. Three engineers were poring over them, discussing animatedly when Kiltman blended into the group. He studied the plans for several minutes, rubbing his gloved hand against his chin pensively. The crowd still remained silent, focused on his cape, unable to absorb the magnitude of the disaster or the fact that this kilted man had taken control of the show.

"Okay," Kiltman said after a few minutes. "The good news is there are a lot of people down there still alive." The engineers looked sceptically at each other.

"Thank God," the DI whispered, eyes closed as he thought of a silent prayer.

"That's the good news. The bad news is that the middle section is very weak and ready to collapse. If it does, it'll bring the rest of the tunnel down on the survivors. It will probably also create an underground canal all the way to Govan and wreak havoc."

"Okay, so we need to start clearing these rocks now from the entrance and get those people out before it completely caves in." A youngish engineer with a name tag identifying him as Jack McGowan was impatient to begin work. His young face was already showing the signs of stress. He knew time was against them.

"No," Kiltman said without turning around. "We don't have time for that. There should be enough air in the tunnel to keep them alive for twenty-four hours at least. What you need to do is give the order to begin clearing the dead weight from above the broken section. Don't touch the entrance as it could easily create a ripple effect and bring the tunnel down. At the same time, evacuate the locals in Govan and move them to higher ground in case this plan doesn't work."

"Let's hold on a minute," challenged McGowan. "Are we really going to believe this assessment without finishing our own investigation? No disrespect, Kiltman, but we know this tunnel better than anyone. My view is that we should finish our checks, and at the same time start clearing this entrance to get as many out as possible. The longer we leave them in there, the greater the risk they won't make it."

"I'm not here to argue or debate," Kiltman spoke deliberately. Turning to the DI, he said, "Your call, officer. What's it going to be? The distressed section is breaking up as we speak. There's no time for further checking."

Beads of sweat trickled along the policeman's temple. He knew nothing about engineering. He was unsure of the true size of the disaster that had taken place. He would love to have been provided with more empirical evidence of the scale of the problem. He needed facts. He also knew that a policeman's true worth was not always in how he interpreted facts, but in how he used his gut instinct when it mattered.

"Do what Kiltman says. Fast!" Kiltman's confidence had convinced him. He looked McGowan in the eye. "I will take full responsibility if this goes wrong, you have my word on that. Let's get started. Now!"

As the DI turned to put the plan into place he snatched a look at Kiltman, noticing a barely perceptible nod of his head. "Good job, officer," Kiltman said. "You made the right call."

Code Green

That Grant MacTavish really has a big hit for himself, Kenny thought, his university friend enjoying the lead story on the ten o'clock news. Still, a bit of personality was not a bad thing considering the gravity of the situation. He had done well for himself since graduating. The irony was that Grant's penchant for an absence of facts came along at the same time as tabloid newspapers loosened the reins on fact-based reporting. The combination had been a wholly new entertaining form of newspaper right up Grant's street. Not being backward at coming forward, Grant had used his success in the printed media to launch himself into television. From what Kenny had seen so far, Grant seemed to have relinquished his fictional reporting style for a more accurate approach. Not a bad thing considering he reported on the news.

Kenny was in the Three Judges pub in Partick, sipping on a can of Irn Bru while munching a toastie. He had taken himself away from the scene and stowed his Kiltman clothes in the bike panier. He had been drawing unwanted attention to himself, and distracting the rescue teams from focusing on the trapped victims. He was only five minutes away from the disaster zone, he could respond quickly if needed.

The pub was full but no-one was speaking, a sense of fear being replaced by foreboding. Grant was holding court, he would have loved to know that.

"We are coming to you live from the Clyde Tunnel, Glasgow. Within the next few minutes the emergency services are hoping to free up the collapsed entrance. The question on everyone's lips is whether there will be any survivors. The atmosphere is beyond tense; no-one dares speak. Everyone is focused on the diggers you can see behind me. Families and friends of those trapped in the tunnel are waiting in a tent erected on the grassy area to my left. Goodness knows what the tension is like in there.

"Rescue teams have been working flat out all day with the primary objective to clear enough rubble from above the collapsed section to avoid the tunnel caving in completely. This seems to have worked so far. For the last few hours they have been focused on the entrance, which is completely blocked.

"This in itself has been a point of controversy today. Kiltman arrived at the scene shortly after the emergency services. Our sources tell us that there was a showdown between Kiltman and the engineers as to what part of the tunnel to work on first. While the rescue services have state of the art equipment, developed, tested and used in coal mines throughout the world in similar situations, the police decided to listen to him. Well, soon we'll find out if this unpopular decision was indeed the right thing to do, when we see whether there are any survivors, and what their condition may be.

"The question still on everyone's lips is what happened to cause this forty year old tunnel to collapse in two sections. Several people have stepped forward to say they heard explosions around the time the tunnel crumpled. If this is the case then we could be looking at the results of a terrorist attack. Currently the police are investigating. Of course, once we have more information we will let you know."

MacTavish touched his ear.

"I am just hearing now that they are removing the final pieces of rubble blocking the tunnel. If there are survivors they should be walking out within seconds. Let's watch to see what happens."

The camera zoomed in on the entrance. Kenny felt his pulse race.

Within moments dusty, weary bodies walked through the haze of smoke. Some walked alone, others helped by their fellow victims. They were a mass of blood, cuts and broken limbs, stumbling along as they coughed the car fumes and dust out of their lungs. Several fell onto their knees before they could be helped into ambulances, the final walk to safety proving too difficult. Others began to use mobile phones which were now able to pick up a signal. They did not realise the family members they tried to call were already rushing across to them from the tent. Screams and shouts continued to grow louder until Kenny thought the pub's television would self-destruct. The cameraman had certainly earned his salary that day flitting in and out, back and forth, to give the viewers a full view of the reunion many despaired for.

For once MacTavish allowed the scene to speak for itself, before the camera zoomed in on him talking to Chief Constable Fraser of Strathclyde Police.

"Chief Constable, we have heard rumours that this was a terrorist attack. Is this true?"

Kenny listened intently, the faint hint of smokeless cordite still lingering in his nostrils.

"Yes, I'm afraid to say that the two collapses in the tunnel were caused by explosives. The who and why will need to wait until we have completed our investigation. Let me assure you that Scotland will put its finest officers on this case. We have already engaged the support of the Special Branch."

Kenny waited.

"All I can say is that we regard this incident as a Code Green breach. I would advise if anyone out there has any information that could be considered relevant, they should call the emergency number. I believe it is now being shown across the bottom of your screens. Any minor detail you feel may be important to our investigation, please don't hesitate to contact us. We will not rest until we have apprehended the people responsible for this horrific act of terrorism. That's all."

Kenny was already running through the pub door onto Dumbarton Road. He tried to be inconspicuous, but he did turn some heads at his rush to the exit. One drinker shouted, "Hey, pal, ah've no seen anyone hurry oot the pub! It's usually the other way round!" This added some light relief to the sombre atmosphere, but Kenny was not in the mood to join in the laughter.

The words "Code Green" were the police department's cryptic message to him requesting his help. He may have already become Kiltman, but the loud belch after downing his Irn Bru proved he was all too human.

Change is a Good Thing

He stepped onto his motorbike carefully donning his helmet to hide the mask he had slipped on as he ran along the cobbled streets of Partick. The bike had been parked in an alley running parallel to Dumbarton Road, Partick's normally bustling thoroughfare. Not bustling tonight, as it had ground to a halt with the closure of the tunnel, cars parked on pavements, owners deciding to come back in the morning.

He wore grey overalls over his costume, no more remarkable than a Kwik Fit garage mechanic after his shift. He had already customised his bike; with a flick of a few switches it appeared to be an average Suzuki 250, rather than a souped up 1100. He had christened it "MacWolf" since it did such a good job of pretending to be a Highland sheep when it wanted. He was also able to change the licence plate from a rather unremarkable combination of characters to KILTMAN.

Melodrama was not something he encouraged in others, but with Kiltman he sometimes enjoyed playing to the gallery, particularly when he had customised the bike to remain anonymous. The disguise and other techniques he employed to retain anonymity were critical to his success. It had been a fascinating two years since he first realised the power of Hair o' the Dog. In the beginning he had invested all his time in understanding what the whisky did to him. Within days he knew that all physical senses had been magnified in potency to superhuman levels. His sight and hearing had been the most obvious. They responded now at will when he needed to focus intensely beyond the reach of any man-made technology.

Smell and taste were probably the most unpleasant for him although no less important in fighting crime and averting disaster, evident in the investigation of the Sauchiehall Street diamond robbery that summer. He had been able to identify the area where the robbers had come from by smelling and unfortunately, tasting, the mud left behind from their boots. When the police gatecrashed their "perfect crime" celebration party, the robbers were far too sozzled to put up a fight. Their choice of hideout had been a shed behind the Ballantynes brewery in Dumbarton. The ground was so saturated with the essence of whisky, Kiltman's nose for a good blend proved to be the undoing of the stupefied robbers.

His sense of touch surprised him the most. How much can you touch something? It is not really like hearing or sight, taste or smell. You either can feel or you cannot. Kenny quickly realised that touch was able to tell him a lot about a particular situation. Just that day, through stroking the tunnel, Kenny could sense where the weaknesses were in the infrastructure. More concerning, he also identified that the explosives used were of a lower detonation velocity, ideal for blowing rock apart. The clear intention was to bring the tunnel down. Thank goodness the DI had made the right decision. Those engineers would have jeopardised the lives of everyone trapped in the tunnel if they had launched their diggers while the walls were crumbling.

But it did not stop there. Touch actually proved to be the most enhanced of his senses. It seemed to work on three levels. He could explore the essence of objects, their molecular construction, merely by running his hand across them. With a lot of effort, he could turn this ability into extraordinary strength. Although this would leave him very weak. He had to sleep for a week after the children's bus incident. Recently, his power of touch had allowed him access to another sense. When he laid his hand on people or objects, Kiltman was sometimes able to see beyond the person or the thing. He could anticipate imminent danger. In truth, he had not quite fully understood this sense, learning as he went along. Half the fun had been in becoming aware of just how much power Hair o' the Dog bestowed on him.

He looked forward to meeting the Chief Constable. He relished these meetings. It had taken over a year for the police to realise they had a crimebuster extraordinaire in their midst. They had certainly not been backward at coming forward in calling him to help in an investigation. Any pride that might hinder accepting help from a kilted superhero had long disappeared. Kiltman had proven on many occasions that his skills combined with a swift, credible police action could put a lot of people behind bars who would still be out on the street upsetting people's lives. This role satisfied Kenny since shortly after he created Hair o' the Dog he had no doubts that payback time had arrived. He had destroyed enough in his life over the years. While he was not able to fully rebuild what he had knocked down, he was committed to making the world a better place for Roddy to grow up in.

On the day Fiona closed the door behind her, Kenny knew he had a mountain to climb. At times, when he was at his lowest, spilling out his troubles to Maureen in Sweeneys, he had accepted he should have been investing that emotional energy in his family. Somehow he had not been able to switch it on. Self-destruction had become all-consuming. Until Hair o' the Dog had barked at him. He had not touched another drop since he created his home brew. At least not another drop of alcohol. He had continued to take his daily Hair o' the Dog medicine. Ironically, once he had fully analysed the whisky, he realised that due to the mineral in MacMeteor, the distilling process did not create alcohol but a potion that gave him his special powers. He had created the first alcohol-free whisky.

Every so often he would feel a twinge of temptation, to remind him that he was all too human. One wee alcohol-laden whisky would do no harm. If his subconscious had cajoled him once, it had coaxed him a thousand times. This was the monkey on his back; he knew there was too much to lose by returning to the self-inflicted misery of before. He fully intended to capitalise on his good fortune by growing stronger with each opportunity he had to help others.

Over time Fiona had allowed Kenny back into their lives for the sake of their son. She knew deep down that Roddy's life would be much poorer if Kenny was not part of it. She herself had moved on, evidenced by the "partner" she kept referring to. Strange expression, Kenny thought. What was wrong with the word "boyfriend"? He was happy for her, his love had moved on to a caring, collaborative level where they shared the same focus. He would do anything for her to offset the sadness he gave her. The rest of his days would be spent correcting these wrongs. He knew she sensed the honesty of his intentions. They had signed their divorce papers together with nearly as much intimacy as they shared that day she had walked down the aisle in glorious white. There was a sense of starting afresh, both realising they had moved into a healthier zone than they had experienced in years.

There were no rules around how often Kenny could see Roddy. Fiona knew the more time Kenny spent with him the better it would be for her son. She had not quite gone as far as giving him a key to the door. And if she had, Kenny would not have accepted it. The last thing he wanted was to turn up with a ball and goalkeeper gloves when Fiona was entertaining her "partner".

Their next trip was for Kenny and Roddy to visit Loch Lomond to walk across the hills of Luss embracing the breathtaking heart of Scotland. Roddy loved the outdoors. He still spent the vast majority of his time analysing the combination of planets within the solar system, but recently he had begun to join the dots, focusing on planet earth and its relationship with the galaxy. Nature was Roddy's teacher in a subject so vast he had already decided to dedicate the rest of his life to understanding it.

Kiltman was never far from his son's lips. If he had asked once about the source of his powers, he had asked a thousand times, as if his dad would know the answer. Roddy's own theory was that he had arrived in an asteroid from another planet, landing in Scotland. He grew up in the Highlands, learning the ways of the world before he joined the human race, hence why his values were so strong. He had learned from the animal kingdom before he joined humanity. He knew he could make a difference. Kenny would smile to himself as Roddy explained his theories, characterising him as a cross between Romulus and Superman. He could never share his secret with his son. His success depended on anonymity and isolation. There was a very distinct line between superhero and father.

He sped along the streets of west Glasgow, enjoying the damp road and warm air circulating around his bike. Even at its greyest, the haunted hew of Glasgow made him feel at home. Shortly before he arrived at Strathclyde Police HQ, Kenny turned off Great Western Road into Saint George's Cross, where he rode to the usual secluded cul-de-sac to change out of the overalls and helmet. It made for a grand entrance when he arrived at Pitt Street police station, but it also carried the degree of gravity the circumstances demanded. Two explosions in the Clyde Tunnel were not just catastrophic in terms of potential loss of life, but in acknowledging there was a mind out there capable of such acts of barbarity. Kiltman knew he would need all his powers to stop this evil maniac.

Cullen Skink

"Evening, Kiltman. Please take a seat. We need to crack on." Chief Constable Fraser was not in the mood for banter. Kiltman pulled up a chair to a mahogany desk that looked out of place in the prefab police station. When he considered his own garb, he realised he was the last person to comment on incongruity.

"Evening, Chief. Let me see what you've got." he liked the sound of his own voice. He had installed a device in the neck of the mask which distorted his speech, giving him a strong Fife twang rather than his easily recognisable glottal Glasgow accent.

"Actually, I'm not going to belabour the meeting by taking you through it myself. DI Wilson has been assigned the Clyde Tunnel case. You've probably not worked together before, but DI Wilson is in the Special Branch with a significant amount of time spent in London assigned to the Met successfully tracking terrorists, experience we'll need in getting to the bottom of this one."

"The more help we can get the better, Chief. I'm already sensing this one has several layers."

The Chief Constable looked back quizzically raising one eyebrow.

"No, Chief, I don't have any special insights. That's just a gut instinct."

"Okay, so let's address that now." Pressing the button on his desk intercom, he spoke carefully. "Sandy, can you send in DI Wilson, please?" Without waiting for a response, he took his finger off the button. Uncharacteristically, he dropped into his chair rubbing the bridge of his nose hard enough to redden the skin. Chief Constable Fraser had become Glasgow's most respected policeman through hard work and patience, with more than a hint of humour. Practically single-handed, he had changed the face of authority from a necessary evil to a trusted organisation. His extensive, grey carwash eyebrows indicated that in a couple of years he would be eligible for retirement. He had been quite clear that he was happy for a younger model to take the reins, allowing Fraser to settle into retirement at a time of relative peace. The statistics on crime fighting had never looked better.

111

The last thing he needed was terrorism on any scale let alone the potentially disastrous consequences of the Clyde Tunnel. The Chief's normally taciturn features looked more haggard in this office light with the world on his shoulders. Kiltman knew he had something major to divulge. He decided to remain patient until DI Wilson arrived.

As the door opened, Kiltman stood to greet the DI. Fortunately, his mask concealed his surprise, and pleasure, when he realised DI Wilson was very pleasing to the eye.

And was also a woman.

"Good evening, Kiltman. It's an honour to meet you." DI Wilson smiled casually as she spoke. Kiltman barely noticed the words, he was captivated by a dimple that seemed to have a life of its own, deepening and widening as she introduced herself.

"The pleasure's all mine, DI." He felt self-conscious at how much he blushed when he extended a blue-gloved hand, trying to smile coyly. Until he remembered he was wearing a mask.

"Okay, let's get down to business. We've a lot to get through here." The Chief Constable was not in the mood for pleasantries. Kiltman snatched a look at the Chief, to notice a slight smirk at his vain attempt to flirt. Something about the mask, kilt and cape made any attempt at flirtation a valiant but comic manoeuvre. It did not take long for him to realise Wilson had not been appointed DI for her looks. She began to describe the landscape, holding a black book, which she rarely referred to. She had her audience's full attention.

"The current status on the disaster site is better than we expected. There are no fatalities. Although there are a number of people still in hospital, three are in a critical condition but expected to pull through. There are another thirty-five being treated for shock, and forty-two have already gone home after treatment for minor cuts and grazes. All in all, we can thank our lucky stars that the timing of the explosions was mid-afternoon rather than rush hour. Otherwise we would be dealing with hundreds of fatalities. The vast majority of the rubble has now been cleared with the emergency services confirming there are no more people inside.

"The tunnel will not be useable for at least three months based on initial estimates by the engineers. The Kingston Bridge is going to become even more of a nightmare than it is currently, with Glasgow's commuters diverted over the water instead of under it. We've already notified the city council to postpone any roadworks on the bridge and surrounding area that can be delayed till after the tunnel has reopened. Glasgow would come to a halt if we had to rely on a bridge beset with unnecessary maintenance. They have agreed to get back to us this week, although there were the usual grumbles of losing the budget if they can't get the works done before the end of March. God forbid, the council might spend under budget!"

She had a sense of humour. Kiltman tried to relax into his chair, but something was irking him. He could not quite put his finger on it although he was sure it would come to him over time.

"Let's move on from the tunnel." Wilson understood from the silence in the room that her audience of two wanted to cut to the chase.

"At three o'clock this afternoon, exactly when the explosions occurred, we received a call that a letter was waiting for the Chief Constable, with specific instructions on how to find it. The letter was pinned underneath a chair in the Glasgow University reading room. I have it here in this folder."

Wilson placed a sealed cellophane folder on the table. The Chief pushed it towards Kiltman. "I've already read it, bizarre to say the least."

Kiltman picked up the folder, angling it to avoid the glare of the overhead light on the cellophane. He read aloud slowly:

"Dear Chief Constable Fraser, it's your lucky day today. Your name will forever be associated with this turning point in Scotland's journey. This country already has a great history, it has produced heroes, inventors, industrialists, and explorers. But what has happened to it? The people have become self-centred, materialistic, bigoted, and selfish. Just look around you, you will see it more than most. Why can you not do more about it? Because you are part of it. You and the rest of the authorities have settled into an era that will be looked upon as the shame of Scotland's heritage. I intend to change that. Your challenge is to stop me.

"Are you up for it? We'll see. No doubt you will rope in that grand Kiltman character to help you. But this will prove to be beyond even his capabilities. He can't even get his belly under control. Ha!"

Kiltman gently touched the spare tyre jutting over his waistband with his free hand. Harsh but fair, he silently acknowledged. He continued reading.

"Who am I, I hear you ask? I am a disillusioned Scot who has experienced little love and understanding in this country. I can be warm and tender, bring comfort to the coldest of souls, but I am also traditional, Scottish to the core. I come from a country where people forged a future for the world. Brave, intelligent men were at one time legendary in Scotland.

"The recent behaviour of our nation has besmirched the legacy they left for us all to enjoy. We are now nothing more than a country of wasters, bigots, drunkards, and junkies. Any pride we had in our country, handed down to us over the centuries by people who sacrificed their all, has been thrown to the roadside like a dirty rag.

"By the time you read this, the Clyde Tunnel will have collapsed; you will know that I am serious. The lives lost in the tunnel will be the first martyrs when the future looks back and understands they were sacrificed to put Scotland back on track. I intend to make our country great again. I will re-establish the base on which to build. Just like when you construct a house you make sure you create a solid foundation, I will do the same with Scotland. I will bring our nation back to the socialist values it once held dear.

"I will be known to you as Cullen Skink, because, Chief Constable, you really are in the soup. Ha! There will be no doubts that I have done the right thing for Scotland, reminding you of the great country you are paid to protect, instead of supporting the layabouts who roam our streets, destroying our national character. I look forward to our little adventure together. I will sign off now, but not before I give you the first clue. What will this clue lead to? Well, you will just have to figure that out for yourselves.

"Enjoy the view, as you
Feel the sway, never a delay
With the jingle of coin, go forth oh collide, your loin
Young man, go west.

Well done, if you passed the first test.
If school were in, it would soon be out,
Enjoy the weekend walkabout.

Sincerely,
Cullen Skink."

The silence weighed upon the three of them. Kiltman studied the typewritten name of Cullen Skink as if it would tell him something other than that this clearly unhinged person had a warped and unfunny sense of humour.

"We have several people working on the letter now, focusing particularly on the clue. It may be the next disaster is just around the corner." Wilson's face was unreadable. Her large, brown eyes seemed to invite discussion while the challenging jut of her jaw made her seem quite formidable.

"The good news," she continued, "if there is any, is that we are not dealing with a terrorist organisation. At least not one of Middle Eastern proportions. This seems to be some sort of home-grown crank, with a gripe against life. What do you think?"

Kiltman accepted his cue. "You're right about the crank. However, I wouldn't underestimate our Cullen Skink. If he has the resources to pull off the Clyde Tunnel job, using what I believe were state of the art high-tech explosives, we are dealing with a very dangerous individual indeed. The clue tells me one thing and one thing only at the moment."

"What's that, Kiltman?" queried the Chief Constable.

"Cullen Skink is no Wordsworth."

Kiltman noticed a rather fetching mole at the side of Wilson's mouth as she tried to hide a smile.

"Sorry about that," he offered. "I couldn't resist it. Listen, we need to get cracking on this, my guess is that we have around fifteen hours to figure it out."

"Come again?" asked the Chief Constable.

"The last two lines of the clue are Cullen Skink's way of hinting at the timing of whatever is going to happen. This is Thursday night, now close to midnight. School, will finish for the weekend tomorrow afternoon. Friday. Cullen Skink is giving us a deadline."

"You may be right, Kiltman." Wilson was on board. "Let me check with my team to see how they are doing on the rest of the clue." Wilson left the room, her absence felt immediately.

"She seems to be the right person for this kind of job, Chief." Kiltman tried to suppress his enthusiasm.

"Glad you think so. You'll learn that she doesn't suffer fools gladly nor does she take prisoners. When the chips are down she goes for…"

"Okay, Chief. I get the picture. One more cliché and you'll have me screaming for mercy. I hope you're prepared for this, because I believe we're in for a rollercoaster of a ride. Cullen Skink has clearly been in this zone for a while. We're in catch-up mode, trying to comprehend the ravings of a madman very much on the back foot, behind the eight ball…"

"Okay, okay, Kiltman. I get it. You don't need to drown me with my own medicine. Allow an old man some indulgences in his twilight years. Fortunately, the worst of mine are a wee dram and the love of flowery description. Must be the Outer Hebrides in me!"

"That's okay, Chief. I'm going to miss you when you retire. You bring a human face to the police force."

"Well, much as I appreciate your comments, this human face is worn, weary, and wrinkled. By the time we get through this escapade, it'll look like a map of Glasgow city centre."

"I know what you mean, Chief. Very grey, full of potholes and big issues showing up everywhere."

"No, Kiltman! I meant lines, wrinkles…" The Chief Constable raised his eyes to the ceiling. If the general public realised how bizarre their superhero was, they would feel a lot less secure.

DI Wilson's timing was perfect. Without knocking, she walked into the office. It seemed as if she had been gone for ever. He had missed the mole.

"The team are still working on the clue but agree with you, Kiltman. Tomorrow at four seems like the right assessment of when. That doesn't bring us closer to the why, where or what."

"Okay, DI. We need to put our heads together." Kiltman coughed. "I mean, we need to think this through and play with a few alternatives."

"Okay, like what?"

"Like, let's go. I think we need some fresh air. Can you find yourself a helmet?"

"Sorry... I don't follow you."

"A motorcycle helmet. We're going for a ride. One thing I've learned over the years is that police stations don't bring out the best in me. Bring the Cullen Skink letter. I'll need to run that through my fingers several times to see if I can get inside his head."

Wilson nodded. No sooner had she left the office than he figured it out. It all made sense. Of course, he was surprised it had not hit him earlier.

The mesmerising dimple, the warm brown eyes, and the mole. Many years before, a frightened lass had walked into the night on the arm of a comforting policewoman, only to return as a fully-fledged DI. Cullen Skink was already proving to be a bizarre adventure.

The Clue

"Do you mind if I call you Lady?"

"Eh, well yes, I guess I do. Why in the world would you want to do that?"

"Well, it seems odd calling you DI all the time. If I apply some home-grown cockney slang, then you would be Lady DI, drop the DI, which would then become Lady."

An unsmiling Wilson stared at Kiltman for several awkward moments.

"Okay, you can call me Lady if I can call you Oddball." She paused. "No, just call me Wilson from now on, just like everyone else in the force."

"I'm afraid to ask why you chose that name for me, but point taken, Wilson it is then."

Wilson's mind was working hard to understand why years of training and frontline experience had resulted in her sitting as pillion passenger not knowing where to put her hands on a middle-aged man in a kilt masquerading as a superhero. Sure, she had read about him. If the stories were true, then she was in the presence of someone incredibly talented. However, she had been around long enough to know the essence and benefits of spin. She was going to be very careful with her kilted partner.

"What are we doing here anyway? Is there a point to this?"

She was struggling to hide her frustration, less despite, and more because of Kiltman's vain attempts to lighten the situation. They had toured Glasgow's city centre and suburbs all night. She had watched him stop the bike on several occasions, walk to a specific point in the town, usually with a strategic view of the city, then ride to the next place. All the while, holding the letter tight in his grasp. When Wilson had suggested he put it in her backpack to keep it safe, he shook his head and said that his fingers were continually working to solve the puzzle. This added to the nervousness she felt as he raced through the streets of Glasgow.

"You've got a right to be inquisitive," he answered.

Wilson bit her lip lest she remind him she appreciated condescension nearly as much as an air of superiority. He seemed to have an abundance of both.

"I've been trying to get under Cullen Skink's skin. While I'm not even close to understanding what's going on, I need to understand his territory."

Wilson's inquisitive eyebrow was enough for him to continue.

"Look. He detonates two highly explosive charges in the Clyde Tunnel. He directs his letter to the Chief Constable of Strathclyde Police Force. He makes a reference, none too complimentary, to me knowing the bulk of my influence, no pun intended, has been here, in Strathclyde.

"Strathclyde is his battlefield, the war zone. He has made this very obvious. He doesn't want to initiate terrorist acts and remain unknown. His aim is to play a game with us on a common chessboard, where he'll be one move ahead of us all the time."

He paused to let Wilson grasp his point. They were sitting on a bench in Kelvingrove Park, the sun rising slowly behind Wilson's back, above the city's proud Victorian skyline, interrupted by the odd carbuncle here and there. Wilson nodded.

"When we know the board game he wants to play, we should be in a better position to understand the clues. Let's look at the letter again."

Placing the clue flat on the bench between them, he spoke slowly, not looking at the document, the poem already memorised.

"Enjoy the view... feel the sway. What sways, Wilson?"

"Trees sway, I guess."

"What else?"

"Tall things. Things far enough away from the ground they are affected by wind. Buildings."

"Exactly. Buildings. Special buildings with a view worth enjoying. Look around you. Is Glasgow with its relatively flat skyline going to give you a view 'to enjoy'?"

"The art galleries, the university?"

"Maybe." He stroked his chin thoughtfully. "Okay, what about the reference to money, 'with the jingle of coin'?"

"That could make it the art galleries. The fact you need to pay an entrance fee. On the other hand, the art galleries don't

119

have a view worth writing home about. I mean, not unless you call the Kelvin Hall a 'view'. Granted you have the university and the park on the other side, but hardly breathtaking after you've looked at them a few times."

"I agree. So we're saying that the coins are jingled where a building sways." He paused. "What if it wasn't a building?"

"A football stadium?"

"I don't think so. Where are the views in Parkhead, Ibrox and Hampden? Lots of tenements and history but not an enjoyable view. As for the park itself, I would hardly call Scotland's current standard of football pleasing to the eye."

"Kiltman. It's the Erskine Bridge! It's a toll bridge." Wilson jumped from the seat in uncontrolled excitement.

"I think you may be right, Wilson. Views of the Firth of Clyde. Maybe that's what the reference is to 'Go forth oh collide…' It's meant to be read phonetically. Let's go."

She suddenly realised by the tone of his voice that he had reached that conclusion long before she had. It made her feel a tad embarrassed at how excited she had become. She was not sure whether to be angry or appreciative that she had been paired with someone quite so inexplicable.

The sun was hovering above the city by the time Wilson and Kiltman arrived at the Erskine Bridge, a couple of miles west of Duntocher. Built over a four-year period, it was opened in 1971, nearly seven hundred yards in length to replace a ferry that could not cope with the number of commuters. Towering above the river, the box girder bridge spans the north and south of the Clyde like an elongated colossus. As if to prove Cullen Skink right, a south-westerly breeze had picked up and there was no denying the sway was in full swing. Within half an hour of their arrival, the Chief Constable stood beside them, an impressive entourage of bomb disposal experts, policemen and detectives fanning out in all directions.

"You're sure about this, Kiltman?"

"No, I'm not, Chief, but nothing else seems to make sense."

"I've already asked the team to close the bridge. This will wreak havoc with this morning's commuters. Both the tunnel and the bridge are out of action. As you can see the guys have been instructed to spread out and search for anything unusual."

"That's a good idea, Chief. Just make sure they are very careful. This Cullen Skink has already shown how nasty his soup can be."

"Do you think we're looking for another bomb?"

"Time will tell. We've got eight hours. DI Wilson and I will keep turning the clue inside out."

"Kiltman, I'm stuck on one of the lines." He had forgotten that Wilson was standing behind him. Just as well he had not explained to the Chief that they had a history together. Also that he found her attractive and how this conflicted with his Kiltman ethical code. Without awaiting a response, she continued. "It's the line 'Young man, go west.' This bridge crosses the river between south and north. If we go west, then we'll end up in the Clyde. Which means the target may not be the bridge but something west along the waterway."

He had already mulled over this line for most of the morning. He was convinced it was the bridge otherwise Cullen Skink would not have played the card he clearly wanted to play to engage his hunters. Turning to survey their surroundings, he studied the collection booths. Each one had been there since the bridge opened in the seventies. In the early days the story went that they would never be able to collect enough money to pay for the bridge's construction and upkeep, the perfect excuse to charge more than the reasonable commuter expected to pay. While many people refused to contribute to the bridge's coffers remaining true to the tunnel, the huge incremental growth in the number of cars meant that revenue budgets were surpassed beyond expectations. The booths were now on their last legs, a recent decision had been made to stop the tariff and allow traffic to flow more freely.

The regular booth workers got to know the commuters and taxi drivers crossing at least twice daily. They spanned the generational gap, from a jovial sixty-year old on the far left to a lad not yet twenty, sitting in the booth on the far right... the furthest west.

Kiltman pointed at the booth. "There's a young man. If he went any further west he'd fall in the Clyde."

Wilson bit her lip, she felt she had been so close, but somehow his suggestion seemed more accurate, in full view of

121

the Chief Constable. "I think you're right, Kiltman. It ties in with the coin jingling as well." It was hard to say "Kiltman" with clenched teeth.

"Spot on, Wilson. I think we're going to make a good team."

"Well, then, get on with it. We'll talk about picking teams later." The Chief struggled to hide his frustration.

Kiltman walked slowly towards the booth, where the youth was finishing his paperwork before heading home on the premature end to his shift. He was distracted by what seemed half the Glasgow police force scrambling around the bridge. He caught a glimpse of blue from the corner of his eye and looked up to find Kiltman approaching the booth.

"Morning, son!"

"Hey, it's Kiltman! I should've known something really bad was going on with police all over the place, especially after watching the news reports this morning about the tunnel. Now it's the bridge."

"Well, we're not sure there's anything to worry about just yet," said Kiltman stretching the truth. "I just need to ask you a few questions. First is what's your name?"

"Jake," the youth nodded. The expression on his face showed the fear of disaster far outweighed the pleasant surprise of meeting Scotland's superhero.

"Jake, how do you know which shift you'll be working on ahead of time?"

"We have this list posted on each of the booths." He pointed with a shaky index finger at the wall.

"And how is it decided which booth you're in?"

"We each have our own booths and the gaffer tries to put us in the same one where possible. It depends really who you share a shift with. This is my booth while the other guys on this shift are usually the same group every time."

Kiltman nodded. Cullen Skink had done his homework. That is, assuming they were interpreting his clues correctly.

"Have you noticed anything odd recently?"

Other than a kilted superhero and scores of police crawling around the bridge? Jake thought.

"No, not really. We always get a few nutters through here in an average day, but apart from taxi drivers it's usually pretty uneventful." Jake managed a half-smile.

"Good one, son. Seriously, has anyone been seen hanging around the booths? Is there anything you would regard as odd?"

"You wouldn't want to have hung around my booth recently, Kiltman. The roof's been leaking like a sieve. I was on at the gaffer for a month before a guy came to fix it. Just last week actually."

Kiltman stepped inside the booth, squeezing past the youth who had inched forward to create space for the superhero's belly. It had not looked quite so generous on the television footage from the tunnel explosion, Jake mused.

Kiltman placed his right hand against the ceiling, closing his eyes allowing the force of his hand to fuse with the plastic material as if the molecules were becoming as one. The burning sensation in his hand told him what he had feared. The ceiling was laced with a concoction of PETN, TNT and cyclonite, enough high brisance explosive material to blow Jake into a lunar orbit. From the side window, he saw the bomb disposal squad unload their equipment, clearly identified by the stark lettering on their bomb-proof overalls. They worked with the efficiency expected of individuals who risked their lives every day.

Running his hand down along the wall of the kiosk, he traced the high-density explosives until his hand was on the floor. Cullen Skink had not placed a bomb in the kiosk. He had turned the kiosk into a bomb, by covering the explosives inside with an identical moulded plastic. This was high-tech stuff. He would be surprised if the bomb squad had seen anything quite like it before.

"Okay, Jake. Why don't you step out of here carefully and let the experts do their job." Jake looked across at the bomb disposal unit. Placing one foot on the floor, he gingerly levered himself from his seat to squeeze past Kiltman and step out onto the bridge. Kiltman stepped carefully from the booth and approached the Chief Constable. From the expression on the older policeman's face, Jake knew he had been very lucky. Belly or no belly, Kiltman got his vote.

The Chief Constable called the head of the bomb squad over. Within minutes, everyone had moved onto the mainland well away from the bridge, where a strategic approach could be employed to deal with the enormity of the impending disaster. Now that the police had barricaded the on-ramps there was no immediate danger to commuters. The remaining police had been despatched to clear a half mile radius, evacuating the surrounding homes and clearing roads of traffic.

"Chief, Kiltman, we're talking about enough explosives to destroy the south side of the bridge," Bob Murdoch, the head of bomb disposal explained. Bob was older than the other members of the team, with a reputation for reading unexploded bomb incidents better than anyone in the business. The worry of years of bomb defusal were written all over him. He had a full head of grey, straggly hair, while the lines etched into a permanent grimace on his cheeks and forehead reflected his high degree of commitment. The brown nicotine stain behind his right ear indicated his addiction required a cigarette close at hand at all times.

"Once that happens, the whole bridge becomes unsafe. It would not collapse, but structurally it would be unfit for a long time to come. It's a finely tuned structure, its strength coming from the box girder design rather than its size. We're talking at least a year."

"If Cullen Skink's aim is to cripple Strathclyde, he's going the right way about it," the Chief spoke measuredly, his face pale and drawn.

"What you talking about, Chief?" Murdoch was more than a tad discouraged by the Chief Constable's ravings about fish soup.

"It's okay, Bob. I'll explain it later. It's not as crazy as it sounds. Well, actually, it is, but in a different way than you think. You can relax, I haven't lost the plot."

Bob was far from relaxed.

"It's just gone one o'clock." Kiltman aimed to get the plan back on track. "Technically we have three hours to defuse this monster. I'm not a bomb expert but my survey of the kiosk indicates that this is infinitely more complex than finding the charger. It's a hot bed of complex wiring and interdependent chemicals."

Bob looked across to the kiosk where three of his best men were applying the most sophisticated tools in the trade. He had been around Kiltman long enough to know they would not turn up much more than he had already identified. Darn, how did he do it?

"So, what do you suggest?" Bob was open to suggestions.

"We've got three hours. I don't believe we can risk Erskine Bridge's future to our being able to defuse a complex bomb created deliberately to confuse us. If you look that way, I think we have our solution." Kiltman pointed west towards the Firth of Clyde.

"Come again?" The Chief had been following the logic until this point.

"Beyond the Firth there's Islay and beyond that the Irish Sea. With one of the choppers, you could have that kiosk facing a watery grave well away from civilisation in an hour."

"Bob, what's the risk?" The Chief was happy to have a plan.

"Well, from what we can ascertain, the bomb is the kiosk. They are one and the same. It's a self-contained unit. It's not earthed. So we just need to detach it from the bridge, manoeuvre it onto a chopper's hook and move like lightning."

The Chief was already on his phone to emergency services.

It took less than half an hour to detach the kiosk and ensure it was safely attached to the chopper. While this procedure was completed, Kiltman felt, through the edges of his costume, the soft drizzle of Scotland's intelligent rain. It never ceased to amaze him how rain always picked the worst moments to strike. He let his eyes drift to the Old Kilpatrick hills, to Wallace Distillers, to his house perched on the summit close to Duntocher. If he was in his house, he would have a clear view of today's proceedings. With or without his supersight. More to the point, if he was a criminal, proud of his work, he would want to take a vantage point strategically well-placed to enjoy the show. He let his eyes scan the hillside slowly but carefully. To a passing onlooker it appeared as though he was enjoying the view, taking in the rolling vista of the hills, Saint Patrick's alleged last home in Scotland before being kidnapped by

Vikings and taken to Ireland. In reality, he was checking every nook and cranny, window and road, until he spoke softly.

"Wilson? Are you still here?"

"Yes, of course I am. Your trusted aide is by your side." Standing directly behind him she had not meant to sound so sarcastic and frustrated.

"Good, because I need you to do something for me. Get yourself a pair of binoculars. Check out the shed above those trees. Through the gap in the middle, you can see some of the tombstones of Dalnottar graveyard on the hillside. It's just above last two lines of graves. Methinks our Cullen Skink is skulking in there."

Wilson adjusted the binoculars to focus in on the graveyard, following the rows of graves until the walled edge. There was a shed two hundred yards above the wall.

"What makes you think he's there?"

"Look at the small window on the left. What do you see?"

Wilson panned slowly to the left, "Nothing... except, hold on. Yes, there's someone there behind the glass. The window is too dirty to make the person out, but it looks like they are holding something."

"A telescope. It's not every day somebody will set up a bird watching spot in a shed above a graveyard, unless they are looking for a phoenix. How quickly can we get up there?"

"Let's go, Kiltman." Wilson had already opened the car door for him. Just when she felt justified in her frustration at him, he turns around to show off a vision better than a pair of 30X binoculars. She had to admit to being impressed ever so slightly.

As they sped across the bridge on the north side, Wilson radioed ahead to open the barricade to let them through. From the left window of the speeding panda car, they could see the helicopter gently lift the booth from the bridge, climb to a height of five hundred feet before speeding west to reach a watery grave somewhere in the ocean, far from humanity. Ecologically it would not sit well with many in the community, countless creatures of the sea annihilated by the shock waves. At that moment, Kiltman thought ruefully, he had much bigger fish to fry.

MacSpiderman

They screeched to a halt at the top of the cemetery, as close to the shed as the road would allow. Two hundred yards, uphill and across coarse terrain, was Wilson's chance to enjoy a taste of one-upmanship as she ran nimbly across the heather. Kiltman's main focus was in not letting her see him fall head over heels. He was not in the habit of showing off his manhood to a DI he barely knew. On reaching the shed he could see she had already taken the initiative. She had opened the flimsy door and stepped into the dark, musty room. When he entered, he knew immediately why his hearing had not picked up a sound when he focused in on the shed from the bridge. Sitting astride a stool wearing a blue Scotland hat, a tartan tablecloth round its midriff, was a blow-up Spiderman doll, leaning against the wall as if taking a break from crime fighting.

Wilson looked from the window towards the Erskine Bridge, following the line of the telescope. While he focused on getting his breath back under control, his heart thumped against the wall of his chest, desperate to escape a body in need of a six-month training programme. Then he heard it. A stifled cough. Adjusting his line of vision, he caught the profile of Wilson against the light shining through the window. There was no mistaking it; she was biting her bottom lip.

"You okay, Wilson?"

Not turning her head, she answered, "Yes, fine, Kiltman. I guess we should…" Suddenly she was taken by a harsh fit of coughing. "Very dusty in here, isn't it? Well, let's call the Chief and tell him what we've found."

"Yes, let's," he began self-consciously. "What exactly do you think we've got here?"

"I'm not sure if this is a crime scene or… a scene from a Marvel comic." Wilson had reached her limit of self-control, shoulders shaking, while holding her sides with unfettered mirth.

"Very good. Always reassuring to see Strathclyde Police have a sense of humour."

"Sorry, Kiltman, but you must admit…"

Kiltman was admitting. He was admitting to himself what he had thought many times before. Why the heck was he dressed in a superhero costume, running up and down Scottish braes? He was also admitting that the situation had a funny side. For the first time they found themselves on the same wavelength.

"Okay, Wilson. You win. Don't worry, one day I'll fit into this bloody costume. Then we'll see who wins a two hundred yard sprint uphill."

"Looking forward to it already," she spoke distractedly, as she detached something from Spiderman's right hand. He noticed that she had already donned her gloves. "There's a note here." She crossed the room to stand in the light of the doorway alongside Kiltman. She read aloud:

"Dear Kiltman, Did you like MacSpiderman? Looks like our roles are now defined – you are the superhero and I am your nemesis. This is getting exciting. Who is that very attractive sidekick you're stringing along for the ride? Lovely girl. I think we will get along well together, the three of us on our adventures." Wilson coughed self-consciously, before continuing.

"When I saw you approach the booth, I knew you had it figured out. Not too difficult, really. You passed the 'school test'. Well done. However, in the process I achieved two things. The first is to convince you that I am serious while very resourceful. The second is that I don't care about loss of life. Glasgow was lucky yesterday. The tunnel proved a bit more robust than I had calculated. Those sixties engineers knew their stuff. From now on things will be a tad more challenging. You will try to stop me, but you will fail. As a result, the blood of many people will be on your hands, since you've accepted the gauntlet laid down on the bridge today. Time is marching on. I intend to deliver against my promises at the brightest midnight, when I will lay the foundation for a new Scotland.

"Where lies the state
of the art
of making love hate.
The place where they make Mum Dad,
they celebrate.

Oh what a wicked web he weaves
where he sets out to deceive
By giving the elbow
To those thug-minded fellows.

Your friend indeed,
Cullen Skink."

There was a cold chill in the shed, supplied by the open door and cracked window pane. It passed through both of them as they let the silence dominate. His mind was racing in several directions at once. Wilson mentally turned the clue inside out, until she was the first to speak.

"This ups the ante. Cullen Skink's now set a time limit on the major disaster he has been alluding to. The brightest midnight must be the night of June 21, the longest day. Today's already the seventeenth. We've got four days." She paused, waiting for a response.

"I agree that's when he's going to push the button. Any thoughts on the riddle?"

"Not at the moment. Seems like his usual amateur poetry, but I can't see anything obvious. What do you think?" Wilson was not sure if she wanted to hear the answer, but she felt she should ask anyway.

He rubbed his chin, clearly deep in thought, before he said, "For all his faults, he seems to appreciate an attractive lady."

Wilson's jaw dropped. Several seconds passed before she managed to say, "Excuse me?" Her expression told him his attempt at humour had not only fallen flat on its face, but had made him look a bigger imbecile than he had done running up the hill.

"Just a joke… but not only a joke. I mean, if we are going to create a personality analysis for Cullen Skink then these types of sub-clues are important to build a picture of whom we are dealing with."

"Kiltman, get real! If you make another wisecrack like that, I swear I'll ask the Chief to take me or you off this case. Where do kiltmen grow up these days? Have you not heard anything about decorum and equality?" Wilson rubbed the back of her neck as she walked towards the door.

"Okay, point taken, Wilson. When we do his identifit, we'll leave sexual orientation out of it."

"Kiltman!" Wilson shouted. "Enough!"

"Right then, glad we sorted that out. Fancy a coffee? I know a nice hotel near here where we can sit in comfort and decipher this clue." Wilson was already out of the shed, walking briskly down the hill, to put herself as far from his weirdness as possible.

Celtic 1967

The walk from the shed passed in silence as Kiltman guided Wilson along a combination of paths and streams through fields and across ditches. In less than fifteen minutes they stood outside a smallish building, a compact hotel on one side with a pub on the other. The hotel had two floors behind a quiet reception room. It seemed to have been built at a different time from the pub. Maybe even a different era or century. The pub was a cube shape, walls speckled with small sharp stones, underneath a flat roof giving the impression of a temporary structure rather than a local bar. The absence of windows made Wilson think that whoever was inside did not want to be seen. Nor did they want to be reminded of the light outside. She made a mental note to send a letter to Tarantino that she had found the perfect setting for a scene from his next movie. There were two doors, one thick, dark, wooden and forbidding with the word "Bar" above it. The other was less moody due to the addition of several panes of glass, with "Lounge" half-heartedly scrawled above the door. Of the two, the lounge seemed a tad more inviting.

"Let's go to the bar," Kiltman said. How predictable, Wilson thought. Show a man a pub, and he will make straight for its dingiest corner.

They walked inside adjusting to the dull artificial light, interrupted occasionally by the flickering colours of an idle fruit machine. Wilson noted that the bar was significantly larger than it looked from the outside. There were a handful of men dotted around the room, at what looked like strategic vantage points, where each of them seemed to have a full view of the others at any one point in time. She wondered if this was deliberate or that she was just being paranoid.

Maureen was drying a glass when they entered, barely managing to hold onto it as she saw her hero walk in. She had dined out many a night on the fact that she and Sarah had been Kiltman's first heroic act, playing along with the damsel in distress angle covered by the media. Despite the fifteen minutes of fame she received, she had not gone to bed since without saying a prayer with Sarah that the good Lord would keep their kilted saviour safe. Interestingly, none of the other customers acknowledged anything amiss with a man dressed in a mask, cloak, and kilt walking into their local pub.

Kiltman smiled at Maureen as he had done so many times in the past. Of course, he realised she could not see his face. She could not ask him any of her searching, personal questions as she had done so often before. The last time he had seen her was when he carried her and Sarah to their safety a couple of years earlier. She looked happy.

"Kiltman!" she said quietly. "It's so good to see you."

He walked behind the bar extending his arms to embrace her. Maureen gladly responded. They hugged tightly.

"You're looking well, Maureen."

"Thanks to you, Kiltman."

They held each other both aware of how much the rescue had meant for each of them in very different ways.

Wilson coughed quietly. Kiltman turned and said, "Maureen meet DI Wilson. DI Wilson, this is Maureen."

"Pleased to meet you, Maureen. So this is Kiltman's local pub, eh?" Wilson smiled, nodding to the gantry behind Maureen's head. The wall was coloured with newspaper clippings of Kiltman.

"No, this is the first time we've seen him in here," Maureen answered. She turned to him and said, "He should come more often to visit his fans. Especially his distressed damsels."

"Of course!" Wilson slapped her forehead with the palm of her hand. "It was you he saved from the fire in Yoker." She had read his file before she met him the previous day.

"Yes, me and my daughter." Maureen was surprised at the tremor in her voice. She saw him tap his fingers on the bar before she said, "Okay, but I'm sure you're not here to reminisce. What can I get you?"

"A couple of coffees, if that's okay with you, Wilson?"

"That suits me fine." The thought of coffee made her relax for the first time that day.

"Nothing to eat?" Maureen asked. "This is on me. And…" She raised her hand as he made a move to protest. "I won't hear any of it! I bet you can do with some nourishment. I'm sure you've been on the go all day since that terrible Clyde Tunnel

132

incident yesterday. The chef's not here at the moment so I'll pull something together for you in the kitchen. Just keep an eye on the bar for ten minutes. I'll be right back."

Before Wilson or Kiltman could say a word, Maureen had disappeared around the corner towards the hotel.

Tap! Tap!

They looked up simultaneously to see one of the customers tap a coin on the bar.

"What does a man need to do to get a drink in here?" Around sixty years old, sporting a flat cap above grey five-day stubble, the man held his pint glass upside down. In a rasping voice, he shouted, "Look! I'm gagging for a drink! Pint of Guinness, when you're ready!"

"I'll get this, Wilson." Kiltman recognised the man as Old Jimmy. He had been called Old Jimmy since he was in his forties because of his old-fashioned attitudes combined with distaste for anyone younger than him. Kiltman walked behind the bar picking up a fresh glass from the shelf below the gantry. Focusing on the angle of the glass, he poured three quarters of the Guinness slowly allowing the correct amount of time before he added the last quarter. He carried the glass to the man and, after a glance at the prices on the wall, said, "That'll be two pounds, please."

He could see the edge of a two-pound coin in Old Jimmy's his hand. A hand decorated with a tattoo that read "Celtic 1967", a reference to Celtic's success in winning the European Cup. The colours had faded, which Kiltman reflected were sadly similar to Celtic's chances of winning it again. Old Jimmy refused to hand over the coin.

"Where's my shamrock?"

"Oh!" Kiltman realised his mistake. "I'm not very good at shamrocks. Next time, I'll do one for you."

"I'm not paying a penny until I get a shamrock on my Guinness. I've been drinking here for years and there's always one on my pint. Maureen doesn't make excuses. So, hurry up. Or I'm going to the pub down the road." A determined sneer had crept into the corners of the man's mouth.

Wilson snorted in the corner of the bar. He refused to look at her as he walked back to the pump. He poured a quarter of the

Guinness into the sink and placed the glass on the pouring tray. He knew that he would have about four seconds to make the shamrock before the glass was full. He felt a bead of sweat trickle down his cheek on the inside of his mask. The pressure was on.

He flicked the tap into the on position. As soon as the Guinness began to pour, he twisted his wrist in his best artistic fashion to carve out a shamrock onto the white of the pint. It was all over before he could complete the third petal of the Irish national emblem. He carried the pint back to Old Jimmy. He placed it on the bar and leant across and whispered, "Cut me some slack, Old Jimmy, there's a good man."

Old Jimmy looked up astonished that Scotland's superhero knew his name. He had not expected to be identified. This changed the perspective of the duel. "Aye, alright, that'll do. More of a sham than a shamrock, but here's the money."

Kiltman prised the coin away from the Celtic hand, before placing it on the till.

"Kiltman, DI Wilson!" Maureen shouted from a passage leading into the lounge. "Here's a wee bite to eat and a coffee. You should come through here. It's a bit quieter." She held up a tray piled high with sandwiches and sausage rolls. "These were left over from a funeral this morning. They're all yours." Maureen smiled, placing the food on a formica covered table in the lounge.

He walked the length of the bar towards the lounge, anxious to avoid looking at Wilson.

"Don't give up your day job, Kiltman," Wilson spoke just loud enough for him to hear.

He walked past her towards the lounge. Before he entered, he turned and said, "Celtic 1967!"

Art of Vanity

"Do you have a newspaper, Maureen? Preferably one with an events or entertainment section," Kiltman mumbled through a mouth full of reheated sausage roll. He felt self-conscious when he ate with his mask on. He would spend hours in the public eye solving crimes and performing heroics, for it all to be wiped away when he had to push food underneath the chin of the mask up into his mouth. He rarely found himself in this position. He normally refused to eat in public. Truth was he could not resist the savoury smell of the sausage rolls. He knew Maureen and Wilson were trying not to laugh at the crumbs accumulating on the Kiltman emblem on his chest and across his conspicuous stomach.

"Sure, hold on." Maureen leant down behind the bar to search for a newspaper. This gave a mischievous Wilson enough time to say, "Can you not invent something to liquidise the food then eat it through a straw?"

"I'm glad you're finding this amusing, Wilson. Even superheroes need to eat. Preferably solids and not baby food. Maybe if there's ever a Kiltboy, he'll be able to eat porridge through a straw."

"Here you are, Kiltman. *Daily Record*. You can't beat it for entertainment! I need to go back into the bar. Old Jimmy wants another drink." Maureen beamed as she walked back through to the bar. This had made her day.

"What kind of 'entertainment' are you looking for?" Wilson asked as he turned the pages, resting at page three for a second longer than the others.

"Oh, right. Okay, maybe I've got it wrong, but what do you think of the clue MacSpiderman left us?"

He placed the newspaper on the table and produced the clue from his sporran. He handed it to Wilson. She studied it quietly for a minute before spreading it flat on the table. "I don't know. It's definitely a clue to a place since he mentions 'where' three times. The rest in between is a mystery to me."

"Yes, it's convoluted to say the least. Some key words that jump out at me are 'love hate' and 'Mum Dad'. Where would you see words like these?"

"Eh, in poetry? Greetings cards?"

"What if you didn't want to send a card or write a poem, but wanted people to know that you loved your mum and dad? Or that you could simultaneously love and hate the world? Or you wanted to boast that your team won the European Cup?"

"Of course! On your body. I've seen many criminals with those words emblazoned on their knuckles. He's referring to tattoos."

"That's what I think. Especially if you look at the last few lines."

Kiltman read them out loud:

"Oh what a wicked web he weaves
where he sets out to deceive
By giving the elbow
To those thug-minded fellows."

Wilson's eyes widened as she clicked her fingers. "Web, elbow, thug-minded fellows. This is a reference to the tattoos those neo-Nazis are famous for having on their elbows. Like a net or web starting from the elbow before working its way out over the rest of the arm."

"Spot on."

"So that's why you're looking in the newspaper. You're hoping to see a reference to a tattoo artist."

"Exactly. So, let's have a quick flick through the paper." Kiltman studied the paper carefully pausing to read a few lines from each article to identify a connection with tattooing. The newspaper was filled with the usual news about horse racing and football with more than a healthy dedication of coverage to movie and pop stars and the preparations for the Edinburgh festival later that summer. They reached the back page without finding a single reference to a gathering of tattoo artists.

Wilson clicked her fingers. "Kiltman, go back to page three."

"Wilson, I didn't realise... "

"Very funny." Wilson took the newspaper from him, turning to page three. She pointed to an article on the preparations for the Edinburgh festival. "Try to focus on this article here and not the pictures." Despite herself, she smiled.

They read the article together as it explained the President of the USA was visiting Scotland as part of his UK visit. To mark his trip the festival committee had worked with the Scottish pipe bands to bring forward a dress rehearsal of the famous bagpipe opening ceremony two months ahead of schedule. The name for this event was spelled out in the title of the article: "President Bush to attend Edinburgh Tattoo".

"Wilson, you've got it. Look…" Kiltman pointed at the last paragraph.

"The dress rehearsal for the Edinburgh Tattoo will take place tonight at eight thirty. All tickets have been sold under unprecedented security for an event of its kind in Scotland. Don't worry if you have not got your ticket to sit alongside President Bush, because you can watch it live on BBC One."

They looked at each other. Wilson pointed to her watch. "It's just gone six o'clock. We've got two and a half hours."

"Okay, call the Chief. Tell him to get the helicopter over here and pick us up from Sweeneys' car park. You should also mention the other small complication of President Bush being at risk."

Wilson had already dialled the number before Kiltman finished speaking. The Chief answered in seconds.

"Hi, Chief, we know where Cullen Skink's going to strike next?" Wilson grimaced when she realised that she had not checked in with him since they had gone chasing up the hill towards the shed.

"Good to hear from you, Wilson. So, we're still on the same team after all. What's this about a next strike?"

"It's in Edinburgh at the Tattoo rehearsal. We need the chopper fast. It's going to happen in just over two hours."

"The Tattoo rehearsal? But, that's…"

"Exactly. President Bush might get more than an earful of pipe music on his visit to Scotland's capital."

"Right! Okay, the chopper is still here with us at the bridge. We'll get it to you now. Where are you?"

"We're at a place called Sweeneys in Duntocher. It's a pub-hotel. Good news is it's got a large car…"

"You're in a pub!"

"Well, we came here to decipher…"

"Pub? We're on the bridge picking up every last scrap of rotten, smelly piece of rubbish, looking on the underside of rocks for clues while you two are off having a wee refreshment."

"Please, Chief, just get the transport over here. We don't have time. I'll explain it all later."

Wilson squirmed in her chair holding the phone several inches from her ear as the Chief moved into top gear in his tirade. She looked at Kiltman for support. He held his hand to his mouth, although she could not see the smile behind his mask. Wilson knew at that moment why Kiltman had asked her to call the Chief rather than do it himself. Revenge was proving quite sweet.

The Tattoo

The castle loomed high in the evening sky. Its majestic presence so impressive the city was known as the Athens of the North. Sitting atop a lump of gruff rock, not surprisingly known as "The Mound", the castle walls reminded the citizens there is a watchful eye protecting them.

They had made good time. In less anxious moments it would have been a scenic journey from the Firth of Clyde to the Firth of Forth, Edinburgh's majestic, calm waterway. Along with Kiltman and Wilson the Chief had sent four bomb disposal experts, who were already in the process of checking their equipment prior to landing. It had just gone six thirty. They would be on the ground in five minutes.

"Wilson!" Kiltman shouted above the noise of the blades.

"What!" She leaned towards him to make sure she heard every last word. They had less than ninety minutes to find whatever surprise Cullen Skink had in store for them.

"The fact that President Bush is here reminded me of the two American tourists who thought it was a great idea to build Edinburgh Castle so near the train station."

"Your point is?" she answered, an unmistakeable shard of ice in the inflection of her voice.

"It's a joke, Wilson. Supposed to highlight the difference in age between our two great countries." He hated having to explain a joke.

"Okay. So what's the game plan when we land?" Wilson felt a tremor of palpitations. She had been a DI for several years now with an impressive record of solved crimes under her belt. Scores of robberies, countless drug busts, armed attacks due to Scotland's growing knife culture and three murders, each brutally worse than the one before. She had noticed a steady increase in disregard for the law over the years. Politicians talked about releasing budgets to increase police presence placing more cops on the beat. All well and good. The reality was the only way to deal with crime as far as she was concerned was at its root. A cliché, but a fact nonetheless. The institution of the family was under attack on all fronts. She grew up being taught the importance of respecting family values and cascading those values through the rest of the community. She had no kids herself but if she ever did she would control the four cornerstones of this decline in the social structure: materialism from branded goods making the young and adults value the wrong things; abuse of technology, from video games to mobile phone addictions from an early age; quality of food since you are what you eat; and respect for your fellow citizen. In some ways she could see where Cullen Skink was getting his gripe.

Several thousand of those fellow citizens were being herded five hundred feet below her from the site of the Tattoo down to a clearing at the beginning of the Royal Mile, the street connecting the castle to Holyrood Palace, where the President was residing as a guest of the Queen. Half an hour earlier the crowd had been excitedly settling into their seats when the call came through to clear the area. Wilson could see from the faces focused on the chopper they were not convinced there was anything to worry about.

The pilot hovered above the square until it had been completely cleared. He looked for confirmation from Kiltman, who nodded his head before landing evenly on the tarmac. Kiltman stepped out, hunched over awkwardly before beginning a jog to a clearing at the side of the chopper. The pilot had turned off the engine but the blades were still whistling above Kiltman's head taking longer to reach a stop. Wilson had already exited walking directly behind him in the same direction. Out of the corner of her eye she noticed his billowing cape was attracted to the suction of the blades. She lunged forward, managing to grab the end of the cape before he became super-minced meat. She continued to hold it tight until they were well clear of the helicopter. The act of rescue went unnoticed by Kiltman, although the sight of Wilson behind him elicited hoots and cheers at a scene reminiscent of a bridesmaid trailing a bride. Wilson knew she should not be concerned about her street cred since they were dealing with a much bigger issue than her pride. But it was certainly taking a battering on this case. Of that, she was in no doubt.

Once she was convinced Kiltman was safe she let his cape blow in the wind leaving him to walk further into the centre of the square. The area was much larger than it looked on television. Wilson had only ever watched the Tattoo once and even then for no more than fifteen minutes. She had thought the spectacle impressive; it had made her proud to be Scottish. However, there was only so much she could take of the traditional celebration. Pipers dressed in full Highland regalia marched with military precision blowing to their hearts' content. Drummers beat a steady rhythm while batons were tossed into a sea of floodlights before coming down to land safely in a gloved hand. The Tattoo was certainly an acquired taste. One that she would need to spend a lot more time acquiring.

On either side of the square were two separate tiered seating structures, erected on scaffolding especially for the event. The stands were colossal, rising up into the evening sky above Edinburgh. Only a few minutes earlier they had been full of people in excited anticipation of the spectacle, awaiting the US President's arrival. No doubt he was now sitting at the Queen's fireside resigned to his night in, ticket shredded, sipping on whatever non-alcoholic beer she had in her fridge.

Kiltman realised that Wilson had held back, which suited him since he had to concentrate on finding any surprises Cullen Skink may have planted. The police had managed to calm the crowd pleading for silence until Kiltman found what he was looking for. Once the silence descended, Wilson noticed how the faces changed suddenly, as if for the first time they understood there was a serious risk of danger. The stillness became tangible when the deafening whirr of the blades slowed to a halt.

Kiltman stood in the middle of the square and closed his eyes. He concentrated on listening intently for any sounds that seemed out of place. He heard the traffic on Prince's Street, Edinburgh's main shopping area several hundred feet below the castle, across a park dominated by evening strollers and teenagers freely releasing cheap lager belches. All a little too close for comfort. He blocked out the high-pitched drone of a private jet approaching Edinburgh airport. The murmuring wind as it wound its way between the castle walls was the last thing he heard before he noticed a soft hum. He listened carefully, straining his ears till he realised there were two distinct noises.

He walked to his left towards the north side seating. The hum was coming from somewhere near the centre of the stand. He exhaled softly as he bent down to lever himself inside the scaffolding beneath the seats. Half-crawling, half-walking, he manoeuvred his way between the jagged, steel pipes towards the sound. He was surprised at how much chewing gum there really was down there. He was not surprised to find that not all dogs were trained to use telephone boxes and parks. Ignoring the hazards of the job, his gloved hands pulled him along the ground.

Below the centre of the seating he found it. A small, black device no bigger than a double-disc CD box had been taped to one of the metal scaffolds. On its front a clock registered the number zero. Kiltman lifted his hand above it pulling gently on the scaffold. Immediately the clock started to register a change in the number. Five, six, seven. He had guessed correctly: the numbers were kilogrammes. The box contained an explosive which would only trigger once a certain weight was placed upon the scaffolding. He had no doubts Cullen Skink had set the switch to wait until the stand reached close to maximum capacity, guaranteeing greatest lethal impact.

Kiltman ran his finger along the side of the box sensing the essence of semtex tightly packed inside. The semtex in itself would not have injured any of the audience. It was so far beneath the seats, the direct impact would have been minimal. Its position at the heart of the stand however would have resulted in the structure collapsing like a pack of cards. The ensuing collapse, panic, stampede and crush of bodies would bring the devastation Cullen Skink had warned of. Kiltman worked his fingers round the edges of the box until he was sure there were no trip wires. He then detached it carefully before placing it inside his sporran. This was one bomb he most definitely did not want to go off, he thought, as he patted the sporran gently.

The hush was tangible when he exited from beneath the scaffolding. For a crowd who had arrived to listen to the skirl of pipes, the silence was becoming unbearable. He walked towards the other seating area before bending to insert himself in the scaffold to once again do battle with chewing gum and canine waste.

It took less than five minutes to reach another black device taped beneath the seats. He detached it as cautiously as before. The thought crossed his mind that Cullen Skink had placed the device as a trap to lure him underneath the scaffold. Once he was in the centre of the structure, if Cullen Skink wanted to, he could have collapsed the whole seating section on top of him. He pushed the thought to the back of his mind as he turned the device over in his hand. On its rear there was a sheet of paper attached.

"Here we go again," Kiltman thought as he removed it. He opened gently lest there may be an unwelcome surprise.

"Kiltman, if you're really underneath the seats and have managed to find this note then I am truly impressed. You are beginning to rise above my expectations. Who would've thought you and that belly would've been able to squeeze through all this metal? Extraordinary! You just keep saving people's lives... does it not get boring? I hope you realise the lives you are saving are on borrowed time. Scotland has a price to pay for its waywardness, a cost that will be counted in people. Such people are an expensive commodity to be invested in our country's future. I shall make that investment on the people's behalf. One day they will appreciate me for it.

"Well, it looks like I will need to up the ante. Obviously I should make things more exciting for you. Bring your sidekick with you on this one as well. She looks as though she would appreciate a bit of culture.

"Enjoy the cappuccino, when you rome the Venice way.
Catholic view, this time is true.
Skinless, Heartless,
My same message from another age
Atop the next directions, sit the voluntary donations.

I hope you've got your passport ready. *Arrividerci, uomo di gonna.*
Cullen Skink."

Kiltman slipped the note and bomb into a tightly packed sporran. He took a deep breath before bending down to crawl out of the maze of scaffolding. He ignored the aches in his elbows and knees while focusing on not banging his head against the metal. The mask's material was resilient but not steelproof. Once through the other side he rose and dusted himself down before waving Wilson and the bomb disposal team to come across to meet him. They walked at a brisk pace trying not to rush lest they incite any degree of panic in the crowd.

First to arrive at his side was Bob Murdoch. "So what we got here, Kiltman?"

Kiltman took the two devices from his sporran and handed them to Bob. "Semtex, Bob. The trigger was in the weight of the audience. If they hadn't cleared the stands before we got here, we would be cleaning up a mess right now. I don't think there are any others. You should have your guys and the dogs check just in case, but I'm convinced there are no more surprises."

"Okay, Kiltman. I'll take these and deactivate them. One of these days you need to tell me how you do it."

"Once I figure that out, I'll let you know. By the way, do you have an old rag I could use?" he was already picking gum from the sleeves of his top. Next invention had to be a non-stick Lycra, he thought.

"I'm sure there is some air freshener in the chopper as well." Bob smiled as he looked at the brown stain on Kiltman's stomach underneath the Kiltman emblem. Kiltman's grunt was enough to encourage Bob not to push his luck.

Wilson approached him with what seemed to be a look of relief. "You had us all a bit worried when you were under the seats. Well done."

"To be honest, I was a bit concerned myself. It's not easy protecting your dignity when you crawl in a kilt." Kiltman waited for Wilson to respond, which arrived in the form of a shake of her head.

"Did he leave us any clues?" Back to business.

"Yes, he did. Here it is." He slipped the paper from his sporran and handed it to her.

She read it slowly determined to identify something that Kiltman may not have noticed.

"Looks like Italy next." She held the corner of the paper delicately lest she interfere with any fingerprints, although she knew Cullen Skink would not have been that careless.

"I think you're right, Wilson. Which leaves me with a big problem." Kiltman scratched his head.

"What type of problem could be bigger than Cullen Skink's next act of terror?" She looked at him quizzically.

"How do I get through Immigration without taking my mask off?"

Rome

"Father, we need your help here." Kiltman spoke carefully.

Father Shuggy Quinn nodded slowly, trying for the life of him not to smile. The Scots College on the ancient Via Cassia north of Rome had been graced with many visitors over the years, from politicians to popes, but no-one quite as surreal as a caped, kilted man asking for help. He had received a call only that morning to be told that Kiltman and DI Wilson would be flying out to ask him for some assistance on a very important case. He was not sure exactly how he could help, since the college was very much a subculture removed from the secular world. There had been a seminary in Rome for centuries, proving to be a strong, spiritual home for many Scots pursuing a vocation. The only crime he was aware of was that of self-indulgence, when the Croatian nuns cooked up a storm each lunch time and evening, evidenced by a cassock with reinforced buttons dangerously close to popping.

The last time Kenny had flown to Rome had been his stag weekend with Tommy. Their agenda had been much more relaxed and self-indulgent than this trip. As the plane circled the airport, he had surveyed the rolling green hills busy in their production of olives and grapes. Only three hours from Glasgow, yet worlds apart. He only wished he had time to walk through the countryside outside the city breathing the dry air, scented with the foliage and nature that made this place so special. Unfortunately, Cullen Skink's deadlines did not cater for idle tourist activities.

"What do you think of this?" Wilson placed the letter on the table in the priests' lounge where they sat anxiously on two soft, recently-upholstered couches.

Shuggy balanced a frail pair of reading glasses on the edge of his nose before studying the note quietly. A couple of minutes passed before he looked up and said, "I'm no literary expert, but it seems you're looking for someone who failed English at school."

"Maybe." Kiltman shifted awkwardly in his chair. This escapade was becoming ever more surreal. Shuggy had changed. He seemed to have settled well into the priesthood, which was more than could be said for the cassock. The good looks were still there, albeit in a rounder format than Kiltman remembered. He also seemed more relaxed than he had been during the post-graduation celebration in the beer bar. Over the years Shuggy had made more of an effort to stay in touch, but Kenny had been so focused on his whisky production that they had only met on a handful of occasions. The meetings became more difficult as Shuggy pressed Kenny on whether his priorities were in the right place. He had become a strict adherent to his vow of poverty, which obviously did not include eating. As he witnessed Kenny going from strength to strength, at least financially, in each reunion he would add even more pressure for Kenny to spend more time soul-searching and praying. In the end Shuggy became so extreme that Kenny made up a myriad of excuses for not meeting until he fell off Shuggy's "save-a-lost-soul" agenda.

Kiltman continued. "We're more interested in where you may think the poem is directing us to go next. You see, we believe there is an Italian connection here, which seems to be either in Venice or in Rome, based on the first line. He appears to connect the two cities somehow. There is also a reference to 'Catholic view' so we contacted the Glasgow archdiocese. They said that we should talk to you as a starting point since you've been in Italy a long time, and know the lay of the land better than most."

When the archdiocese had recommended Shuggy, Kiltman nearly fell off his chair. He had not looked forward to the meeting since Shuggy reminded him of all the things he should feel guilty about.

"I'm flattered, I must say. I hope the Archbishop holds my spirituality in as high an esteem as my role as a tour guide." He returned to the letter, musing over it carefully. "Well, let me think. There's really not much I can say. Except for one thing."

"Yes?" Wilson was slightly uncomfortable sitting in the seminary. She was not sure if it was because Father Quinn had no experience of crime fighting, or she had not visited a church in years. She was still reeling from arriving at Fiumicino airport with a masked man in a kilt, expecting the Italian immigration authorities to take him into custody, to be left to deal with the

147

clue on her own. However, when Kiltman provided a letter from the Italian embassy in London, combined with their knowledge of his by now famous escapades in Scotland, he was given a welcome only provided to heads of state. A carabinieri bulletproof limo transported them from the airport directly to the college.

"Don't assume that 'Venice way' means somewhere in Venice. You see, in Italian, as you no doubt know, the word for street is 'via', which comes directly from Latin. It also translates as 'way'. It just so happens that we have a very famous street in Rome called Via Veneto. The street's not too long, you can get there in half an hour by taxi... or by bulletproof limo. I would suggest you go there, and 'rome'. Can't say too much for this guy's spelling. As for the rest of the clue, I'm sorry but I can't think of anything else that might help you."

Kiltman and Wilson exchanged glances. They rose from the couch at the same time.

"That'll do nicely, Father. We'll be in touch if we need anything else." Wilson was in a hurry to leave.

"Just one more thing, Father. What do the words *'uomo di gonna'* mean?" He had to ask.

"Literally, it means, 'man in a skirt'." Cullen Skink was raising the stakes. He was becoming increasingly more personal. "Although, to be honest," he continued quickly, "there isn't a word in Italian for kilt. So over here you'll probably be known as *Gonna-uomo*... eh... Skirtman." Father Quinn realised by Kiltman's silence he had not liked the interpretation. "Now, now. Let's not fall victim to the sin of pride. It's not what others think or say that matters, it's what's on the inside. Behind our masks, if you pardon the analogy. Anyway, I'm sure you must be on your way. Next time, please stay for lunch, the sisters makes an exquisite lasagne."

"Thanks, Father." Wilson nudged Kiltman.

"Oh yes, thanks, Father. Very helpful." Skirtman! Kiltman was guilty as charged. Pride and a latex costume were odd partners. His penance for this cardinal sin was Cullen Skink. He only hoped he would not have to complete the penance in full.

The Bones Church

The limo made it as far as Piazza del Popolo to the north of Via del Corso in the centre of Rome. The piazza was a huge, oxymoronic, circular square with streams of cars careering into it from all sides. In the centre a fast-flowing fountain dominated the scene, quietly ambivalent to the frenzy of competing vehicles. They arrived in the middle of a watertight traffic jam, which some would argue was an essential part of the Italian experience. The numerous cars, taxis and buses seemed to squeeze into every available space until there was no room left to manoeuvre. Gridlock became semi-permanent. Time was slipping away. "Well, Kiltman, you up for another jog? We're about a mile away from Via Veneto. I've figured it out on the map."

"Okay, Wilson, there's nothing else for it. Just take it easy on me this time." Kiltman groaned quietly inside his mask. Wilson's suggestion was easier said than done. The traffic was so tight the carabinieri driver shrugged his shoulders before pressing the button to open the window. Wilson was halfway out the window before Kiltman had summoned the energy to loosen his seatbelt. He followed her lead, first thanking his lucky stars they were not in a cinquecento. Wilson bounced from one car bonnet to the next, followed by a cacophony of horns and whistles. He followed her trail across the cars listening to the increasing volume of noise as trapped drivers enjoyed the momentary entertainment. While Italy models itself on being a country at the leading edge of fashion, no-one had previously considered as catwalk appropriate a mask, skirt and cape on a middle-aged man. If they had, they probably would have added a pair of Dolce and Gabbana sunglasses to protect his identity.

Kiltman jumped from the car, trying not to think of how many commuters may have had the dubious pleasure of witnessing a true Scotsman through their windscreens as he bounded across their vehicle. Wilson was looking back at him, running backwards as she waved. Just as he caught up with her, she turned to run even faster. He seemed to be in constant catch-up mode. After an eternal ten minutes, Kiltman leant against a wall trying to control a now familiar heaving chest, gasping for polluted Roman air. Wilson was resting on her haunches, the map flattened on the pavement.

"Kiltman, Via Veneto is not very long. It bends up round the corner in an 'S' shape as far as the Villa Borghese. It's a..."

"Park overlooking the city. Thanks, but I have been here before."

Wilson looked up from the map, her mouth open in surprise.

"Sorry, but even superheroes can become a little tetchy." He raised his hand in the air in apology. For the first time since meeting this bizarre man two days earlier she felt a twinge of affection.

"So where do we start?" she asked, looking back at the map. No point in making it obvious how she felt.

"Okay, let me think." He paused for a few seconds. "The other part of the clue points towards something to do with cappuccino, but from what I remember, this street is littered with cafes, very expensive cafes. It has to be something oblique. Let's start walking and listening."

Kiltman walked up the Via Veneto, apparently at home in one of Rome's most fashionable streets. Several outdoor cafes added calm to an air punctuated by the cacophony of car horns. The cafes were populated by scores of tourists with chairs facing the onslaught of battling vehicles, spellbound by the artistic confusion of Rome's commuting hour. The two worlds seemed to coexist happily, emotionally entwined but physically separate. He listened to a myriad of conversations coming at him from all directions. He could even hear the people standing outside the American embassy a couple of hundred yards away. His mind analysed every word at a speed computer chips would envy. Many of the conversations were in languages he could not understand, but there was no shortage of English coming at him in Australian, American and British accents. He let it flow through his mind until one phrase jumped to the fore. "What's this Cappuccini Bones Church all about then?"

Cappuccini?

He picked up pace until he arrived at the source of the comment, an American posse of tourists bedecked in light-coloured "pants" and chequered shirts. They were in a huddle outside one of Rome's many churches, as common to the city as traffic lights in Glasgow's city centre. They walked up a short flight of stairs following scores of people who seemed to move with purpose. Kiltman noted that instead of visiting the church, they were being directed into the crypt halfway up the steps. He decided to follow them into a dark, musty, low-ceilinged entrance. He dropped a few notes from his sporran into the collection box on the table at the door, before leading Wilson through to the darkness. He nearly missed the old monk sitting in the chair at the entrance, layers of dust gathering in clumps on his brown cassock.

Once their eyes adjusted to the lack of light, he heard Wilson's purposeful cough. She raised her eyes to the ceiling as she leant forward to whisper in his ear. "Please tell me I'm imagining things."

Kiltman wanted to tell her that it was not real. However, she was not imagining the thousands of human bones and skeletons arranged in designs and patterns worthy of a skeletal botanic garden. She was not imagining the endless rows of skulls, femurs, and pelvises stacked high and deep. He was not imagining the wet whisper when her lips grazed his ear. Nor her warm breath on the back of his neck. They were in a church. He was unsure what Father Shuggy would have said about that.

Respecting the silence of the crypt, he leaned across to her ear. "No, this is a cemetery. The bones belong to four thousand Capuchin monks who died several centuries ago. They are designed in this way to highlight the brevity of life, reinforcing the starkness of death. The bones are laid bare to show how we are all going to end up after a relatively short period on this earth. Funnily enough, the word cappuccino comes from the colour of the robes worn by these monks. That'll make you think the next time you go to Starbucks." Despite the ugliness of the crypt, Kiltman sensed an unspoken intimacy as they wandered through the Bones Church. He hoped at that moment, whatever happened with Cullen Skink, Wilson would remain a part of his life. Was it possible to find romance in a boneyard? For that matter, was it possible for someone who had never seen his face, someone who had an issue at being partnered with a man in a kilt, to find him the least bit attractive?

151

"Maybe this is Cullen Skink's message when he refers to the line 'My same message from another age'. Not a lot of 'skin' around here, most certainly a pretty 'heartless' exhibition! He intends to make life short for the few so that the many can learn from mistakes made by others in the past. This crypt may represent his picture of what Scotland will look like when he has his way. But what exactly he is trying to achieve is beyond me." Wilson shivered. Kiltman nodded.

"This place gives me the creeps," Kiltman said. "I've just realised where the next clue may be lurking. Let's leave the dead in peace." Kiltman shuddered involuntarily.

The Vatican

Kiltman manoeuvred past the stream of visitors, startled by the incongruence of a caped crusader in a cryptic tribute to the art of bone. The last two lines of the clue were now as clear to him as the light of day, which they were both desperate to see again. He squeezed his way back to the entrance. Without waiting for the old monk acting as doorkeeper to agree, Kiltman lifted the money box and looked at the bottom. Shaking his head, he placed the box back on the table. Lowering himself under the table oblivious to the blusterings of the monk, he lay on his back. He slithered along the mottled floor of the crypt until he was directly underneath the centre of the table. He knew he had got it right when he looked up and saw an all too familiar sheet of white paper attached to the underside of the table. Detaching it gently lest he lose a precious word, he tucked it into his sporran and reappeared from the other end, the particles of dust clinging to his cape, highlighted by a stream of sunlight from the doorway.

The old monk had given up complaining and was now sitting restfully in the chair beside him looked entirely nonplussed, most likely contemplating which corner of the crypt his bones would decorate one day.

"Arrivederci e grazie!" Kiltman whispered while dropping a few coins into the box, before nodding at Wilson to make an exit. Back in the sunlight, Wilson smiled at him. For the first time in a long time, he sensed a part of his life slip out of control. He was enjoying it. Standing on the steps, he looked into Wilson's deeply comforting eyes enjoying the warmth of the moment. Wilson stared back at the blue and white mask wondering if she could ever find latex the least bit attractive.

"So, what does it say?" She had to keep them focused. She had felt it. There was something between them she could not explain. She had met her fair share of men. She was always very careful. Hurt, or the fear of it, made her nervous. It had been the end of every relationship she had begun over the years. Not the type to go to therapy, she had analysed herself a thousand times. All roads led back to that night in her teens when her innocence was threatened in a Glasgow alley.

"Here we go." He had already read the detail, but focused on reading it carefully for Wilson's benefit.

"Dear Kiltman and sidekick Starling (Robin has been used by that other superhero! Ha! Ha!).

"I hope you enjoyed the Bones Church. Why did I send you there? So that you could see my view of humanity. Life is short, the human body comes from dust and to dust it will return. You're running out of time, the clock is ticking until the brightest midnight, when Strathclyde will see havoc and devastation wreaked in volcanic proportions. I will make an example of the Catholic Church to show you just how easy it is to destroy the human spirit. The body comes soon after. You will have the blood of many on your hands, the faith of millions laid bare at your door. I will be helped by the true Kings of Scotland, who led the meagre forces of a bedraggled and poverty-stricken nation against the might of the English.

"The Stuart line, drenched in wine
Gazed upon apostles, those religious fossils.
Plaque removal finds approval.
Not so sweet the smell, of a church's death knell.

"Tick, tock, tick, tock.
Cullen Skink."

Somewhere deep in the recesses of Kiltman's mind, a tiny spark of clarity tried to break through. There was something he recognised in this clue but was frustratingly out of reach.

"I've got a suggestion."

"Fire ahead, Wilson."

"Let's google it."

Kiltman waited for the joke.

"Google what?"

"Follow me." Wilson ran out onto the Via Veneto. She turned left onto the pavement and sprinted towards the end of the street where the traffic exploded onto Piazza Barberini. She had already disappeared through the doors of the Bristol Hotel before Kiltman had reached the piazza.

"Look, sir, I'm a Detective Inspector with the Scottish police. Can I please use a computer to check the internet?" Wilson leant her elbows on the reception desk.

"*Ma signora*, you need to be resident in hotel." A surly concierge with a handlebar moustache was obviously not impressed with Wilson's badge, waved officiously in his face.

"Excuse me, sir. We have an international crisis here. We need your help." Kiltman stood behind Wilson.

"Ah-hah! It is the skirtman from Scozia. Yes, but of course. Follow me." The concierge had changed from surly to willing because of a man in a skirt. Wilson's bemused look showed she did not appreciate the disrespectful attitude to the Scottish badge. While Kiltman's grimace at his Italian nickname made him realise he had suddenly developed onomatophobia.

It took Wilson less than five minutes to google a combination of Stuart and Rome. One day, she thought, this googling idea will be much faster. Top of the list was something neither Kiltman nor Wilson had previously realised. For some reason in the eighteenth century, the Catholic Church deemed it appropriate to create a monument in Saint Peter's Basilica to the Stuart dynasty of Scotland, where James, the son of King James II of England, and seventh of Scotland, had been buried in the eighteenth century with his two sons, Henry and Charles. While their bodies were buried underneath the cathedral in the crypt, a monument had been erected near the entrance in their memory. Henry was an understandable addition to the Vatican's limited space due to his decision to become a cardinal in the church. Charles, on the other hand, famed for being the Bonnie Prince, failed in his 1745 rebellion to win the British throne. Kiltman and Wilson looked at each other.

"Incredible," Wilson spoke softly. "This also explains the reference to the apostles."

"Yes, a great way for Cullen Skink to assassinate many of the Pope's cardinals, priests, nuns and pilgrims. It wouldn't do a lot for Scotland's international reputation." Kiltman's voice displayed the nervousness he felt at the thought of the Pope and the HQ of the church sitting on top of a cocktail of explosives.

To the backdrop of car horns and whining bus engines, they ran onto the street while poring over a crumpled map. Two Italian youths dressed in leathers sat astride a Vespa scooter, barely concealing their mirth as they pointed at skirtman, a thumb pressing the horn to the beat of their shouts. Their good fortune at being in the right place at the right time had provided the opportunity for a belly laugh they had not enjoyed since Berlusconi's hair transplant.

Ten minutes later as they sped through the cobbled streets of Rome's historical centre, he was surprised at the complete absence of guilt he felt. He was sure the lads were unhurt on bouncing off the street when he realigned the balance of the Vespa. Two good things came out of that moment. A couple of Italians received a lesson in respecting elders – especially those in the superhero profession – while Kiltman had another opportunity for Wilson to put her hands on his waist as he revved the Vespa to max speed around the corners and squares of Rome.

The kilt flapped freely and revealingly in the wind during a knuckle-numbing, buttock-clenching ride across cobblestones. He screeched to a halt and parked the scooter alongside the colonnades of Saint Peter's cathedral. They had arrived at peak time with a long queue snaking halfway across the square, pilgrims and tourists waiting patiently to enter St. Peter's. With no time to waste, they ran through the crowds bumping and manoeuvring their way to the entrance. He led Wilson to the checkpoint and X-ray machine nearest the huge, bronze cathedral door. He nimbly detached his sporran and belt before feeding them along the conveyor. Fortunately, the crowds of people were good natured, their cheering convincing him that a kilt was the perfect queue-jumping aid. Wilson followed immediately behind him. By the time they were entering the cathedral, the belt and sporran, which contained the all too important Hair o' the Dog, were back in place.

As they stepped across the cathedral's threshold, a large man in a black suit and dark sunglasses stepped in their way, hands raised. He spread his legs in a manner that showed he was not in the mood for discussion. In a slow staccato voice, he said, "You cannot enter. You must wear trousers."

"Sorry?" Kiltman had not expected this.

"No short skirts allowed."

"Skirt? This is a kilt! It's not a skirt."

"Your legs. Not possible for men's legs bare in cathedral." Wilson's stifled cough told Kiltman all he needed to know about his street cred in Rome.

Kiltman was faced with a choice. He could walk away searching for someone he could convince to lend him a pair of trousers. Not good for his image, to say the least. Alternatively, he could enter into a discussion with the bouncer as to the kilt's role as Scotland's world-renowned, iconic image, hence why it was completely appropriate, in fact necessary, he should wear it when he entered the universal church's HQ.

Instead he opted for a swift kick to the bouncer's privates, not hard enough to do permanent damage, but sufficient to give Wilson time to gag and handcuff him to the door's large circular handle. They had bought themselves a precious few minutes. Once the onlooking pilgrims realised the Kiltman scene was not the Vatican's idea of entertainment to cheer weary travellers, the Swiss Guards would be called to unleash their spears and swords. Time was not their friend.

The Stuarts

They sprinted into Saint Peter's cathedral, turning to the left, following the description provided by Google. There were no doubts they had arrived at the right place. Two lion rampants dominated the top of the monument, above three stern faces sculpted into the marble bearing a Latin description that made little sense to Kiltman or Wilson. It was enough that the inscription bore the Latin names of "Karolo" and "Stuard". They had found the final reference to the ancient, interrupted bloodline of Scottish royalty: Charles and the Stuarts.

Wilson was already scanning the outside of the marble by placing her head at an angle, her ear flush to the wall searching for evidence of a bomb or even a sheet of Cullen Skink's white paper. Kiltman stepped back and looked at the ceiling. Wilson started when she heard the force with which he slapped his gloved hand off his forehead. "Of course! How could I be so stupid?"

"What, Kiltman? We've not got time for…"

"Fermarsi! Fermarsi!" Six Swiss Guards and three bouncers were running across the cathedral towards them shouting manically for them to stay where they were.

Kiltman decided not to waste precious time analysing whether the guards really were Swiss, considering how animated they had become. Instead, he pulled Wilson towards him and whispered, "Go, get the Vespa. Meet me outside in five minutes." He slipped the key into the palm of her hand.

"But what are you…"

"Just do it. I'll meet you there. Now go."

Wilson used her turn of speed to lose herself among the hundreds of pilgrims now gripped by the showdown of Kiltman versus Swiss Guards in what could have been a Vatican competition for the most bizarrely dressed.

"It's okay, let me explain." Kiltman opened his arms in a gesture of surrender. "Really, I can explain."

Melodrama was to be the order of the day considering the surreal nature of the confrontation. The Swiss Guards and bouncers stood silently in a semi-circle around him, his back against the Stuart tomb, until one of them spoke. "Give us your weapon. Then lie on the floor."

"I don't have a weapon."

"Look! Don't argue. Do it now!"

"I cannot lie on the floor. Kilts and floors don't mix. I don't think the Church would appreciate its worshippers being obliged to witness something quite so revealing."

"What are you saying? Lie down! Immediately!"

He reckoned he had three more minutes.

"My manhood is, how can I say, unprotected. This is a house of God. You will not want such obscene pictures in the newspapers tomorrow, desecrating the holiness of the cathedral." Kiltman pointed towards the tourists turned paparazzi, busily capturing the unique moment.

"Listen! Lie down! Do you hear me? I have a stun gun here and I'm prepared to use it to incapacitate you." The Swiss Guard, who appeared no older than a schoolboy, produced an oversized pistol. This changed the playing field.

"Okay. I need to remove this belt before I lie down."

"Hurry up. I have lost patience with you." The pistol was pointed at his stomach. By aiming at his midriff, the guard knew there was not much chance of missing. The proverbial barn door crossed Kiltman's mind.

He slowly unbuckled his belt. Without looking down he detached the glass tube affixed to the inside of the buckle. He dropped the tube onto the marble floor. The sharp crash was masked by the hiss of gas released into the air creating a dense cloud of mist which enveloped him completely. Dropping onto one knee he felt the bullet pass overhead, followed by a groan from an overly inquisitive tourist behind him. Spinning swiftly, he ran in the direction of the door, knocking a disoriented Swiss Guard to the ground, before pushing through hordes of dumbfounded onlookers. He burst out onto the square in the middle of a billowing fog of smoke, to find Wilson gaping at him astride the Vespa, the high-pitched engine squealing. She was puzzled by the swirl of smoke exiting the huge cathedral doors, but knew this was not the time to ask questions.

"Go! Go! Go!" he shouted as he jumped behind her, groaning slightly as he landed squarely on a scuffed leather seat. The last thing the Swiss Guards saw as they ran from the cathedral was a blue and white cape with matching kilt disappearing through the colonnades.

"Where are we going?" Wilson shouted over her shoulder.

"Let's head in the direction of the Trevi Fountain. I remember the way so just follow my directions."

"What was that smoke thing all about?"

"Just a wee something I use when I want to make a hasty exit." It was actually a by-product of a whisky experiment that failed miserably in Wallace Distillers in his first couple of months, practically blowing up the lab. It was the closest Wullie had come to firing him before... he fired him years later. It seemed like that life had belonged to someone else as he slipped his hands around Wilson's delicate waist.

The Prince

"Use the horn!" Kiltman shouted above the frenzy of camera clicking, laughing and chitter-chatter of hundreds of tourists crammed into a space no bigger than a pub. The object of attention was arguably the most visited monument in Rome, an extensive fountain with semi-circular pond, grotesque yet extraordinarily beautiful.

"Do you have any coins for the Trevi, Kiltman?" Wilson shouted as she manoeuvred between an international array of human shapes, colours and sizes.

"Unfortunately, no, but I'll bring one for the next time we pass here."

"So you want to come back to Rome?"

"Who knows what might happen once we put Cullen Skink behind bars."

Wilson decided not to react to any hidden connotation in his comment, speeding past the fountain, careering up a sidestreet before he pointed. "Down here to the right."

"Where are we going? More to the point, when are you going to explain this sudden need to tour Rome's sights? The Vatican is probably sitting on a bomb, and we're…"

"I'll explain. Stop here." Wilson screeched the Vespa to a halt before propping it up against a wall.

Kiltman walked briskly through an elegant doorway into an aula leading to a small courtyard circled by stairs, sparsely decorated with exotic trees. "Look." He pointed to a marble plaque with chiselled lettering. Wilson's Latin was non-existent but the last line struck her: *'s'estinse la dinaste de' stuardi'*.

"This is where the Stuarts lived when they were in Rome. I came across this place years ago when I was a tourist, as opposed to a thug who steals scooters and fights with the Pope's bodyguards. I did a bit more research on it later. The Stuarts received this building from Pope Clementine XI as a gift. Bonnie Prince Charlie lived here after the 1745 rebellion. He ended up dying an alcoholic, 'drenched in wine'."

"I'm not convinced yet, Kiltman. I don't see much in the way of apostles around here. I think we should be back at Saint Peter's. After all, he was an apostle."

"If my memory serves me well, I can show you the final piece in the jigsaw." Wilson followed him out to the street, turning right onto an elongated square. Wilson saw the name of the square, elegantly etched in marble above a window, Piazza dei Santi Apostoli. He pointed above the square to a row of statues dominating the skyline atop a church, clearly dedicated to the apostles.

"Touché." Wilson was surprised at how acceptant she was becoming of him outguessing her.

"Okay, so let's go figure out what he's got planned." He could sense that this time Cullen Skink had a surprise waiting.

They hurried through the aula of the house. He immediately began to run his fingers along the plaque's marble surface perched high on a ladder that had been conveniently nestled under the stairs. The discolouration in the seam where the plaque sat snugly in the wall showed that some reconstruction had been performed here a lot more recently than the eighteenth century. Within minutes he had found a temporary seal round the edge of the plaque and, using a Strathclyde Police biro, began to excavate a hole big enough to slip his fingers through. Working it from side to side, he eased it from the wall. The plaque was significantly larger than the tiny section visible to the public. He had wanted to lower it down onto the ground but had not counted on it being so heavy. The noise it made when it crashed to the floor would have wakened the prince himself from either the dead or his most wicked bender.

He could see a small, cylindrical bottle nestled in the back of the fresh hole, sitting atop a square black box the size of an egg cup. He closed his eyes and took a deep breath, focusing on ignoring any scents or smells other than those provided by the contents of the hole. The strong acidic odour of gelignite from the box was clear. No surprises there. He looked directly at the cylinder and captured the essence of the smell by concentrating on the space between the cork and the rim, engaging his brain to process its chemical contents until the word "anthrax" registered. Placing his hand in the hole, he searched for a trip wire. Comfortable that it was another stand-alone device, he removed the box and cylinder carefully avoiding the sides of the hole.

162

"Wilson, hold onto this ladder. If I fall, the Catholic Church will lose something quite invaluable. The church would be left with a vacuum. It would take generations to rebuild the knowledge. Can you imagine the church defending its teachings without its brain?"

"What are you talking about?" Wilson understood he was holding an explosive, but it was so small it could hardly have damaged anything outside the immediate building. Also, they were nowhere near the Vatican so what was the melodrama about the church?

"Okay. This little box is gelignite. You see this tiny clock here? That shows it will go off at twelve noon. We have just over half an hour. While it may knock us for six and shake the walls, it is not intended to damage on a scale of the explosives in the tunnel or on the bridge. At least not directly. Ironically this bomb is made as low impact as necessary to shatter the cylinder. If it's too strong it may reduce the impact of the endgame he is trying to achieve.

"This cylinder contains bacteria known as anthrax. It would be released into the air to poison anyone or anything within a half mile radius. This building is no longer used by Stuarts but happens to be the Pontifical Institute of Biblical Studies, a lot more cerebral than in Bonnie Prince's last days. The building one hundred yards from here is the Gregorian University, run by the greatest minds in the Jesuit order. Their living quarters are connected to the university. Cullen Skink's objective is to take out the very essence of the church. Apart from the huge loss of life, Catholics would lose the core of their interpretations of scripture and theological direction. It could potentially collapse into chaos. Or as Skink put it 'Not so sweet the smell, of a church's death knell'."

Wilson had a thousand more questions. Not least, how did he know what was in the container without opening it? She decided the only way to answer the question was to open the cylinder, which would most certainly defeat the purpose of the quest, if indeed he was right. "Okay, so what next?"

"Let me separate the timer from the explosives before we talk about next steps." He closed his eyes. He ran his finger around the edge of the clock thankful for the silence of the aula helping him keep a steady hand.

He concentrated on finding the connection, oblivious to what was happening below him. He had not expected Wilson's perfume to attract a large, frisky dog to the scene. The dog was oblivious to the ladder blocking the corridor he normally bounded along. He bumped into it with enough momentum to propel him into freefall. The cylinder and bomb slipped from his hand following their own trajectory towards the concrete floor. He tried to snatch them as he fell to the ground but they were frustratingly out of reach. When the cylinder hit the concrete floor, the anthrax would go to work and create the deaths and mayhem he had been trying to avoid.

Wilson had played sport throughout school and had won medals in the police academy due to her stamina and speed. As she watched the dog hit the ladder, she moved into reaction mode. Whether it was the tiredness settling into her joints or the surprise of the moment, she felt her mind moving much faster than her limbs. She seemed to be stuck in an invisible quicksand trying to move faster than her body would allow.

With an almighty effort her athleticism was tested to the full as she dived underneath a flailing Kiltman, both arms extended in front of her. An inch from impact, her palms facing upwards, she caught the cylinder with her left and and the bomb with her right. As she closed her fingers tightly around them she saw a dark shadow fast approaching.

Thump.

He rolled off her as fast as his dazed mind would allow. She had broken his fall. While he felt relatively unharmed Wilson lay unconscious, her fingers now open around the offending objects. He gently moved them from her limp hands and placed them gently where the wall met the floor. He lifted her into a sitting position then slapped her cheek gently. When she came around her face was two inches from his.

"Thank God. Are you okay?" he asked.

"Yes, just a bit bruised, but I'll be alright," she groaned.

"That was a very brave thing you did diving underneath me."

"You're no Twiggy, Kiltman. I'll give you that. I guess we managed to save them from exploding?"

"We didn't, Wilson. You did."

"Well, I had to contribute something at some point on this investigation. Come on, let's go." She stood unsteadily, brushing herself down. She could feel the bruise on her back already beginning to form.

Kiltman picked up the bomb and cylinder. He had to do something to take the focus off his bumbling accident. He knew he should not have taken a chance with the lethal concoction while on the ladder. That was a mistake. Examining the device carefully, he touched two wires, one red, the other slightly thicker and blue. He slid his finger slowly back and forth along the red wire before he pulled the blue, wider cable from the gelignite. They waited for an impact. The best they could have hoped for was silence. Which is what they got. He had successfully broken the connection and defused the device. Through a soft whistle, he let Wilson know her time had not yet come.

"How did you know which colour to choose? Were you able to sense the connection?" Wilson was clearly impressed.

"No. I just chose the colour closest to my kilt."

"What?"

"Only kidding. Come on, let's go. We need to get back on track." They may have thwarted Cullen Skink's attack on the world's biggest religion, but they had been left clueless. Literally.

June 19

"Kiltman, I don't know what superheroes do to ease tension, but I'm desperate for a glass of wine." She would have preferred a bottle of chardonnay in front of the television, lying on her couch in Glasgow's fashionable Kelvinside. Lately she had been prone to whiling away her leisure time migrating seamlessly from *Countdown* and *Deal Or No Deal*, to *Emmerdale* and *Coronation Street*. She had become a post-modern victim of quizzes and soaps which somehow seemed the perfect foil for crime fighting and now, superhero shadowing.

"I'm ready for a double espresso. You do realise that it's six in the morning." He was desperate for a caffeine injection.

They hastily exited the carabinieri headquarters, where they had surrendered themselves the previous afternoon. They had no option. Wilson could have blended into the tourists swarming around Rome's labyrinthine streets, but no number of people could hide a technicolour Kiltman. The hullabaloo when they entered the station had all the drama of Mediterranean passion and exaggeration. Once he explained that they were giving themselves up and not blowing the place apart, a sense of calm settled on the station.

They had been interrogated throughout the night by various inquisitors from the Vatican, Interpol and Rome's secret police. When the cylinder was finally analysed and found to contain the anthrax germ, their story fell into place. Chief Constable Fraser ended up participating in a conference call from Glasgow at four in the morning to establish the credibility of the story, which made him value his retirement even more than he had already.

The Italian and Vatican authorities were particularly unappreciative of the fact they had been saved from slaughter and unimpressed by the saving of the Pontifical Institute of Biblical Studies. They had made it clear they did not want Scottish laundry washed in their streets. Wilson and Kiltman left somewhat berated, licking undeserved wounds. Their immediate concern however became much more basic as they were met by the smells of an Italian bar at daybreak. Directly across the road from the carabinieri offices fresh coffee and freshly baked pastries beckoned them inside.

Wilson agreed to put the wine on hold. She went to the bathroom to "put her face back on". He was concerned she might put it on upside down considering how tired she was. He ordered two large espressos accompanied by a plateful of nibbles and toasties. With one eye on the bathroom door, he removed a silver, round flask from his sporran. He eyed the flask, thinking to himself if ever he needed a good buzz from Hair o' the Dog, this was it. Cullen Skink was proving a handful, keeping him and Wilson on the back foot. He needed his daily top up more than ever. Pressing a secret catch on the side of the flask, the top popped open. He raised it to his lips enjoying the strong aroma of his creation. It had barely reached his throat when Wilson walked out of the bathroom.

"Ah-hah! What's this then? I'm not allowed a glass of wine because 'it's six in the morning'." She made a reasonable impersonation of him, hands in the air making invisible inverted commas. "But oh no. Kiltman can have a wee dram when he wants to. There's no justice in the world."

"Eh, just a small pick-me-up. Do you want a glass of wine?" He was cornered.

"No way. Then I'm only having a drink to keep up with you. Forget it. That coffee smells scrumptious though." She was not nearly as aggrieved as she pretended, realising that with her low blood pressure a glass of wine would have had her either sleeping or singing "O Sole Mio" on a table top. They had not eaten since their flight twenty-four hours earlier. The energy provided by an airline's cardboard sandwich and chocolate biscuit had been used up by the time they made it through passport control. They both felt incredibly tired, the caffeine barely helping. Neither of them wanted to admit to the lethargy creeping through weary muscles and creaking joints. The weight of exhaustion was exaggerated by the absence of a plan. They had lost contact with Cullen Skink.

"Do you think there is any point in us staying in Rome?" Wilson broke the silence.

"No, not any more. Cullen Skink's made it clear that Strathclyde is the ultimate target. But he's left us in the dark."

"Yes, I know, although we would've been in the dark anyway." Wilson spread her hands to convey how obvious this was.

"What do you mean?"

"If his germ attack had been successful, we would still not know what he had planned for Scotland. If he intended to stay true to form, then he must have been planning to find a way to communicate with us. It doesn't make sense that he would leave us hanging now."

"You're right." Kiltman desperately wanted to remove a very distracting and seductive fleck of pastry attached to her upper lip. She let him out of his misery when her tongue unconsciously licked it away. He started to concentrate again. "Maybe he's intending to send another message to the Chief. If he doesn't then we will have to rely on feedback from the forensic team back home in analysing the meagre evidence we've collected, but I wouldn't hold my breath."

"Signor." The barman was pointing to the corner.

"Yes?"

"Call for you."

Kiltman darted a glance at Wilson then moved swiftly to the corner of the bar, where an old-fashioned, rotary telephone sat atop an Italian directory. At another time he would have found the anachronism comforting. He grabbed the receiver hastily. "Hello?"

"So we finally speak." The voice was soft, controlled, with a hint of a Scottish accent.

"Who are you?"

"You know me as Cullen Skink."

"Cullen Skink." He repeated for Wilson's benefit. She had settled down beside him, her ear touching his temple. "When can we meet to talk about what's going on here?"

"Meet? Yes, that's a good idea. Maybe one day. However, that's not why I am calling. I thought I would let you finish your breakfast before I sent you on your merry way again." He listened intently. Wilson placed her ear closer to the receiver, her warm breath making the hairs on his neck stand on end.

"You thwarted my plot in the House of Stuart. Part of me thought that you might win that duel. I was willing to accept that since it helped me gauge you and your ability when truly under pressure. You on the other hand continue to see how serious I am. Not only that, you also understand how resourceful I can be."

"Of course we can see that you are capable of mass destruction. You don't need to keep proving it to us. Let us help you. Is there not some peaceful way we can help you achieve your goals?"

"My goals? My goals? They are not my goals. They are Scotland's goals. Or at least they should be. Strathclyde is a sewer pit. Don't pretend you don't see it. Drugs, drink, bigotry, violence. The goal, if you want to call it that, is to wipe the slate clean. Start again. You will not be able to stop me. But I want to give you a chance to at least try. At least in future generations they will say that Cullen Skink played a fair game."

"Okay, so what happens now?" Kiltman did not want to upset him. He could sense the impatience creep into Skink's voice.

"Ah, good. You still want to play. Next, my kilted warrior, is for you and Starling to take another journey. Your clue this time is a little ditty which I regard as my best. Are you ready for it?"

"Ready as I'll ever be." He had snatched a pen and sheet of paper from behind the bar. Cullen Skink spoke deliberately, conscious that Kiltman was scribbling the detail.

"Be tall in this town.
Exiled Scots pioneering thoughts,
Pushing boundaries, curtains to Russkies.
There is no name, bar the shame
The nuclear holocaust ensures you're not lost."
Click.

"Cullen Skink, wait!" It was too late, the line was dead. Dropping the receiver, Kiltman rushed to the door. He must have been infuriatingly near, but Kiltman realised the impossibility of a search when he stumbled outside. In the last half hour the street had filled with cars and people rushing in competing directions. He returned to find Wilson studying the paper. "There's no way we'll find him in the middle of that chaos. Thoughts?" he asked.

"Your writing's terrible!"

"Yes, but the other side of my brain works much better. What do you make of this?"

"Well, it doesn't seem to refer to a place in Scotland, with the 'exiled Scots' reference. You need to 'be tall in this town'. It doesn't make sense to me. The 'boundaries, curtains to Russkies' may mean something to do with one of the ex-Soviet bloc countries, or even Russia itself. The proverbial needle in a haystack comes…"

"You're a genius!" He grabbed Wilson spontaneously and kissed her on the cheek.

Wilson reddened, reeling with barely concealed surprise. "Next time you try to kiss me like that, at least take your mask off. My cheek feels as though it's been waxed. And why am I genius by the way?"

Kiltman lowered his head slightly. "Sorry, I got a bit carried away." He realised that what he had intended to be a show of affection proved to be more about him sticking his latex nose in her ear while exfoliating her cheek. Although some may have found this erotic, Wilson was obviously not in that camp.

"You hit the nail on the head. Ex-Soviet bloc. Pioneers. Over the last ten years against which former eastern bloc country has Scotland played more football matches than any other?"

"Do I look like someone who follows the tartan army?"

"Okay, I'll tell you. Estonia. Don't you remember the game that never was, in Estonia? It was an international between Scotland and Estonia back in 1996. FIFA ruled that the lights were too poor to play, and the game was rescheduled for earlier in the day. The Estonians refused to turn up since they were extremely hacked off at the timing change, so the Scots played against a non-existent team. They kicked off, the game was abandoned due to lack of opposition, and the points were awarded to Scotland. At the time there were numerous television programmes and magazine articles about the Scots' influence in Estonia."

"Excuse me, but is this relevant?"

"Not really. Except, what is the capital of Estonia?"

170

"Kiltman, you are really starting to annoy me. This is not *University Challenge*. We're chasing a potential mass murderer. We need every minute."

"Okay, sorry. I just enjoy that kind of thing. The capital is Tallinn. Get it? 'Be tall in'. Scotland played its first match against Estonia in May '93, shortly after the Iron Curtain came down. A handful of Scots stayed after the match deciding to start a new life there. Over each of the years after that, whenever Scotland played a game against Estonia, Russia, Finland or Latvia, they always made Tallinn their tartan army HQ. Each time they would leave more Scots there, who would become pioneers in what became known as the 'eastern frontier'. I knew someone who went there some years back. He used to talk about the fact that lots of Tallinn girls spoke English with a Scottish accent. Cullen Skink may be using this as an analogy of how Scots should be perceived versus the bitter view he has of those at home. Whatever the case, we need to get to the airport. Time is a precious commodity, becoming more valuable by the minute."

"Couldn't agree more." Wilson was exasperated at his long-winded explanation of Tallinn as the next port of call. And tickled by his latex kiss. She wondered if he would ever remove the mask for her one day when they were back at home. She also wondered if they would have a country to go back to.

They walked from the bar onto a street searching for a taxi to transport them to the airport. Before they had moved from the shadow of the door, a bright light dazzled them into semi-blindness. They both raised their arms to shield their eyes from the sharpness of the artificial light after a night in a darkened interrogation room.

"Kiltman, good morning! I'm Grant MacTavish. You're live on BBC. What can you tell us about your escapades at the Vatican yesterday? Does it have anything to do with the Clyde Tunnel and Erskine Bridge incidents in Scotland?"

Kiltman began to focus on Grant's terse correspondent features, every inch the on the spot reporter. He had landed an exclusive. He fully intended to milk it dry.

"Good morning, Grant. Strathclyde Police will be issuing a statement this morning." Kiltman provided a response he had seen after practically every incident ever reported on the news. If they were not intending to provide a statement before, he was convinced they would now. "I suggest and urge you to wait for that statement. There will be an opportunity to answer questions then."

"Can you at least tell us if there is a connection between what you are doing now and the terrorist attacks we are seeing in Scotland?"

"Grant, considering your experience in reporting across the world, I am sure you more than anyone understands all too well that there are moments in any investigation when the confidentiality of information has to be maintained." To the average viewer it may have sounded like a rebuke, but Kiltman's comments were based on his awareness of Grant's love of self.

Grant's face struggled with Kiltman's deliberate challenge. A long three-second pause preceded his energetic response. "Absolutely! We all have a role to play in fighting terrorism. We look forward to picking up with Strathclyde Police later today. We're right behind you!"

Grant turned to face the camera and wind the report down. Kiltman felt a subtle but determined tug on his sleeve. He turned to see Wilson wave down a taxi. Without a single *arrivederci* they ran towards it. Kiltman held the door open for Wilson to jump into the back seat, before he joined her.

"Airport, drive! *Presto!*" He pointed straight ahead in an effort to snap the driver out of the shock of picking up "Gonna man". He was also aware of the cameraman's lens pressed against the window of the taxi.

"Si, signore! Andiamo!"

The taxi lurched into the flowing traffic as if an available spot had been there all the time. In seconds, they were far away from a reporter who was far too conveniently in the right place at the right time.

Tommy

"This is really strange." Wilson looked skywards as she exited Tallinn airport, coming to terms with daylight at night time. A blue-white sky sat above a placid Lake Ulemiste on the other side of a busy main road. She could scarcely believe they had welcomed the morning in Rome. It had taken them the best part of the day to catch a flight to London for a connection direct to Tallinn.

"I know what you mean. Not unexpected, since we are two days away from the longest day of the year, when Tallinn has nearly twenty-four hours daylight. The brightest midnight."

The lake's mystical calmness added a welcoming softness to the evening. Kiltman knew more about Estonia than he had first realised when he had boarded the plane. His detailed read of the Estonian Air inflight magazine brought back to life a book he had read shortly after Tommy left for Estonia describing the country's harsh history. The lake was home to some of Tallinn's oldest folklore. If you were asked whether Tallinn was "ready yet" by an old man with a grey beard, you would no doubt be talking to Ulemiste the Elder, who was thousands of years old. Whatever your reply, you should not say "yes", since he would flood the city in seconds. Kiltman found it ironic that such a sense of doom hovered over a city that had recently won its independence.

Estonia had enjoyed an all too brief period of independence between the first and second world wars, only to be first invaded by Germany then "saved" by Russia. Its close proximity to the Great Bear had ensured the second half of the twentieth century was dominated by its oversized neighbour. The Soviet bloc had quickly swallowed up this country of just over a million people, entering into a fast-moving Russification process that added hundreds of thousands of Russians to the population by the early nineties. Once the tide had turned, the roles reversed. The people had lived through hard times until 1991, when they were handed the keys to their own country. While these were still difficult times, there was a renewed sense of purpose and hope. From all accounts the economic books remained balanced, the country moving from strength to strength.

Strangely, if Tommy had not gone there, Kiltman would have not taken the time to read about Estonia. Snuggled up beside Finland and Saint Petersburg at the junction between the Baltic Sea and the Gulf of Finland, it was remote enough to stay off most travellers' radar screens. Why Cullen Skink was interested in it was something they would need to find out. Fast.

Their walk through Tallinn's terminal would have been an experience altogether much more enjoyable under different circumstances. He was greeted by shouts of "Kiltman! Kiltman!" by the travellers, many of whom were holding copies of various British tabloid front pages, showing him escaping from Saint Peter's in a cloud of smoke. He had read several newspaper articles before landing, realising that between the Italian media, police, and Grant MacTavish, most of the details of their investigation had been made public. Cullen Skink was now a household name. It identified him not only as the terrorist behind the attempted germ release in Rome, but also the Clyde Tunnel explosions as well as the Erskine Bridge and Edinburgh Castle scares.

The Chief Constable had been berated throughout the press for not doing enough to catch the mastermind behind the terror. Even the RSPCA had raised a formal complaint about the number of fish, porpoises, and dolphins left floating in the Irish Sea after the Erskine Bridge bomb was exploded offshore.

Many people in Strathclyde had spent that day fleeing Glasgow and surrounding towns to stay with friends in other parts of the country. The television in the airport terminal showed convoys of cars backed up across the Kingston and Erskine Bridges. The authorities were doing their best to convince them to stay at home with assurances the threat was being managed. The truth was they were probably better off being as far from Strathclyde as possible. Cullen Skink was controlling the show, his finger firmly on the button. So far, none of his threats had been empty. He clearly had a special agenda for Scotland. By creating several high-profile incidents, he had stirred enough terror to hamper the investigation process. The Chief Constable seemed to be spending most of his time dealing with the press and government officials, while Kiltman and Wilson were jetting around Europe, no closer to finding the maniac.

"Let's go to a bar in the centre of the town. It's called Terviseks, which means 'cheers' in Estonian. Good name for a bar since it lends itself to double entendre moments, particularly when the ever-hopeful Brits are in town. It was opened a couple of years ago. I was given a tip that the owner may help us figure out what the rest of the clue refers to."

The rusty Lada taxi sounded as though it was moving a lot faster than the passing buildings showed. It gave them a chance to take in the medieval architecture of this beautiful Baltic city, while the driver was determined to hit every pothole and cavity in the road. Wilson gagged at the stench of stale cigarettes and vodka in the cab. Kiltman wondered how he should best conduct the next meeting. He felt more nervous than he had in a long time.

The taxi pulled up outside a building on the edge of the main cobbled square, its walls and décor boasting five hundred years of age. It nestled comfortably on the street, surrounded by several buildings of the same age. Arriving in the town centre was the equivalent of stepping back in time to a greater and more respected medieval period in Estonia's history when it had been a force to be reckoned with.

Terviseks was painted in colourful lettering across the window on the ground floor of the building. On the other side of the window two very attractive blonde girls sat sipping what looked to be champagne. They were engaged in a lively chat which added to their carefree image, giving the bar significantly more appeal than the façade would otherwise warrant. Simultaneously they caught sight of the kilted crusader stepping out gracelessly from the Lada. By the time he stood breathing the fresh northern Baltic air, the girls had arrived on the pavement.

"Tere! Tere! Kiltman!" they shouted in unison. He had to look twice to make sure they had not been greeted by the Cheeky Girls.

"Tere, girls." He hoped Wilson was impressed by another of his five words in Estonian, learned courtesy of an *Evening*

Times article on the Baltics. He nimbly sidestepped the welcoming committee leading Wilson by the arm into the bar.

"Excuse me, is the owner here?" he asked an attractive, blonde, blue-eyed barmaid, while realising that the bar was full of attractive, blue-eyed blondes. He was beginning to realise why Tommy had been so excited to come to Estonia.

The barmaid seemed captivated by the caped Kiltman. She smiled shyly. "No, not here. He is on holiday. Not sure when he come back. You want drink?"

"It's okay, Anu, I'm here." A voice came from inside the storeroom. A man stood in the doorway of the dark storeroom. He waited for a brief second before he walked slowly towards the bar. He wore a green tartan kilt and a Scotland football jersey. "Well, well. What an unexpected pleasure. Kiltman! This is just what we need to increase the week's takings. What would you like?"

"Hi, I'm Detective Inspector Wilson of Strathclyde Police. Your name is?" Wilson was clearly becoming frustrated at sitting on the back seat of the case she was supposed to be leading.

"I'm Tommy MacGregor, the proprietor of the best pub in Tallinn. I hear you two have had quite an adventure. I'm just back from a week off and have read the papers today. You must be shattered. Any closer to catching this nutter?"

Kiltman was pleased to see Tommy. He looked relaxed, still with a twinkle of good nature in his eye. He realised that he had missed him over the last few years. He had let their friendship drift into extinction because he had been so self-absorbed. Once Cullen Skink was dealt with, he had a friendship to revitalise. He was confident his voice was distorted enough to conceal his identity. "That's why we're here. The last clue seems to lead to Tallinn. We called the British consulate before coming here. They recommended we talk to you since you seem to be an expert on the city."

"Well, I do keep my ear to the ground, if that's what you mean. In a place like this you have to be careful. Lots of shysters ready to drag you down. I need to watch my back."

"You can still afford to take a week off in what's obviously high season." Wilson's antenna was up.

"Can a man not have a holiday? Listen, there are no pockets in a shroud, darling. You can't take it with you. So, how can I help?"

"Here's the clue. Can you tell us anything?" Kiltman was uncomfortable at Wilson's approach. They needed Tommy's help. They were not there to hassle him.

Tommy took the note. He read it several times, humming an unrecognisable tune at the same time. Handing it back, he said, "This note is interesting. Lots of ways to interpret it, but I'm not sure what you want to hear."

"Look, Mr. MacGregor, we don't have time to play games. Is there anything you can see in there that might point us in the direction of somewhere in Tallinn?" Wilson's hackles were up. Tommy was getting to her.

"Jeez, keep your knickers on. Actually, one line jumps out at me. 'There is no name, bar the shame'. There's another pub here called Nimeta Bar. It's along the road towards the other side of the square."

"But what's the connection?" Kiltman was intrigued.

"Nimeta Bar in Estonian language means 'Bar With No Name'. It was founded by a few Scottish lads back in the mid-nineties. They spent that long trying to find a name for it they ended up calling it Nimeta. Quite smart actually, it appeals to the Estonian sense of humour."

Kiltman and Wilson looked at each other knowingly. A bar founded by Scots pioneers, called "no name bar". They were on the right track.

"Mr. MacGregor, can you please show us where the bar is? We might need to run a few other things past you."

"Okay, let's go. As long as you don't buy anything there. It's going to look really bad for me if I take my customers to another pub. Especially when one's a celebrity. The other is a very lovely lass with big…"

"Be careful. Mr. MacGregor. I might not be in my official neck of the woods, but I can still wait for you to come home." Wilson felt the stubbornness take root.

"Eyes! I was going to say eyes!" Tommy could barely conceal his glee. His timing had been perfect.

"Very funny." For some reason Wilson was trying hard not to like Tommy.

Kiltman was grateful the mask concealed his smile. Tommy had still not lost it after all these years. The ability to charm and upset at the same time, in equal measure.

"Let me finish what I was doing back there. I need to take stock out to the bar. I'll be back in a second. Anu, give my friends a drink. Thanks." Tommy returned to the storeroom.

Wilson shook her head. "No thanks, I'm okay. If I had a drink I would fall over."

Kiltman accepted an Irn Bru, partly because he was thirsty but mainly out of surprise at finding Scotland's other national drink so far from home.

"Wilson, why are you giving Tommy such a hard time?"

"Apart from the fact he has male chauvinist written all over his cheeky face? Is that not enough?"

"Not really, considering the size of the issue we're facing here. We need all the allies we can get."

Wilson picked up Kiltman's Irn Bru and drank half the contents before putting it back on the bar, stifling what would have been a very unladylike belch.

"I guess you're right. It's just that, well, as a policewoman sometimes the gut reacts before the brain."

"I can see that!"

"Very funny. You know what I mean. Sometimes you sense something is not right but can't put your finger on it. So you start a few ripples just to see what will surface."

Kiltman nodded. He had a deep respect for gut reaction, especially when there was very little to go on. If only Wilson knew about his friendship with Tommy. Not to mention the brief liaison he had with her in the alley all those years ago off Byres Road. He would not have been there to save her if Tommy had not arranged the kilt night. Her gut told her something was not quite what it seemed. She could not have been closer to the truth. Her gut was proving to be a very reliable part of her anatomy. One day he hoped to be comfortable telling her that.

The Bar With No Name

Kiltman followed Tommy and Wilson as they walked briskly through the olde worlde streets of Tallinn. He pondered what he knew of its colourful history. He could sense the heritage with every stride of a city critical to the success of the Hanseatic League of trading partners all those centuries before the Russians absorbed it into their sprawling, haphazard empire. It was clear why Cullen Skink had chosen Estonia as a location for a clue since it reinforced the sense of loss he felt at Scotland's social demise, being put in the shadow of the regeneration of countries like Estonia.

Kiltman could see the chronic weariness in many of the faces he passed. Yet for every worn expression, there seemed to be someone with a young, energetic smile. The new generation was already beginning to enjoy its taste of freedom – the icing on the cake being superheroes roaming the streets. He began to feel like the Pied Piper, a convoy of interested observers trailing behind him.

Tommy looked over his shoulder, pointing a finger towards a bar. He waited with Wilson at the entrance for Kiltman to snap out of his daydream.

"You've certainly caused a stir here. This is becoming the biggest event since the game that never was. Anyway, this is Nimeta Bar." Kiltman could practically hear Tommy's teeth grind as he introduced them to a competitor. He sensed this was the thin edge of a fierce battlefront.

Without a word, Wilson stepped forward into a smoky pub packed with people. Kiltman closed his eyes, focusing on the noise. He could hear many different languages, primarily from the Baltic and Scandinavian nations.

"Terviseks, Kiltman! Can I buy you a drink?" A man wearing a bra, suspenders, and a black, leather mask with a zip for a mouth put his arm on Kiltman's back. Kiltman saw the obligatory whip leaning against the bar. The picture was complete.

"No, but thanks for the offer."

"I know you think I look a bit strange, but this is my stag weekend. We're all here from London. I'm absolutely polluted.

Terviseks!" The man swayed slightly. "I think we would make a great team. I can see the headlines now: 'Kiltman and S&M man clear up the town'. Kiltman captures the criminals then S&M man tortures them to find out where they stashed the loot or hid the body."

"Thanks, S&M man. I'll keep that in mind if I ever need a partner. Now, I need to…"

"I know, I know. You're looking for, what ya m'call him? Killing Stink, that's it. It's all over the papers. Go get him, tiger! But what you doing over here in Estonia? Don't you know this is the land of gorgeous women and stag parties?"

"Aye, it's a pity we can't have one without the other." A grim-faced Tommy was pulling Kiltman towards the edge of the bar. "We get these numpties every weekend now. Used to be that we felt we were bringing something new and special to Estonia. Now it just seems as if we're making it as bad as back home."

"Okay, so let's look at the rest of the clue." Wilson's voice barely hid her exasperation. She read slowly: "The nuclear holocaust ensures you're not lost. Any thoughts, Mr. MacGregor?"

"Are you going to start being nice to me?" Tommy most definitely had not changed.

"Yes, I will be nice to you. But later. Right now we're running out of time. Do you have any idea what this means?"

Tommy turned his back to them. He placed three fingers in his mouth and wolf-whistled at such a pitch Kiltman expected the Estonian dog population to come running to the pub. A momentary silence descended on the bar.

"Come on, folks. Can you move aside just for a minute? We need to let Kiltman and Detective Inspector Wilson through." Tommy spread his hands as if he were Moses separating the Red Sea.

Cheers and screams rippled through the bar as Kiltman became the centre of attention. Then a silence descended as the customers realised he was still investigating the terrorist who had a habit of leaving bombs in very public places. The crowd split moving to both ends of the wall in curtain fashion. He would have commented on the irony of this, except he was captivated by the wall they had exposed.

Along its full length there was a painting of a rough terrain, speckled with the empty shells of buildings that seemed to have once stood tall and proud. It was a chilling scene of devastation across a barren, lonely landscape.

"What is that?" Kiltman asked in astonishment.

"When they opened the pub back not long after the curtain came down, they engaged a couple of Estonian artists to create a mural. This is what they came up with. It depicts how they think Tallinn would look after a nuclear blast. How relevant is that to the atmosphere you want to create in a pub? Beats me." Tommy scratched his head theatrically.

The lack of reaction from Kiltman and Wilson was enough for each of them to know what the other was thinking. It was inconceivable that anyone would even consider nuclear as an option, yet Cullen Skink's recent track record had proven nothing was beyond him.

"It's a tourist attraction here in Tallinn. People come from far and wide to see the mural. It's as if they capture a glimpse of their own destiny. The Cold War is still very fresh in their minds, when they lived under the constant threat of American aggression. Do you know that the kids had gas masks in their desks? They used to have drills as to what to do in the event of a nuclear attack. In some ways they hoped it would happen so that they could wipe out the Russian oppressors before starting all over again. You could call it the Ulemiste strategy." Tommy appeared to be transfixed by the apocalyptic wall.

"Oh, really? You think they were right?" Wilson's eyes were unblinking in their survey of Tommy's face.

"Who me?" Tommy stretched his arms in front of him, palms facing skywards. "I'm just someone who's trying to make a living. If I had a wall big enough for a mural, I would make sure it was a lot cheerier than this Omega Man apocalypse. That's what you expect here in Tallinn: lots of death, doom and destruction. The grim reaper seems to be behind every corner."

"Let's check this out. Skink must have left a clue somewhere." Kiltman stepped carefully away from the soon to be S&M husband, experiencing a massive surge of pity for his future wife. The hubbie looked far too comfortable in the underwear and leathers.

Underneath the mural there was a row of letters which appeared to follow no logical order. Tommy noticed Kiltman focusing on them. "That strip of letters shows the names of the people who were around in Tallinn, all connected with the Scottish lads who opened this place. It goes all round the bar, not just on that wall. You can pick out names if you work from letter to letter. Actually…"

"Just a second." Kiltman had stepped forward to kneel in front of the wall. "There is a section here that's been added recently, covering up the original strip of paper." They looked at the strip, from where he had placed his left hand until they reached his right. The letters were no longer identifiable as names but read as: thiswallspacescotlandsfuturefacefreedomsoughtwhenhefoughts cotlandsmartyrhislifebutbarterironicmemoryinholyinfirmaryyou rtimeisslippingsorryforspspelling

He traced his fingers along the strip, muttering softly, combining syllables and letters in varying combinations. "Wilson, do you have…" She had a notebook and pencil under his nose before he finished. Writing carefully, fully conscious of his unreadable handwriting, he followed the rhyming syllables to create another ditty in Skink form. He read slowly:

"this wall space Scotlands future face
freedom sought when he fought
Scotlands martyr his life but barter
ironic memory in holy infirmary
your time is slipping
sorry for sp-spelling."

He walked to the wall, closing his eyes, forcing himself to absorb the scent of the mural, running his hands carefully over every inch of the painting. The smoke and alcohol fumes consumed by the wall over the years filtered into his nasal passage. Delicately touching the colours, he could see, through the brushstrokes, the artists' fear of a nuclear attack. The emotion was wrapped up in every fibre of the wall. In the background he ran his fingers over a volcano spewing lava into the air, but this was different. Fear had been replaced by anger and despair.

Eventually he said, "The artists who painted this were not very happy. Lots of passion has gone into this painting."

"Kiltman?" Tommy was pointing towards the volcano. "The volcano is new. I've never seen it before. There isn't a volcano in Tallinn, never has been."

"This could've been added by anyone," Wilson spoke carefully. "Did you sense anything that we should be worried about?" Wilson was conscious of the bar full of silent, fearful people.

"I don't sense any kind of explosive device, if that's what you mean." Kiltman was less diplomatic. The rumble of concerned voices in the bar made him realise he needed more privacy. "Wilson, can you join me outside?"

Sensing the rising panic, he raised his hands in an effort to calm the atmosphere before addressing his audience. "There's nothing to be alarmed about. Just carry on with your night out. Also, there's one word of warning I need to give you."

Silence engulfed the bar. The nervousness was tangible.

"Make sure you drink plenty of water before you go to bed tonight. Enjoy yourselves."

Ironic Memory in Holy Infirmary

Wilson was engrossed in the poem playing with the corners of the notebook, when Kiltman approached her outside Nimeta Bar.

"Wilson, that wall is Skink's real message. As the writing underneath the mural says, 'this wall space is Scotland's future face'. He is giving us a picture of what's coming. I know we don't want to consider it but it seems to shout nuclear annihilation from every burnt-out building."

Wilson's mole was even more pronounced when her face drained of blood. "I was hoping you wouldn't say that."

"Well, that's what he seems to be saying. Also, the volcano has only been painted in the last week; the smoke in the bar has had a lot less impact on the volcano than the rest of the painting. Whoever painted it is harbouring a deep anger and frustration. We need to find something else in there that leads to our next clue. Any thoughts?"

"Why has he written 'sp-spelling'?" Wilson rubbed her chin thoughtfully. "I've never known anyone to stammer when they are writing."

"Actually, it was me that hyphenated the word. In truth what he wrote was 'spspelling'."

"Need any help here?" Tommy stepped through the door onto the street clearly relishing his role in the adventure.

Wilson looked at him carefully, before she spoke, "What do you think of 'sp-spelling'?"

"Well when I was at school, our teacher used to write 'sp' to show you had made a spelling mistake. I think it was a standard teacher abbreviation. I should know, I got plenty of them."

"And your point is?" Wilson needed a good eight hours sleep.

"Well, maybe this guy has made a deliberate spelling mistake."

Wilson studied the poem. "There is only one other 'sp' in the poem, in the word 'space'."

Kiltman clicked his fingers. "If you erase the 'sp' in space, you get the word 'ace'."

"And the word before it is wall. If we assume the 'sp' is a spelling mistake and should not be there, we end up with the word 'wall-ace'." Wilson was suddenly regaining her energy. "That would explain the reference to freedom and Scotland's martyr. I'm not an expert on history, but the Hollywoodised version certainly brought William Wallace to the fore in recent years. Where does that lead us?"

"I agree with the Wallace connection. The only other line we haven't explained is 'ironic memory in holy infirmary'." Kiltman felt they were so close, yet as far away as when they had started. There was one way of potentially getting to the bottom of the clue. The idea had been floating around in his head for a few minutes. He knew that what he needed to do would be difficult, as he would need to deal with the demons of the past.

"Wilson, can I borrow your mobile phone?"

She handed it to him, not questioning what he had up his sleeve. Somehow she sensed that was the best reaction.

"I'll be back in a minute." He walked around the corner into the stunningly proud, colourful Raekoja Plats, the main square, taking up position in its centre to ensure no-one was within earshot. He remembered the number easily. He should have done. He had called it many times lately but never waited for the ringtone to start. He had lacked the courage. He would never have a better reason to call than now.

He deactivated his voice adjustor before he dialled.

"Hello?"

"Hi, this is Kenny. Kenny Morgan."

The silence on the other end seemed to last an age. He felt his heart fall with the weight of guilt and hurt he knew he had caused.

"Thank God. Kenny, is it really you?"

"Hi, Wullie. Yes. It's me. It's been a long time. How you doing?"

"I'm grand, young man. It certainly seems like a lifetime since we went our separate ways. How the hell are you?" Wullie still had that booming, I love the world, voice.

"Great. Really great. So good that I'm, eh, working on a project at the moment. Actually, I'm calling because I hope you could help me."

"Fire ahead. You're not on *Who Wants to be a Millionaire?* are you? Ha! Ha!"

"Unfortunately, no. It's just a personal thing, nothing special. I'll fill you in when I'm back in Scotland. I'm on holiday at the moment but really looking forward to getting together. We've got a lot of ground to cover."

"We certainly have. Okay, fire ahead. What's the question?"

"It's to do with William Wallace."

"Aye, a grand man. Do you know that I'm descended directly from him?"

"Of course, you mentioned it once or twice." Or five hundred times. Kenny smiled. "The thing is, I need to find where his memorial is, but I haven't a clue where to start looking. Any ideas?"

"Well, let me see. There are many monuments to the great man, laddie. I wouldn't know what direction to point you in. If you were looking for his tombstone, then you'll struggle to find it."

"Why is that?"

"Because his body was chopped up into pieces then placed on skewers all over London to show any future rebels the fate they faced. Aye, the English were not the friendliest bunch of oppressors, well before the Geneva Convention. Having said that, there is a plaque which commemorates the place where his life was brutally taken from him by the English torturers."

He was beginning to sense a grain of hope. "Where would that be?"

"In London. Towards the east end of the city. They've actually built a hospital next to where he was executed. How bizarre is that?"

"Very bizarre," Kenny answered, remembering the poem.

"The hospital is called Saint Bartholomew's. It's famous, you know."

Ironic memory in holy infirmary.

"Wullie, you're a star! You've solved it. Look, I need to run, but thanks a lot. I'll give you a shout when I get back."

186

"You better do, young man. By the way, are you having a dram these days?" Kenny took both barrels of the loaded question in the gut.

"No, Wullie. I'm on the wagon. To be honest, I've never felt better."

"That's the best news I've heard in years, Kenny. On you go, get on with whatever you're working on. Don't be a stranger!"

"You bet!"

"Oh, before you go. Did your friend ever contact you?"

"Which friend, Wullie?"

"Some guy came around here looking for you. Must have been a couple of years ago asking what you were up to. I thought it was strange at the time, since he only had to go to your house."

"Did you get a name?" Kiltman was intrigued.

"No, well, yes, I suppose I did. My memory's not what it was. Too many brain cells ruined by the odd dram here or there. Ha! Ha! I do remember what he looked like though. Couldn't forget that."

"I'm all ears, Wullie."

"He had a big black beard reaching halfway down his chest. However, it was his clothes more than anything I remember. He wore a black gown from neck to toe with a weird mushroom-shaped hat. I would say he was some sort of monk, but he seemed to be foreign. Middle Eastern I would imagine."

"Hassan! Was his name Hassan?"

"By Jove, Kenny! You're right. That was him. Surly fellow. Didn't have too much to say for himself. When I offered him a dram, he nearly fell off the chair. He couldn't get out quick enough. Did he ever come to see you?"

"No, actually, he didn't. Strange. Look, Wullie, I'd love to chat but need to go. Thanks a million. Take care of yourself. I miss you, you know."

"This is the best call I've had in years. Keep in touch, son. Bye."

As he clicked the phone closed, he felt a twinge of guilt at not staying in contact with Hassan. He would put it on top of his to-do list whenever he got to the bottom of the Cullen Skink affair. The last he had heard about him was through Shuggy shortly after they graduated when Shuggy met him at a world religions symposium in Rome. In Shuggy's opinion his trip to Afghanistan had changed him beyond recognition. He had become intolerant of others in a manner bordering on violent. Shame, Kiltman thought, the Hassan he remembered had a heart of gold.

Right now, however, he needed to concentrate on Cullen Skink. Time was marching on. Cullen Skink was leading them a merry dance, now inserting another link in an endless chain of clues and red herrings. The Chief was not going to appreciate the next update. Glasgow and surrounding areas were in chaos, without a real direction on how to catch the madman. How could they allay the fears of over a million people who were unsure what their immediate destiny held in store for them? He needed to see positive developments in the search. He was not getting them. Kiltman, rather than provide hope to the Chief, was going to advise him that he and Wilson were headed for London. To look for a monument to William Wallace. While Wallace had a brave heart, the Chief would need every ounce of strength not to have a heart attack.

Rush Hour

"So why did you become a policewoman?" Kiltman was intrigued by Wilson, but also knew she was waning. Lack of sleep and regular nutrition were bad enough, but the real issue was lack of results. This goose chase made them feel like hamsters on a wheel, given a couple of nuts every so often to keep them treading.

"It's a long story," she answered.

"They all are. You don't think I was born wearing a Kiltman costume? I grew into this outfit."

"You certainly did!" Instinctively she reached across aiming to pat his belly. The plane shuddered on landing with Wilson's hand landing on his sporran for the briefest of seconds.

"Eh, sorry!" she said quickly. "I meant to…"

"It's okay, I know. My belly's my next project." They shared the embarrassment in equal measure. Although he was sure he had enjoyed it more than her. "So why did you join the force?"

"One day I'll tell you the story. Funnily enough, I think you'll find it particularly relevant. Let's just say for now that someone helped me by giving me a sense of purpose."

He knew she was not going to say any more than that. "I'm glad you made that decision, Wilson. You're a very special person. It shines through in how committed you are to doing the right thing."

"Thanks, Kiltman. That means a lot." Wilson's confidence had never felt as bruised as at that moment landing at Gatwick. She had invested so much yet received little return. He had said some sweet things, but in truth she knew that she had underperformed on this venture. He could have done it on his own. She may have guided him on a couple of clues, but he would have got there anyway. Somehow it mattered that he had a good opinion of her and her abilities. Now that she was on home territory, she aimed to bring her hard-earned policing skills to the fore.

On exiting the plane, they were pleased to see two Detective Inspectors from the Metropolitan Police waiting immediately inside the terminal.

"Kiltman, DI Wilson. Welcome to London. My name is Smith. This is DI Stevens. We've got a car outside to take you into London."

"Thanks. Much appreciated." Kiltman was grateful for the support of the metropolitan's finest.

"You've made quite a stir over here in the news. The tabloids have offered prizes, big money prizes, for photos of you in action trying to catch this Cullen Skink character."

Smith produced a copy of *The Sun*, half of the front page covered by Kiltman standing in Nimeta Bar, arms extended in front of him as he addressed a room full of frightened faces. Behind his back the mural was clear, showing the obliteration of Tallinn. The headline read: "KILTMAN STANDS BETWEEN PEOPLE AND HOLOCAUST".

"That, we could have done without." Kiltman grimaced. "It only happened last night! How the heck can they turn a newspaper around in that time?"

"They probably keep their front page open for you. Not too many colourful superheroes around looking for attention these days."

He decided not to react to Smith. He let him continue.

"Strathclyde is fast becoming out of control. Increasing numbers of people are uprooting, fleeing for higher ground. Looters are everywhere. Worse still, the vigilantes are having a field day. There have already been a score of casualties with people taking the law into their own hands. There's a strong sense this investigation is spinning its wheels."

"This is proving to be a difficult case," Wilson spoke up. "We're flying by the seat of our pants. Any help you can give us will be a tad more appreciated than criticism. It's already June 20th. This disaster, whatever it may be, is planned for midnight tomorrow night."

"Then let's go. There's no point in us standing here chewing the fat. Lead the way." Kiltman pointed towards the exit signs. Smith had a lot more to say. It was not often he got the chance to extract the Michael from a superhero. Yet something in Kiltman's manner told him he should back off for the time being. He did not see Kiltman's fist scrunched in a ball while he closed his eyes counting to ten.

Half an hour later they were in the back of a panda car nose to tail in commuter traffic inching into London. Wilson had never seen so many cars pointed in the same direction. It rendered the Kingston Bridge at rush hour as innocuous as a Tesco car park. They rounded a bend onto a long stretch of motorway extending as far as the eye could see. The traffic was backed up to a standstill.

A motorcyclist was trying to negotiate his bike between the wing mirrors of cars, weaving an enviable path through hordes of angry drivers. Kiltman turned to Wilson, who was also looking at the motorcyclist. "You thinking what I'm thinking?"

"Lead the way, Kiltman."

"Smith, thanks for the lift but we don't have time." Not waiting for a response, Kiltman and Wilson prised themselves from the car. The motorcyclist was only two cars in front when Kiltman tapped him on the shoulder. He immediately removed his helmet to reveal a young, friendly face. He beamed a smile at Kiltman, extending his hand. "Unbelievable! How are you, Kiltman? Traffic's a nightmare!"

"That's why we need your help."

"Sorry?" The motorcyclist's smile disappeared as quickly as it had appeared.

"Can we borrow your bike? You can enjoy the experience of arriving at work in a panda car. They'll drop you off at the front door. You probably know that we're working on a very important case, that's why your cooperation is vital to its success."

The biker paused for a second. "My mother and father live in Glasgow. I spoke to them on the phone yesterday once I saw the news. It was so frustrating not to be able to help them. So you know my answer." The biker stepped from the bike, handing his helmet to Wilson. "Go, get him. I know you can do it."

He squeezed the biker's shoulder as he lifted his leg across the bike. "Your folks will be safe. Make sure you tell them how you helped, they'll be proud of you. We will make sure you get the bike back tomorrow. DVLA will help us find you. You're a good man."

Wilson snuggled up behind Kiltman, wrapping her arms around his waist. He manoeuvred the bike onto the hard shoulder crunching it up the gears in seconds. With the bike speeding along the side of the road, Wilson shouted in his ear, "How the hell did you get away with that?"

"Now you're starting to learn the power of the kilt, Wilson."

Braveheart

Prior to his whisky-induced powers he had never been an expert bike rider. He had been competent at best, more of a Mr. Bean than Evil Knievel. Gear crunching and loss of balance were routine. Wilson would never have believed that as she clung to Kiltman's waist with all her strength. She hoped he was capable of managing the bike as it hurtled between cars and trucks, flitting from hard shoulder to central reservation. Truth was in situations like this, he focused his eyes and ears on monitoring the traffic ahead and on either side of the bike, picking up on the slightest sounds and visuals that would cause him to react. The intense focus improved his reaction time such that he could manoeuvre the bike around and through the tightest openings measuring and calculating space and mass as he rode. Morning commuters barely registered the flash of blue as his costume and cape whisked by their windows.

They made good time into the centre of the city while breaking the vast majority of Highway Code regulations at the same time. It was a dull, overcast London day, black clouds hovering above a ragged skyline. The Thames nurtured a thick, mushy, green-pea colour washing choppy waves against barges and a scattering of boats. It was not London's most inviting day.

The bike negotiated alleys and one-way streets the wrong way, Kiltman following Wilson's guidance on how to reach Saint Bartholomew's hospital towards the east of the city. Saint Paul's Cathedral loomed large on their right. He had not appreciated just how huge it was. It completely dominated the east end of the city centre, tourists already milling around snapping happily at its off-white pigment against a dark, brooding sky. A few minutes later the expanse of Saint Bartholomew's appeared in front of them, the sound of multiple ambulances in the background indicating that every hour is rush hour for a hospital.

Instinctively, he pointed the bike to the left of the hospital. He slowed down to allow them a chance to survey the walls for any memorials to Scottish warriors from the thirteenth century. After a hundred yards Wilson pointed at a white plaque snug against the hospital wall. They parked the bike on the street before walking towards the hospital to see what Cullen Skink had in store this time. Considering he had died eight hundred years earlier, Wallace was still very much alive in many people's minds. Scottish saltires, cards, letters and flowers decorated the memorial. They scanned them carefully. One card stood out above the rest. The front showed a picture of Batman punching his right hand against his left with a caption that read: "Holy unacceptable, Robin!"

Wilson picked it up. Kiltman saw from her terse expression that they had found the next clue. She read aloud: "Dear Kiltman and Starling, how many air miles have you clocked up now? I hope you're grateful. Not to worry, your mission will soon come to an end. I know you can't decide whether to love or hate me. Here I am wreaking havoc all over Europe, but at the same time giving you hope of finding a solution. Yes, giving you a chance to stop me. Let me tell you now: you won't. You will come close, very close, but you will be thwarted. You will be left with a bitter taste in your mouth, to be wracked with guilt for the rest of your lives. If you survive, it will no doubt spell the end of your career, Kiltman, since the world will know just how limited your powers are.

"Anyway, they will have more important things to worry about in trying to rebuild Strathclyde. By the time you read this, Scotland will be less than two days away from its fate, but this fate will give birth to a future of hope. William Wallace knew this when he sacrificed himself for our country. As the memorial states in our great language, 'Bas Agus Buaidh', Death and Result. This is what I will achieve, just like Wallace did. In generations to come, historians will look back on this century. They will credit Cullen Skink with saving the face of Scotland, putting it back on the map as a nation with values and principals.

"But you know all that already. So without further ado, here is your last clue. If you survive my legacy to Scotland then our paths may cross, but I do not expect either of you to be around after the brightest midnight. You don't seem the type to desert a sinking ship, and believe me, Strathclyde is going down.

"Dumb as you are, Saint
Bartholomew's flaking paint
On starting to define,
The beginning of those lines,
Vulgar place,
Can you save face?
"We both know what is destined to happen very soon.

Yours truly, in partnership for making Strathclyde a better place to live.
Cullen Skink."

Kiltman paced up and down in front of the memorial, assessing, rearranging the words in the poem. "What do you think, Wilson?"

"I'm beginning to agree with your original assessment."

"Which was?"

"This guy is no poet. I guess that irks me nearly as much as this tour of Europe. He's playing with us, but doing it in such a coarse manner."

"I know what you're saying, but I think this is in our favour. His clues are pretty easy to digest; they seem to get easier rather than harder. This tells me one thing."

"He's leading us into a trap?"

"Exactly. We have become part of the message he wants to deliver. He's using us to drive panic, create a media frenzy. By reacting to this clue as per the others, we'll play right into his hands."

"But do you have any idea what this clue is about?"

"Not yet," he lied. "But let's not worry about it here. We need to get back to Scotland. We have to prepare for the showdown."

June 20th Late Afternoon

"Is this a real castle, Dad?" Roddy could not contain his enthusiasm, eyes darting back and forth trying to take it all in at the same time. "Was it once full of soldiers and knights, holding out against the enemies? Who were the enemies? Were they English?"

"Well, where do I start? Actually the castle is more than fifteen hundred years old. They took a bit of a chance building it here on Dumbarton Rock, a volcano. Even then they probably knew it hadn't erupted in ages, but still they didn't have the benefits of our scientific techniques today."

"A volcano! Cool!" Roddy imagined molten lava gushing out from between the stone slabs on the floor carrying the castle down the steep sides of the rock into the river. Steam hissed as the lava met the water beneath a volcano bubbling ferociously.

"The name Dumbarton means the Fortress of the Britons. It became the capital of Strathclyde back then because it was a strategic point in defending against the invaders who sailed up the Clyde. No-one understood this better than the Vikings who attacked us over a thousand years ago, resulting in a siege that lasted for four months."

"Four months! But how did they capture it in the end?" Roddy pictured Viking spears bounce off the walls of the castle, the odd one sneaking a path through a window, fatally wounding a warrior, dropping onto his back screaming his last breath.

"The usual way that sieges end. They ran out of food and water. Eventually they had to open the gates otherwise they would have died of malnutrition. Several centuries later the castle was used as a prison where they held the Jacobite rebels."

"Were they the ones who wanted to bring the Stuart kings back to Scotland?" He pictured the prison beneath their feet, proud men with beards down to their ankles holding the iron bars firmly, defiant to the end.

"Good boy. Yes, they tried but failed. Even William Wallace was kept prisoner here until they sent him to London for his trial. He was betrayed by his fellow countrymen after making Scotland a proud nation once again. They repaid him by handing him over to the English."

"How could they do that to a hero, Dad?" He pictured Mel Gibson dropping a dirty, bloodied rag onto the ground screaming, "Freedom!"

"They were different days then, son. Life was cheap, loyalties mixed up." Not so different, Kenny thought.

Roddy shook his head slowly as he walked towards the window overlooking the Clyde. He could see the Viking longships sailing along the centre of the waterway, their trademark horned helmets atop fuzzy-haired warriors. He imagined himself with a bow and arrow, aiming at the captain of the first longship. He would take him out first then throw the Vikings into confusion. He hoped his men had the hot oil ready. He would get the servants to check. He would need to put a plan in place to ration the supplies, to survive the siege.

Kenny watched him. He could imagine what was going through his son's head as he faced the challenges of defending the rock. The innocence of youth, he thought ruefully. He dearly hoped that Roddy would still be able to enjoy his youth in two days time. Kenny had become more and more nervous as the deadline approached, realising that he stood between his son and his son's future. The duel with Cullen Skink had become more than personal. As they drove to the castle, there was evidence of the panic gripping the region. Towns normally bustling with people had been evacuated, many deciding not to wait for the realisation of Cullen Skink's threats. Police were everywhere with the key objective of protecting property from looters, while trying to unearth some clue as to the whereabouts of Strathclyde's number one enemy. On certain strategic roadways the army had been employed to retain order amidst the chaos of thousands of vehicles packed with boxes and suitcases. Each vehicle contained panicked individuals doing their best to protect their families from an evil they did not comprehend. Although they knew enough to drive as far away from Strathclyde as possible.

Fiona and Kenny had discussed that morning what they should do with Roddy. Fiona was nervous but felt that if Cullen Skink was to terrorise Strathclyde then he would do the same to other parts of the country. Maybe he was pretending to target Strathclyde but was actually going to do something nasty to Edinburgh or Aberdeen or the Highlands. One thing she felt strongly about was that he could not be trusted. She had talked at length with Lulu. They had agreed they would sit it out in Lulu's apartment in Glasgow. Fiona had recently broken up with her partner before Kenny had the chance to meet him. Kenny knew Roddy had not been impressed. He tried not to be pleased that Fiona stuggled to fill the vacuum he had left.

She had said that if the worst did happen, they would be with a good friend. She had suggested Kenny join them. The evasiveness of his answer made her believe he was high-tailing it out of Strathclyde. He did not attempt to resist her line of logic. It fitted easily into her impression of her ex-husband.

Roddy was neither up nor down since he was convinced Kiltman would catch his nemesis before he had a chance to implement his evil plan. Fiona raised her eyes to heaven when Kenny had said in front of Roddy, "Let's keep our fingers crossed Kiltman will catch Cullen Skink before he does something very bad."

It had been a breath of fresh air for Kenny to arrive at Dumbarton. The rock never ceased to impress him, standing proud and powerful on the edge of the river. He had been there many times when he came to watch Dumbarton FC play football in its shadow. It may not have been the San Siro, but fewer stadiums had such a breathtaking landscape. The local team was one of the first football clubs to be established in Scotland, receiving the pet name of "The Sons", as in Sons of the Rock. The area was steeped in history capturing the essence of the country's long embattled history. The new chapter it now faced might prove to be its most challenging yet.

Kenny had agreed with Wilson that they would split up during the afternoon. She needed to study the forensics, see what clues could be surfaced from the various places associated with Cullen Skink. He said he would go away to work on the William Wallace monument clue. He felt a tad guilty. Part of him wanted to tell Wilson what the clue meant. However, if he had done that, she would have been obliged to advise the Chief Constable. Fraser would have galvanised the troops with the objective of going after Skink. All hell would have broken loose. Kiltman had worked out the clue immediately when he read it outside the hospital in London.

"The beginning of these lines" was the key to unlocking it. Also, the short name for Saint Bartholomew's helped him realise he was on the right track. Saint Bartholomew's was known as Saint Bart's. By taking the first syllable of the first three lines, it spelled Dumb-Bart-On. The last two lines started with Vul-Can. Vulcan was the Latin word for volcano. That was when it all fell into place. The volcano on the mural in Tallinn had been added later. Also, over the centuries the castle had connections to the Stuarts and William Wallace. All roads led to the rock.

An estranged father and son on an outing to the castle made the perfect ruse for Kiltman to inspect it while incognito. If Wilson knew what he was doing, she would have gone berserk. He accepted this was a discussion he would need to suffer. He could not take the risk of playing directly into Skink's hands with an onslaught of police and military descending on them, creating another siege scenario. It looked odd enough as it was, a father and son on an outing to Dumbarton Castle when the vast majority of the region was fleeing in panic. If confronted, he was ready to adopt the nutty professor, absent-minded scientist persona.

While Roddy fired imaginary arrows at the Vikings, Kenny walked along the inside wall tracing his hand along the brickwork. He closed his eyes to listen, letting his fingers connect with the bricks. He concentrated on excluding the sounds of the ships' horns on the river, rising above Dumbarton's congested, fleeing traffic. He focused on the inside of the castle and the rock. He let his ears drift down into the bowels of the extinct volcano. The gurgling lava deep inside rumbled, bubbling far enough away that there was no concern of an eruption for many millennia. The people of Dumbarton could rest easily knowing that nature was not their enemy.

His ears did not provide much more of an understanding than Roddy would have read on the internet before they left the house. He decided to let his fingers do the walking.

Until the lights went out.

"Dad! Dad!" Roddy shook Kenny's head roughly by the ears. Kenny opened his eyes to see his son's frightened face looking back at him, his nose practically touching his. "Speak to me! Are you okay? What happened, Dad? You fainted!"

"It's okay, Roddy." Kenny hugged Roddy close to his chest. He felt an enormous surge of love for his son and his concern. He also feared that his son's excitement might result in him losing at least one of his superears. "I was just a little lightheaded. I'm okay now."

He lifted himself to a standing position, while his legs still felt wobbly. Roddy's worrying look of despair made Kenny smile. "Wee man, don't fret yourself. I'm okay now. One hundred percent. Go over there. Check out the cannon. I'll be with you in a second."

"Okay, Dad, but just be careful!"

Kenny retraced the moments before he collapsed. He had let his hand fuse with the wall. It soaked up the essence of the castle down through to the rock itself and its contents. There was a surge of energy, a mass of unleashed power he had never been in contact with before. There was no mistaking what it was. It was Strathclyde's horror and potential apocalypse. It was highly enriched uranium, with enough suppressed power to knock him out.

Underneath their feet lay a nuclear bomb with enough explosive capability to wipe out Dumbarton, Glasgow and the neighbouring countryside. Dumbarton's close proximity to Faslane and the Holy Loch naval bases made the devastation cataclysmic. While both locations were heavily guarded under the auspices of the navy, it was widely known that the contents of the bases included nuclear submarines. Cullen Skink may have focused on Strathclyde as his target but his homemade nuclear bomb would create a potential chain of nuclear explosions with a force similar to a massive asteroid crashing against Earth. It could upset the planet's finely tuned balance to the point of shutdown, akin to the death and extinction experienced prior to the Ice Age. Kenny suddenly felt cold.

The Rock

"Roddy?" Kenny called from the doorway Roddy had walked through to inspect the cannon. He waited to see an excited Roddy burst back into the main hall to grab his dad's hand. Earlier he had dragged him outside to witness a Clyde littered with imaginary longships. The doorway remained empty reflecting a gnawing sensation rising in the pit of Kenny's stomach. He listened. He heard the usual sounds of nature and humanity mingling together outside the castle walls. He also heard the cascade of small pebbles as they bounced down the uneven surface of the rock. Then he heard Roddy's voice, but not the energetic, bubbly sound of his son enthralled by the magic of the castle and its history. It was a barely imperceptible whimper.

Kenny ran to the cannon. He knew immediately what had happened. Why had he let him go out there on his own? Roddy had found a hole in the outer wall barely large enough for a small dog. Somehow he had squeezed his little frame through it to realise his fantasy on the other side, pouring boiling oil on top of the Vikings. Kenny saw it clearly.

"Roddy!" he shouted.

He continued to hear the whimpers, but no response to his call. Roddy's fear crushed Kenny's heart to the core. Kenny placed his feet and hands on strategic holds on the outside wall trying frantically to scale it. He managed to work his way to the top. Peering down over the edge, he saw Roddy trapped on a large stone protruding at a forty-five degree angle. Both hands were clamped round the stub of a tree growing out from between the rocks. His feet were trying desperately to find purchase on the stone but they slipped under him with each attempt to push himself up. His grip on the tree was the only thing stopping him from falling directly onto the ground, a perilous two hundred feet below, with little in between other than jagged juts of rock. Kenny had never felt so nervous and helpless. His son's fragile arms would not be able to hold his body weight much longer. Several dislodged stones lay ten yards above where Roddy held on for his life. Kenny's mind's eye could picture Roddy slipping on those stones just before he thrust a hand out to catch the tree. It had saved his life. Kenny had no time to spare.

"Roddy," he shouted. "Hold on! Don't look up or down, just hold tight. I'm coming to get you."

He crawled over the edge seeking out hand and foot holds to lower himself down. As he reached the bottom of the wall, he placed his feet carefully on the uneven surface. Like father, like son, was all he could think of when the soft, mushy surface yielded against his weight dropping him like a stone in the direction of Roddy. As he landed, Kenny focused on placing one hand around the tree shrub, the other around his son's waist. He was fully aware that the shock of landing on top of him could easily dislodge his son's weakening grip.

"Ummpphhh!" The air shot from Roddy's lungs despite Kenny's efforts to take the strain on his feet and knees. Kenny's hand grasped both the shrub and Roddy just as his son's hands opened and he began to slip. Kenny's weight and grip proved solid enough to pin his son to the rock, albeit gasping for breath.

"Oh, Dad! That hurt! Why did you jump on top of me, you nearly knocked me off the tree to fall down into the river?"

"It's okay, son, just take deep breaths." Kenny was whispering a silent prayer to every god known to mankind. They had nearly perished. He had nearly killed his own son. The tragedy of that moment would have obliterated the last obstacle in the path of Cullen Skink and his nuclear bomb. The information would have died with Kenny. They lay there together in silence, until his son spoke up.

"But now we're both stuck here. How are we going to get back up?"

Roddy could not believe his father could be so clumsy. Kenny's mind was racing. There was no option other than to attempt the climb back up the wall. One slip on the damp rocks would have one or both of them heading downwards. He could feel the phone in his pocket. A 999 call would save their lives, give his son a chance of a future. The flipside was that the pandemonium would alert Cullen Skink to something amiss at his nuclear launch site, forcing him to trigger an early response.

As if in answer to Roddy's question, the tail end of a grey rope landed beside them. Looking up they could see a head above the wall, where the other end of the rope disappeared. "Who's that?" Roddy asked. Kenny knew immediately but was too astonished to explain.

"It's a good Samaritan, son. Now, let's get this rope round your waist." As Kenny looped the rope around Roddy, his mind raced. He forced himself to let the questions stay in the recesses of his mind until his son had reached safety. He chose a bowline knot to be sure the rope did not tighten around Roddy's middle. Looking up, he tugged on the rope and shouted, "Pull! Pull!"

At the other end of the rope the figure silhouetted against the sky pulled slowly. Roddy gripped tightly, walking his feet up the side of the rock and then the castle, trying to take the weight off the rope. Kenny fought back a lump developing in the back of his throat, watching his pride and joy exercise a composure he never knew he had. After fifteen minutes, Roddy climbed to safety over the other side of the wall.

The rope dropped again at Kenny's feet. He slipped a significantly larger loop around his waist before attempting to climb. The rope tightened as it was pulled from above the wall. Pride made him work industriously to climb back up. By the time he reached the top his arms were shaking with the exhaustion. He made a note to self to include upper body strength in his new fitness regime alongside cardiovascular exercises. On reaching the top, he gratefully accepted the hand extended to help him over the lip of the wall, to drop down on the other side to where Roddy was sitting on a rock chewing his nails.

"Dad!" Roddy ran towards Kenny and hugged him tightly. "You nearly crushed me. What were you doing?"

Kenny did not have time to explain to his son what his game plan had been. Turning away from him, Kenny pointed to the figure jumping down beside them from the top of the wall. "Roddy, do you remember your Uncle Tommy?"

Tommy Again

"Roddy, I would never have known you, you've become so big!" Tommy ruffled Roddy's mop of thick, red hair.

"Uncle Tommy!" Roddy hugged Tommy's lower abdomen.

"Dad told me you were in Estonia."

"I was, but I decided to come back for a wee while."

"What made you come back?" Kenny asked. "Have you not seen the latest news about this Cullen Skink character? He plans to blow up Strathclyde."

"Of course I have. That's why I'm here. I would rather spend this time with the people who matter most to me than out in the back of beyond. Someone else can look after the pub for a while."

"So you decided to visit Dumbarton Rock?" Kenny was trying not to sound suspicious, but was struggling to piece the facts together.

"I phoned Fiona and asked where you guys would be. I didn't think I would end up having to save you. A wee bit of gratitude wouldn't go amiss."

"Sorry, Tommy. I'm still a bit shaken up. With everything else that's going on, these aren't normal times. I really don't know how to thank you." Kenny reached out and hugged him. His friend's half-hearted, reciprocated embrace would not have won any prizes in the I Need a Hug Club. Kenny's mind was still racing through the facts. He was trying not to appear as if he had seen Tommy the day before, albeit as Kiltman. "What's been going on?"

"Where do I start, Kenny? Maybe we can sit down this afternoon for a blether. If we can find a pub open I'll buy you a pint. It might be our last chance." Kenny sensed a lack of sincerity in the gesture, as if Tommy was going through the motions of long-lost friends getting back together.

"I'm on the wagon these days. It's a much better life." Kenny spoke in hushed tones, while Roddy sat on a seat near the entrance leafing through the pages of a tourist brochure lying on the ground.

"That's great news, pal. Drinking is just not for some people. I'm afraid you're one of them. Since I started managing the pub, I've seen lots of people throw away what matters to them for the sake of a drink. I'm proud of you."

Kenny wanted to enjoy Tommy's words and company. He desperately wanted to stop the clock, to take pleasure in their reunion, one he could acknowledge openly. "Cheers, Tommy. Problem is I can't meet this afternoon. I need to run a few errands after I take Roddy back home. How long you going to be around?" He could see his disappointment, or was it suspicion?

"Not sure yet. We'll see what happens with this Cullen Skink fella!" He took a pen and notebook from his pocket. Writing quickly, he said, "Here's my number where I'm staying in Glasgow. When you've got a bit of time, give me a call. I'll run on for now." Tommy passed the paper to Kenny, barely making eye contact.

"Thanks again. You know you probably saved our lives." Why did he find it so difficult to say that? He watched Tommy pinch Roddy's cheek before he walked briskly through the doorway. Wilson had been suspicious of him from the minute she met him. Kenny had felt it unwarranted, believing that certain personalities are more like oil and water rather than haggis and neeps. He had to acknowledge that Tommy had acted bizarrely in Estonia. He had never been difficult to read, but now he appeared somewhat darker, a much more concealed personality. Despite the help he had provided, he seemed more withdrawn than Kenny remembered. Somehow more calculating.

"Can we go home, Dad? Mum will be getting worried." Roddy's shocked state was written all over his pale features. The T-shirt Kenny had bought him at Loch Ness the year before had a rip across one of the monster's humps. A streak of black stretched unbroken across the shirt onto his beige shorts just above two small knees adorned with an array of scratches and fast-developing bruises.

Kenny was not looking forward to his next conversation with Fiona.

Fiona

"You what? You asked Roddy to go and play with a cannon?"

"No, Fiona. I said to go and look at the cannon." For the past several minutes Kenny had been failing miserably in Level One Explaining to a Mother How Her Child Nearly Fell off a 250 Foot Rock.

"Oh, sorry! *Look* at the cannon!" Fiona had closed the door lest Roddy hear. She paced around the kitchen table running her hands through her hair.

"The cannon's hundreds of years old. It's not live." Kenny grimaced thinking that if Fiona only knew about the nuclear bomb, she may be a tad less concerned about a rusty old piece of hardware.

"Thank goodness Tommy was there." Kenny suddenly felt inadequate. How could a few words hurt so much? In a costume he put himself forward as the man who would save Strathclyde, potentially the planet, but as Roddy's father he was a failure. Before they had arrived home, Roddy had asked Kenny whether they should tell his mum what had happened. Kenny appreciated Roddy's question since he knew he was trying to protect his father from a dressing down. He desperately wanted to avoid the conversation, but he knew this was one of those moments when Roddy would learn the importance of honesty. Rather than the advantage of lies.

"I know. He just appeared from out of the blue. Very strange."

"Strange? Tommy saved your and Roddy's lives! Hardly strange."

Kenny wanted to explain that his comment was in the context of Kiltman's visit to Estonia and how Tommy had appeared somewhat suspicious on a Dumbarton rock with a nuclear bomb in its intestines. Fiona would immediately request some sort of court order to prevent the mad father from seeing his son, on the grounds of the poor man thinking he was a superhero before he then jumps off a rock onto a stone where his son is holding on for dear life.

"I don't mean strange. More like bizarre. Timing's everything, eh?"

Fiona's look told him she was not in the mood for euphemistic clichés. While over the years she had settled into the mother role quite naturally, Kenny had always felt she was a tad overprotective. He had struggled with Fiona driving Roddy to school in the morning then picking him up in the evening. Some of Kenny's most memorable childhood experiences were when he walked to primary school with his friends. They would have missed the chance to hang out at the building sites to see how the tradesmen rebuilt the areas blown apart during the blitz in World War II. They would never have had the unique experience of finding a bomb still live after nearly thirty years. On second thoughts...

"Maybe it is better I leave you two for today. I get the sense I've fallen into the *persona non grata* category." He did not wait for her response. She needed time to be with Roddy, alone in the house.

As he walked to the door the silence had become unbearable for Kenny. For Fiona, it was an opportunity to reload her weapon – her tongue. Roddy walked into the kitchen holding a postcard of Dumbarton Rock they had picked up at a petrol station on the way home. He looked purposefully at his mother, handing the card to her pointing enthusiastically at the picture. "Mum, look, this is the stone I was lying on just under the castle. If I had fallen off, I would have landed in the bushes below. I would have been okay."

Kenny did not know whether to gag or hug his son. His effort to make Fiona feel better about the accident only provided a perfect colourful picture of her son's dice with death.

"I don't want to see that just now, Roddy. I'm talking to your father."

"But Mum, Dad did what he could. If he was Kiltman then maybe you could have expected him to see the danger before it happened. Considering he's merely human, Dad did really well."

"Look, Roddy. It's got nothing to do with Kiltman and his special powers. You should not have climbed through the hole in the wall, and your father should have been a little less distracted. God only knows what you can find of interest in a centuries old, rundown castle."

Roddy looked at his dad. He waited till his mum looked at the ceiling before he shrugged his shoulders. Kenny returned the look and winked. Nice try, Roddy, he thought. Final result of the family analysis of the problem was that Dad, bless him, was altogether far too human.

Wilson

"I think we've figured it out, Kiltman." Wilson was standing with her back against a whiteboard in the Pitt Street war room. There were four whiteboards dominating the room, each covered with a mass of writing, scoring out, arrows and pictures of bridges, tunnels, and a rather infantile drawing of the Vatican thrown in for good measure.

He eased himself onto a chair at the edge of the table. It was the evening of June 20th. He felt tired, exasperated and more than a little inadequate. Roddy had tried to stand up for his father, only to be reminded of his father's frailties. He pushed the dysfunctional parenting to the back of his mind. He would have plenty of time to gain Roddy's respect, once he had dealt with Cullen Skink.

"Hi, Chief. Looks like we're getting close. Fire ahead, Wilson. You guys seem to have been busy making the whiteboards a lot less white."

She smiled at him while the Chief Constable barely registered his comment. The strain was showing on his weather-beaten features. He was not yet aware of the surprise Kiltman was about to unleash. He would have to pick his words carefully.

"It's Dumbarton Rock. Something's happening there. If you take the start of each line in the clue… you are… able to… spell out…" Wilson slowed to a halt. She could see from Kiltman's body language that she was not telling him anything he did not know already. "You've figured it out already, haven't you?"

"I've got a confession to make." He shifted in his seat. "I went on an incognito recon visit to the rock today to check it out. I'm sure you'll understand why I kept it to myself. I thought a subtle approach would be best." Which included, of course, a father and son team hanging off the rockface, saved by a rope and reverse-abseiling. Very subtle.

Wilson's first reaction was to be angry. However, the professional in her kicked in forcing her to look at the situation from Kiltman's perspective. Cullen Skink already knows what she looks like. If they roped in undercover policemen, it would take too long bringing them up to speed with the current status of the case.

209

"But surely you're a lot more recognisable than me?" She was still going to make him explain.

"I'm the master of disguise. Have you ever seen *Mission Impossible?*"

"More like Inspector Clouseau!" The Chief Constable smiled.

"Well, okay. Let's just say that I didn't go there as Kiltman."

"Okay, I'll buy that. What did you find?" Wilson looked stressed.

"Our worst fears have been realised."

"Nuclear?" The Chief Constable walked towards him.

"Yes, a nuclear bomb big enough to take out Strathclyde and beyond. From what I could tell, it's somewhere inside the rock, sitting deep under the castle."

"Are you sure?"

"Chief, I found enough highly enriched uranium to create Hiroshima several times over. It's nestled deep in the rock, ready to blow."

"Oh my God." The Chief Constable began to pace the room, pinching the bridge of his nose.

"Dumbarton Rock will not be extinct for much longer if we don't find a way to defuse that bomb and put Skink out of action."

Wilson found her voice again. "First thing we have to do is make sure the area is clear of nuclear weaponry. As you're well aware, the bases at Faslane and the Holy Loch may contain nuclear submarines. I've already notified them to clear out. They're running it through their chain of command as we speak. Hopefully they will treat this situation with the seriousness required of a clear and present danger scenario."

"Well, we'll just need to make sure they pay heed to our warning. I've got several influential contacts both there and at government level. I've already warned them this may be coming. Let me get on the phone now to confirm what we've found." The Chief's worst fears were being realised. Retirement had become a distant dream, replaced by the impending doom of mass nuclear attack.

"Chief, can I give you one word of advice?"

"Shoot, Kiltman."

"Keep this information very low key. We don't know who Cullen Skink is, or whether he has insider connections. There's nothing to stop him bringing forward the detonation timing if it suits him."

"I'll bear that in mind." The Chief Constable strode from the room wearily. He left a silence Wilson and Kiltman were both very conscious of.

"How you doing, Wilson?" Kiltman was genuinely concerned. Her eyes seemed to have taken up shop three inches deeper into her skull than the last time he saw her.

"Tired. Very tired. And to be honest, frustrated."

"We're in the eye of the hurricane now. It's a bit like sitting an exam. We've prepared so well, foregone days of sleep. We're now about to enter the exam hall to see what the paper looks like."

"Eh, apart from mixing your metaphors, not a bad analogy, Kiltman. Except we don't know if the exam hall will still be in one piece or we'll still be able to hold a pen when the 'exam' ends."

"That's the spirit, Wilson. Good old positivity and optimism, you can't beat it." He forgot she could not see his winning smile as he tempered the comment with his tender loving care expression.

"Oh, it's sarcasm now, is it? Look, Kiltman, we've got to work together for only another couple of days. Whatever happens. I would appreciate if you could keep your comments professional and helpful." Her chin was unnaturally scrunched. She was trying not to cry.

"Okay, Wilson. I was actually trying to be a tad light-hearted. I'll take your point on board."

Were superheroes supposed to be rebuked by Detective Inspectors? He had got into the habit of thinking that all he had to do was throw out a quip before the police force smiled in the comfort of having him around. He would definitely need to work on his approach before he engaged on witty repartee with Wilson again.

Wilson pulled a tightly rolled map from behind the desk. She spread it carefully on the desk not looking at him. Placing the paperweights, aka coffee cups, on each corner, she wanted to kick herself. She had over-reacted, which had annoyed her. She had lost self-control, and in her heart of hearts she knew he did not deserve it. If one of them did not try to be light-hearted there was the risk they would implode. She wanted to apologise but could not find it within herself. This added to her exasperation, since she could normally apologise to others quite easily when she realised she had done wrong. The only people she struggled to say sorry to were the ones who had got under her skin. Kiltman was well and truly in there, as prickly as a rash in high summer.

Between a Rock and a Hard Place

How could he begin to explain to her about his meeting with Tommy? No matter how he approached the subject, she would be suspicious. Tommy was the last person in the world he had expected to see as he dangled high in the sky, his son trapped beneath him. He had saved their lives. Not a lot of other options were available to Kenny when that rope arrived.

How could Kiltman broach the topic without giving away his identity? Oh yes, Tommy came to see his old friend whom he had last seen as an alcoholic but who had now recovered so well that he was a superhero. This was a can of worms he did not want to open, yet he felt obliged to tell Wilson that her newfound Estonian-Scottish 'friend' was there. There was only one way to handle it. Tempered honesty would have to be the best policy.

"There's another thing, Wilson."

"Oh, yes? You ARE full of surprises this evening, Kiltman." Wilson was trying to stay in control of an investigation where she was feeling more and more like a spectator.

"Tommy was at the rock today."

"What? Tommy MacGregor? What in the world...?"

"He was walking around, just like any other visitor to the castle. He wasn't acting particularly suspicious."

"Oh, of course not. What would be suspicious about the guy we met in Estonia yesterday just turning up on top of a nuclear bomb factory? So did he explain why he was there?"

"Well, truth is, I didn't get into too much detail with him."

A conversational vacuum was always worse for the person who had spoken last. The silence ached for a spoken word until Wilson snapped a pencil. He struggled to conceal his reaction to the noise, his senses revved to max. They had been like that since this afternoon. He was more stressed than he had realised.

"Do you not at least see the relatively massive coincidence going on here?" Wilson had picked up a pen and was clicking it rhythmically with each syllable as she worked to control her nerves. He decided not to stop her as the distraction meant she had an ounce less energy for crucifying him.

"Let me line it up for you then. The facts are as follows. Tommy helped unlock the Nimeta Bar clue faster than you could say Terviseks. Cullen Skink believes Estonia is a good example of the true nature of the Scots, when there are a million other places in the world where he could show Scottish exploration at work. Tommy has been on holiday the same week Skink's leaving clues around Europe. Based on our passport investigation he was in Rome over ten years ago, he then disappears to Estonia. He now turns up on the exact spot where Cullen Skink has placed a nuclear bomb. He didn't mention once to us that he was thinking of going to Scotland, let alone to an extinct volcano where barely anyone goes unless they want to take a photograph.

"Maybe if you had let me into your secret trip, we could have taken him in for some questioning. Do you have any idea where he might be now?"

Kiltman felt suitably berated. While he had been economical with the truth, at least he had not told an outright lie.

"In case you had forgotten, Wilson, there's a nuclear bomb sitting under the rock. If we don't make that the centre of our attention, then it really doesn't matter a hoot about Tommy, whether he is Cullen Skink or not."

Wilson sat on the table placing her hands underneath her legs, eyes fixed on the floor. He knew he had pushed her too far. He sensed the walls close in, the hunt had taken its toll on both of them. Wilson and Kiltman had joined forces only four days earlier. Since then danger had presented itself to each of them in equal measure. They could have perished together in Rome but they had survived, each because of the other. They had snatched parcels of sleep on flights across Cullen Skink's clue-laden landscape. Her head had nestled against his shoulder from Rome to London. He had enjoyed the sense of comfort in the closest contact he had shared with a female in years. A spark had been ignited somewhere along their journey, and while he was not an expert, he liked the thought that Wilson might feel it too.

She raised her head slowly. Steel of eye, strong of jaw, there was no doubting her commitment and determination. "Okay, Kiltman, your call. One thing I've learned over the last few days is to trust your instinct even more than my own. What's next?"

"Oh the Clyde, the Clyde, the Wonderful Clyde." He sang an exaggerated version of the river's age-old anthem.

"What did you do with the money?" Wilson asked, eyebrows askew.

"Money? What money?" he replied, caught in mid-chorus.

"The money your mother gave you for singing lessons."

Close Call

My dream is very close to being realised. God created the world in six days, yet I am going to destroy Strathclyde in one. Tomorrow night will witness the apocalypse needed to shake Scotland out of its wicked ways. The next day will be the next genesis, as this beleaguered country picks itself back up and creates a newer, better place.

Kiltman has not disappointed me, he has understood each of the clues as quickly as I expected and planned. He is no doubt at this moment trying to understand what will happen at Dumbarton Rock. He knows my threat is nuclear. There is a whole wall dedicated to it in Estonia. As I watched him decipher the clue and realise the horror of what I had in store, I knew I had him in the palm of my hand. He will not underestimate Cullen Skink. He will also know that I gave him every chance to stop me, but he has just not been good enough.

I yearn to see how he will try to impregnate the rock. This rock has become my pièce de résistance. The years of investment and perseverance have turned an old volcano barely capable of a sneeze into a world-changing colossus. The surprises lying within are designed to defy one as determined as Kiltman. I relish the opportunity to let him try until he fails in his quest. His overgrown self-esteem and ridiculous superhero status will be smashed in his face as he witnesses my monster, my dear Permian. She has developed a life of her own over these years. She will now wreak the same destruction that created the Permian age 250 million years earlier, the greatest cull of life on our god-forsaken planet. Not an insect survived. Barely a fish was left swimming. Land lost three quarters of its residents. It was the mother of all destructions. To this day no-one knows whether it was an asteroid or volcanic eruption on a mass scale, but no-one will be in any doubt as to what my bomb will do. My Permian will be the mother of all manmade destruction. One day it, and I, will be worshipped in the same way as the Christian God is supposed to arrive in all his glory on a chariot to end the world.

My legacy will continue for a long time after I am gone and Scotland has become the sacrificial lamb for the whole world to see and learn from.

Underwater

Wilson sat at the controls as if she had been doing this kind of thing for years. The sense of isolation in the two-man submarine was exaggerated by the dark, chilly waters of the Clyde. She guided it along the centre of the river as close to the bed as possible. Once a small salmon river, the industrial revolution had dredged the Clyde to allow ships laden with raw materials and goods to pass each other daily without risk of collision. Wilson was fully aware of the river's renowned status over the last couple of centuries as she negotiated the sub between rusted remnants of ships, boats, and tugs, testament to Glasgow's ambition to lead the world in the nineteenth century. The Clyde was a veritable graveyard of sunken dreams. The radar panned a three-mile radius around them indicating how well stocked Davy Jones's locker was in the west of Scotland, white dots blipping randomly across the screen.

The minisub had been Wilson's idea. Kiltman had been more than a little sceptical about her being able to negotiate underwater from the Broomielaw in central Glasgow as far as Dumbarton Rock. A two-year secondment to the Royal Navy, part of a training programme inspired by a government initiative to improve collaboration between the police, military, and naval forces, was enough to convince him she knew what she was doing. Before leaving Pitt Street they had argued vociferously with Chief Constable Fraser that he should not engage any other resources to approach the rock. If they approached Cullen Skink with a blunderbuss, he would activate the bomb immediately. They had to retain an element of surprise. He felt for Fraser. He was caught between the devil and the deep blue sea. If it was perceived he had not put the full power of his resources against Skink, then it would seem he had failed in his responsibility. Yet by doing so, he might trigger the reaction they were working to prevent. In the end he had succumbed to Kiltman's logic that the only way to beat Skink was to play by his rules until the moment when they could turn the tables on him. He had accepted only Kiltman and Wilson should play this game, nobody else. They had to keep it that way.

Wilson flicked switches, turning sturdy dials at will, managing the course of the sub against the buffeting of swelling currents. The wind had picked up strength exaggerating the force of the rain. They both realised the elements might add their own personality to the night's proceedings.

"You're doing well, Wilson. We'll be there in another ten minutes."

"Bet you didn't think a woman driver would be able to do this." She clearly relished her role in the sub.

"To be fair, I am impressed as long as you don't try to reverse around a corner or parallel park."

"Very funny." She flicked another switch.

They sat in silence until they slowed to a slither, barely moving in the water, but with enough pace to manage the currents massaging the sides of the sub.

"Up periscope!" Kiltman announced. "I've always wanted to say that," he added when he saw Wilson raise her eyes heavenwards. She had already pushed a button to activate a video screen. As the periscope, actually a video camera on the end of a collapsible lance, broke the surface of the water, the screen changed from black to dark blue.

"ACTIVATE INFRA-RED?" flashed on the screen.

Wilson responded with the yes button. Immediately they saw a mesmerising scene of uncoordinated lights and shapes along the north bank of the river. She turned a dial to aim the camera at the rock, barely perceptible due to the absence of surrounding light. It seemed as remote and dull as any rockface could be, not a hint of activity to indicate the weapon of mass destruction in its belly.

"Are you ready?" Wilson asked as she carefully zipped up a tight, one-piece, black costume. Kiltman felt he had just got to know her a whole lot better.

"Ready when you are. By the way, is this standard issue?" he asked.

"Well, yes, it is, if you expect to secretly climb the outside of a rock in the middle of the night. Why?"

"You ever thought of doing singing telegrams at the weekends?"

219

Realising she was becoming adept at ignoring his inane comments, he watched her place a pair of infra-red goggles over her eyes before grunting, "Let's go."

She flipped the location setter switch to activate the computerised anchor. Rather than carry a cumbersome iron weight on a small sub, the pre-programmed ballasts on the ship would self-regulate to ensure it stayed at exactly the same location until they returned.

He had chosen his own attire for the occasion. He had donned the top half of a wetsuit he had personally converted by blending various fabrics into the material enhancing its strength while rendering it more lightweight and flexible. The adding of a subtle Saint Andrew's cross to the back, with the Kiltman logo on the front, were the only marks to show that it belonged to a superhero. He had also donned a rubberised, waterproof version of his kilt made from non-absorbent materials. Not exactly Highland tweed, but at least it would help him stay afloat. Pleased at his creation, he looked at himself momentarily then smarted at how unflattering the wetsuit was. While Wilson looked like Diana Rigg from *The Avengers*, he felt more like a disoriented penguin wearing a kilt. Thank goodness I'm not vain, he mused, as he stepped from the sub onto land.

A short semi-circular grassy area separated the rock from the river. They negotiated it carefully, running at a brisk pace. The wind and rain had whipped up into a fierce storm. He found he was able to keep up with Wilson only because she was holding back for him.

They had studied maps before they left Pitt Street. The castle had been built there for a strategic military reason: the walls were sheer from the river all the way to the castle. Their Pitt Street assessment identified a route up the south-west corner of the rock. On a good day it was never going to be an easy climb. On a night pummelled by weather of biblical proportions, the route to the top would be treacherous. As the Chief and Wilson had discussed the best way to scale it, Kiltman knew their plan would need strong, agile climbing skills. He had stepped back from the discussion at that point saying a silent prayer he would have the strength to follow Wilson. Once this was all over, he promised himself he would convert his attic into the gym he had planned for ten years earlier. No excuses.

At the bottom they leant against a small ridge protecting them from the ferocity of the wind. The elements would be unforgiving during the climb. Wilson handed him four suction caps, for his feet and hands. While these were standard issue SAS equipment, he was impressed by how effective they were, particularly against the increasingly irritating storm. Within minutes he found himself climbing faster than he thought possible. He reflected that the suction caps could be further enhanced by mechanising the vacuum creation using a small trigger beneath the forefinger. Moving his limbs carefully he made a note to self to investigate this for his own armoury, while wondering if that would make him an inventor of suckers or a sucker for invention.

The Corridor

The last thirty feet proved difficult for him before he lifted his legs over the edge onto the same boulder he had become acquainted with only half a day earlier. The climb did not need to be so tough for him. He could have used the same trick he had employed the previous year when he pulled the schoolchildren's bus from the edge of the cliff. He had accomplished it by channelling the power of all his senses into his muscles. It was a risky option but he had no choice, the bus was slowly shifting weight onto the wrong side. The downside was that he had to spend the next week in bed barely able to lift a finger, realising he had not fully understood this element of his superpowers. If he tried the same tactic on the rock he would be useless afterwards, and he could not take that risk with what lay ahead of them.

Wilson was already on the boulder, adjusting the suckers to carry her over the remainder of the climb.

"The wall is going to be more difficult. There doesn't seem to be much in the way of smooth surface for the suction pads to cling to." She surveyed the wall directly above their heads studying the infra-red image to map out a route.

"That won't be necessary," Kiltman shouted into her ear against the maelstrom of wind. "There's a hole just up there on the left-hand side at the bottom of the wall. It's very small, but I've brought something to make it wide enough for me to get through. Which means four of you could get through." He showed her a mechanical chisel strapped to his leg.

"How on earth did you know about that hole?" Wilson bent her head slightly to the side.

"It's a long story. One day when you're drunk enough not to remember it the next day, I might tell you. Come on, follow me."

His bones were already aching with the cold and effort of stretching and pulling. The last section proved to be tougher due to the hole being further round to the west of the rock, directly battered by the full brunt of the storm. Holding on with one hand, he used the other to work the chisel round the two bricks in the lower end of the wall. He created enough space to push them inside. It was surprisingly easy considering they had been there for so many centuries already. He felt a twinge of guilt at defacing the wall, but was sure the Architectural Heritage Society of Scotland would understand that two bricks were a small price to pay for at least a whole region.

He squeezed his frame through the hole before watching Wilson lever herself to the other side like a curvaceous panther stalking its prey. They sat leaning against the inside of the wall concentrating on controlling their belaboured lungs and heart. After a couple of minutes, they nodded to each other. Kiltman led the way into the castle. Inside was pitch black. Wilson compensated with her goggles, while he allowed his sight to adjust automatically to night vision. Hair o' the Dog had thought of everything.

Running his hand along the wall, he ignored the draining force of uranium and concentrated on finding a passage into the intestinal gut of the castle. Further back in the room his hand had sensed significantly less density behind the wall. Breathing deeply through his nose, he detected the hint of oil. It seemed to seep through deep cracks, filtered by decaying plaster and dust. Pressing gently against the bricks, he noticed a gap between them much newer than the centuries old castle. He pushed carefully until a brick swivelled on its axis. The gap in the wall allowed more of the oily smell to drift into the night air. A lever sat flush inside the space left by the brick, a veneer of damp showing it had been used recently. He sensed Wilson's breath on his neck for the second time in a few days, a welcome respite from the rain that stung him only minutes earlier.

"Well done," she whispered.

"What did you say?" he asked.

"I said, well done," she repeated as she leant closer towards him. He sighed, a tad guilty at already having heard her the first time.

He pulled the lever downwards just before a whirr of machinery interrupted the stillness of the room. Wilson's first thought was that they may have activated the bomb, but as the wall and section of the floor moved, she realised they had found what they were looking for. In Dumbarton Castle's ancient version of the revolving door, they were gently swivelled behind the wall into a room which had rarely seen light. The darkness was haunting. A stone, spiral staircase disappeared down through the floor inviting them to descend the steps.

They edged forward to begin their descent, hesitating only to be sure they were alone. He counted the steps as they gingerly followed them down through the innards of the castle. Six inches in depth each, once they passed the two hundred mark he realised that they were halfway down deep inside, the castle far above them. The air was dank and lurid, reminding him of a perfume he had smelled many years before. He promised himself never to return to that bar again.

They approached the bottom of the steps; a plain, oak door waited for them, no handle in sight. He placed his foot on the final step. His foot sensed a mechanism as ancient as the castle itself kick into motion. The pressure caused the door to spring open automatically. Considering it was nearly centuries old, this would have been cutting-edge technology. He was impressed. He looked back at Wilson. "Do you want me to carry you over the threshold?"

Wilson provided an involuntary shudder which he understood had nothing to do with the cold getting into her bones. If he was ever fortunate enough to make it back to the lab, he would prioritise charm improvement techniques before suckers, he decided. He lowered his head slightly to pass through. Wilson followed close behind. They walked carefully down a corridor which seemed to offer nothing more appealing than several dead rats. At the end of the walkway, he could see an iron grille. Leaning over his shoulder he whispered, "We've found the dungeons."

Kiltman touched the bars. He noted they were considerably younger than the rest of the castle, made of a cast iron newly strengthened in recent years. Peering through the bars, he saw the corridor continue on through the rock. He felt along the walls on either side of the grille searching for a switch. Wilson was already down on her knees scraping sections of the wall looking for the same. Then it hit him.

"We need to get out of here, Wilson, this isn't a dungeon. It's a…"

The thud was loud in its own right but the closeness of the walls and low ceiling magnified it to an intensity that hurt his ears. A cast iron grille had dropped from the ceiling to block access back to the stairs.

"...trap."

Trapped

"We're well and truly sealed in here." Wilson's assessment did not surprise him. He was fully aware of the trap they were in. The corridor had turned into a cage, a distinct absence of pickable locks on two iron grilles on either side of them reaching from floor to ceiling. A lock would have given Wilson a chance to display another skill she had most probably learned in what must have been an accelerated development plan in the Strathclyde Police. He had certainly never known any member of the constabulary to have the bag of tricks she had at her disposal. Unfortunately, they did not extend to covering their current plight. Kiltman wished he could pull something from his own bag, but he had not developed a Gelleresque ability to bend metal. At least not without reducing him to a quivering bedridden wreck. He had to think.

Wilson had already tried her mobile phone to contact the Chief, but the density of the rock on all sides snuffed out any hope of making or receiving calls. They sat down against the iron grille, glum, gloomy, and disillusioned.

"You ever seen the game, Mousetrap, Wilson?"

"Yes, I have. I know what you're going to say, but what could we have done differently?"

"Maybe a distance of, say, twenty feet would have made a difference."

"Are you saying I screwed up by sticking too close to you?"

"Steady, Wilson, it takes two to tango even though I've got two left feet at the best of times. I was encouraging you to keep in step. I should've thought he would have a simple trap like this. He knew if he lured us deep down inside, we would not be able to make contact with the outside. He wants us to sit here and wait it out until the bomb detonates. It'll be light outside now, it's already six o'clock. We've got eighteen hours to go."

In the darkness of the cave, he leant his head back against the wall, cursing his naivety. They had walked into an elementary trap. They now found themselves in a situation more surreal than Kiltman could remember. Wilson was looking at him through goggles more akin to a first world war fighter pilot, which would have been funny in any other situation. Wilson touched his hand. At first, he thought she had misjudged the distance in the dark, but she left it there, resting on top of his. He let his fingers slip naturally into hers. He turned to look at her. "Wilson, we're going to get out of here."

"Kiltman, you are everything people say you are. Even much more besides. This time there's nothing you can do. Skink has kept placing the cheese nearer and nearer until we felt too comfortable in his trap. The only hope we have is that Fraser sends in the cavalry when he hasn't heard anything from us by noon."

"You know as well as I do that it will be all over the very moment the uniforms turn up here. Skink will push the button as soon as he sees a risk of his plan being foiled. He has us in all directions. Our only chance is to get out of this cage. Let's think."

Kiltman heard it before her, a slight shuffle of feet on the steps, someone treading carefully. He put his finger to his lips. He peered through the bars towards the door they had walked through minutes earlier. As the steps came nearer a glimmer of torchlight played on the other side of the door. Wilson had to remove her goggles, the intensity of light hurting her eyes. The figure entered the corridor. Kenny saw who it was immediately. They heard the steps come closer to the cage, the torchlight bathing them in a sullen yellow.

"Well, what do we have here then?"

Wilson recognised the voice. "MacGregor, I knew it!"

"Knew what, lass? You really don't know anything if you ask me. I don't know why our esteemed national hero teamed up with a cocksure upstart like you in the first place. There's no accounting for taste, eh? By the way, you left the door open. Anybody could've got in here. Just as well it was me, eh?"

"Tommy, you've been drinking, haven't you?" Kiltman was never one to ignore the obvious.

"I've had a few drams alright. Celebrating the last day, having a wee blowout before we're all blown to smithereens. You should've done the same rather than mess around playing dungeons and dragons... no guesses for who's the dragon. Ha! Ha!"

"Tommy, let us out of here!" Kiltman was shaking the bars, fists clenched with barely suppressed anger. "This has gone far enough. Now come on, help us. Please!"

"Help you? Oh, aye, right. See you. Bye." Tommy turned. He walked back towards the door chuckling and talking to himself. The beam of the torch bounced and ricocheted against the walls of the corridor as he disappeared through the door.

They heard it slam behind him as the light disappeared.

"Coincidence?" Wilson shouted. "Are you now going to tell me this has all been a coincidence?" She had already pulled her hand away from his on hearing the footsteps. Otherwise she would have done it then.

He wanted to defend Tommy, but did not know where to start explaining it to Wilson. Could he talk about the years they had spent together from when they were kids at school through till when Kenny started in Wallace Distillers? How Tommy had been there through thick and thin? How the roles were reversed when Kenny lost everything and Tommy went to seek his fortune? How Tommy had searched for him and Roddy the day before? Or had he? He had not asked Fiona if indeed Tommy had called before going to the castle. Wilson's doubts were founded on facts while Kiltman's opinions were just that, based on the relationship of two very different people a lifetime ago.

"It just doesn't stack up, Wilson. I can't explain it but..."

"I don't know why you're defending MacGregor. Maybe if you hadn't been quite so trusting and a bit more challenging this..."

They heard the sound of metal rubbing against metal. It came from the ceiling, directly above their heads; small chrome-plated pipes protruded through a handful of holes, hissing mechanically. He climbed onto the iron grille trying to reach the ceiling to block them with his hand, but even as he did so he realised it was a futile attempt to stop the inevitable. He heard Wilson slump to the ground behind him. Seconds before he lost his grip on the iron bar and fell backwards onto the floor.

Skink Unplugged

He was drowning. Sinking deeper and deeper into the depths of the river. He tried to pull with his arms and kick his feet to fight the current sucking him under. He had no power, he felt as if the water was turning to tar, its cold dampness against his face. Another wave of water rushed into his nose and mouth, causing him to splutter. He tried with all his might to fight against it but his body would not react, would not pull him to the surface. Willing himself to win this battle, he forced his eyes open.

He was surrounded by bright lights. He was still in the corridor, lying on the floor of the cage, alive with bulbs protruding from the walls. He stared at the ceiling, working on salvaging his consciousness, which seemed to want to let him fall into oblivion. His legs did not seem capable of taking the strain let alone raise him into a standing position. He tried to reach out for the bars to help in the process. Nothing moved. Not a muscle or a joint responded below his neck. He turned his head to the side to see if Wilson was okay. She was gone. A damp patch was the only clue as to where she had lain unconscious in her wetsuit. A trail of water drifted along the floor to the door indicating where she had been dragged to the exit.

"Well, well, Kiltman is coming back to life!" The voice seemed very far away, yet right beside him. He could feel the breath on his cheek. As he stared back towards the ceiling, a dark object interrupted his focus. The head and shoulders of someone silhouetted against an overhead light. He was wearing a mask, one of those Venetian carnival types. The features seemed fishlike, large eyes and bloated lips. Behind the lips was a voice-modifier, delivering the words with a mechanical overtone.

"It's a pleasure to meet you after all this time. Do you like my mask? Or is it out of 'plaice'? Ha! Ha! By the way, I am shaking your hand at the moment. Really, I am. You can't feel it because you are paralysed from below your neck by a cocktail of nerve gases I created, taking all the best bits from the chemical agents, tabun, sarin, and soman. You may have heard of them, the best paralysers money can buy! I even tested them on myself one day when I had nothing better to do."

He paused and scratched under his chin, where the fish mask was scraping against grey stubble. He then started again with renewed gusto. "When I woke I was starving! I was immobile for forty-eight hours. You don't need to worry about being paralysed for so long because you will be dead in ten hours. Yes, it's now two in the afternoon. I forgot to mention that I added some chloroform to the gas today to give me some time. Also, of course, to let you have a well-deserved sleep after all your gallivanting."

"Look, Skink! You can still stop this, you don't need to go any further. You've proved your point already."

Despite no sensation below his neck, Kiltman was surprised at how well his vocal chords worked. They were the only weapon he had left.

"Oh, no, Kiltman. There's more to come. Why do you think I needed time? As you will see, your sidekick has disappeared. She is neatly tucked up in bed, although not quite conscious yet. When she does come round, she will be pleasantly surprised to see what I have in store for her. You brought her to me, just as I expected you would. She became a key part of my plan on that day you brought her to Erskine Bridge.

"I've enjoyed working with both of you over the last few days. You saved Rome from a horrible disaster, but I bet no-one has really thanked you for it. That, my friend, is the world we live in. It was fun to watch you decipher the nuclear clue in Nimeta Bar. Your face was a picture. By the way, in case you haven't figured it out yet, I was the man on the stag night. You know, the man dressed up in the bondage gear. You even spoke to me but didn't notice that none of the other men in the room seemed to know who I was. Took your eye off the ball there, didn't you?"

He tipped his head back and said in a strange childlike voice, "Kiltman missed the ba-all! Kiltman missed the ba-all!"

After pausing to take a deep breath, he continued. "And then your hop, skip and jump over to London to pay homage at the monument to one of the greatest men Scotland has produced. An example to millions, yet he only becomes famous when some Australian-American turns him into a money-spinning exercise. What has our heritage, our world, come to?"

"Please, Skink, bring a halt to this madness now. You can still choose not to do this."

"Madness? My dear Kiltman, this is not madness. Madness is hundreds of thousands of people killing themselves with drugs, drink, bigotry and hatred. Madness is not looking after the weaker members of our society, while encouraging materiality as a god to be respected. Madness is building a system around all of this to protect it while making it even worse. Don't talk to me about madness. I have a medicine for this insanity. As you know, we are sitting on top of it right now. You will be the first to benefit from its healing powers as it spreads its wings to heal Strathclyde, and potentially further afield if I can create the chain reaction I'm hoping for."

"Look, let's be…"

"Reasonable? Ha! Yes, let's start being reasonable. Let's start by me seeing who I've been dealing with over the last few days. So who is Kiltman? How human is he really? I'm feeling quite nervous now. You have a well-earned reputation. It's a pity more people like you didn't try to make a difference by helping us fix this world we live in. Unfortunately, all you are doing is making sure the status quo doesn't change. You have the best of intentions, but you are directing them against the wrong things. So let me see what you really look like. I'm quite excited."

Cullen Skink reached down to Kiltman's mask. He waited a second before he tore it roughly from his head, oblivious to the pain he caused to the only part of Kiltman's body with feeling.

"What the…?" Cullen Skink reeled backwards. He collapsed down onto one knee. Kiltman watched him from the corner of his eye. Skink nervously rubbed his arm, shaking his head from side to side. He could not see Skink's facial expression but recognised the symptoms of a maniac about to explode.

"It can't be! It's preposterous!"

Skink stood and walked to the wall where he punched his fist against the uneven surface. He laughed, then shouted, howled, then squealed. Kiltman watched him. His nemesis was a lot madder than he had given him credit for. He was completely deranged. Skink turned back to face the horizontal superhero.

"Kenny. Kenny Morgan. The guy who nearly drank himself into an early grave. Whose wife and child left him because he couldn't look after them. Suddenly this disaster of a human being decides to become the saviour of mankind. How bizarre is that?" Skink smacked his hand loudly against the wall before kicking the iron bars, letting a loud, wolfish howl escape from his lungs.

"Look, Tommy, let's work this out. It's not too late to fix this mess. You've still got a chance."

"Tommy? Please, don't insult me. No, my friend, you've got it all wrong. Your intuition has most certainly let you down on this occasion, because your nemesis is…"

Cullen Skink had his back towards him. Slowly slipping the mask from his head, he waited a few moments before he turned to reveal his identity. The last time they had met was on graduation day.

A History Lesson

"Of all the traps in all the rocks in all the world, he walks into mine." Cullen Skink laughed manically, his head and hands raised to the ceiling as if thanking God for his good fortune. Lowering his head to study his motionless ex-classmate, he spoke in measured tones, forcing himself to control his excitement. "So, how did this happen? You were a miserable down and out. A pathetic creature loved by no-one, obsessed with nothing except booze."

Kiltman was confused. There was no doubt the man staring at him was his university classmate.

Donald Mackenzie.

"Aw, you're full of compliments, Donald. Who needs Friends Reunited anyway? Although, I don't think even they could bring people back from the dead."

He tried to put the shock to the back of his mind. He hoped he had not overdone it on the blasé approach. Time and nuclear weaponry permitting, he would deal with it later. There was no doubting that the monster standing above him was Donald. He had lost his Einstein hairstyle. Instead, he sported a billiard ball bonce. His hefty waistline showed he had continued to treat physical well-being as a "distraction from genius", his university catchphrase for any interruption from study.

"Kenny, my dear boy. My 'suicide' was easily faked. A couple of life-changing payments to the right people and, hey presto, I'm dead. The easiest way in the world to become a non-person. Which I had been anyway, long before I 'died'. I actually went to Gartnavel Royal Infirmary for over a year before then, being prodded and poked by a myriad of white coats. But you wouldn't know that, since you never tried to visit me."

Skink shook his head, and his features distorted into an anger Kiltman had not witnessed on a face before.

"No grapes or Lucozade, what kind of friend were you?" Skink spat the words. "When I realised, they could do nothing for me, I decided to become the undead. It was easy. By that time, my Russian comrades had made direct contact. They helped me achieve my plan and then escape."

"Russian comrades?"

"How little you remember, Kenny. I told you, they were my biggest fear at that time. Technically they were Soviets, but I preferred to stick to calling them Russians."

"But I thought…"

"Yes, you thought I was losing the plot, blabbering on about fictitious enemies. Please! As if I didn't have enough problems with nervous breakdowns, obsessive compulsive disorder, and schizophrenia. Do you really think I needed to invent other issues?"

He sat down on the ground beside Kiltman, leaning forward, beginning to relax into his story, enjoying the sound of his voice. "A faction of hardliners, unhappy with Gorbachev's pandering to the Western world, took me back to Russia just before the Iron Curtain came down. They had followed my university success and knew I could help them. Recognising my talent, my superior intellect, if I say so myself, I was to play an important role in bringing the communist ideal to the rest of the world. After a year of intensive treatment, they helped me cope with my illnesses. I learned that in fact there was very little wrong with me. My problem was that I was too normal. Ha! You may raise your eyebrows, Kenny, but it's true. My issues were born out of my reaction against a world that had lost control. I saw it before anyone else. I understood the scale of corruption and evil. This has helped me channel my intelligence into making the world a better place."

"A better place? Creating nuclear weapons makes the world a better place? Come on, Donald." His mind was working vigorously to find a way out of his impending doom.

Skink continued as if Kiltman had not spoken.

"My Russian friends helped me create my precious Permian. She waits expectantly below us to give birth to a new world. We worked very closely together building our own ideals and objectives around the Soviet dream, ready to bring a new age to the West. We converted the rock to be the nest for our nuclear egg. It was the perfect location to wipe out the nuclear submarine sites. Faslane and the Holy Loch were sitting ducks. In the midst of the panic created by this bomb, we would then activate nuclear strikes against New York and Tokyo. The world would have been thrown into chaos, allowing the USSR to step in and take control.

"But just as the Iron Curtain came down in the early nineties, my so-called partners let me down. The ideals they had espoused, even built an empire around, proved worthless when they had the chance to live in the West. They were too tempted by the materialism and waste they had spoken against for so long. I am proud to say I took great pleasure in bringing each of their short worthless lives to an end. The hardest, yet most rewarding, was in disposing of my wife, Yelena. She was closest to my heart but still could not see through my eyes. She will have the honour of being the catalyst to create the new world. Her spirit will become part of the atmosphere for all time to watch over her creation of a new genesis when Permian comes to life."

"Why didn't you invite me to your wedding, Donald? Ceilidh music and Russian dancers would have been a hoot." Kiltman's superhearing picked up a sound from the top of the stairs behind the door he and Wilson had entered, diagonally opposite the door his nemesis had come through. Confident that Skink had not heard it, he concentrated on distracting him.

"Kenny, it's not like you to be funny. You haven't even heard the half of it. How was your stag weekend in Rome? Did you enjoy your bottle of champagne from an anonymous stranger?"

"You bought us that bottle?" This time he did not feign a response.

"I hated you, Kenny. I hated your success and how you wore it so well. You managed to find a balance in life despite, or maybe because of, the hard work and studying. You found a good woman and a real job. You became all the things I wanted to be but couldn't, because I was paying a price for my sensitivity to the problems in the world. Problems you were oblivious to."

"But, Donald, I regarded you as a friend. I wanted you to be successful."

Donald wagged his finger. "You were half-hearted in your friendship. I would've trusted you if you had let me. But you kept me at a distance. You dangled your friendship in front of me like a sardine to a cat then pulled it away when I moved towards you. I decided to invest my time in following you to see how I could destroy everything you had created. I wanted to make you suffer enormous loss and a painful end. I knew this was selfish, but this was the one weakness I allowed myself because I was becoming stronger by hating you. I needed the strength."

He paused before taking a deep breath. "At the same time, bizarrely, I kept an eye on you, to protect you from harm."

"Why on earth would you want to protect me?" Kiltman perceived someone breathing on the other side of the door.

"Because I wanted you to die my way. I wanted to be the one who pulled the trigger to send you on your way to meet your maker. That way, I would absorb your power and make it part of me."

"So why didn't you?"

"I didn't need to, Kenny. When I saw how much of a washout you had become, I knew you were no longer worth it. You couldn't hold on to a beautiful wife and child because of your fondness of whisky. No, at that stage by killing you I would have absorbed your frailty. I decided to leave you to die in your own self-hatred and misery."

"Sorry to disappoint you, Donald. I guess you got it wrong that time."

"Yes. But look what's happened? You've been presented to me on a plate. Destiny is telling me that my life's work has been recognised by letting you walk into my trap. What I had hoped to do all those years ago has now returned in glory. At midnight tonight I will absorb your spirit in mine. The powers of Cullen Skink and Kiltman will become as one."

He stopped and smiled. It was not a pleasant sight. Two rows of stained yellow, some blackened, teeth.

"But before I go, I must thank you for bringing me Wilson. We both know when you met her the first time, don't we?"

"What are you talking about?" This was becoming more like *This is Your Life* by the second, only Michael Aspel was nowhere in sight.

"Stop pretending to be stupid. You were a very close second to me in university so I know you are not that simple. Do you think it was a coincidence she was attacked that night? I was sure that when you went to her aid, as I knew you would, you would be the victim. I learned a big lesson. When you hire help, be prepared to pay for the best. Those two idiots got far too carried away with the girl. Their distraction gave you the chance to defeat them."

"What? You hired two men to attack her? What kind of monster are you?" Kiltman would have given anything for one chance to lay a fist squarely on Skink's chin.

"What kind of monster? Ha! I think you know the answer to that. She was just another tax-guzzling student, ten a penny in Glasgow. Don't forget, I'm the kind of monster who can blow up Strathclyde. Do you remember a busker that night?"

"How could I forget, it was worse than putting a cat through a ringer."

"Yes, that was me. In the end I called the police; my plan had been foiled. I couldn't let you and the girl walk into the night together. It would've hurt too much. It was the next day that I signed myself into Gartnavel Royal Infirmary. I was so consumed by you that I had to escape into a mental institution. You drove me to that. Now, guess what? You've brought me the damsel in distress all these years later. The victim you saved is now mine. And I can do with her what I want."

"You dare…!"

"Oh, for goodness sake, Kenny. Don't insult me. My plans are much more long term and fulfilling." Cullen Skink paused for several moments, scratching the back of his head while staring at Kiltman's elongated, stiff body. Kenny's attention was drawn to Skink's right hand as it moved slowly, stroking something he could not identify.

"Ah, I see you've noticed my beads. Do you like them? Or more to the point, do you recognise them?"

"Beads? I don't get it, Donald. Since when did you find religion?"

"How little you understand, Mr. All-knowing Kiltman. Remember your friend, Hassan? Of course, how could you forget? He was someone else you were half-hearted in befriending."

"What are you talking about?" Kenny was struggling to fit this piece into a jigsaw he had already completed in his head.

"Hassan's bark was worse than his bite. When I was searching for the critical components for my nuclear baby, who did I find doing exactly the same thing but a group of Taleban extremists from Afghanistan. Their ringleader was none other than your bead-wielding friend." Skink smiled, rubbing his hands together.

"What did you do to Hassan, Donald?" Kiltman already knew the answer since he could not imagine Hassan being separated from his beads willingly. Skink's face contorted into a grimace of unbridled venom.

"I would've done nothing if he had been true to the cause he had been fighting for in the wilderness of that Soviet enclave he called a country. His loyalties were so confused that he decided to break a confidence." Skink waited for Kenny to speak. Kenny had no words.

"Your silence tells me that you have guessed what happened next. Your friend realised that I was planning to wreak nuclear devastation in Scotland. He pleaded with me not to do it, his memories of Glasgow and friends too much of a burden on his conscience. Ha, he was quite willing to blow up other parts of the world, but oh no, not his precious Glasgow."

"Did you murder, Hassan, Donald? If I could get out of..." Kenny felt a tear trickle down the side of his cheek. He was not sure if it was anger or grief. Or frustration. No matter how much he tried to move his limbs he felt more glued to the floor than before.

"Oh, shut up, you pathetic freak show of a superhero! Hassan went to visit you hoping to convince you to speak to me. He felt that you had a special 'connection' with me and you would make me see the light. I saw the light alright – when I torched him in his car after he had been to find you at your house. Of course, not before I managed to play with him. By the time I had finished he was in tears, especially when I confiscated his precious beads."

"You barbarian!" Kiltman wanted to scream a string of obscenities at Skink but bit his tongue instead. Further antagonising this madman would just add fuel to an already raging fire.

"Are you not listening to me? Don't you understand that Hassan was a murderer in waiting? You should be thanking me for saving thousands of lives. Not bemoaning the loss of a terrorist. So maybe I did torture him a bit, but I needed to find their plutonium resources. He fell into my lap thanks to you, Kenny. Imagine, I may never have created my nuclear weapon if he had not come looking for you. How do they describe it in the gangster movies? He sang like a baby. Thanks a million, you helped me bring my plan to life."

Kiltman felt the words sting. He knew the logic was flawed, manipulative and ludicrous. Surely, he could have done something? Seen something? Not let it get to this stage.

"Well, this has been the best conversation I've had in a long time. As you lie here, there's a lot for you to think about. You have tried hard, but there is nothing you can do to avoid the huge loss of life in Scotland. But then you know just as well as I do that the value of all the chemicals in a human body amounts to less than £5. So what's the big concern?

"It has been lovely talking to you, Kenny-Kiltman. Goodbye! Thanks for making this so worthwhile. I will let you die in dignity, if you can call lying on the floor defeated, dignity."

Cullen Skink took Kiltman's head in his hands, looking in his eyes as if waiting for a response. He leaned forward and kissed him tenderly on the mouth, holding the position for several seconds. Kiltman closed his lips tight waiting for him to finish. It tasted nearly as bad as when his Auntie Liz kissed him on passing his exams. Skink picked up the two masks. He replaced Kiltman's over the horizontal superhero's head, making sure to put it back in the correct position. He leant forward and studied his handiwork, adjusted the edges and stood up, smiling.

He moved to the far end of the corridor and activated the iron grille with a remote control he produced from his pocket. As he disappeared through the open door, he shouted back, "Enjoy your well-deserved rest, in peace. Ha! Ha! Ha! Ha!"

He heard the laughter disappear into the darkness as the iron grille descended back into place. Skink was only gone a few minutes when Kiltman turned his head towards the other door leading to the stairs. He called in as loud a whisper as he could muster. "Hurry up! Put your feet on the bottom step."

The door sprang open to reveal a bleary-eyed Tommy struggling under the weight of a supersized pair of mechanical scissors.

Escape

"My head's nipping!" Tommy's rasping voice and sunken eyes bore testament to the fact he had been trying to go out with a bang. "I could've drunk myself into a nice coma, just let it all happen, but oh no, you and little Miss DI had other ideas. It was going to be the perfect drinking session. Absolutely hammered and no worries about a hangover."

"Look, Tommy, just focus on prising those bars open, there's a good lad. I promise I'll make it up to you one day." Kiltman could feel nothing below his neck, while his head was a beehive of activity.

The sound of cast iron being mangled out of shape hurt Tommy's ears as he worked the mechanical scissors against the grille. After he had left Kiltman and Wilson earlier that day, he had entered into his own mini-adventure.

He had gone to Dumbarton Fire Station to ask for help in a drunken haze. When he asked them for a piece of equipment to cut through iron to free Kiltman, they laughed him off the fire station. He could hardly string two words together without losing his train of thought. They accused him of being a looter who had decided to be more sophisticated than the others, which seemed to contradict the fact he could barely stand on two feet without swaying.

He had left there and found a café on Dumbarton high street. It was empty but the doors had been left open in the owners' haste to escape. Tommy had spent an hour there gorging on coffee and water. He sobered up enough to wander out onto the street and wave down a taxi patrolling the streets looking for looters. The driver had decided not to run for the hills but protect the neighbourhood from being ransacked.

Tommy's cock and bull story about needing to go to Duntocher Fire Station on an errand proved effective in convincing the driver. It was not long before they had parked outside a compact, brick building that could only ever have been a fire station, evidenced by five red, metal doors pulled all the way up, awaiting action. Tommy had exited the car before it had stopped before running around to the back of the station. Within minutes he came back with a giant pair of scissors that could have been a prop on *Gulliver's Travels*. When Tommy dropped the contraption on the back seat of the taxi, he said, "On the way back to Dumbarton, I am going to tell you a story. Kiltman needs our help. Trust me when I say, I would not be able to convince the fire station to give me these beauties if I wasn't telling the truth."

The truth was there was no "convincing" involved, he had snuck in and grabbed them when the firemen were watching the news on TV, wondering where and when their services would be required. The driver dropped him at the rock and continued on his way to stop looters. Tommy had smiled at the irony.

The "scissors" were a highly sophisticated, hydraulically powered tool used to prise open vehicles in accidents by widening the size of the hole or cutting through metal. He had learned of its power in a documentary about the San Francisco earthquake in 1989, when it allowed the firefighters to release people trapped in cars beneath a collapsed highway. He knew it was made to measure for Kiltman's predicament.

He had made it back down into the "dungeon" within minutes. When he had heard Kiltman calling him, he placed his foot on the bottom step and jumped through the door as soon as it sprang open. He had wasted no time in placing the machine flush against two central iron bars. On the other side Kiltman lay motionless on the paving stones. Once he was sure the scissors were in place, he flipped the ON button. The machine expanded, pressing against the bars with an unnerving power as if nothing could withstand its strength. It did not take long to create a gap big enough for Tommy to climb through.

"Where's Wilson?" Tommy asked, leaning down beside Kiltman.

"It's a long story. Thanks for coming back. I knew you would." Which was a half truth, he was not sure if he would come back as Skink or Tommy.

"No problem. Only twenty-four hours ago I saved a father and son from falling to their death. They weren't particularly appreciative, so I decided to crack open a bottle to while away the remaining hours until doomsday. Then you and Wilson turned up. I was watching you when you found the lever on the wall."

Tommy pulled from his backpack an empty bottle of The Rising, a Wallace ten-year old Kenny had created using the earth and water of Glenfinnan where Bonnie Prince Charlie's 1745 rebellion had started.

"This is what has been keeping me busy, in case you wondered."

"Look, Tommy, we don't have time for this just now. I'm completely paralysed and I need your help."

"Paralysed? Oh my God..." Tommy's anguish was genuine. Kiltman wondered if he had even noticed that he had been lying motionless on the ground staring at the ceiling the whole time he had been bending iron.

"Just focus, please. On the back of my sporran you'll see a four digit number with a series of dials underneath it. Turn the dials until you get 1402." Valentine's Day, but more importantly, Roddy's birthday.

"If you get the number wrong, then we'll have to wait an hour before we can try it again, so be careful."

Tommy stopped asking questions and gibbering. He was sobering up by the second beginning to understand he had a role to play in averting disaster. His fingers shook as he turned the sensitive dials. Nerves combined with the hangover made the exercise more difficult than it needed to be. When he completed the number, the clasp popped open.

"Good man. Now, inside you'll see a flask. Take it out and press the back, a third of the way down in the middle of the circle on the Celtic cross."

Tommy extracted the silver hip flask, mesmerised by its beautiful design. On one side there was a relief carving of a man and boy standing in the light of a sun shining on a lush glen, bordered by three mountains of equal height above a loch glimmering in the warm sun. On the other side was the Kiltman logo etched into the silver, with a Celtic cross to its left. Tommy pressed the cross and the lid sprang open.

"Now, pour a decent-sized dram down my throat. Once you've done that, close the lid and put it back in my sporran. Then snap the sporran shut. I'm warning you, Tommy, don't even think about taking a drink."

"Aw, come on. Just the one. I'm gasping for a wee dram."
Tommy was enjoying the aroma of the whisky as it wafted
around the corridor. "I'll get you your own case of whisky later if that'll please
you. For now, just listen to me. Okay?" Tommy nodded, he
knew when he was pushing his luck. He placed his hand under
Kiltman's head and lifted it to a forty-five-degree angle. He
gently lifted the bottom of the mask enough to allow access to
his mouth. Kiltman gulped thirstily as Tommy poured a hefty
dram from the flask. Letting his head down gently, he
murmured grumpily before he replaced the lid and sealed the
flask back in the sporran. What a pity, he thought. He had never
smelled anything quite so hypnotic and mouth-watering.

Kiltman enjoyed the taste of the whisky before it meandered
through his stomach into his bloodstream. He concentrated
intensely willing Hair o' the Dog to drift purposefully through
his veins and arteries to attack the nerve gas. He had never done
anything like this before. He was not sure if he could make it
work, but it was his only chance. Suddenly his right leg shot
into the air causing it to spasm, kicking erratically in all
directions. Tommy leapt forward on instinct to hold the leg as it
frantically lashed the air around his head. Suddenly all four of
Kiltman's limbs were jerking, thrusting everywhere, his body
arching upwards in a scene Tommy remembered from *The
Exorcist*. The power in the limbs was too much for him to
control, so he rolled off Kiltman waiting for the seizure to come
to an end. Kiltman opened his mouth wide and released an
almighty howl that lasted for what seemed an age.

The nerve gas escaping through his throat in a torrent, he
enjoyed the strength rushing back into his limbs. It took several
minutes for him to stop shaking. Once his body had settled
down, he stood up groggily leaning against the bars until he
was confident his legs would support him. He felt the rush of
blood bring on a torture of pins and needles he had not
experienced since he had fallen asleep in that hedge. Pre-
Kiltman days.

"Come here, you!" he shouted at Tommy, who had taken up
refuge in the corner. His friend approached gently, unsure of
whether the nation's superhero still controlled his own body.

He wrapped his arms around Tommy and hugged tightly. "Tommy, you're a star."

There was so much Kiltman wanted to say to his lifelong friend. That would need to wait till another time, another place and another costume. He was riddled with guilt at even considering Tommy could have been Cullen Skink. One day he would find a humorous way to tell him of his suspicions. The other part of his brain was dealing with Donald and his madness. At university he was renowned for his eccentricities, but how eccentric did he need to be to threaten the world with a nuclear bomb? Donald had not been the most loquacious or communicative of students, but should Kenny have worked harder with him? Half-hearted in his friendship, he had said. Worse than no friendship at all. He had not visited Donald in hospital, unconsciously washing his hands of him. Donald was partly right in his attitude to Kenny. However, a punch on the mouth or letter of indignation would have been an acceptable measure of retaliation. Did he really need to follow him around the world plotting to kill him? No, Kenny concluded, Donald's warped mind had used a hammer to crack an egg. If he could not stop him in his tracks, the yolk would be all over Strathclyde.

"I didn't know you were so affectionate, Kiltman." Tommy prised himself from Kiltman's arms, Scottish embarrassment competing with the exaggerated show of affection. Kiltman realised he had let his mind wander settling into more of a cuddle than a hug.

Pointing towards the iron grille on the other side of the corridor, Kiltman coughed and said, "Let's set those scissors loose against that one now. We're going to find Cullen Skink's wife before she finds us."

Permian

The corridor grew damper and more claustrophobic with every step. The walls dripped a green, watery slime onto the stone floor, transforming it into a slippery slope, a metaphor he was only too well aware of. He led the way with Tommy keeping an eye behind for any unwelcome surprises. They communicated with each other through hands and head movements conscious of another Cullen Skink trick around one of the corners. Kiltman also wanted silence because Tommy, the residue of a bottle of The Rising floating in his system, was far from Scotland's quietest whisperer.

After half an hour of snaking through moist, dimly-lit corridors Kiltman raised his hand beckoning his friend to stop. Death was very near. It was so palpable he could taste it. Literally. Tommy's startled expression told him that his friend was now sobering up, becoming fully aware of what he was involved in. Loyalty and commonsense are not necessarily complementary qualities.

Kiltman approached a dark wooden door. He placed a hand against it gently. The scent was coming from behind the frame. He touched it with his forefinger. The door was at least five inches thick, locked tight with a basic mortice deadlock. He peered through the keyhole searching for signs of life on the other side. He was not surprised to see the room was empty.

Tommy tapped him on the shoulder and said, "Can we use this?"

Kiltman turned to see him holding the lifesaving scissors. It had been Tommy's idea to bring them. Kiltman had agreed as long as his hungover friend carried them. All those years of cross-country running were coming in very handy.

Kiltman nodded. "Yes, but just give me a minute first." He leant his ear against the door and listened for signs of power, whether electrical or battery operated. He detected nothing other than wood contracting infinitesimally with the drop in temperature as night drew in. It was already eight o'clock. Four hours till detonation.

"Okay, do your stuff, maestro." He stepped out of the way to let Tommy insert the teeth of the machine against the jambs on either side of the door. He looked to Kiltman for acknowledgement. He nodded knowing that this was their only chance. It took the hydraulic motor several minutes before the machine expanded to fill the breadth of the doorway. Tommy flipped the switch to increase the pressure. The machine continued to widen until both jambs burst out of the wall in an explosion of wood and stone. With the walls disintegrated on either side, Kiltman pushed the door easily watching it fall with an almighty clatter onto the concrete floor. He was not concerned about making a noise since Cullen Skink would have reacted earlier to any sounds if he had still been around. He had flown the coop taking Wilson with him. Kiltman felt the gnawing sense of loss and guilt rise in the pit of his stomach. He worked hard to ignore it; she needed him alert and focused.

The room was larger than the small door had led them to believe. Each wall was decorated with an array of electronic equipment, interconnected through tubes and pipes. They had found Skink's lab. Kiltman closed his eyes imagining Skink create anthrax, nerve gas and bombs of all shapes and sizes, with the *pièce de résistance* his nuclear monster. Talking of which…

Kiltman followed the aroma of death across the room till he reached a three-foot high glass case nestled in the middle of the floor. Inside it he saw the letters "Permian" attached to a metal box that continued into the floor below them. He could sense the highly enriched uranium nestled under their feet waiting to say hello to Strathclyde. Below the letters, a digital clock displayed a row of neon numbers. He expected to see midnight and today's date on the display but instead saw the numbers count down from 2 mins 35 secs, to 2 mins 34 secs, to 2 mins 33 secs.

He rolled his fist in a ball and looked to the ceiling, cursing Cullen Skink with all the energy left in his broken, exhausted body. The door had somehow been linked to the bomb. The only time Cullen Skink had used a trip wire was on the one that truly mattered. As soon as it opened, a three-minute countdown had started. Tommy, on his shoulder, comprehended the situation as soon as he saw the display and Kiltman's reaction.

Lifting the scissors high above his head, he dropped it like a brick on top of the case, shouting, "Skink, you monster!"

Shards of thick glass cut into their legs, arms and body. Barely registering the blood trickling from their wounds, they swept the glass from the top of Permian. 2 mins 10 secs. Tommy waited silently for Kiltman to make the next step. He wanted to scream with the frustration building like a pressure cooker inside his head. He would have traded it in for that morning's hangover in a heartbeat.

Kiltman ran his fingers underneath the metal rim of Permian until he found a release catch. Pressing gently, the top of the bomb slid to one side leaving a mass of wiring and the same display of neon numbers.

1 min 45 secs.

A golden casket nestled in the middle of the wiring. On its side they read the inscription "My dearest Yelena, you shall be the salvation of Scotland as your ashes grow like a phoenix into the new world. All my love, Donald".

"How touching!" Tommy's grim face was deathly white as he stared at Yelena's burial urn.

Kiltman studied the mess of wiring and contact points looking for a clue to disable the trigger. He had only one option: there was no time to explore beyond what intuition told him. Placing his hands gently on the casket, he lifted it from its cradle. Holding the base with a steady hand he tried to twist the the top off. It was jammed closed, refusing to budge against Kiltman's efforts. The veins and sinews in his neck bulged with the strain. It was not moving.

Tommy touched him on the shoulder and slipped the casket carefully from Kiltman's hands conscious it was still connected by an array of coloured wires to Permian. Withdrawing a substantial penknife from his pocket, he rapped its handle against the rim of the casket, while twisting gently. Handing it back to Kiltman, he said, "Have you ever opened a stubborn jar of marmalade in the morning after it's been in the fridge too long?"

Kiltman lifted the casket and twisted. The lid came off easily. "Well done, partner," he whispered. "Sometimes superheroes make things more complicated than they need to be."

1 min 5 secs.

He peered into the casket. It was half full with a very dusty and blackened Yelena resting happily in her cremated ashes.

"Sorry, Yelena, but we need your bed for a wee while," Kiltman said, pouring her ashes on the floor beside him.

At the bottom of the casket, a microchip nestled in a bed of circuitry. He inserted Tommy's knife slowly, aimed at the microchip. Placing the knife delicately underneath, he looked directly at Tommy. "You ready?"

45 secs.

"Of course I'm not ready! Just do it!"

Kiltman made sure the knife was in place before he took a deep breath. He held his hand steady for several seconds and then twisted his wrist, levering the microchip out of its position. It bounced from the casket onto the floor nestling in the middle of Yelena's ashes at the same moment the clock stopped at 30 seconds. As they stared silently at Yelena scattered across the floor, Tommy whispered, "Looks like Yelena's had her chips."

The Lair

"How do you feel, my pretty young lady?"

"What the hell is going on? Who is that?" Wilson stared at the ceiling. An industrial whiteness flickered from the light of the fluorescent tube directly above her. She turned her head to the side to a wall covered in photographs. As her vision adjusted quickly to the artificial light, she gasped involuntarily. The photos were stuck to the wall in chronological order from when she started on this venture with Kiltman. Both of them sitting in the light of the rising sun in Glasgow. On the Erskine Bridge, talking animatedly with Kiltman. Preventing his cape from slipping into the helicopter's blades against the backdrop of Edinburgh Castle. Steering a Vespa around Rome. Admiring the William Wallace monument. Sipping a coffee in Starbucks when she sat alone the day before trying to understand the implications of the last few days. The intense scrutiny she had unknowingly been under made her feel vulnerable. This quickly moved to panic when she realised her arms and legs were trapped in a vice she could not budge.

The owner of the voice moved into view between her and the overhead light. It took several seconds for her to adjust to the silhouette. She quickly realised she was a prisoner and her captor was no oil painting. She had seen many faces in the prisons over years of police work. She had developed a game to match the face against the crime, measuring the number of scars and broken bones to the degree of severity of the offence. In most cases by studying the face she could guess the crime. Cullen Skink's face was different. It was free of blemishes, except for extraordinarily bad teeth, while seeming childlike in a Chucky the killer doll kind of way.

"Where is Kiltman?" she asked, surprised at the nervousness in her voice.

"Poor Kiltman. Your romantic superhero. I'm afraid he reached the limit of his powers and finally realised that he is just as fallible as any other mortal. And believe me, he is very fallible." Skink smiled more to himself than for Wilson's benefit.

She prayed this could not be true. He could not be dead.

"My fair lass. Don't worry, he is still alive. At least, he will be for one more hour. He will then join the rest of Strathclyde in donating their DNA to the atmosphere. Who knows, if your efforts to clear the nuclear weaponry from the naval bases were not successful, then we will be dealing with a particularly larger dent in the ozone layer than just above Strathclyde."

"What have you done to me?" Wilson concentrated on controlling the panic rising in her throat.

"Cute, very cute. You ask me about your kilted superhero before yourself. It must be love. Ha! Ha! Some people might say that the two of you were destined for each other from a long time ago. Those people will no longer be with us tomorrow, so who cares what they think."

"What are you talking about?"

"It's not important, Yelena. That's all in the past. We must now look to the future. Our future." A twisted grin flashed across Cullen Skink's face as he leaned closer to Wilson.

"Yelena? Who the hell is Yelena?"

"You sound just like a jealous wife should do. Music to my ears. Yelena, my dear, will soon be you, and you will be Yelena."

He saw the confusion and fear in her eyes. Touching her cheek with his forefinger, he said, "Now, now. Don't worry. Soon none of this will be important. You will get your body back and be able to walk, talk and chew gum at the same time if you want. When that happens, the world will be a very different place. And you, my dear, will be a very different person."

Cullen Skink looked towards the table where he had delicately placed a syringe containing the mind-bending drugs so carefully and successfully perfected in the torture chambers of Moscow's KGB headquarters. Wilson would become Yelena, he was quite sure of that. He would enjoy recreating his wife in this perfect specimen of a woman. He would instil in her malleable mind the ideals and beliefs that he had grown to live his life by.

Wilson was able to follow his line of vision to the table. She realised that she was not going to have a quick end. Whatever he had in store for her required medical instruments and drugs. For the first time in her life, she prayed for death.

251

Turning his head to examine his surroundings, he smiled. The five rooms and warren of corridors would be perfect. The two-foot thick leaden walls and ceiling would protect them for the next five years, when he had calculated it would be safe to resurface for the beginning of a new life on the face of the planet. In the meantime, there was enough food, drink and mind-moulding literature to keep them occupied. He had also built an extra couple of rooms for the newcomers he was quite certain would arrive. He estimated the first would be there in less than a year. The master race would begin its manufacturing process very soon, creating the perfect family.

"Won't we, my love?" Wilson winced as Cullen Skink leant forward, his putrid breath invading her nostrils while he kissed her forehead and stroked her cheek with a crooked thumb sporting barely a millimetre of nail, chewed to the quick a long time ago.

Finding the Lair

Kiltman saw the relief in Tommy's face. It had been there for the last three hours. Cullen Skink's lab had become infested with Strathclyde police officers in white plastic suits, some opening drawers and reviewing files while others dusted machinery for prints, collecting DNA samples from keyboards and discarded eating utensils. Fraser had decided to take the risk of Skink spotting them. He had no choice. Wilson had been abducted and it was already 11 pm. There was no more time on the clock to hang back.

The fact that Skink had not reacted meant he was otherwise distracted. Kiltman knew what would have interrupted Skink's surveillance, but he chose not to mention it to Fraser. He was sure Fraser was thinking the same thing. Wilson.

The investigation of Skink's lab would not reveal anything, other than what they knew already, which was that Donald Mackenzie had worked on his own, no forwarding address supplied. Kiltman let them continue nevertheless since any clue, however small, might provide a chance of identifying where Cullen Skink was holed up with Wilson. He was sure she would still be alive. At least for one more hour.

Kiltman and the Chief Constable had spent longer than they could afford poring over maps of the area trying to identify a potential hiding place. They were looking for somewhere that could disguise a nuclear bomb shelter and protect Skink from the explosion and radioactivity.

No suspicious aircraft or boats had been picked up on the radar around the castle in the last couple of days, let alone hours. Skink would not dare use the roads considering Wilson's immobility and the mass of traffic building up on the key junctions. The Chief Constable had assigned scores of officers to crawl all over the rock, inside the castle and around Dumbarton. They had reached the conclusion that his lair would be within the vicinity of the castle, but far enough below ground level not to be impacted by the explosion. They had drawn a blank on every square within the grid on the flattened map. Not a single, secret shelter could be traced anywhere.

They had been running checks on Donald Mackenzie for a couple of hours but found no location in Scotland other than the flat he had used as a student years before. Not surprisingly he had disappeared from all networks and files, having "died" many years earlier. He had told another white lie when the Chief questioned how he knew Cullen Skink's identity. He pretended that Skink had provided a brief biography before he left the fortified corridor to allow him the pleasure of knowing who his nemesis had been so that he could die in peace. The alternative, the real explanation, would have been the beginning of the unravelling of a finely knitted sweater.

Kiltman was trying to think straight but could not erase the image haunting him of a paralysed Wilson in the hands of Cullen Skink. There must be some way of identifying where he would be concealed. Somewhere in the pattern of everything he had shared with his nemesis, whether as Cullen Skink or Donald Mackenzie, there was a clue. He had known Donald as a young, confused student. Many years later the same person had become a cruel, evil fanatic. Many years later. Same person but a different time. Same place but a different time.

Kiltman slapped the desk with his left hand before making a clicking sound with his right. Chief Constable Fraser raised an eyebrow and looked at him waiting for some words to accompany the percussion.

"Chief, it's eleven o'clock. In one hour he's going to know that we spoiled his fireworks show. When that happens all bets are off. He'll not want Wilson as a dead weight holding him back from escaping. Her coat is hanging on a shoogly nail, she's running out of time. I have an idea."

Chief Constable Fraser looked at Kiltman. Part of him wanted to reach out and hug him for finding and stopping the bomb. The other part wanted to punch him on his latex chin for making him sweat it out all day waiting for the green light to raid the castle. He understood that Kiltman did not have much in the way of options, particularly when he was trapped and paralysed, but he should have found some way to get him a message. My God, he was able to defuse a nuclear explosive with only thirty seconds on the clock, yet he could not find a way to update the Chief Constable. He had been minutes away from descending upon the castle all guns blazing when Kiltman had called him from MacGregor's mobile. They had been camped a few miles from Dumbarton for the best part of the day, frustration and fear playing havoc with their nerves. All he could think to say was, "Chief, where you been? The party's almost over."

"Okay, what's the idea?" The Chief threw his overcoat onto a chair.

"These maps of the area are all recent, aren't they?" Kiltman paced around the lab.

"Yes, of course they are." Kenny smiled at the hint of pride in the Chief Constable's tone. "We update them monthly to ensure we have the most current picture possible."

"Sometimes, though, it's better to be a bit less up to date."

"Sorry?" That hint of pride had disappeared.

"Cullen Skink must have started this project years ago when he had the help of the Soviet agents he was working with. When they built a nuclear shelter, they would have worked around the landscape and buildings in existence at that time."

"Makes sense," acknowledged the Chief Constable. "Okay, let's see what we can do here. Detective Urquhart, can you please stop what you're doing and access the archives?"

Detective Urquhart had been downloading Skink's hard drive in the hope of finding a clue, growing increasingly exasperated as the majority of files included pages of formulae and diagrams. Any budding terrorist would have a windfall if he was allowed access to these files.

Several minutes passed as Urquhart's fingers worked mesmerisingly across the keyboard, the screen responding and changing just as quickly.

"Okay, sir, that's me in." Urquhart was a young policeman who had been assigned this exercise due to his computer sciences background, combined with a natural ability to decode just about any virus attached to police files. The kind of computer geek you wanted as an ally, not a foe. "You want the maps for this part of the Strathclyde region?"

"Yes," Kiltman said. "Access the maps from around ten years ago."

In seconds they were looking at a map of the area, both north and south of the river. They studied the same topographical spaghetti they had been reviewing for hours, the typical mix of contours, symbols, roads, villages and the river running through the centre. Kiltman's attention was drawn to a series of blocks and greenery on the opposite side of the river in the village of Langbank. "What's all that? I don't remember seeing it on the other map."

Urquhart clicked on the symbol. Immediately the map expanded into an increased level of detail. It showed a church surrounded by larger buildings, interrupted by empty patches of land, some kind of sports fields. Beneath the church, they read: "Saint Vincent's College, Langbank".

"Saint Vincent's College. That description's definitely not on the other maps. Any ideas what kind of college that used to be?"

"I remember that," the Chief Constable said. "It was a seminary for the Roman Catholic priesthood. A couple of young lads from my parish went there around twenty years ago. It was supposed to be one of the last junior seminaries in the world."

"Junior seminary?" Kiltman asked.

"Yes, where boys between twelve and fourteen years old would go to test their vocation to the priesthood before they moved into the more serious seminaries. Back in the eighties they were not getting sufficient numbers to justify keeping the place open. So they sold the land and buildings. They've now been replaced by some nice houses. Although I believe the church is still there today. Langbank is just a quiet picturesque village where nothing happens. Usually…" The Chief Constable was impressed at his powers of recall. Maybe his wife was right, retirement was a tad premature. Or maybe she just liked to have the house to herself.

"That's it!" Kiltman slapped his hand against the Chief's back. He ignored the look of shock from underneath the forestry eyebrows.

"Cullen Skink studied there when he was a young boy. Somehow he, eh, mentioned it when he was telling me his biography. I'd forgotten about it until now. You can get your folks to check it, but I'm sure as the Pope's a Catholic that he attended that seminary. Not surprising really. Cullen Skink is not the only person to want to become a Holy Father and come out a

256

Holy Terror, opting to create mass murder, sending souls to heaven a lot quicker than they otherwise should've gone."

"Like who else?" Fraser was pinching the top of his nose, barely following Kiltman's ramblings.

"Hitler and Stalin apparently spent time in a seminary. But if Cullen Skink has his way, he will go to the top of the directory of Murderous X-Men of the Cloth. He would become the most infamous Scotsman since Pontius Pilate."

"While I appreciate your understanding of history and your logic, there's one thing escaping you." The Chief Constable took mental note to check Pontius Pilate's Scottishness later, rather than have Kiltman digress even further.

"What's that?"

"Those buildings haven't been around for years. Other than the church, they were demolished to make way for a new housing development."

"I thought you might say that, Chief. Have you ever been to Rome?"

"Well, yes. Why?" He decided not to divulge that he had gone there after the attempted assassination of the Pope in the early eighties to offer assistance in the investigation, which they impolitely refused.

"Did you go to the catacombs?"

"Yes, but…" The Chief Constable remembered the dank, clammy closeness of the walls and passages deep underneath Rome where the early Christians used to pray in the company of the corpses buried far beneath the prying eyes of the Romans. He had been glad to walk back up the steps to fill his lungs with fresh air.

"Were they not nearly two thousand years older than the buildings that sit on top of them now? Looks like we may have our own west of Scotland version of a catacomb."

Without waiting for the Chief Constable's response, he patted Detective Urquhart on the back. "Great job, Urquhart." He paused and took a breath, feeling a rising sense of optimism, and turned to Fraser.

"Chief, can you get the minisub ready for a trip across the Clyde. We've only got forty-five minutes left before Cullen Skink realises the bomb has been defused."

Urquhart looked at his boss for affirmation. The Chief Constable nodded then looked at Kiltman. "I hope you're right. It's Wilson's last chance."

Kiltman winced. He could handle pressure, he just did not like to be reminded of its consequences.

Langbank

The minisub dropped to the riverbed in seconds. Urquhart was designated pilot; his technical mastery also included submarines. Another high flyer, Kiltman thought. The police force was becoming more like the SAS every day. He asked Urquhart to focus on keeping the submarine steady following a straight line to where the seminary used to be. Kiltman listened intently to the water, the sound of changing currents, the swaying of plant life, whatever nature was left after years as an industrial waterway. He noticed nothing other than the Clyde meandering through its valley after a hard day's wind and rain. Forcing himself to concentrate on the riverbed, he smelled the vegetation sprinkled along the dredged area in its centre feeling the silt and mud merge and separate, driven by competing currents. At any other time, this would have been a fascinating experience, learning and enjoying how another world functioned.

"We're not far from the south bank, sir," Urquhart spoke softly.

"Go as close to the bank as possible. Try to just sit there directly on top of the line from the castle to the seminary church. Turn your engine off. Let's just float making as little noise as possible." He began to sense something but was not sure exactly what it was or where it was coming from.

Sweat trickled down into Urquhart's eyes causing him to blink, but his hands never left the controls. Seconds ticked by. "Okay, that's as close as we can go. From here to the bank, around one hundred yards, the water's extremely shallow because the tide's out. You'll have to walk across a muddy, waterlogged sandbank before you reach the village."

Kiltman lay horizontally on the floor and pressed his hands against the metal of the sub. There was something. What was it? He was straining every sense in his body to ignore everything except the one thing that would seem totally out of place. Then he got it. Through his fingers first, the vibration. Then he heard the hum of the engine. The generator to be exact. The sound seemed to come from underneath the riverbed, but it was very faint. It was originating from inland towards Langbank village. He could not be one hundred percent sure but was confident the

259

sub was sitting directly above a tunnel leading from the rock to Langbank on the opposite side of the river. The sound of the generator with nowhere else to go was drifting through the tunnel in a haunting, tuneless hum.

"Bingo!" Kiltman said quietly. "Let's surface so that I can go ashore. I need to follow this line. Once you've done that, tell the Chief Constable to get his team across here. They need to be ready to pounce. Tell him he should keep his distance until I've engaged with Cullen Skink. If he disappears back into his lair then we'll face a hostage situation which will have only one outcome. Have you got that?"

Urquhart nodded, trying not to risk his parched throat letting him down and showing his fear.

"Relax, Urquhart, it could be worse."

"Could it, sir?"

"No, not really, I was only joking! Now move this baby to the surface."

Urquhart steadied the sub as best he could to allow Kiltman as short a space as possible to step onto the bank, freshly exposed after the tide's withdrawal earlier that evening. He placed each foot gingerly in front of the other to ensure he maximised his balance by spreading the weight evenly. The walk was tricky across the wet, loose sandy mud, but he felt confident with each step that he was winning the battle. Until his left leg gave way and he slipped clumsily into a pool of river isolated on all sides by mud and weeds.

Lying in the water, he looked up at the challenge in front of him. The village lay on the other side of a mushy beach, sprinkled with pools of river water and debris. The weakness and tiredness sat heavily in his legs, the toll of the last few days beginning to win the battle.

He lifted the mask up to his forehead and cupped his hands before dipping them in the cold water. He threw several handfuls onto his face and neck until he could feel the blood pound in his temples. The impact was enough to intensify his concentration and ignore the massive build up of sleep trying to take control of his body. He looked at his watch and rose to a crouch position, prepared to negotiate the riverbank. Twenty-five minutes to midnight. He promised himself never to worry about time again after that night whatever the outcome would be. Every moment was proving precious.

Within minutes he was hurrying through the streets of Langbank, a picturesque Clyde village dotted sparingly with bungalows and gardens serviced by a couple of shops and a train station. Nice place to raise a family, he mused, or train a priest. The village was silent. It appeared stoic in its disregard for the panic going on across the Strathclyde region. Chief Constable Fraser had not advised the press that the bomb had been defused lest it cause Cullen Skink to act prematurely. On closer inspection Kiltman could see very few cars around and no lights in any of the homes. Langbank villagers had also headed for the hills.

He jogged around a sharp bend on the road to make his way to where the seminary used to be. The road wound its way from the river up into a cluster of houses and narrow streets. Struggling to control his rising heartbeat and breathing, he ran up the hill staying close to the edge, shaded from the moonlight by an overhang of trees. After several hundred yards he stepped onto the edge of a clearing that the older map told him was once the courtyard of the seminary. Eyes closed, he allowed his senses to capture the atmosphere of the area. He could sense the energy and emotion of thousands of Scots lads "testing" their vocation over the years as they played, prayed and studied, preparing themselves for the ironic gift of celibacy.

At the edge of the courtyard, he saw the church. The Chief had been right, it was still there. It was smaller than most houses of worship he had visited, but was still a rugged, imposing structure defined by the strength and neatness of its solid blocks of stone. Kiltman was surprised not to sense a spark of spirituality in the building until he saw the intercom. God's house had been tastefully decorated and transformed into apartments with "oblique views of the river" and "aspects on the hills". Twenty yards from the church's steps, a row of trees disappeared into the darkness. Stepping carefully towards the wooded area, the soles of his feet tingled. The density of the earth beneath him seemed to change. There was a distinct hollowness underfoot. In the darkness of the trees, he sensed he was standing above a deep shaft, reaching far below Langbank's peaceful village. Bending to inspect the ground, he spotted a discolouration in the earth, where hot air habitually oozed upwards into the moist grass. It was five minutes to midnight. The rat was in its lair.

Midnight June 21

"Don't worry, Yelena. I will help you drink it. Only two minutes to go." Cullen Skink had placed two glasses of Moet Chandon on the bedside table. He had propped her into a sitting position facing the wall of the shelter before he crawled into the bed, wrapping his arm around her waist. Life did not get much better than this, he thought. All those years ago when he had tried to become a priest to please his parents, it was of no consequence that the other boys had treated him like a pariah. It was during one of those secluded afternoons when he was exploring the alleyway behind the refectory area that he had found an anonymous and rusted iron grille, sitting horizontally across what appeared to be a well. It had taken several hours of prising and oiling to open it, but the prize for his efforts was the realisation that he had found a shaft leading down to a tunnel stretching across to Dumbarton Castle. His only conclusion had been that the Vikings had built it over a thousand years earlier to counteract the failings of a besieged castle.

When they built this escape route from the enemy, they created the perfect nuclear shelter for Cullen Skink. The seed of the plan to change the world was born that day as he walked through the tunnel, deep below the Clyde.

"I will hold you when the earth shudders, my sweet. Don't worry, we are two hundred feet underground so the impact will be minimal. Yes, the earth will move, but it won't be the last time for us, Yelena, I can assure you. We are within the last minute of the old world." He waved his watch in Wilson's face. It glared in bright neon: 11.59.

"You're mad, Skink. You can never get away with this." Wilson's words belied her true emotion. Her mind raced furiously to find a way out of the shelter once she had control of her body. She knew that even if she did escape, she would enter a radioactive world with nowhere to go. However she considered her situation, she was trapped.

"I have got away with it, darling. Don't you see? But let's not go over old ground, let's plan for the future, which is about to begin in ten seconds. Nine, eight, seven, six, five, four, three, two, one! Yeeeeessss!" His voice climbed to a crescendo while he hugged Wilson ever more tightly lest she fall from the bed with the impact. Wilson closed her eyes, prayed for the souls two hundred feet above her and waited. The silence grew from ponderous to hope-filled and then relieved when Cullen Skink screamed, "Aaaggghhhh!"

A crazed look on his face betrayed his agony. He jumped from the bed and flipped a switch on his computer. It took him a few minutes to get a signal but he eventually found a connection to BBC World News.

Just as Grant MacTavish spoke. "As you can see, we are standing here in George Square, Glasgow. Or rather, we're STILL standing here in George Square. Many people who decided not to flee their homes and loved ones are gathered here, to be together when Cullen Skink dropped the bomb. It's already a few minutes past midnight. The people are cheering and screaming. I haven't seen such euphoria since I witnessed the Berlin Wall coming down. That night in Germany will remain with me forever, but in terms of magnitude of impact tonight has replaced it as my memory of salvation and hope delivered on a massive scale.

"I can barely hear myself think, the noise is deafening. I'm telling you, even if the world ended right now, the spirit of the people would live on. Cullen Skink has failed. I'm sure I speak on behalf of the crowd behind me. I've got one message for the monster who tried to terrorise our country. You might try to destroy our buildings and bridges, but you will never squash the heart of the Scottish people. If you're watching, you pathetic failure, then just look at this. These are the people you tried to destroy. The Scottish people: good, genuine, generous, happy, amazingly altruistic and kind. Quite simply the best people in the world!

"Come on, Scotland! We love you!" he shouted, completely out of character. But Grant did not care how emotional he sounded. The relief and pride in his voice was one hundred percent genuine, evidenced by the tears streaming down his cheeks.

Whether his recounting of witnessing the fall of the Berlin Wall was quite so genuine was neither here nor there at the omment. As the camera panned behind his shoulder to show thousands of Scots packed into the square, Grant knew that they had lived and grown through the same sense of love for family and friends as he had done over the last two days. Most of the men proudly swirled their kilts while women had painted their faces in the colours of Saint Andrew's cross. Billboards were propped up against lampposts while their owners danced a spontaneous ceilidh linking arms with anyone and everyone until the dancing spread through the square like a forest fire. At the same time, a long flowing rumba had started and was gaining momentum as it snaked round the outside of the square. The camera continued to close in until it levelled on one of the billboards: CULLEN SKINK, YOU'RE A DAMP SQUIB. KILTMAN RULES!!

"Noooo!" He whirled around to confront Wilson. "Shut up, you BITCH! Stop laughing! Do you hear me, stop it. Now!"

Even if she had wanted to, Wilson could not prevent the relief from showing, seasoned with the pleasure of an angry and frustrated Cullen Skink. Kiltman had done it. How, she might never know, but thank God he had. He jumped on the bed. He wrapped his fingers around her throat and began to squeeze, his face two inches from hers.

"You will die, right now. I have no further need for you. You would never be as good as my Yelena, anyway. Goodbye and good riddance."

Wilson could feel her larynx crush. Forcing herself to speak, she managed to squeeze out the words, "Insurance... me... think... about... it..."

She saw the message register in his fiery eyes. His face was so close to hers she could taste the moisture of his breath on her lips. The two or three seconds she waited until he released his fingers felt like minutes. He let her head fall awkwardly onto the pillow before turning his back on her. He rose slowly from the bed barely registering the sound of Wilson's splutters and painful breaths.

Over his shoulder he muttered distractedly, "On this occasion you might be right. But it's only a matter of time before you pay the price for Kiltman's actions."

He reached into the desk drawer and withdrew a pistol. It glinted in the artificial light of the lair before he checked it was loaded. He slipped it into the inside pocket of his jacket before leaving the room to approach the crude elevator he had built in the shaft. He had to see this for himself, to acknowledge that Permian and Yelena had not been allowed to fulfil his mission. His composure was beginning to come back. Just like this pathetic policewoman, he thought, these idiots have only bought themselves a stay of execution.

Showdown

The elevator raced upwards, his mind spinning. He did not have a contingency plan, he needed time to think. He would hide out underground until the searches stopped. They would never find him. They would not find the castle entrance to the tunnel, it was too deep below the rock for them to even consider it. No local maps or historical studies had ever acknowledged or recorded it.

The door, built into the roof of the elevator, opened onto a still, pleasant night on the Firth of Clyde, the air a little salty from a westerly breeze. The entrance to the shaft had been camouflaged by a large cluster of bushes and strong, thick trees. He stepped out onto the grass, infra-red binoculars already in hand to study the castle across the river. Raising the glasses to survey the rock, he saw the police and military forces crawling all over it like cockroaches on a mouldy cheese. The fools were always several steps behind him.

"Good evening, Donald. The game's a bogey." Kiltman stood behind Cullen Skink in the darkness of a withered tree.

Several moments passed before Skink said, "Well, well. You are full of surprises. One minute I leave you paralysed behind bars. The next you are up and about challenging me on my own turf. How very resourceful, Kiltman." He spoke without turning. "So, what happens now then?"

Kiltman walked towards him, standard issue handcuffs in hand. "You're going to see what being behind bars is like, Donald. It shouldn't be too different from what you would have ended up doing for the next few years anyway, if you'd had your wicked way. But rats like you enjoy small lairs, so maybe you'll be at home in prison."

Cullen Skink moved quicker than Kiltman had anticipated. He dropped the binoculars. Before they hit the ground, he had pulled the pistol from his inside pocket and aimed it directly at Kiltman's chest. "Typical, foolish Kiltman. You didn't know I was the fastest draw in the west... of Scotland. You don't even have a weapon. This is going to be easier than I expected. What do superheroes do in the afterlife?" Skink began to squeeze.

267

Kiltman smiled as he pressed his belt buckle. The dart that he had been keeping in there for a special occasion such as this flew sweetly and accurately into Cullen Skink's bloated stomach. The concentrated diazepam on its tip reached the receptors in his brain in less than a second. Cullen Skink collapsed to the ground in a heap. Kiltman heard the pleasing crack of his arm as it broke underneath him on impact.

"We eat fish like you for breakfast, Donald. That's what we do." Kiltman placed the handcuffs on his nemesis' wrists just as the sound of the police siren interrupted the chilly, post-rain evening. As the car screeched to a halt in a clearing near the trees, Kiltman stepped down into the elevator and pressed the button. Whatever he was going to find down there, he wanted to be on his own when he found it. The elevator plummeted like a stone until its hydraulic brakes forced it to a shuddering stop. The door opened automatically to reveal the lair, in the middle of which lay an abandoned and immobile Wilson.

"Nice digs you've got here, Wilson. Champagne? But you didn't know I was coming!" Kiltman stepped into the room.

"I would pour you a glass, but I hope you understand. You got him?"

"Yes, they're packing him into the police car as we speak. So how did you two get on in your love nest?"

"Not my idea of how I expected to spend the next few years, but, hey, any port in a storm!"

Kiltman had reached the bedside. Sitting down on the edge of the bed, he lifted the bottom of his mask and kissed her tenderly on the lips, stroking her soft hair with his fingers. He took his glove off especially for the occasion.

"I was worried about you," he whispered.

"You should've seen it from this end," she smiled, unsure whether she should be enjoying her vulnerability.

"Let's get you back up on solid ground, young lady. There is an antidote to this nerve gas. You will be up and about again in a couple of hours." He looked at her to make sure he was not imagining this moment, and whispered, "Just don't ever do that to me again!"

"What? Let you kiss me when I can't stop you planting your mask on my face?"

"No... I mean... You know what I mean." She really did know how to make him blush. Thank goodness for masks.

"I know. Next time someone paralyses and kidnaps me, I will tell them to stop immediately."

He placed his arms under her legs and neck and lifted her easily from the bed. He walked towards the elevator, trying to ignore the syringe and drugs on the table, the unspeakable horrors Skink would have committed. As the doors closed, she said, "Up, up and away, Kiltman." The bitter revulsion rising in his throat disappeared when he saw the cheeky grin he had grown to love.

V

Lucky Man

Uisge Beathe

"Dad, what will happen to Cullen Skink now that Kiltman has put him in prison?" Roddy was playing with plasticine models he had created of Kiltman and his nemesis fighting. From what Kenny could see, Kiltman was certainly much more agile in Roddy's mind than the original version.

"He'll go to a high security prison for a very long time."

"Did Uncle Tommy really help catch him? Or was he just making that up?"

Tommy had visited them two days earlier. He had spent the evening regaling Kenny and Roddy with the role he had played in helping Kiltman. Considering the room for embellishment, Kenny was impressed Tommy had kept his version of events closer to the truth than he would have expected. He had to bite his tongue on one occasion. He knew he was lying on the floor staring at the ceiling when his rescuer had used the scissors to bend the iron bars. However, he still would have noticed if Tommy had bent the first couple with his bare hands before he realised the hydraulic scissors were more effective. He let it slide for the sake of secrecy.

They hugged affectionately when Tommy left that evening to go back to Estonia. Their friendship had been revitalised and they both appreciated it. On leaving, he squeezed Kenny's hand and said, "It's good to see you back on your feet, Kenny. I'm glad you got yourself sorted out eventually. I hope things work out with you and Roddy."

Kenny was sure Tommy had no clue who was behind the Kiltman mask. He had no doubts he could trust him implicitly, but it was better for all concerned that his secret remain intact. The only person who knew his secret was Cullen Skink. The latest reports he had received were that Skink had become demented, foaming at the mouth as he screamed obscenities at the other inmates. He rarely slept, constantly pacing his cell, mumbling and muttering, punching his head with his hand, the other locked in plaster, to fix the bone broken in the dual with Kiltman. Kenny was not concerned that he would disclose his identity. No-one would believe, let alone listen to him.

"Roddy, if it hadn't been for your Uncle Tommy, Cullen Skink would have done some very nasty things. He was very brave."

"But, Dad, if you had been Uncle Tommy would you have done what he did?"

"Maybe, Roddy. Who knows?" Tommy had avoided mentioning the bottle of The Rising, that had been forgotten in the midst of all the shenanigans.

It seemed an age since they had hung out together, Kenny sipping tea while Roddy devoured ice cream soaked in Irn Bru. They were enjoying the peace and quiet of Uisge Beathe.

A loud ring echoed through the house.

"I'll get it, Dad."

"Okay, son. I'll put the kettle on for another cuppa."

Kenny could hear the footsteps in the hall as Roddy and the visitor walked towards the kitchen. Roddy entered first, not attempting to conceal his excitement. Behind him stood a woman, her beauty intensified by the air of nervousness she failed to hide.

"Dad, look! Look! It's Detective Inspector Wilson. She came to visit us. How cool is that?"

Roddy turned to Wilson, and said, "Can I just say, you are even more beautiful in real life? We can't stop watching you on TV now that you've put the Skink away." Roddy had become an expert on the Kiltman/Skink encounter through watching numerous TV news programmes.

"Well, thank you, young man. You've made my day." Wilson smiled and ruffled Roddy's hair.

"Eh, Detective Inspector, this is a surprise. To what do we owe the pleasure?" Kenny's mind was working at warp speed to understand the implications of Wilson's visit.

"Thanks, I'm fine now. A few aches and pains but just happy to be up on my feet."

She looked at the floor for a few seconds before she lifted her head. "I hope you don't mind me arriving here unannounced, but I had to see you."

Roddy knelt on a chair at the table, head resting on his hands, mouth open wide. Wilson's face had been in every paper and magazine for the last week. Now here she was sitting at his dad's table.

"To be honest, I'm speechless. Cuppa?" Kenny's eyes moved slowly to his son. He was all too conscious of Roddy's presence.

"Yes please."

Thank goodness she had given Kenny an excuse to turn his back and busy himself with cups and spoons.

"I came here because I had to thank you."

"Thank me?" Kenny asked over his shoulder.

"Thank him?" Roddy wanted in on the act.

"Roddy, your father is a very brave man. I hope you know that." Wilson looked at Roddy.

"Is he?" Roddy had a picture of his father falling on top of him on Dumbarton Rock.

"Mr. Morgan..."

"Kenny is fine, no ceremony in this house."

"Kenny, you saved my life. Or at least you saved me from a fate worse than death." Wilson's eyes welled with tears. "I'm sorry, but this is not as easy as I convinced myself it would be."

Kenny handed her the last square of kitchen towel from the holder as he gave her a mug of tea.

"Thanks. This whole Cullen Skink adventure has made me think. When I was trapped by him deep underground, I promised myself that if I ever escaped I would do something."

"What was that?" Roddy had practically crawled across the table to Wilson.

"Roddy, let the Detective Inspector speak." Kenny was not sure he wanted to hear what she was about to say.

Wilson breathed deeply, before she spoke in a slow, precise tone. "I became a policewoman for a reason. The reason was that someone many years ago saved me when I was attacked in an alleyway in Glasgow by two thugs."

When Kenny's sigh of relief was much louder than he had wanted, it quickly turned into a coughing fit.

"You okay?" she asked.

"Yes, tea went down the wrong way. Keep going."

"When that man saved me, he breathed life into me. I realised I had a role to play in helping others. I needed to try and make the world a better place." She looked at Roddy's enthralled face. "That man was your father, Roddy."

"Cool! Dad, you never told me about that!" Roddy had jumped off the chair, needing to find something to do with his legs.

"It was a long time ago, Roddy. It's a faint memory. I'm no spring chicken remember." He was finding this conversation excruciatingly painful on many levels.

"It has not been easy for me to come here today. I hope you don't mind, but I got your name from the police archives. I wanted to find you on lots of occasions but didn't have the courage until now. This time I had so much more determination. It was important that I see you as much for my own peace of mind as to thank you. I really would never be able to move on until I met you again. The passing of time can make certain memories less real. I can't afford to lose the turning point in my life. You made it happen, Kenny. I will not be able to thank you enough for having the gallantry and bravery to not walk away."

Roddy was looking at his father, tears welling in his eyes.

God, Kenny thought, how much discomfort could one man suffer?

"And one last thing, Roddy." Wilson, looking less anxious, turned to his son and smiled that captivating smile. "Do you know that your father wore a kilt that night? He was Kiltman before Kiltman was Kiltman."

"Dad was Kiltman! Wicked!" Roddy was mesmerised. "But that was a long time ago, Dad, wasn't it?"

"Yes, son." Kenny patted his belly. "The only villains I'm fighting now are the high calorie ones."

Roddy ran into the living room to re-enact another Kiltman-Cullen Skink fight scene. They let a minute's silence fill the air before Kenny said, "Thanks for coming today. I know it must have been hard for you."

"I'm a lot better now that I've come and said my piece. And been able to say thanks. You have a wonderful son. You're very lucky."

"Yes, I know. I'm a lot luckier than anyone can imagine." Kenny began to fidget with his cup.

Wilson found herself being drawn towards this strange Kenny Morgan. She could not explain the warmth she had felt sitting in the kitchen with him and his son. Before she could stop herself, she asked, "Are you and Roddy doing anything on Friday?"

"Friday? Me and Roddy? Doing anything?" Kenny nearly dropped the cup on the floor.

"Well, it's just that Chief Constable Fraser is having a retirement bash. I would love you two to come. Roddy would be in his element. You never know, Kiltman might even turn up."

"It would be an honour. We would love to go." Kenny paused. "We could maybe even go for some dinner later if you fancy, Detective Inspector. Our way of thanking you for saving Scotland." Kenny's stomach had turned into a tumble dryer.

"Just call me Maggie, Kenny. Dinner sounds great, as long as there's no fish soup on the menu."

He smiled, she smiled. She wondered, and he hoped.

Still Fishy

It could be worse. Food's good, conversation's non-existent. Perfect. The only downside is the carbolic soap I use to create the foam tastes terrible. A small price to pay to have them where I want them. They are already falling into a false sense of security.

Once I'm no longer fish of the day, I will strike. These flimsy walls and bars were built for mere mortals. When the time is right, they will not stand in my way.

Kiltman, wherever you are, I'm coming to get you. I know who you are, and this knowledge is my greatest weapon. Ha! Ha! Ha! Ha!

Acknowledgements

Where do I start to recognise the many people who helped breathe life into Kiltman?

Our incredible mum, for her strong hand always firmly on our backs, her strength of character and love of a good story alive in our memories. Every minute of her life was about her family. Self-sacrifice does not begin to describe what she did for her "weans".

Gorgeous Georgie, for our love, her quirkiness and boundless energy, who gave me the greatest gifts conceivable (pun intended): Max and Bruce, with more imagination in their little pinkies than their dad could dream about.

My amazingly resilient brothers and sisters, each a character with a story to tell; George is in heaven but left us with a huge vacuum we filled with unique memories of his wonderful character; Anne, who gave so much for us as we grew up, a second mother even to this day, yes, every family needs an Anne; Angie, an inimitable blend of sweet kindness and bold tenacity, our family's unconscious comedian; Margaret, a child at heart and kind to a fault, always there when I made life-changing decisions, who edited many of these pages, preventing me from embarrassing myself any further; John, a true character, a walking compendium of jokes and stories, dates and trivia, who 'knew Bishopbriggs when he was a curate'.

Then a host of my many friends who may recognise elements of themselves or shared experiences in these pages. To name but a few: Jack McVitie, Beannie Muldoon, Paul Gunn, Adrian "Scragg" Quinn, Stevie Love and Roddy MacDonald; through thick and thin we helped bring each other up, one way or another.

My buon'amico, Stuart Beaumont, for his artful naming of Kiltman's nemesis: Cullen Skink.

Tom Brucato, for his friendship and unstinting support in Kiltman's early stages.

Martin Delve, for his scrupulous attention to detail in helping identify logistical and logical anomalies in the plot. A born editor and a good friend.

The fellow seminarians, nuns and priests who will hopefully recognise the Langbank and Rome references.

Appreciation in abundance too for the early-90s Scots pioneers and our Estonian friends who re-invented bars, bingo and bonhomie to eschew Tallinn's post-Soviet hangover.

I could not forget the people of Duntocher and Clydebank who taught me how to pour a pint of Guinness and opened my eyes to the real world. To a person they truly are the salt of the earth.

Last but not least, a heartfelt thanks to Phelim Connolly for turning my flimsy descriptions of Kiltman into character-filled drawings. It has been a pleasure to see a true genius at one with his gifts, applying them to Kiltman, a tartan, patchwork quilt woven in reality, embroidered with fantasy.

Printed in Great Britain
by Amazon

27071569R00159